A Family Affair

BY THE AUTHOR

The Bulls and the Bees

A Family Affair

A
Family Affair

ROGER EDDY

THOMAS Y. CROWELL COMPANY, NEW YORK

A Family Affair

one

WHEN HE REACHED THE NICKOLS SCHOOL, A BLOCK NORTH OF THE AVENUE, he lingered for a moment and stared in at the vacant windows. The building was empty and quiet, deserted for the summer, and the only sound in the schoolyard was the buzzing of the cicadas in the elm trees.

Miss Nickols, he knew, had finally died. Years before, on his way home from the public school, he'd often hide himself in the hedge that surrounded the Nickols playground and peer in at the girls as they played field hockey, all of them dressed in orange and gray, with small felt hats. Once Miss Nickols herself, in bloomers and middy blouse, had flushed him from the shrubbery and ordered him off down the street. She had nothing to fear from him. He meant her girls no harm. He envied them their ivy-covered world and the large black cars that rolled up every afternoon at five to whisk them all away.

On past the school, across Thompson Street, he reached the park. A hundred yards away he could see the duck pond. It was matted with lilies and summer slime. The ducks were all up on the bank, preening themselves, the ground covered with their feathers.

Farther along two girls were playing tennis. When he paused, watching them, they started to giggle, and their game dissolved into confusion. It was wartime, 1944, and the shortage of young men was acute.

He left the park, crossed Buckeley Street, and started up Lawn Street Hill. It was the beginning of another blazing hot day. Already the tar along the curbstones was melting, and the air was limp with humidity.

The next two weeks, he suspected, would be dull. There was no one in the city who interested him any more, and it was not the place to spend a two-week leave from the army. Perhaps, he thought, he'd stay around just another two or three days and then drift on down to New York. His aunt might be disappointed, but she'd understand. She'd know he was bored.

Also he'd met a girl on the train coming up from Texas, an army brat she called herself, a general's daughter. She was heading for New York and acting school. "Call me," she said when she left the train at Penn Station. She handed him a slip of paper. On it she had written her name and a telephone number. He'd spend just a day or so more with his aunt, he decided, and then go on down to New York.

When he reached the top of the hill he stood on the sidewalk for a while, looking at the Olanders' house. It was one of the city's landmarks, with eleven chimneys and two stone turrets. Built in the 1890s, it was a relic of an era when people still dared admit they weren't poor.

Over the Olanders' slate roof he could see the entire city spread out to the east, the buildings shimmering in the July heat. Off to the right the gold dome of the state capitol reflected the morning sunlight, and he could see automobiles, like ants, moving across Capitol Park. The river cut the city in two and disappeared to the south, through the flat, green farmland. Far in the distance, across the river, he could make out the tobacco fields, like gray lakes, covered with their netting.

He crossed over to the west side of the street and looked at a large gatepost. Embedded in the stone was a bronze name plate. "L. C. Chalmers," he read to himself. How old would he have to be, he wondered, before the name Chalmers failed to cause a sudden tightening in his chest? Where was Polly Chalmers now? She must be married, he decided. No girl as beautiful as she had been at seventeen would still be living alone at twenty-four.

Then he said, "What the hell," and walked in the Chalmers' driveway. He had nothing to do. At least he could find out where Polly was. If she were home, and still unmarried, he'd ask her to play golf. But if she had moved away, then that would be the end of it. It would be a relief to have the dream shattered.

Someone in the Chalmers family, he could see, loved the lawn. There were nearly two acres of it, sloping toward the house, a thick, green, velvet sod, not a weed in sight. The house itself was a large oblong chunk of brownstone, an ancestral warehouse, with a slate roof and narrow casement windows. A mat of ivy covered the walls and curled out over the gutters. Between the house and the garage there was a small greenhouse, and over the greenhouse he could see the golf course in the distance, a rolling expanse of green.

A brass lion stared out at him from the center of the Chalmers' front door. In its jaws was clutched a brass ring. He lifted the ring and let it strike against the lion's mane. Then he placed his ear against the door and listened. He heard nothing. The house seemed empty and deserted.

The Chalmers must be away, he decided, turning around and looking out onto the lawn. What did Mr. Chalmers do for a living? He was wealthy. That much was obvious. But he also must work. That was the tradition in this city. Pauper or millionaire, you worked.

It was a good tradition too, he thought. That's why all the houses on The Lawn Street Hill remained, year after year, decade after decade, solid and strong. This was no society where people sucked wealth from the ground and then moved on when the hole ran dry. Here work had created the wealth, not oil or gold, lumber or cotton. This city might never have flowered, but for the same reason it had never withered and died. There was nothing here to interest the historian, and no romance to excite an artist. Here nothing would ever go with the wind, or if it did, it wouldn't much matter, as the loss would be well covered by insurance.

"Can I help you?" a voice asked through a crack in the door.

2

He could see only a single dark eye, a few freckles, and a lock of sandy blond hair. It wasn't Polly. Polly had dark hair and smooth white skin.

"I'm sorry to bother you," he said. "I was looking for a Polly Chalmers."

"Oh. You mean my sister." The door opened wider. "I know you vaguely, don't I? Aren't you Charlie somebody?"

"Yes," he answered, nodding. "Charlie Webb."

Polly had two sisters, he remembered, both of them older. This one seemed to be about his age. She was short and a little chunky. She was wearing gray flannel shorts and a man's white shirt with the sleeves rolled up. Her face was one which women call interesting and men can't remember well enough to describe. She seemed determined and efficient, poking a long chin out at him through the open door and looking at him appraisingly with her pale blue eyes.

"I'm Lucy Chalmers," she said, letting the door swing all the way open. "And now I remember you. You used to caddy at the club."

He nodded. "That's where I knew your sister Polly. I caddied for her a few times. I was going to ask her to play golf with me today."

"What a shame. Polly lives in New York now."

"Is she married?" he asked, feeling clumsy and foolish.

"Polly? Ha. Won't you come in? The house is closed up. Everyone is down at the Island."

"You wouldn't happen to have Polly's address, would you?" he asked, not moving from the door. "I'm going to New York in a day or so."

"I wish I could help you," she answered, "but I can't. Polly's like a tumbleweed. She moves around all the time, and I never do know where she's living. Just somewhere in New York. Won't you come in?"

"I guess not," he answered. "I have a few things I ought to do."

"Such as what?" she asked him casually, smiling at him for the first time. She had nice teeth, white and even. She looked almost pretty when she smiled.

"Nosy, aren't you?" he answered, smiling back at her. With Polly, he would have been tongue-tied with embarrassment. With her sister Lucy, he was completely at ease.

"Not nosy, just curious," she answered, unabashed.

"If you must know, I have an extremely important appointment down in the park. I'm going to feed the ducks." He started backing toward the driveway.

"Do you like ducks?" she asked, following him.

"I used to."

"I have an absolute passion for them. I really do."

"Then we have something in common."

One word from him, he realized, and Lucy Chalmers would go with him. She might even provide the stale bread.

"What are you doing these days, Charlie?"

"Army," he answered vaguely.

"Are you back on furlough?"

"Leave," he corrected. "I'm an officer."

"Well! Well! I beg your pardon. A general?"

"I'm a captain," he answered, blushing. She was obviously kidding him. She seemed terribly anxious for company. "What are you doing these days?" he asked.

She shrugged. "All sorts of things and nothing in particular. You know what girls do. I just came up from the Island to water mother's plants."

"To do what?" he asked incredulously.

"Water plants. Someone has to do it once a week, or they all die. The gardener is on vacation, so I had to do it. Would you like to see them?" She glanced toward the greenhouse. "We really have some rather beautiful things."

"I guess not. I wouldn't know a geranium from a daisy."

She looked disappointed. "Then run along and feed your ducks. It was fun seeing you again. Do you know what I remember about you, Charlie? Your golf swing. It was absolutely beautiful."

"Do you really remember that, or are you just saying it?" he asked, terribly flattered.

"I really do. Didn't you win the caddy tournament once?"

"As a matter of fact I did."

"It's odd," she answered. "I really remember you quite well. I'm holding you up," she added, waving her hand. "Go feed the ducks."

"I was just thinking that perhaps you would play golf with me."

"Me?" she asked, innocently.

"Why not? You play, don't you?"

"Well, sure I play a little. But you didn't come here to ask *me* to play, did you?"

"I'm asking you now."

"All right, I will, if you really mean it. Give me two seconds while I grab my clubs."

"I'll meet you at the club at one o'clock," he answered. "I'll have to walk home to get my own clubs."

"Walk?"

"I don't have a car."

"Well, I do," she answered. "I'll take you home."

"I'd rather walk."

"But that's utterly ridiculous. Go climb in my car, and I'll be right out." She started toward the house.

"I'd rather walk," he repeated.

She cocked her head at him thoughtfully, her hands on her hips.

"Suit yourself. I'll meet you at one. Incidentally," she asked, as he started toward the street, "do you mind me playing in shorts?"

"Why should I?" he answered, pausing, glancing at her legs for the first time. They were short and muscular, strong and efficient, but hardly legs that would cause a traffic jam.

"Mother thinks girls look slightly indecent in shorts."

4

Perhaps some girls did, he thought, coldly appraising her, but not this one. Lucy Chalmers would have trouble looking indecent wearing nothing at all. Why did he let himself get involved with her, he wondered. His leave would be short enough as it was. But it was too late to back out of it now. He'd play eighteen holes of golf with her and then say good-by.

"You look fine to me," he answered.

"Thank you, sir." She bowed low, as though he had paid her a compliment. "I play much better in shorts. Run along home. I'll see you at one."

two

IF EVER HE HAD A DAUGHTER, CHARLIE THOUGHT AT ONE THAT AFTERNOON AS he watched Lucy Chalmers drive off the first tee, the ball traveling straight down the fairway two hundred and twenty yards, he'd teach her to play a good game of golf. Tennis courts, beaches, swimming pools, and even the ski slopes were now dominated by women. Only the game of golf still seemed to baffle them. The girl who could play golf without making a fool of herself was rare. Yet Lucy sank a four-foot putt on the first green for her par.

She had the figure for golf, he thought, admiring it for the first time. A low center of gravity, which must have annoyed her on a dance floor, was useful for the game of golf. She had little or nothing to get in the way of her backswing, and her short, sturdy legs provided an excellent base for her pivot. She was good. He told her so as they teed off for the second hole.

"I probably learned it from my father," she answered, removing a wooden tee from behind her ear and placing it expertly in the sod. "He plays a pretty good game. Anyway it's about all I've been doing since I got out of Smith." She smashed another drive two hundred yards down the middle of the fairway.

"I mean you're really good," he said five minutes later, when she sank another putt for her second par.

"Well, thank you, sir," she answered, scooping her ball out of the cup. "As I remember, you once played a pretty fair game yourself."

Her use of the past tense didn't escape him. It was the first time he had held a golf club in his hands for over three years. He had played a good game once. He'd won some tournaments about the state, and he played on his college team for two years. Of one thing he was certain. In all the years he had played golf, no girl had ever beaten him. In fact the girls he had played with had never even *tried* to beat him.

Lucy Chalmers didn't seem to know the rules, however. Not only was she trying to beat him, she was succeeding. At the end of the first nine holes he was five down.

She acted like a professional, concentrating on each shot, lining up her putts from both ends, and tossing a few blades of grass into the air as she walked along the fairway to test the wind. Par for the first nine was thirty-six. Lucy shot a forty, he had a forty-five. Lucy Chalmers was out to take him, he decided.

The day was hot. Both of them were drenched with perspiration when they started the second nine. They had caught up to a foursome ahead of them, and they sat waiting on a bench near the rear of the tee.

"I might play a little better," he said, "if we were playing some sort of a match."

"But we are playing a match," she answered, holding her hair away from her neck, letting the breeze cool her skin. "We're trying to beat each other."

"Are we?"

"Aren't you trying to beat me?"

"I thought this was a social game."

"You can be social and still beat people."

"Your honor," he answered, smiling, amused at her vehemence.

"Seriously," she continued, as they were walking down the fairway, "why shouldn't women be allowed to beat men?"

"Most men find it slightly unflattering."

"Oh, pish. Do women have to flatter men all the time?"

"Don't you like to be flattered?"

"I just like to win," she answered. "That's the only real kind of flattery, anyway."

"I still think we ought to play for some sort of stake. I need more incentive."

"Name it," she answered, watching him.

"All right. If you beat me I'll buy you a dinner tonight."

"And if you win?"

"You buy the dinner."

"I can hardly lose on that. I was hoping we could have dinner together anyway."

"That's a form of subtle flattery right there," he answered.

"Maybe it is, but I mean it. I like you. Do you like me?"

Lucy Chalmers was a strange girl, he decided.

"Yes, I do like you," he answered, surprised to discover he meant it.

"All right. The bet's on."

A moment later she topped an approach shot. It was the first poor shot she had made all afternoon.

He won that hole, the next, and the next. On the seventeenth hole he was even with her. As his game improved, hers got worse. The eighteenth hole was a short par four. Charlie gambled and drove straight for the green, aiming his shot over a grove of trees. The ball sailed out into the sunlight, bounced on a hard patch on the fairway, and rolled onto the green, straight toward the pin. A moment later he sank a six-foot putt for an eagle two.

"Looks like I won," he said casually, writing the figure 2 down on his scorecard with an exaggerated flourish. He looked at Lucy, grinning. She stared back at him with a mixture of expressions—admiration, annoyance, and frustration.

"I hope you weren't just letting me win at first, Charlie."

"I've been trying to beat hell out of you since the first hole," he answered. "I don't mind being beaten, but not by a girl. Where do we eat tonight?"

"I had an idea. We have this farm outside the city. It's not really a farm. I mean it used to be before we bought it, but now it's just a place where we have picnics and things like that. Why don't I drive you back to your house and you can change your clothes, and then we can go buy something to eat. Maybe some hamburg and beer. Do you like beer?"

"I love it."

"Then how does that strike you? We could just slop around out there until supper time."

"All right. Except that I'd rather walk home from here."

She opened her mouth to argue, then thought better of it. "All right. Whatever you say. Where shall we meet?"

"I'll be at your house at five."

Lucy Chalmers improved on acquaintance, he decided as he was walking home. The more he saw of her, the less he minded that she wasn't pretty. She was pleasant and intelligent, and he really liked her.

"Who with?" his aunt asked him when Charlie told her he'd be out for supper. His aunt dressed too well for her years; her hair was a shade too blue, and she wore too much makeup. She had arrived back from her dress shop just as he was going out the front door.

"With a girl named Lucy Chalmers," he answered. "I don't believe you know her."

"Wasn't it a Polly Chalmers you were once so crazy about?"

"This is Polly's older sister."

His aunt nodded and said, "I remember her now. She was rather short and plump as a little girl. I always had a terrible time fitting her. Did she tell you I used to make all her dancing school dresses?"

"She didn't mention it," he answered coldly. Then he added, "I've got to go. I told her I'd meet her at five."

"Why don't you rent a car?" his aunt called after him.

"Lucy has a car."

"All the more reason for you to be independent," she said.

But he didn't answer, and walked away up the street.

He reached the Chalmers' house just before five. There was a note tacked on the front door.

"Off buying food," he read. "Be back soon. Walk on in."

The house had been closed up tight, and the air smelled musty and damp. He walked across the front hall and looked into the living room, a huge, dimly lit cavern that extended half the length of the house. The west curtains had been drawn, and sunlight slanted through cracks in the material, sending beams of yellow light across the room to the opposite wall. The rugs

7

had been taken up for the summer, and the oak flooring had heaved in the dampness. At the center of the ceiling there was a large brown stain, as though years before a tub had overflowed above and leaked down through the plaster.

The room reminded him of an antique shop. The dominant mood seemed to be one of expensive shoddiness. All the furniture—chairs, sofas, two large carved oak chests, numerous tables, a long upholstered footstool by the fireplace, three ancient wing chairs with faded slip covers, corner cupboards with glassware and china—all was stored in the room rather than arranged with any sort of comfort in mind. We have these things, Mrs. Chalmers must have said, and therefore they must be displayed. Tucked away in a corner, as though it was hoped they would weather for a generation before being introduced to the world at large, were two new and comfortable reading chairs. Here was the island in the room where people lived. The rest of it was merely space where heirlooms were stored.

Where did people like the Chalmers spend their money, Charlie wondered. They had no yachts, no stable filled with racing horses, nor did they sponsor such things as the opera or plays. It wasn't done around here. No one went fox hunting, gambled, or gave large parties. What did they do with their bank accounts besides balance them once each month? Nothing?

Inherited money made cripples out of people, he decided. It carried with it a legacy of guilt. If you were born rich you must plead poverty. Only the man who made it himself could truly enjoy his good fortune.

He walked over to the curtains at the west side of the room. No one without a great deal of money would have the nerve to leave rags like these hanging, he thought. They were in shreds. If he so much as touched them, he suspected, they would dissolve into antique dust. That was the tradition here. Keep things until they fell apart, wear suits until the light shone through. If you must boast, boast only of the holes in your socks. And if you must buy, buy only the very best, because your grandchildren would be using it too. Live quietly amid dusty luxury, and pass it on intact to your children.

He walked back into the hall. The walls were covered with portraits. Ancestors, he judged, gazing up at them. Directly opposite the front door a choleric-looking individual with bushy sideburns stared disapprovingly out of his expensive gold frame, his eyes narrow and mean, his mouth a thin hard line. Here was the start of it all, Charlie decided. Here was the man who must have planted the original seed. What did he do? Whatever it was, it was plain that this man had lived and died with an accurate set of books.

"Do you approve of my great-great-grandfather Hadley?" Lucy asked, coming in the front door.

"Banker?" Charlie asked.

"Guess again."

"Beggar man, thief?"

"Blacksmith."

"I don't believe it. Blacksmiths don't rate portraits."

8

"This one did. Great-great-grandfather Hadley, bless his greedy little soul, invented a better horseshoe nail."

"Seriously?"

"Seriously. Did you ever hear of The Hadley Company?"

"Oh, so that's it."

"So that's what?" she asked, cocking her head at him.

"I mean, is that your father's company?"

"My mother was the Hadley. Shall we go?" she asked, changing the subject. "Well, well, well," she shouted, noticing his uniform and his captain's bars for the first time. "How impressive."

"I just thought I ought to prove it to you," he answered, blushing. "If it embarrasses you, I'll——"

"Why should it embarrass me? You look magnificent." She took his arm and headed toward the door. "I'll lock up. You drive."

"Poor father," Lucy said as they were driving north out of the city. "He wanders about the countryside buying himself retreats. Then we move in, and he has to retreat to somewhere else."

"What's he retreating from?" Charlie asked.

"I don't know. What do men retreat from? Women, I suppose. Us. A wife and three daughters."

"What's he do in his retreats?"

"None of us really know. Reads, I think. Reads, and thinks, and polishes his furniture."

"Polishes his what?"

"Furniture. Antiques. Didn't you notice our house was filled with them?"

"To me, antiques are just old furniture."

"Well, they are old furniture," she answered, laughing, "but not *just* old furniture. Turn here," she said, putting her fingers on his arm and pointing to a side road. "It's about five more miles. I hope you won't be bored out here. It isn't much of a place. Mother has absolutely no interest in it, and it's more or less running downhill."

They drove for a while through the tobacco fields. The plants were already six feet tall, lush and dark green.

"Father once actually talked about all of us moving out here," Lucy said, giggling. "Mother put the damper on that in a hurry."

"She didn't like the idea?"

"You've never met my mother, I gather."

"If I have, I don't remember it."

"If you had, you would remember her. She's a rather positive person, and she hates rustic living. She likes servants, twenty rooms, and her greenhouse."

"How about you?" he asked, suddenly interested in her answer.

"I'm supposed to be quite a bit like my mother," she answered.

"Then you wouldn't like to live in the country?"

"I was born in the city, and I like the city. Quaint little farmhouses are just fine for other people. I like comfort. Now," she said, putting her hand

9

on his arm again, "here's the driveway. It's another half-mile in from here."

They crossed a small stream, the car rumbling over a narrow wooden bridge. Then they came out into a clearing, an old field that had started to grow up with cedar and birch. At the far end of it was the house. It was red, a salt-box with a gray stone wall near the front door and a well near an old maple tree. A century before, lilacs had been planted at each corner of the house. The bushes had now joined along each wall.

"This," Lucy said, opening the car door and stepping out, "is it. Be it ever so humble. You never came out here with Polly?" she asked.

"I never went anywhere with Polly."

"I used to suspect Polly did some rather swift things out here a few years ago. She's that type. Where shall we sit? Inside or out?"

"Whatever you say."

"Then let's sit outside. It looks like a wonderful evening."

There was a stone fireplace near the wall. They cooked the hamburger and drank beer, sitting on the wall. It was warm and completely still. Overhead, hundreds of swallows glided back and forth across the sky, swooping down over the open field, gathering in the insects. The field was dry and smelled faintly of sweet fern.

"How about you?" Lucy asked.

"What about me?"

"Would you like to live in a place like this?"

"It's pleasant tonight."

"Tonight, yes. It's wonderful in summer. But how about the winter? Oh, sure. It's fine for the man of the house. He goes off each morning. But the little woman sits at home in splendid isolation and wonders if the romance of it all is worth it. Give me neighbors."

"The trouble is," Charlie answered, "that if you live in the city you more or less have to live just like everyone else lives."

"What's wrong with that?"

"I'm not sure I like the idea of being confined."

"It's all just semantics," she answered. "We're civilized people, and civilized people visit the country and live in the city. Let's go for a walk."

three

THEY CARRIED THEIR BEER WITH THEM AS THEY WALKED ACROSS THE FIELD to the brook. There was a stone dam near the bridge. The water was stained dark brown from the evergreen trees upstream.

"I can't see why you all don't do something with this place," Charlie said when they were standing on the dam, looking at their reflections in the water.

"As a family we don't like to do things with places," Lucy answered. She slapped a mosquito on her arm. "Let's keep moving or we'll be eaten alive."

It was nearly dark when they returned to the house. They sat inside, on a sagging brown couch that faced the fireplace. As it gradually grew dark outside, they drank beer and listened to the radio.

After a while Charlie asked casually, "What's Polly doing in New York?"

"None of us really know," Lucy answered thoughtfully, as though she were trying her best to be kind. "She says she's acting, but I honestly don't think she's doing anything. Polly's trouble," she continued, "is that she went to the wrong college. Bennington ruined her. She got mixed up with some sort of a theater group up there, and she hasn't outgrown it. I mean, you know every girl goes through a period when she thinks she'd like to be an actress or have some kind of a career. That's all right. It's supposed to be healthy. But then most of us outgrow it. Polly never did. My younger sister," Lucy added, smiling toward the fireplace, "just can't stand the thought that she might be just like everyone else."

"What's everyone else like?" he asked.

"I mean normal. Polly's determined not to be normal."

"She certainly was a beautiful girl."

"I suppose she still is," Lucy admitted reluctantly.

They were quiet for a while. Crickets were singing outside, and Charlie's face burned. He loosened his collar.

"I'm about to fall asleep," he said.

Lucy stood up and crossed the room to the radio. She turned the dial until she found music. Then she opened two more beers and handed him one. When she sat again on the couch she was closer to him.

"You have another sister, don't you?" he asked.

"Anne."

"What's she like?"

"A mess. She's living down in the slums of Philadelphia."

"Why the slums?"

"From the time she was about this high," Lucy answered, "Anne has had a mania to espouse causes. It started with stray cats and dogs. Our house used to be alive with them. Then when she went off to Bryn Mawr, she graduated to people. God," she added, shaking her head, "Anne used to drag home the oddest collection of human misfits. Christmas at our house when she was at college was like a settlement house. You never knew who she'd bring home. She'd meet people in railroad stations, and on street corners, and insist that they join us for Christmas. In theory that's fine, but it made for some damn sticky Christmases."

"What's she doing in the slums?"

"The same thing, more or less. She got all fouled up with religion. I know that sounds terrible when I say it that way, but that's really what happened. She damn near turned Catholic. It was touch and go for about a year. She wanted to be a priest," Lucy exclaimed, as though she still couldn't believe it. "A woman priest."

"She could have been a nun."

"She wasn't quite that neurotic. When she found she couldn't be a priest,

11

she settled for a minister. That's what she is. A woman minister. And she also married one. Clyde's a minister too. They run a private settlement house. I honestly don't really know *what* it is. They feed people and encourage people."

"What do you mean, private?" he asked.

"Anne does it with her own money. That's the nub of the whole thing right there. That's always been Anne's trouble. The fact that we have a little more money than other people has always made her feel guilty. She's determined to give it all away. Do you know what my sister Anne needs?" she asked, turning toward Charlie. "She needs children."

"I gather she doesn't have any?"

"She doesn't want any. I mean it. She doesn't. It's all part of her being fouled up with religion. She says quite frankly that she won't ever have a baby of her own because she wants to be a mother to everyone, and not to one or two children in particular. She apparently talked it all over with Clyde before they were married, and he agreed."

"She sounds rather interesting," he said thoughtfully.

Lucy smiled at him. "That's the way they used to describe us, the three Chalmers girls. Polly was the pretty one. Anne was the interesting one." She paused.

"What were you?"

"I was the dull one," she answered in a tone of mild defiance.

"What does that mean?"

"That I never wanted to act, or have a career, or uplift the poor, or do anything but find myself a husband I loved and have a family."

"That makes you dull?"

"Apparently."

They were quiet for a moment. In the distance, a dog was barking.

"What are you going to do when the war is over?" she asked.

"I'll probably just get some kind of job."

"No big plans of reforming the world?"

"I like the world the way it is."

"Hurrah. So do I. More beer?" she asked.

He shook his head.

"I don't need beer when I'm enjoying myself."

He could feel her melt as he spoke. She leaned back and rested her head against the couch, her face turned toward him.

"Where do you want to work when the war's over?" she asked.

"It doesn't make too much difference."

"Would you like working around here?"

"There are worse places."

"I love my home," she answered. "I love it, and I intend to live here always."

Their eyes met then. She could be kissed, Charlie decided. He had kissed enough girls in his twenty-six years to recognize the signs when he saw them. He could kiss Lucy Chalmers if he wanted to. Instead, he stood up and walked across to the fireplace.

12

"Let's drive somewhere," he said. "We could put the top down on your car, and drive."

"Such as home," she answered, her hands folded tightly in her lap.

"I didn't mean that."

"You seem to forget that gasoline is rationed. We used up two weeks' supply just getting out here. Anyway, you're bored, so let's go home."

She stalked toward the car.

"I wasn't bored," he insisted, when they were driving toward the main road. "What made you say that?"

"Because it's obvious that you were bored. I talked too much, and I've bored you to tears."

She sat quiet and sullen all the way back into the city, her head against the window on her side.

"You're terribly quiet," he said finally, as they drove into the city.

"I think it's time I kept quiet, don't you?"

"I enjoyed hearing about your family."

She continued to stare out the window.

"You said something this afternoon about going back down to the Island tomorrow."

"I probably will."

"I thought we might play golf again."

She was quiet for a moment.

"Is that an invitation?" she asked.

"I meant it to be."

"I thought you were going down to New York."

"I can change my plans."

"When would you like to play golf?"

"Tomorrow."

"All right."

"And I have another idea. Why don't we play golf every day for the next two weeks? At least, why don't we do something together every day?"

"You shouldn't say things like that if you don't mean it, Charlie." She had turned away from the window.

"But I do mean it. I don't remember another day I've enjoyed as much as today."

"I've enjoyed it too," she answered, as he turned in at the Lawn Street driveway. "You're not going to walk home in the darkness, are you?" she asked, when he stopped the car.

"Yes."

She reached across and took one of his hands. "Listen to me," she said firmly. "I know where you live. You live on South Franklin Street. I know all about it. I looked up your address in the phone book, and this afternoon I drove right past your house. I also know your aunt runs a dress shop, and she also used to make my dresses when I was young. You're ashamed of it, aren't you?"

He sat speechless with embarrassment.

"Aren't you?" she repeated.

"I don't think you know what it's like," he answered.

"Oh, posh," she answered harshly. "Who cares if you don't have a father who's a vice president of moving papers from one insurance file to another? And who cares if you were brought up by an aunt who had to work for a living instead of spending her life making flower arrangements? It's you who are the snob." She twisted his hand. "Why did you drop by to see Polly? Did you really want to see her, or did you just like the thought that you know someone who lives on Lawn Street Hill?"

"I am a snob, Lucy."

"Well, you're honest about it."

"I've always envied families like yours."

"Oh, posh, posh, posh," she shouted. "All this makes me wonder if you really like me."

"I like you," he answered, looking at her. Her shoulder was touching his. "I like you as much as I've ever liked anyone in my life."

"And I like you," she answered, her voice catching. "Now listen to me. And don't argue with me. I want you to take my car. I mean it," she insisted, when he started to shake his head. "I mean it, and when I say I mean something, I mean it. You take my car. I will *not* have you walking up here every day to meet me. If we're going to play golf together, and whatever else we decide to do—anyway, my car is now yours, and let's have no further discussion about it." She smiled. "Except that I don't expect you to run off to New York with it."

"I won't," he answered. "And Lucy . . ."

"And Lucy what?" she asked.

She had a beautiful mouth, he noticed. A thin delicate line, very straight and strong.

"Thank you."

"Well, you're welcome, I'm sure," she answered, surprised. She slid out the car door onto the driveway. "Tomorrow," she said. "Come for breakfast if you like. Throw stones against my window. It's around in back."

She stood in the driveway, watching her car disappear. Her knees felt weak and rubbery. After a while she turned and went into the house. There was a fresh quart of milk in the icebox, and she sat at the kitchen table drinking it, trying to decide what it was about the day that had been so completely different.

"My God, I'm in love," she said harshly, pushing away from the table, nearly spilling the milk.

It was true, she decided. She was violently in love. There had been a moment earlier that evening when she had been sitting next to Charlie on the couch, when if he had so much as touched her she would have thrown herself into his arms. For the first time in her life she had wanted physical love.

"My God, my God, my God," she muttered, opening the icebox door, and replacing the milk. "You're mad. You're mad. You're mad," she whispered to herself as she ran up the stairs into her room.

She undressed slowly, standing in front of the open window. There was a faint breeze coming in from the west. She could smell the flowers in the terrace garden. Then she stood naked in front of the mirror on her closet door.

What made men want to marry girls? she wondered. Men always wanted to marry her sister Polly, and no one had ever wanted to marry her. Why should beauty be so important? Wouldn't she make a much better wife than Polly? I want to be married, she thought. I want to be a wife. Could a man want more than that?

She ran across her room and lay face down on her bed. Downstairs one of the clocks struck the hour. It was eleven o'clock.

"Eleven o'clock and all is well," she said aloud, feeling silly.

She rolled over on her back and reached out toward the ceiling with a bare leg, pointing with her toes.

"You're going to marry me, Charlie Webb," she whispered to herself. "You don't know it yet, but you are going to marry me."

four

LIKE MOST UNMARRIED GIRLS, LUCY CHALMERS BY THE TIME SHE HAD REACHED her twenty-sixth year had received a good deal of unsolicited advice from her mother on the subject of how she might make herself more attractive to men. Lucy had listened attentively but hadn't taken any of the suggestions too seriously.

It wasn't that she was an arrogant person, nor was she under any illusions about her natural physical charms. She had been blessed with the minimum, and she knew it. It was simply that she was certain that when the right man finally came her way, she would get him.

Her chief assets were of the spirit, she knew, not of the body. She was neither beautiful nor even particularly attractive, but she was a competitor. Salesmen didn't make sales because they were handsome, nor did women necessarily have to be beautiful to end up with a husband. Persistence and determination must be reckoned with in all things. Men in general had never really interested Lucy. Since growing out of the girlhood crush that had hit her at nineteen, she had thought of herself as saving her energy for one man in particular, the right man when he came along. When he appeared, she'd enter the game with a will to win, and there was not the slightest doubt in her mind that she'd walk off the field with the prize.

"If we're lucky," Charlie said as they stood on the first tee the following Thursday afternoon, "it will veer off down the river." He pointed with his driver toward a small black cloud on the horizon to the west. "Anyway, let's take a chance. I think this is going to be my lucky day."

Lucy agreed without enthusiasm. It was the fifth day of a heat wave, and she was exhausted. During the last five days she and Charlie had played a total of ninety holes of golf. It had been her suggestion that noon, when they were eating lunch in the kitchen, that they spend the afternoon on the terrace, sunning themselves and spraying each other with the hose. Or they might sit about the house and play records, she suggested. Or read. Anything but play more golf. She was sick of golf. She had never before realized just how public a private golf course could be, and how little chance there was for intimacy on one hundred and fifty acres of open ground.

If they started discussing some interesting subject, something of a personal nature, Charlie would be sure to slice a shot a hundred yards away, and she wouldn't see him again for five minutes, and by then the mood would be completely shattered. She had always loved golf. Now she hated it. She stopped keeping her score, conceded herself long putts, giggled when she missed shots, and in general acted like any other girl on a golf course. Golf had ceased to be the game she was playing.

Charlie had found the change in her baffling. He did his best to revive her interest, giving her helpful hints, changing her swing slightly, and making it a point to compliment her whenever she hit a good shot. Her game seemed suddenly to have gone to pieces, and it puzzled him. That she was in love, that her knees nearly buckled every time he came close to her, never occurred to him.

Since their first evening together at the farm, he had seen to it that there was no repetition of the scene on the couch. Lucy had become a good friend, and he wanted it to stay that way. This would be one two-week leave from the army he wouldn't mess up with some emotional crisis with a girl. Girls didn't take their emotions as casually as men, he had discovered. This would be one girl he'd say good-by to without an ugly or embarrassing scene.

He hoped Lucy would write to him. He planned to suggest it before he left. He liked her. She was honest, sincere, and genuine. One night, while they were sitting in the Chalmers' kitchen eating a late supper after golf, he had paid her what he considered a great compliment.

"You're going to wear well," he said. "Forty years from now you'll look just about the way you do tonight."

"Well, thank you," Lucy answered angrily. "Just like the Great Stone Face you mean, or a tombstone."

"Seriously," he answered, embarrassed. "I like your looks because they're so durable."

"Good old durable Lucy. Salt of the earth."

"I didn't mean it that way," he answered, completely confused.

"Then how did you mean it?"

"I mean I like your looks, and I like you."

"Then say it that way," she answered, suddenly pleased.

Charlie's conduct was equally baffling to Lucy. What did a girl have to do? she wondered. Short of coming right out and saying it, how did she get the point across that she loved him? He was treating her like a sister, cool and painfully respectful. He did like her. She was certain of that. She saw it

16

occasionally in his eyes. What was holding him back? If she sat next to him, he'd get up and move. If she brushed the back of his hand while they were walking along together, he'd pull back his hand as though she had burned him with a cigarette. And his mania for golf drove her wild. As her game fell apart, his improved daily. All he talked about was his next shot, and when the round ended, he'd talk about how he could have improved it. When finally, that Thursday, she'd gathered enough courage to suggest that they do something else besides play golf, he had looked so disappointed that she gave in instantly, afraid he'd go off to play alone. She resigned herself to another three hours of frustration.

"How long do you think you'll stay in Texas?" she asked, when they were walking along the second fairway.

"Two weeks. Maybe a month at the most. We're on our way overseas."

"How can you be so sure?"

"You can sense it. We hear rumors of Italy."

"A month isn't very long," she answered thoughtfully.

"Frankly, I'll be glad to go," he said. "I'd like to see something of the world, even if I do get shot at while I'm doing it. At least I'm single," he added. "The people I'm really sorry for are the wives who get left behind."

"Oh, pish," Lucy exclaimed angrily. "That's utter nonsense. Men are such fools. If two people want to get married, they should do it, war or no war. Even if they have just a single day together, or even an hour. You should never put things off, even a marriage. If you do, it never takes place."

A moment later Charlie hooked a brassie shot, and they didn't meet again until they were on the green. The conversation about marriage was not resumed.

By the end of the first nine, the thunderhead in the distance had increased in size. It now covered most of the sky to the north and the west, and there were flashes of lightning. It was moving fast, black and menacing.

"I suppose we ought to pick up and go home," Charlie said, watching the cloud. "I hate to, though. I'm playing pretty close to par."

The rain came when they were midway through the thirteenth hole. It started with a sudden blast of cold air. Then a deluge, driven by the wind, swept horizontally across the course, drenching them both instantly.

Lucy scooped her ball from the turf, and squealing with terror and delight, she darted for a small shelter behind the green.

She could really run, Charlie thought approvingly, watching her race down the fairway. She held her skirt well above her knees and lifted her knees high, like a halfback. She didn't shuffle, and she didn't skip, and she didn't hop. She ran. He liked that. Then he finished out the hole, keeping his hands dry in his pockets, and sinking a long putt through the standing water on the green for his par.

He found her curled up on a pile of burlap bags. She was still breathing hard from her exercise, and she was soaked to the skin.

"You were right," he said, standing over her. "We should have stayed home. This has been building up for days."

"Sit down and watch it," she ordered, pulling at his shoelace. "It's absolutely beautiful."

The rain was blowing in continuous waves across the course, like squalls across open water. The ground had been baked hard, and the water collected in puddles, then ponds, and finally lakes. It was dark inside the shelter, a gray light that was shattered occasionally by the flashes of lightning.

There was a pulse beating at the base of Lucy's neck. He put his finger against it.

"I'm freezing," she whispered, shuddering.

"You don't feel like it," he answered.

"What do I feel?"

"Just wet." He kept his finger on her neck.

"What are you doing?" she asked, leaning toward him, her face turned against his shoulder.

"Feeling your heart."

"What's it saying?"

He never answered. He was kissing her, and she was kissing him, violently, her arms around his neck, her body pressing against his.

"Why do we do this?" he whispered, his lips against her ear.

"Don't you want to do it?"

"You know I do."

"Then why shouldn't we do it?"

He kissed her again, lowering her onto the burlap, his arms under her shoulders, his chest against hers.

"Is this forever?" she whispered.

He nodded, searching for her lips.

"Forever?" she repeated.

"Forever," he whispered, not quite sure what she meant.

"Do you love me, Charlie? I love you."

"Perhaps I do," he answered.

"You must know," she whispered.

"I guess I do."

"Only guess?"

"I do," he answered. A few kisses wouldn't involve him too deeply, he decided. He'd now have to sign his letters with love instead of with sincerity, but it might not ruin everything if he was careful.

"Darling," she whispered, stretching, her entire body suddenly against his. She ran her hands down his back.

"You know what this makes me want to do, Lucy?"

"I know," she whispered. "But I think we can wait, don't you?"

"I suppose we can," he answered, not sure what she meant.

"Come on," she said, struggling to her feet. "We've got a jillion things to do." She reached for her golf bag and pulled him out onto the course, still holding his hand.

"Where to?" he asked, noticing that she was heading not toward the fourteenth tee, but straight for the clubhouse. The rain had stopped, and even though he felt a little limp, he still planned to finish out the eighteen holes.

She turned toward him and put her clubs down on the grass. Then she placed her hands on his shoulders, tilting her face up toward his.

"I don't want to wait, darling. I don't want to be engaged to someone in the army. I want to be married. I meant what I said earlier. I don't mind being left alone. I want to get married right now."

Had he said anything about marriage? he wondered. He walked with her toward the clubhouse. He really was in a jam now. What had he said when they were together in the shelter? As far as he could remember, only that he loved her. He should have realized that love meant marriage to a girl like Lucy Chalmers. She was no one that he could toy with without expecting a reaction. She meant it, he thought miserably. She considered herself engaged, and now they were on their way to be married unless he stopped it. But how could he stop it? He was in a terrible jam.

"I adore it after a storm, don't you?" Lucy asked, looking at him.

He nodded. The warm ground was steaming in the cool air, and a flock of starlings were moving about the sod, digging for worms and grubs. The sky to the north was already blue, while the storm rumbled off to the south down the river.

Perhaps he ought to marry her, he thought. He liked her. She was the nicest girl he'd ever met. At least he could let the whole thing go along for a while longer, while he thought about it. Right now he was confused. He'd let things take their natural course, and it would come out all right in the end. Girls were sensitive, and the proper way to handle them was not by slapping them in the face.

"What are you thinking about?" she asked.

He stopped and turned her about until she faced him.

"Are you sure you want to marry me?"

"Yes, I want to marry you," she answered soberly.

"But why? I'm nothing."

"What do you mean, you're nothing. I won't have you thinking that any more. You're the man I love, and that's all that matters to me."

"But your family——"

"My family will be pleased," she interrupted. She hugged him, her face against his chest.

"Then you really love me?"

She nodded. "Do you love me, Charlie?"

"I think I do," he answered. "Yes, I do," he repeated.

"Then let's get married. Isn't that what we ought to do?"

"I suppose we should. But shouldn't we wait a while? I mean, there isn't much time."

"I don't want to wait," she answered. "And don't worry about the time. We'll make it." She pulled down his head and kissed him. "I knew this was going to happen. I knew it practically from the first moment I saw you. How long ago was that?" she asked, her lips close to his. "It seems like ages. I've got to call Mother right away." Then she laughed, a completely happy sound. "My poor father. Something always comes up to ruin his vacation."

"Say hello to Mother," Lucy said less than a half-hour later, handing Charlie the receiver.

"Now you two children hold your horses," Mrs. Chalmers shouted. The connection was poor. Her voice sounded a thousand miles away. "Mr. Chalmers and I are leaving here tomorrow morning. You and Lucy won't do anything rash, will you, Charlie?"

"We won't," he answered.

"And give my very special love to your aunt," Mrs. Chalmers added earnestly. "Tell her how terribly fond of her I've always been."

"I will, Mrs. Chalmers."

"Now put Lucy on again. She and I have a few things to work out."

He heard Mrs. Chalmers giggle nervously at the other end of the line.

"Now where?" he asked Lucy, when she had finished speaking to her mother. She was heading out the door.

"To your house, silly. We have to tell your aunt, don't we?"

"I suppose we do," he answered.

"Of course we do. Would you mind terribly, darling, if we don't have a huge wedding?" She turned and looked at him earnestly. "Mother said, and I agree, that on such short notice a family wedding will be just about all we can manage. Will that be a terrible disappointment to you?"

"It seems sensible," he answered. He still found it impossible to believe that this girl who was now gazing up at him, her eyes sparkling with excitement, would shortly be his wife. It's really a joke, he kept thinking, a game that he and Lucy were playing. In a while she would start to laugh, then he'd laugh, and it would all be over.

"Mother's absolutely marvelous at organizing things. She thought next Monday. That gives us four days. If you're worried about announcements," Lucy added when she noticed his startled expression, "we can mail those out later. It's done all the time."

"Is it?" he asked weakly. The matter of announcements hadn't crossed his mind.

"Promise me you're not disappointed."

"About what?"

"About not having a big wedding."

"I've never thought too much about it."

She hugged him happily and tilted her head back for his kiss.

"Your aunt hasn't even met me," she giggled.

"I know."

"You've told her about me, haven't you? I mean she knows you've been seeing me lately?"

"She knows," he answered.

"Good. It would be simply terrible if you hadn't said anything."

Now would be the time, he thought. Now would be the time to face it

20

and tell Lucy the truth—that the whole business had gotten out of hand, that he didn't love her and didn't want to marry her. Right now, he thought, looking at her. He should tell her right now or else it would be too late.

They were standing in the hall. Over Lucy's shoulder he could see great-great-grandfather Hadley looking down at him from the wall. Would he approve of this? Charlie wondered. The chances are he would, he thought. The man who had owned that pair of cold eyes would approve of any arrangement as long as there was profit in it.

"What are you thinking now?" Lucy asked.

"Just about how happy I am," he answered. "Let's go break the good news to my aunt."

five

"CHARLIE," HIS AUNT SAID AT NINE-THIRTY THAT EVENING, "BEFORE YOU GO off to your room, I'd like to have a talk with you."

He settled into a chair. He knew what was coming. They had all eaten dinner together, and Lucy had just left to go home. As she left, she had asked his aunt to make her a wedding dress.

"You hardly seem like the happiest of prospective bridegrooms," his aunt continued, seating herself at her sewing machine.

"Are any prospective bridegrooms happy?" he asked.

"You don't look happy at all."

"How do I look?"

"Let me ask you," she countered. "How do you feel?"

"Stunned," he answered. He smiled uneasily. "You didn't expect me to say that, did you?"

"This whole thing has come as a complete surprise to me, Charlie. I just don't know what to say."

"Does that mean you don't approve of it?"

"Not at all. I'd just like to know whether you love this Lucy Chalmers."

He rose from the chair and walked to the window.

"I'll be completely honest with you," he began. "Probably the main reason why I'm going to marry Lucy is because I think it's a good idea."

"What in the world does that mean?" his aunt asked him. She was looking through a book of dress patterns, turning down pages.

"During the last three years," he continued, "I've met at least a dozen girls I probably could have married. Everything from a waitress to this general's daughter I came up from Texas with on the train. I wasn't in love with any of them, but I probably could have married them, and made out all right."

"Go on," his aunt said, when he paused.

"I'm being completely cold-blooded now, but I've always envied families

21

like the Chalmers, and maybe I just like the idea of marrying a girl named Lucy Chalmers. Does that shock you?" he asked.

"Not at all," she answered promptly. "And now I'll be honest with you. One of my worst fears has always been that you would get yourself blinded by a pretty figure somewhere and end up married to a complete nobody. If you had done that, I would have felt that everything I'd ever done for you would be wasted."

"I've turned into a terrible snob," he interrupted.

"Of course you have, and I'm glad of it." She looked across the room at him for a moment. "You've always been a little ashamed of me, haven't you?"

He didn't answer.

"I'm not blind," she continued, her voice showing no bitterness. "After all, it's been me that has pushed you. It was me that made you go to good schools and to a good college. It was me who used to freeze out any girl you brought back here who I didn't approve of. And Lucy Chalmers is exactly the sort of girl I've always hoped you *would* marry. That's the main reason why I've been working myself so hard for the past twenty years. Just so you wouldn't have to marry someone like me."

"I've never appreciated you," he answered quietly.

"Of course you haven't. I didn't expect you would."

"Then you approve of my marrying Lucy?"

"Where do you plan to live after the war is over?" she asked, not answering his question.

"Probably back here. It doesn't make too much difference to me, but I know Lucy wants to stay here."

"She'd be foolish to live anywhere else. Let me tell you something about these so-called good families like the Chalmers, Charlie. And this applies to all of them up there on Lawn Street Hill. They're big frogs in an extremely small pond. Thirty miles away from here they're nothing, just tadpoles like everyone else. If you married Lucy Chalmers," she continued, "and took her out to Chicago or to Denver, she'd be just another rather ugly little girl from somewhere back east. The only place the name Chalmers means a thing is right here. So if you think the magic name Chalmers is going to be a dowry for you, you'd better plan to spend your life right here."

"Now who's being cold-blooded?" he asked.

She moved back to her sewing machine. "When you come back after the war is over, I won't be here. I'm going to move away."

"To where?" he asked, surprised.

"I'm not sure. Probably to Florida."

"Why?"

"For two reasons," she answered. "First, because I hate it here." She paused a moment for her words to register. "To like this place you almost have to be born here, and I wasn't. This is no city to move to unless you've married into some family like the Chalmers. That's the main reason. The other is because I don't want to be in your way. Now, don't look shocked. You know perfectly well what I mean. I will not have Mrs. Chalmers patronizing her son-in-law's aunt and feeling she has to explain to me why I can't be made a member of all her clubs. I will not be an embarrassment to anyone if I move to Florida."

"What will you do down there?"

"The same thing I've done here. I'll open another shop. I'm really looking forward to it. I've lived here with you for nearly twenty-five years, long enough to give you something I never had. Roots. I've made this your home, but it's never been mine. Don't worry about me. I'll get along all right. Perhaps you'll name a daughter after me if the Chalmers don't have the names for all Lucy's children already picked out."

"I hope I've absorbed at least a few of your traits," he said quietly.

"You have," she answered. "You're more like me than you realize. I think the Chalmers family may be in for quite a surprise with you for a son-in-law. All these families around here can use a little new blood. With you, Lucy and the rest of her family might just get more than they bargained for." She tightened her fist and pushed it against his chin. "Lucy asked me to make up a list of family and friends we'd like to ask to the wedding. Do you have any names?"

"Not a one," he answered.

"Neither do I. I think you and I will uphold the Webb family honor all by ourselves. I've got to get right to work on a dress for Lucy," she added. "Wasn't it sweet of her to ask me?"

six

AT ELEVEN-THIRTY FRIDAY NIGHT, LOWELL CHALMERS FOUND HIS WIFE LYDIA sitting alone at her desk in the alcove off her dressing room. She looked tired, and Lowell was certain she was. From the moment she had arrived home at noon that day, after the four-hour trip from the shore, she and Lucy had been on the go without a moment's rest. Lydia was pale under her summer tan, and there were circles under her eyes. Lowell Chalmers had never considered his wife beautiful, even on the day he had married her. Her appearance commanded respect but hardly adoration. Tall and poised, she possessed an air of queenly confidence that after forty years of marriage Lowell found more satisfying than mere beauty.

Secretly he often mentally compared her to a colonial antique, a clock or a chest of drawers that looked just right in a setting of luxurious simplicity. In different surroundings, in Texas or California, she might have looked out of place, as cold and severe as an icicle, but here in her own house, and her mother's house before her, she looked as correct as a polished hardwood floor.

"I know you're tired," he said, "but I'd like a few words with you on a serious matter."

"Of course," she answered, putting aside a list of names Lucy had given her. She knew what was coming.

"Has Lucy gone to bed?"

"Yes, poor child. She's exhausted."

Lowell Chalmers stood by the open window, looking out over the terrace. His hair, once black, had thinned, and was now a silver gray. The July sun had turned his skin pink instead of brown. He still wore his dinner clothes, a soft, unstarched shirt, a black bow tie, and a red sash about his waist, an extra touch that he had been affecting during the last few years.

He was a mild man, much given to sitting quietly in his study with a book, or wandering about the house with an oily rag and his personal bottle of furniture polish. For all his opportunities, his education, and the wealth he had both married and inherited, his life might have been considered wasted. He had neither added to his wealth nor lessened it. He served on boards of directors only if he or his wife held substantial stock in the company. He had never been asked to run for elective office, and the city's park boards or water commissions had felt no need of his services.

Had he not been born a Chalmers, and had he not married Lydia Hadley, he doubtless would have lost himself in a bank or an insurance company, there to work faithfully and quietly, perhaps rising to be a vice president a year or so before his retirement. He was a tolerant man, not a competitive one. His own life had been smooth, and if he could wish anything for the world at large, it would be that it all could go smoothly.

"Yesterday afternoon," he said, choosing his words with care, "you and I were sitting exactly one hundred and seventy-three miles from here enjoying a pleasant breeze off the harbor. The phone rang, and Lucy broke the news to us that she wanted to marry someone named Charles Webb." He turned toward his wife. "I'll be quite honest, Lydia, and admit that I had never heard of this person. Had you?"

"Many times," Lydia answered brightly. Her expression was one of calm determination.

"His aunt runs some sort of dress shop, I understand. And you apparently have bought some dresses from her."

"Very good dresses, too," Lydia answered. "I wore one at dinner tonight. Perhaps you heard me talking to Ruth about it."

"Ruth," he exploded. "So we're already calling her Ruth."

Lowell Chalmers felt then as he always did when he discussed something with Lydia. It had been the same for forty years. Talking with her was like playing chess with the world's foremost expert. While he could make just one move at a time, she jumped ahead, poised and confident, ready and waiting to sweep him off the board. After forty years he expected to be beaten by her. If he argued with her about anything, it was more to exercise his mind than it was because he thought he was right. He respected her judgment in all things, and particularly did he respect her ability to analyze the most complex affairs coldly, objectively, and without sentiment.

"I'll continue," he said. "We returned from the Island as a result of that call, and tonight we had dinner with this Charles Webb and his aunt who runs the dress shop. Where are his parents?" he asked, interrupting himself.

"I believe they are both dead," Lydia Chalmers answered promptly. "I really know nothing about them, except that he was raised by his aunt."

"I see. Not exactly a good inheritance, would you say?"

"What exactly are you trying to say?" she asked.

"Simply this. I think this whole affair is hasty, ill conceived, and extremely impractical. Let's grant that Lucy is in love with this Charles Webb, and he's in love with her. Why can't they wait a little while? Great Caesar's ghost," he exclaimed, uttering the oath he reserved for moments of great emotional stress. "Great Caesar's ghost," he repeated, "marriage lasts a long time. Lucy meets this boy last Saturday, and she wants to marry him this Monday. Aren't we letting our daughter down if we don't point out to her that being hasty about something like this may very well ruin her whole life?"

"Isn't underneath all this, Lowell, a feeling that Lucy shouldn't marry someone whose aunt runs a dress shop?"

"Well, dammit, perhaps it is," he agreed harshly. "Is that necessarily being unrealistic?"

"Did you like Ruth Webb, Lowell?"

"Oh, good Lord," he answered. "What difference does it make whether I liked her or not? I neither liked her nor disliked her. Frankly, Lydia, what amazed me tonight was the act you put on. Yes, act," he repeated. "You almost looked as though you were anxious to sell something."

It was a harsh thing to say, and Lowell Chalmers knew it. But Lydia's actions had surprised him that evening at dinner. Lydia, who was apt to be reserved and quiet with friends she had known since her school days, had been gay and outgoing—almost gushing, he thought at times. More than once during dinner, Lowell had felt they must be entertaining royalty. Under normal circumstances he would never have had the opportunity to meet someone like Ruth Webb. Certainly he would never expect to entertain her at a small dinner at his own house. If he had run into her at someone else's house, and had been allowed to form an independent judgment of her, he would have found her a little cheap and brassy. He might have spotted her for exactly what she was, the proprietor of a dress shop.

Lydia stood up and crossed the room.

"Sit down a moment, Lowell. I'm going to tell you something about being a parent. Lucy," she began, when her husband was seated, "is twenty-six years old. She'll be twenty-seven this September. Now, unless I am mistaken, and I hardly think I am, she has never had a serious suitor in her whole life. She never has been popular with the young men her own age, has she, Lowell?"

"You make Lucy out to be some kind of misfit," he answered hotly.

"Not at all. Not at all. But we do have to face facts, and the fact is that now, at the age of twenty-six, Lucy is in love with someone who apparently is in love with her. She wants to marry this boy, and he wants to marry her."

"But let them wait a while. Why this tremendous rush?"

"I'll tell you why," Lydia answered. "Twenty-six is hardly an age when a girl like Lucy can afford to be casual about marriage opportunities. Lucy wants a husband. She wants a family, a house, and a husband. If we persuaded her to wait until after the war, and the war lasts two more years or even longer, Lucy might be nearly thirty by the time she could have her family, and for that matter this boy Charlie Webb might never come back to marry her anyway. He might marry someone else. Those things happen, Lowell."

"You make it sound completely cut and dried," he answered angrily.

"But, dear one, it is rather cut and dried. I've thought about this," she continued. "I started thinking about it the moment Lucy called. Perhaps Charlie Webb isn't exactly the sort you and I might wish for our son-in-law, but I think he'll make Lucy a very good husband, and it's Lucy I'm thinking about."

"Do you like him, Lydia?"

He was watching her when she answered. As often happened when Lydia thought about a subject that was unpleasant to her, her expression changed. Her face became a little pinched, and her eyes narrowed. It was at times such as this that Lowell Chalmers often noticed his wife's remarkable resemblance to old Mr. Hadley who hung on the downstairs wall.

"No," she agreed reluctantly. "I hardly think I did like him, but then it's not me he's marrying. I found him rather cold, Lowell."

"Precisely," he agreed. "That is exactly what I thought. He seemed to be glancing around our house as though he were an appraiser." They were both quiet for a moment. Then Lowell said, "I just wish all our daughters could have been as pretty as Polly."

Again Lydia's eyes narrowed. The subject of Polly's beauty was intensely annoying to her. From the moment she was born, Polly had always taken after the Chalmers side of the family.

"I would remind you," Lydia answered tautly, "that by Monday next Polly will be the only one of our daughters who doesn't have a husband. In the long run it doesn't make much difference how many men you *could* have married. What matters is whether you *do* get married, and whether you *do* raise a family."

"I know," he answered surrendering. "As usual, you're right." He took a deep breath. "Well, it seems as though you have everything under pretty good control. If there's anything I can do before Monday, please let me know." He started toward the door.

"There is one thing," she answered.

"Oh?" he looked pleased. He was used to not being needed.

"Rice," Lydia Chalmers said, consulting a list. "We ought to have at least a little rice, don't you think?"

"Rice," he repeated, extracting a notebook and a pencil from his jacket. He wrote "Rice for wedding" under a column he called "W.P.A." All the things Lydia asked him to do he put under this heading. It was a small joke he had had with himself since the early days of Franklin Roosevelt.

seven

IF ANY AMONG THE MORE THAN SIXTY RELATIVES GATHERED IN LYDIA Chalmers' living room on Monday afternoon thought they saw a look of surprise pass across Charlie Webb's face at the conclusion of the wedding ceremony, they were not mistaken. It happened just as Lucy lifted her veil to be kissed. He closed his eyes. It was an involuntary act. He always closed his eyes when he kissed a girl. Then as he felt Lucy's lips pressed against his, cool and dry, and as he felt his hand against her shoulder, for a moment he had a weird, dreamlike sensation that he was embracing a golf bag. He had no time to analyze it, as the instant he opened his eyes Lucy was there smiling at him, her elbow poised, waiting to be escorted out onto the terrace for the reception.

For the next half-hour, as he and Lucy stood in the reception line at the edge of the terrace lawn, the feeling grew inside Charlie that, as a party, his wedding was a terrible flop. He had never much considered what his own wedding ought to be, but at least he hadn't expected to be bored. Weddings meant gaiety, champagne, music, and singing. The trouble here, he decided, was with the guests themselves. Most of them looked as though they had come straight from a convalescent home or a hospital for the aged.

A Mrs. Talcott Wells, well into her eighties, deaf and apparently senile, lingered in front of him, grasping his hand as much for support as in greeting, mumbling something he couldn't understand.

"What's she asking me?" he whispered to Lucy.

"Say No, you're afraid not," Lucy whispered back at him.

"No, I'm afraid not," he shouted into Mrs. Wells' waiting ear.

"A pity," she mumbled, losing all interest in him, tottering away.

"What *did* she ask me?" he asked Lucy a few moments later during a lull.

"She wondered if you played the violin. She gave me piano lessons, and she founded the music school."

That must explain the music for the wedding, Charlie decided. Mrs. Wells had doubtless had a hand in choosing it—four elderly men, two violins, a cello, and a piano, all of them striving mightily, but pleasing no one but themselves.

Mrs. Olander from across the street—Mrs. "Eleven Chimney Olander," he wanted to call her, unable as yet to realize that these people were now his relatives, that by marrying Lucy Chalmers he had become one of the family—Mrs. Olander engaged him in a two-minute conversation about her grandson whom she was certain Charlie must know, since they were both captains in the army and both stationed in Texas. It turned out, however, that the

27

Olander grandson was in the Air Corps and stationed at a camp five hundred miles from his.

Where were the men, Charlie wondered. If they were smart, they were out playing golf. The few he noticed moved rapidly through the line, then headed just as rapidly for one of the colored waiters with the champagne. What men there were looked bored and miserable, sending meaningful looks toward their wives, doubtless wishing they had had the foresight to come in separate cars.

Most of the time, Mr. Chalmers wandered about the terrace looking unnecessary. Having been assigned no specific task, he made work for himself, following along behind Mrs. Newell Goddard. Mrs. Goddard weighed two hundred pounds and wore high heels, apparently to prove that she could still do it. As she walked, she bored holes in the terrace lawn, and Mr. Chalmers pressed them down with his feet, like a nervous greenskeeper at the National Open.

There was champagne, there was food, there was music, and there was a bride, but the party never jelled. By the time the last relative had passed through the line, a third of the guests were already departing for their cars.

Polly Chalmers was a little tight when she headed toward Charlie. He was standing with Lucy near one of the rose beds. It was the first time he had seen her in over six years, and she had changed. There was a New York look about her. She wore black, and her dark hair was glossy and smooth, like a cat that was fed only cream. She stood out among the Chalmers and Hadley relatives like a piece of satin in a bundle of old rags. She planted herself directly in front of Charlie, smiling crookedly, twisting a champagne glass by its stem, her head tilted on one side.

"I want to ask you a question, new brother-in-law," she purred, "if sister Lucy will let me."

"Ask him anything you wish," Lucy answered, tightening her fingers on Charlie's arm.

"What I want to know is," Polly continued, enunciating carefully, "did you ask Lucy to marry you, or did she ask you to marry her?"

Lucy stiffened. Polly had two spots of color on her pale white cheeks, and her eyes were shining with wicked delight.

"Really, Polly," Lucy protested.

"And I have now another question," Polly continued, paying no attention to her sister. "Didn't you used to be my caddy?"

"Why don't you go drink some more champagne?" Lucy said sarcastically. "Even though you've had too much already."

"Very well," Polly answered, handing Lucy her glass. "Go fill it for me and I will."

Lucy took the glass and walked rapidly away, not however toward the champagne but toward her mother.

"Weren't you?" Polly asked.

"Yes, I was," Charlie answered.

"So that's why your face was vaguely familiar. Well, well. You used to carry things for me for money. Now you'll be carrying things for Lucy for nothing." She grinned at him and tucked her arm through his.

Charlie started to enjoy himself for the first time that day.

"So did you, or did she?" Polly asked again. "Whose idea was this, anyway? Yours or Lucy's?"

"Mutual," Charlie answered, laughing.

"Listen, old caddy of mine," Polly answered, "how did the dull one get you?"

"All your relatives have been telling me what a lucky fellow I am."

"Lucky, ha! What's your name again?" she asked.

"Charlie Webb," he answered, completely delighted with her.

"All right, Charlie Webb." She pointed out over the terrace with her hand. "Behold the camp of the Amazons. Behold the family where the women reign supreme. Not a man do you see out there. Not one. Do you know what happens to the men in my family after they have been married for a few years?"

"They get eaten?"

"No, they don't get eaten. Not quite. I'll tell you what happens to them. They are given vests with embroidered ducks."

"Given what?" he asked.

"You just wait. A few years from now you'll be wearing a vest with little ducks on it. That's so people will know you're a man. I'll make a little bet with you, Charlie Webb. Do you want to make a bet with your sister-in-law?"

"Lucy doesn't seem to be bringing back the champagne," he answered.

"Don't worry about Lucy. You're stuck with her for life. You're only stuck with me for two more minutes. I'm going to make a little bet with you. Ten years from now you'll have been maneuvered into the following list of things. One: you will be working in the family business. Two: you will be a member of the golf club. Three: you will have a seven-room house on a street that is lined with other seven-room houses. Four: you will have a well-clipped lawn, flower beds, a two-car garage with two cars in it, and only one little place where you legally can be alone, a damp little corner in the cellar which you will call your den and which either Lucy or her cleaning woman will investigate once a week to be sure you're not up to anything original. You're doomed, old caddy of mine. The female tide in this family will sweep over you, and all you'll have left is a vest with ducks on it to show you once were a man."

"Maybe you're wrong," Charlie answered.

"You will, Charlie Webb. You will. You will. Polly knows. Polly was born into this family, and Polly knows this family. Such a pity, too. You were such a good caddy. One thing I forgot. You will also have a ring in your nose like a bull." She giggled. "Oh, oh," she whispered, noticing her mother and Lucy bearing down on them from across the terrace. "Here comes the U. S. Cavalry." For a moment she hummed the overture from *William Tell*. Then she turned slowly and faced him. "What I really wanted to say," she took his hand in both of hers and squeezed it, "is Welcome, sucker. Welcome to the clan."

29

"Polly dear," Mrs. Chalmers said with acid sweetness, her fingers biting into the flesh on Polly's arm, "do come along with me and talk with dear old Mrs. Wells. She does so want to hear what you've done with your cello."

"You tell that dear old Mrs. Wells," Polly answered, extricating herself from her mother's grasp, "that I pawned my cello when I was a sophomore in college. Cheers," she said, winking at Charlie, and departing toward the champagne table.

"Poor Polly," Lucy whispered a moment later. "We've all become a little sorry for her."

"She's certainly lost none of her beauty," Charlie answered.

"Honestly, it *is* embarrassing to have your own sister the *only* person at the wedding who drinks too much."

"At least someone drank too much," he answered.

She led him along the terrace toward the house. The reception was rapidly breaking up.

"Mother was wondering," she added, "if you'd made any arrangements for tonight?"

"I thought we could just drive until we decided to stop," he answered.

She giggled. "We might end up sleeping in the car. Then you haven't made reservations anywhere?"

"No."

"I didn't think so. Mother says she and father have some sort of an arrangement with the Plaza in New York. I mean we can always go there, and they'll see to it that we get a nice room. All we have to do is mention Father's name."

"Would you like that?"

"I really would, darling."

"Then it's fine with me."

"And don't you think we ought to get ready to go?"

"It more or less looks like it," he answered.

As he left the terrace and went on into the house, Polly caught his eye. She ran a finger across her throat and then toasted him silently with a half-filled glass of champagne.

A few minutes later Lydia Chalmers walked rapidly toward her husband, who was still wandering about the terrace mourning his ruined lawn.

"The rice, Lowell," she exclaimed. "Lucy is all ready to leave. We need the rice."

"Oh, my God," he answered, hitting his forehead with the heel of his hand.

"You didn't forget it, Lowell?"

"I did, my dear. I did indeed."

"But it was the only thing I asked you to do," she wailed angrily.

"I know it. I know it. Wait a moment. Perhaps all is not lost." He turned and ran off toward the kitchen.

Nutmeg, garlic salt, cinnamon, salt, sugar, pepper, everything but rice, he muttered to himself a moment later as he pawed through the kitchen drawers. Waxed paper, paper towels, dish towels, old newspaper. "Can I help you, Mr. Chalmers?" one of the waiters asked, hovering near.

"Rice," he shouted. "We need rice."

For the next three minutes the kitchen and the pantry seethed with activity while every drawer and every shelf was turned upside down.

"Puffed rice," one of the colored men shouted. "How about puffed rice, Mr. Chalmers?"

"You mean cereal?" he asked scornfully.

"It's rice, Mr. Chalmers."

"All right, give it to me," he answered. He ran toward the front hall. He found Lydia was outside on the driveway. "Now I know it isn't what you wanted," he said thrusting the box of puffed rice at her, "but it's rice."

"It doesn't really matter," she answered, patting him on the arm. There were tears in her eyes. "They've already gone."

Charlie awoke the next morning with Lucy standing at the foot of the bed. She was smiling at him, her expression one of complete happiness.

"Wasn't this better than sleeping in the car?"

He nodded sleepily.

"I'll take the first shower," she said. "Then the bathroom will be all yours." She moved next to him and kissed him on the forehead. "I love you, darling." She disappeared, and in a moment he heard the water running in the shower.

He lay on his back, staring at the ceiling. It was New York after all on his leave, but under slightly different circumstances than he had planned. It was New York with a wife instead of with an address book. There would be no time spent on the phone calling people he knew, and there would be no call to the girl he had met on the train. He rolled over and reached out to the chair next to the bed. His wallet had fallen onto the floor. In one of the inside compartments he found the slip of paper she had handed him at the station ten days before.

Helen Gruber. Not a pretty name, but she was a pretty girl, and that was all that mattered. She'd probably haunt him, he decided. Not that she had made more of an impression on him than at least a dozen other girls he'd met in his lifetime, but Helen Gruber would haunt him because she'd remain a loose end, something he couldn't tie up neatly. Here he was in New York, as he had promised, and he couldn't see her or call her on the phone. Or could he? he wondered. He heard Lucy singing softly in the shower. Lucy certainly wouldn't hear him make a phone call. It probably wouldn't be the most sensible way to start a honeymoon. He probably ought to tell Lucy what he was doing. But would she understand? He doubted it. Or she'd be completely noble about it, insisting that he make the call while she stalked out of the room, removing all the pleasure from it. He reached for the phone.

"Get me Canal 6–4075," he said to the hotel operator.

The phone rang for a long time. Finally a sleepy voice at the other end said, "Hello."

"Hello yourself," he answered, his voice almost a whisper. "It's Charlie Webb."

He could almost see her coming awake.

"Well. Well. Are you finally in New York?"

"Yes."

"Where?"

"At the Plaza."

"How fancy."

"Where is Canal 6–4075?" he asked.

"Practically in the river," she answered. "Way downtown."

He hesitated. The water was still running in the shower.

"I was beginning to think I wouldn't see you again, Charlie."

"You probably won't," he answered, suddenly feeling extremely sad.

"Oh," she answered. Then she laughed. "That's what I get for making it completely clear that I want to see you again. Why won't I see you?"

"Because I'm married," he answered bluntly.

She said nothing for a moment.

"I heard you correctly, didn't I? You did say you were married?"

"You heard me correctly."

"When did all this happen?"

"Yesterday afternoon."

"Who in the world hooked you? You mentioned nothing about a home-town sweetheart."

"It was rather sudden," he answered.

"Well, it certainly must have been. Not that I planned my whole future around you, but it comes as a shock so early in the morning."

"I really didn't know I was going to get married, Helen. It was just one of those things."

"Who did hook you?" she asked again.

"Just a girl I met at home."

"Just like that. I don't believe it."

"It's true."

"Without even a struggle?"

"Not much."

"The females in your home town must be deadly."

The water in the shower had stopped. Lucy was still singing, and Charlie could hear her rubbing herself with a towel.

"I'm sorry," he said quietly into the phone. "I'll have to hang up now."

"The little woman returns?" she asked sarcastically.

"I'm afraid so."

He hung up just as Lucy appeared from the bathroom. She was naked.

"I am merely following some sage advice from Colette," she giggled when she noticed his startled expression. "A man should see his mistress completely dressed or completely naked. Never halfway in between." She danced gaily about the room, her body pink and white from being rubbed with a towel.

Colette had been thinking of mistresses, Charlie thought, watching her, not wives. Either wives should be completely dressed, or it should be dark.

"Who were you talking to on the phone?" Lucy asked, as he rolled out of bed.

"My secret love," he answered. He patted her head gently as he went on into the bathroom.

"Seriously," she asked him when he reappeared, "who *were* you talking to?"

"My secret love," he repeated. He had no intention of lying to her, but he wished she'd let the subject drop. Did Lucy have any loose ends lying about from her first twenty-six years? he wondered. The chances were she didn't. She seemed much too efficient for that.

"And who is your secret love?" she persisted.

"You are," he answered. "I was only joking, Lucy."

"But who were you talking to? You were talking to someone because I heard you."

"All right, I'll tell you. And don't get upset about it. I was talking to a girl. Her name is Helen Gruber. I met her on the train two weeks ago when I was coming north from Texas. I told her I might look her up if I ever got to New York. I just called her to tell her I was married."

He had started to put on his shirt when he heard Lucy cry. At first he thought it must be someone in another room. Then when he saw her lying face down on the bed, her face buried in a pillow, her shoulders shaking, he just stared at her incredulously.

"For heaven's sake," he said, standing over her helplessly.

"You called another girl on our *honeymoon?*" she wailed.

"I told her I would call. So I did. That's all there is to it." He put his hand on Lucy's back and sat next to her. "You asked me to tell you, and I did. Would you rather have me lie to you? I could have said I was calling room service. Do you want me to hide things from you?"

"I'd prefer that you didn't do things you had to hide."

"But I'm not hiding anything. Please stop crying," he said miserably. "Please, Lucy."

She rolled away from him on the bed. "You wish I weren't here, don't you?" she wailed. "You wish you were all alone in New York so you could go see this girl?" She looked at him, her cheeks wet with tears. "You didn't . . ." she paused, then said, "You didn't enjoy *sleeping* with me last night, did you? I wasn't very much fun."

"Oh, for God's sake, Lucy."

"It's true, Charlie. You really don't love me. You love this girl you met on a train."

"I'm sorry I called her, Lucy. It was stupid of me. And please stop crying. I do love you. I really do."

She reached for his hand and pulled him next to her on the bed. "Don't you ever again call another girl," she ordered fiercely. "Ever. Ever. You belong to me."

"I know," he whispered. "I'm sorry I did it."

"From now on there's no one for either of us but each other. That's fair, isn't it? Tell me if it isn't fair."

"Of course it's fair," he answered. "And there isn't anyone else. There never has been."

She sat up quickly in the bed and wiped her eyes with her hand.

"I'm such a ninny," she said, laughing. "There I was crying on our honeymoon."

Again he stared at her in amazement. She had turned off her tears as suddenly as she had turned them on. She seemed able to control her emotions as easily as a faucet. Had she merely been testing him? he wondered. He knew she wasn't that sly or mean. She was just tired. For her it had been an exhausting week.

She reached up and hugged him, her face pressed against his chest.

"It's just you and me, Charlie. You and me for the rest of our lives."

"I know, I know," he whispered, holding her tight. "I'm sorry I made you cry."

eight

"YOU'RE CERTAIN YOU NEED ME ALONG?" LYDIA CHALMERS ASKED LUCY FOR the second time that morning. "I won't just be in the way?"

"Please come," Lucy answered, a note of pleading in her voice. "I'll feel much better if you do."

Lydia nodded and looked at her daughter fondly. Charlie had called an hour before. He was out of the army, and he was flying to New York the next day. Lucy hadn't seen him in over a year, and she was nervous about it. She wouldn't be much of a mother, Lydia thought, if she couldn't understand that.

"All right, Lucy. We'll have Joseph drive us down early tomorrow morning. Naturally you plan to take the baby?" She glanced toward the crib.

"I thought I ought to, or do you think I shouldn't?"

"By all means take her. Charlie must be dying to see his daughter. And she is such a pet, Lucy." Lydia reached into the crib and scooped her granddaughter up in her arms. "Oh, you little cutie," she cooed, rubbing noses with her namesake. "Oh, you little *darling*. Honestly," she added, turning again to Lucy, "won't Charlie be thrilled? Imagine coming back to a three-months-old baby you've never even seen."

Lucy looked glum and sat on the edge of the bed.

Lydia smiled. "You're rather upset about something, Lucy. Would you care to tell me what it is?"

"What if he doesn't like his baby, Mother? What if he doesn't even like me? He's been away a whole year."

"Look at me," Lydia answered, putting a finger under Lucy's chin. "This whole thing won't be nearly as bad as you seem to think. Husbands have been returning from wars for thousands and thousands of years."

"But we hardly know each other. We were together exactly one week, not counting the time before we were married. What would happen if he didn't like me?"

"But he will. How can he help it? Now listen to me," she said firmly. "I know how dull it's been for you all alone for the past year, and I know how lonely you've been. Here you were married and still *not* married. Then you had your baby, and there was no father here to share her with you. It hasn't been easy for you. It hasn't been easy at all." She sat next to Lucy on the bed. "But you've done your job without a single word of complaint. Perhaps no one else will ever compliment you for this, but I will. I have been proud of you during the last year."

"Thank you, Mother. You've been wonderful too, Mother."

"And now it's all over. Charlie's on his way home. Starting at noon to-morrow you'll have a life of your own. And don't you worry about his not liking you." She laughed meaningfully. "He'd better like you, my dear. So stop worrying, and start making plans for tomorrow. I think we'd better start at eight in the morning. That should give us ample time for La Guardia. He'll like you," she repeated as she walked out of the room. "He'll like you as much as I do, and that's a great deal."

This was one of the more interesting sides to being a mother, Lydia Chalmers thought as she walked to the kitchen to tell Joseph that he and the Packard would be needed at eight the next morning. She had three daughters, and she loved them all because she had given birth to them and they were her children. But of the three she really *liked* only Lucy. Lucy was the only one who needed her, and it was satisfying to be needed. What the other two needed she didn't quite know, but it certainly wasn't their mother. She'd lost both Anne and Polly the minute they'd gone off to college.

Anne had finally left home blaming her mother and her father for their complacency, and Polly had just found her parents boring. That was the fashion these days among the young, Lydia knew. Not to look inside yourself for deficiencies, but to blame your parents. Well, so be it, she thought. Let Polly and Anne carve out a life of their own. If they could do better with their lives than she had with hers, she would wish them well. In the meantime it was nice to have Lucy. Lucy had always needed her, and it seemed likely that she always would need her. Not that this meant Lucy lacked spunk. Why people thought that any child who didn't turn like an ungrateful rattlesnake on her parents at a certain age showed a lack of spirit, she couldn't understand. What was wrong with liking the world the way it was? Without people like Lucy, the entire structure of society would collapse overnight. Let Anne and Polly follow their will-o'-the-wisps. Thank the Lord for Lucy, who seemed to know what really mattered in the world.

Much the same thoughts were passing through her mind at noon the next day when she watched Charlie walk into the airport waiting room. She sat well in the background, on a bench against the wall. Tears welled into her eyes as she watched Lucy pass the baby into Charlie's arms. Charlie laughed and held young Lydia at arms' length, his face a picture of joy.

Then he put an arm about Lucy's shoulders and hugged her, standing completely still, just looking at her. It was classic. The soldier from the wars returning, the scene that had been repeated a million million times since the world began.

Unfortunately, however, it was just at that moment that Lydia noticed her son-in-law's suit.

It was without doubt the most hideous garment she had ever seen. It was ghastly. The shoulders looked four feet wide, heavily padded, and extending inches out into nowhere. Down the front of the coat there was a row of pearl buttons, and the waist was drawn in with a cloth belt. The trousers waist was pleated, and the creases looked sewn in. The trousers cuffs were at least a foot across. It was the color, however, that shocked her most of all. It would have caused raised eyebrows even in Hollywood. A greenish-blueish white, with a sheen to it that changed color as she stared at it, like a diseased liver in bright sunlight.

Lydia's heart sank. With horror she realized she had never seen Charlie dressed in anything but a uniform. He had looked fine in that, just like any other captain in the army. But the war was now over, and Charlie had returned dressed like a tout. There was no point in being coy about it. She and Lucy had work to do. In England, she knew, people were judged by their accents. In America it was the clothing, and Charlie looked *awful*.

"Welcome home, Charles," she said formally, extending a cheek so he would have no embarrassing moments wondering if he should or should not kiss her. "I trust you're pleased with your daughter. We think she looks like you."

"It's hard to tell," he answered, grinning. The baby was screaming, her face the color of raw meat.

"Well," Lydia asked, "are we just about ready to go?"

She led the way out of the waiting room. Halfway across the parking lot toward the car, she stopped suddenly and snapped her fingers.

"Charles, be a dear and walk on ahead. I have a little secret I'd like to discuss with Lucy."

He said, "Of course, Mrs. Chalmers," and walked on alone toward the car.

"It's his suit," Lydia hissed when Charlie was out of earshot. "It's the most frightful thing I've ever seen."

Lucy looked uneasy. She had noticed the suit, and she hadn't liked it either. But Charlie himself had looked wonderful, and at the moment that had seemed enough. For a whole year she had been remembering a shy, rather clumsy boy. But in a year he had grown up.

The meeting had been graceful too. None of her fears had come true. Charlie seemed to know instinctively how she must feel. For one thing, he hadn't kissed her. Had he wished to, she would naturally have let him, but she had hoped he wouldn't want to. Not yet. When he merely put his arm around her shoulders and hugged her, it had been just right. When she, Charlie, and their baby had been together in the waiting room, Lucy wished her mother had stayed at home. She hadn't needed her after all. Charlie was home, and that was enough.

"Surely you must have noticed it," Lydia persisted.

"I noticed it, Mother. But there isn't much we can do, is there?"

"I think there is, darling. What I thought we might do, with your permission of course, would be to have Joseph run us into New York. I've been planning some sort of homecoming present for you both, and the thought occurred to me that the best thing I can do, under the circumstances, would be to buy Charles a new suit. We could have it fitted in a matter of minutes, and then you and he could drop down some week end to pick it up. He'd be thrilled," she added, when she noticed Lucy's look of uncertainty. "And I promise you I won't eavesdrop when you two pick out the material. You say it was your idea, if you wish. He won't even have to know that I'm paying for it."

"Why don't you handle it?" Lucy answered morosely.

"Very well." Lydia started walking toward the car. "Really, Lucy, that suit is too awful for words. We simply have to do something about it."

"It's one of Mr. Chalmers' favorite sayings," Lydia said after her announcement to Charlie that they were on their way into New York to buy him a suit, "that being well dressed is just a matter of charge accounts." She laughed, certain that Charlie would immediately grasp the significance of what was a Chalmers family saying. When he looked blank, she added with her first touch of annoyance, "What he means, of course, is that if one is careful to open charge accounts only in the better stores, one will never end up wearing . . ." her voice faded into uncertainty. She had, she realized, talked herself into a trap.

"You mean a suit like the one I'm wearing?" he asked good-naturedly.

"Mother didn't mean that at all," Lucy interrupted, springing to her mother's defense.

"Of course she meant it. And she's right. Have you ever done much traveling, Mrs. Chalmers?"

"I beg your pardon, Charles." Lydia Chalmers' tone was frigid.

"I mean, have you ever been in a foreign country, and found yourself getting carried away with something you see in a store? This is silk," he said, rolling his suit material between his fingers. "I bought it in Florence, and it looked fine over there because that's what everyone else wears. I had a tailor make it up for me, and the moment I put it on I knew it was a mistake. Maybe I should have thrown it away, but I thought Lucy might get a kick out of it." He settled back against the seat. "Anyway it's nice to be home, terrible suit and all." He winked at Lucy.

"It occurs to me," Lydia said primly, "that you two hardly need me along on this suit-buying expedition. Why don't you take Charles down to Brooks, Lucy, and use our charge account? Joseph and I can wander about the city with young Lydia, and pick you up in an hour or so. Lucy can sign my name," she added, glancing at Charlie.

37

"I can sign my own name," he answered. "I'm sure my old charge account is still good." Again he winked at Lucy. "Your mother doesn't seem to believe me," he added, "but my clothing was perfectly proper before the war. I'll show her some of my old suits when we get home."

Lydia Chalmers stiffened. Then she leaned forward and opened the glass window that separated them from the chauffeur.

"Joseph," she announced sweetly, "there has been a change in our plans. We will buy no suit for Mr. Webb today. You can drive straight on through the city and head up the parkway for home."

That night as she went to bed, Lydia Chalmers did what was for her a most unusual thing. She asked her husband Lowell for some advice. It was necessary to keep her voice low, as Lucy's room, with Charlie now using it with her, was just down the hall.

"Tell me honestly," Lydia asked, "did I do the wrong thing? I thought he would have been thrilled with a new suit. Wouldn't you have been?"

In their whole married life, Lowell Chalmers had never known Lydia to be any closer to hysteria than she was that afternoon when she had arrived home. She had been numb with rage, and he had wormed the story out of her only by persistent questioning. He wasn't sure why, but after he had found out what had taken place that afternoon, what it was that had made Lydia so furious, he had found himself more amused than sympathetic. Not that he took Charlie's side in the matter. Charlie had acted rather crudely, he thought. But what amused him was Lydia's violent reaction. Nothing he had ever done in over forty years of marriage had ever made Lydia as angry as her son-in-law had made her that afternoon.

"It was as though I had set out to insult him openly," Lydia continued, when Lowell didn't answer. "I was trying to be nice, and he thanked me by being rude. He *was* rude, Lowell," she repeated, raising her voice.

"Really now, Lydia," he answered quietly, "aren't we making quite a thing out of this suit?"

"Perhaps we are. But his attitude disturbed me. Does it occur to him, I wonder, that we have been supporting his wife and his child for a whole year while he has been traipsing about Italy? Did he consider that?"

"That's hardly fair, Lydia. We were delighted to have Lucy stay with us. Charlie was sending her money. She could have lived somewhere else if she wanted. And he was hardly traipsing about, as you put it. He was a soldier in the army."

Lydia turned on him angrily. "Why are you taking his side? He acted like a boor, and here you are defending him."

"I'm sure he did act like a boor," Lowell answered, backing down. "But shouldn't we let the whole thing drop?"

Then Lydia did something that she had never done in Lowell Chalmers' memory. She started to cry.

"I don't like him," she wailed. "I don't like him at all."

38

"But he's married to Lucy, Lydia. Not to you. *I'm* your husband. Have you forgotten?"

"He was just beastly to me. He really was," she wailed.

He cupped her face in his hands and made her look at him. She looked rather appealing with tears streaming down her cheeks. "I have an idea," he said. "I suggest that from now on we let our son-in-law pick out his own suits, and I suggest that we let him decide when he needs a new suit. And I now suggest that we both go to bed and forget the whole matter."

Lydia drew away from him and moved to her bed. For a while she lay on her back and wept silently to herself. Lowell knew he shouldn't just leave her that way, but he didn't know what else to do. He suddenly felt hungry. If he hadn't suspected it would make Lydia even angrier, he would have gone down to the kitchen for some milk and graham crackers. It was a little late in life to learn what to do with a crying wife. What did other husbands do? he wondered. He had still not made up his mind by the time he had fallen asleep.

He might have felt somewhat better had he known that Charlie was having a similar experience thirty feet and two walls away. Before she had started to cry, Lucy had also kept her voice low.

"Mother was terribly upset today," she began.

"She seemed to be," he answered. "Was it something I said, or what?"

"Oh, Charlie," she said, her voice catching.

"Oh, Charlie, what?" he asked angrily.

Why, he wondered, had this silly business about the suit been able to spoil something he had looked forward to for a whole year? He had been nervous about meeting Lucy. He might not recognize her, he thought. And he might not like her if he did recognize her. Then she had looked wonderful standing in the waiting room, holding their baby in her arms. He had planned not to kiss her, and he didn't. But he had wanted to kiss her. She looked good. He had wanted to throw his daughter high in the air and roar with laughter. The emotion he had least expected to feel had overpowered him. He felt like a husband to a woman he scarcely knew, and a father to a baby he had never seen. It was his family waiting to greet him. His family, and he had wanted to hug them half to death.

Then he saw Mrs. Chalmers, and the life had gone out of the whole thing. There had been no reason for him to feel this way. She had a perfect right to meet him too. But her presence had infuriated him none the less. He wanted to see his wife and daughter, not his mother-in-law. If Lucy had come alone, he would have taken a long way home. He might not have arrived home for another week. They might have gone somewhere. Anywhere. It didn't much matter. They could have learned to know each other again, gradually, and had fun while they were doing it. Mrs. Chalmers had spoiled everything.

She hadn't fooled him for an instant about the suit. He knew what was passing through her mind. She was sure Lucy had made a terrible mistake in her choice of a husband. Maybe she had. But he could learn. He had no charge account anywhere. If Lucy hadn't liked his Italian suit, he would have gladly ripped it into shreds and put on his uniform again for a few days. But Mrs. Chalmers' expression when she saw it made him want to wear the suit for the rest of his life.

"Oh, Charlie, what?" he repeated.

"Mother was just trying to be nice."

"She chose a mighty funny way of doing it. Why in hell didn't you come to meet me alone, Lucy? What did we need your mother for?"

Lucy started to cry then. "But you didn't have to insult her."

"And she didn't have to insult me." He turned his back to his wife and walked to the window. "Tell me something honestly. Was your mother planning to give me a new suit all along, or was it just something she dreamed up on the spur of the moment when she saw me? Answer me honestly."

Lucy just wailed. He turned to look at her. Her face was buried in the pillow.

A few months before, a fellow officer who was also married had given him some advice on how to handle women's tears. "Tears," he had said, "are a woman's weapon and not a state of mind. The only defense against tears is silence."

Charlie said nothing, standing with his back to the bed, looking out the window.

Good advice was one thing, he thought, but being able to follow it was something else. Lucy's crying reminded him of being on the front line during an attack. You didn't know how you'd react until you were there. She was crying on their first night together after more than a year apart. She was crying because of something he had done. Perhaps he had been wrong, he thought. Perhaps he should have swallowed his pride and let Mrs. Chalmers buy him a suit. The whole thing was out of control.

He moved back to the bed. Lucy was wearing a new pink nightgown. "I'm sorry," he said. "I'm sorry I insulted your mother. I really am."

Lucy stopped crying and turned her face toward him.

"Would you tell Mother that, Charlie? Please. That's all I ask."

"Isn't it enough that I tell you?"

"But it was Mother you hurt. Not me. And she's been just wonderful to me, Charlie. You don't know how good she's been to me all the time you've been away."

"All right," he answered. "I'll apologize to your mother, and I'm sorry I made a mess of things."

She kissed him then and pulled him down on the bed. "I'm glad you're home," she whispered happily. "It's been a long, long year."

nine

"You seem cheerful," Lowell Chalmers said to Lydia late the following afternoon when he returned from the factory. He had nearly bumped into her as she walked through the downstairs hall. As usual, she was carrying a vase of carnations.

"Why, darling," she answered in mock horror, "aren't I always cheerful?"

He went on into his study without answering. He supposed he would never fully learn all the facets of Lydia's personality. Less than twenty-four hours before, he had seen her lying on her bed, sobbing bitterly. Now she was sailing serenely through the house, singing, busy with her favorite hobby, that of arranging the flowers she raised in her greenhouse.

He collapsed wearily into his reading chair and spread out his newspapers on the floor. There were four of them in all, the *Christian Science Monitor*, the New York *Times*, The Manchester *Guardian* air edition, and the *Wall Street Journal*. He had browsed through the local paper earlier in the day, at his office. Behind him the mantel clock ticked steadily, and next to him on his desk he had a pair of scissors and a supply of paper clips.

It had been his habit, since his daughters Anne and Polly left home, to cut out clippings that interested him and then send them on to them in his twice-monthly letters. Both the girls had absorbed some rather leftish views while they were at college, and newspaper clippings seemed a good way to keep in touch with them, and also a way to give them some advice without appearing to do so. He kept a thick file of clippings, mainly from the *Wall Street Journal*, and he would send them along with a letter, which Mrs. Fleck, his secretary, would type up in duplicate. It was a technique that more fathers might adopt, he thought. Children often resisted advice simply because of the source. A good editorial writer often put a father's thoughts into print, and a child could then read them and be influenced in spite of himself.

When Lowell had finished reading and clipping his papers, a half-hour still remained before dinner. Lydia had placed a new novel on his reading table. It was not Lowell Chalmers' habit to read novels until they had been in print for at least two decades. Things that were well said, and worth saying, lasted at least twenty years. Reading a new book just because it was new seemed to him like drinking fresh wine before the dregs had been removed. There was such a thing as literary alcoholism, and Lydia was a victim. Her appetite for books appalled him. Not only did she read every bit of slush that appeared on the market, she also took it upon herself to urge him to do the same thing.

He slid the novel off the table and glanced through the pages. The book was much too heavy, he thought, weighing it in his hands experimentally. That was another theory he had about literature. Books were like Christmas

41

presents. The best ones usually were small. This book weighed at least three pounds.

While he was skimming through the pages, he heard scratching across the room. He pushed his glasses back on his head. A mouse had struggled up through the floor, fighting its way through the hole made by the radiator pipe where it passed into the cellar. He watched as the mouse walked slowly across the rug toward his chair. It must be either a very young mouse, Lowell decided, or a very stupid one. Possibly both. Experienced mice never exposed themselves to such certain death.

He closed the novel silently and took aim with it. When he retrieved the book he found the mouse under it, dead, flattened against the rug, a warm bit of twitching gray fur.

Now why had he done that, he wondered, smoothing the mouse's fur with his finger. One killed things smaller and weaker as a matter of course. But what a horrible way to die, he thought whimsically. Crushed by three pounds of historical fiction.

"That's a remarkable book, is it not, Lowell?" Lydia asked, breezing in from the hallway.

"It most certainly is," he agreed, closing his hand quickly over the dead mouse.

Lydia pinned a carnation in his buttonhole.

"Pretty, aren't they?"

He nodded without bothering to glance at it. Lydia's carnations were always the same.

Lydia seated herself on the footstool near the fireplace.

"Our son-in-law Charlie apologized to me today."

"Well, now," Lowell said cheerfully.

"He did indeed. Just before he, Lucy and little Lydia went off this morning, Charlie admitted to me that he had acted rather poorly yesterday. Incidentally, Lowell, I insisted that he and Lucy open up our house at the Island. Charlie had some ridiculous idea about staying at an inn. Why, I asked him, with a ten-room house lying completely empty, should he spent his money at an inn?"

Lowell started to answer. Then he thought better of it and merely nodded.

"Anyway," Lydia continued, "I think the air is nicely cleared with our son-in-law."

"That's fine," he answered.

"But that isn't what I really wanted to talk about," she continued. "Could you possibly put the book aside for a moment?"

He let it slide to the floor.

"I think it's time we considered a job for Charlie, and that's what I'd like to discuss with you now."

"I'm sure Charlie must have some ideas of his own on the subject, that we ought to listen to first."

"I don't think he does. Lucy as much as told me this morning that he has nothing definite in mind."

"What are you getting at, Lydia?" Lowell let his head tip back, resting it on the back of his chair. The mouse was still twitching in his hand.

"I assume you'll want him to work for The Hadley Company."

He didn't answer.

"Not that I wish to interfere with your business in any way. But I know Lucy hopes Charlie will want to work for the Company. I thought you and I should discuss it in advance."

"In advance of what?" he asked quietly.

"Before you ask him to work for the Company."

"Then you think I should ask him?"

"But of course I do. Don't you?"

"Lydia," he started angrily. Then he stood up and walked to the fireplace. The mantel clock had started to strike six. He waited until the room was quiet. "The Hadley Company is no longer a place for a young man," he said when the clock was silent.

"What on earth do you mean by that?"

"Exactly what I say. We would be misleading Charlie if we urged him to go to work out there. The Company just doesn't have much of a future. Wait a moment," he continued. "Let me finish. It isn't only the Company's fault. It's my own fault. I've let the Company slide downhill, and it wouldn't be fair to tell Charlie anything but the truth about it."

"Haven't I heard all this before?" She smiled patiently. "Unless I'm mistaken, we'll all vote the usual dividend at the annual meeting."

"Yes," he answered, "we'll vote the same dividend. But it won't represent any profit on the part of the Company." He turned and faced her. "We're down to well under a hundred employees out there, Lydia. We really don't need even that many for the orders we have on hand. The Hadley Company just isn't the company it once was, and we might as well face the facts."

"There have been times like this before. Aren't you merely in a period of adjustment after the war?"

"The war has nothing to do with it. We're not much more than a shell out there. We should have sold out years ago, and if another opportunity comes up I will most certainly recommend that this time we go through with it. Which is another reason why it's no place for a young man to start. If there's a chance that we might sell, where would that leave Charlie?"

"You're just tired, Lowell."

"I'm not tired. You asked to discuss this matter, and I'm trying to discuss it fairly. It's my fault that the Company ought to be sold. I've never been fitted for the work I'm doing, and I know it better than anyone else. Someone like your father would have kept the Company up with the times. I've just let it slide. I should have been a teacher, or I should have worked on a newspaper. The main trouble with The Hadley Company has been me, Lydia."

She tightened her lips.

"You always say this, Lowell, as though you blamed me for urging you to work for the Company in the first place. If you'll think back, you'll remember that you just thought you wanted to teach or work on a newspaper. You never made a move in that direction."

"That's quite true," he admitted. "That's quite true."

"Let me tell you something rather sweet that Lucy confessed to me." She walked over to Lowell and put a finger under his chin. "She said she could wish for no better life for Charlie than the one you had had, and she said she could wish for no better life for herself than the one you've given me. How many children say that to their parents, Lowell?"

"Lucy is a very satisfying child," he admitted.

"Then won't you ask Charlie about it when he returns?"

"I wish you would do it. I'm afraid I'd paint too discouraging a picture."

"Then you wouldn't mind? You won't feel as though I'm meddling into your affairs if I suggest to Charlie that he work for you?"

"I leave it entirely up to you, Lydia. But please be fair about it. Tell Charlie what he may be getting into. Tell him we nearly sold the Company a few years ago, and that there is always the chance we might sell it again. And let him make up his own mind. Don't urge him. Just tell him he can work for us if he wants to. That much I insist on, Lydia."

"As you wish," she answered. "I'll bend over backwards to be fair, and naturally I won't put any pressure on him. What possible pressure could I exert, anyway? I'm sure any decision he makes will be entirely his own." Then she looked at him sharply and said, "What on earth are you holding in your hand?"

"It's just a mouse, my dear."

"Where in the world did you get that?"

"I killed it with that remarkable book you left on the table."

"You silly boy," she giggled. "Give it to me."

She took the mouse by the tail and started for the door.

"Oh," she said, stopping suddenly, "I knew there was something else I wanted to ask you. What is a shakedown cruise?"

"A what?" he asked, staring at her.

"When Lucy and Charlie were leaving this morning, I told them I hoped they would have a most successful second honeymoon. Charlie said he didn't think it would be as much of a honeymoon as a shakedown cruise."

Lowell Chalmers burst out laughing.

"A shakedown cruise," he said, "is a naval term. It means a trial run under battle conditions."

He was still laughing as he climbed the stairs to wash up for dinner.

Charlie and Lucy returned two weeks later, on Sunday afternoon. That evening Lucy had a talk with her mother, and the following morning Mrs. Chalmers joined both of them at the breakfast table.

"I understand you children had a fine time," she said, addressing the statement to Charlie.

"Yes, we did," he answered.

"That's wonderful. I'm so glad you took the trip. You'll find it becomes

44

increasingly difficult to get away when you're older. A lot of petty responsibilities make trips impossible. It's sad, but true."

"I suppose that's right," Charlie answered. Mrs. Chalmers had impaled him with her cold blue eyes.

"Mother," Lucy said suddenly, as though on signal, "I think I'll run along upstairs and give Lydia her bath. You don't have anything in particular to say to me, do you?"

"Not a thing, darling. You run along and attend to your chores." She watched fondly as Lucy left the dining room. "Lucy is a wonderful mother, Charles. You haven't had much of a chance to appreciate her as yet."

He waited. Mrs. Chalmers was leaning forward over the table, her eyes never leaving his face. She reminded him slightly of a bird of prey, an eagle or a hawk about to pounce on a rabbit.

"Now, Charles," she began, "Lucy tells me you plan to look for a job."

He nodded.

"She also tells me you really have nothing definite in mind."

"That's true, more or less," he admitted. "I have just a few vague ideas."

"Would you care to tell me of a few of these vague ideas?"

"They're still pretty vague at this point."

"I see," she answered, smiling a little. "That hardly gives us much to go on, does it?" She reached out and rearranged a carnation in the centerpiece. "Lovely, aren't they?"

"Very pretty," he answered. Mrs. Chalmers was looking at him again.

"You know, Charles, it's always a terrible temptation for an older person like me to try to influence the young. We feel we have learned certain things in our lifetime, and we like to believe we can pass on what we've learned to our children. You know the saying about only a fool learns from experience, while the wise man learns by the mistakes of others."

"Have you made some mistakes, Mrs. Chalmers?" he asked, hoping to relieve the tension.

"This business of choosing a job," she continued, not listening to him, "is one of the most important decisions you'll make in your entire life. You must realize this."

"Yes, I do," he answered.

Elsa had opened the pantry door, hoping to clear away the breakfast dishes. Recognizing from Mrs. Chalmers' expression that she didn't wish to be disturbed, she backed out again.

"The last thing in the world either Mr. Chalmers or I wish to do is to influence you one way or the other. Wherever you decide to work, and whatever job you take, the decision must be yours, and yours alone."

"Thank you," he answered, beginning to feel as though he were about to suffocate.

Mrs. Chalmers leaned back in her chair. "Do you know much about The Hadley Company, Charles?"

"Only that they make horseshoe nails."

"Now good Lord," she exploded, "who told you that?"

"I assumed it from something Lucy once said."

"Horseshoe nails. My dear boy, we haven't made horseshoe nails for forty years. The Hadley Company makes knives, Charles. We make the highest-quality steel knives that can be found anywhere in the world. Horseshoe nails," she repeated, laughing. "That's like saying the Standard Oil Company makes oil for lamps. Is that all Lucy told you about our Company?"

"I didn't ask her anything more about it," he answered.

"This is the company my great-great-grandfather founded," she continued. "You can see his portrait out there in the hall. He made quite a name for himself in his time. He went to Washington as a senator, and he gave his name to the town of Hadley. The Hadley Company is our family company, Charles. It has a long tradition behind it. It's been going for one hundred and seven years."

"That's a long time," he said quietly.

"And I might add that never but once during that one hundred and seven years has the company failed to pay a dividend, and that was during the Civil War, when every cent was put back into expansion as a matter of national interest."

"That's quite a record," he answered.

His mind was racing ahead to the moment when Mrs. Chalmers would come out and offer him the job. He planned to refuse, and he hoped he could do it gracefully. The trouble was he couldn't think of any good excuse why he didn't want to work for The Hadley Company. There were a number of little reasons, but no one perfect excuse. For one thing, he didn't like being fitted into the family tradition. If he wished to avoid being completely swallowed by Lucy's family, his first move should be to stay away from the family company. Then, too, making knives sounded pretty boring. He wanted to get into something where he could use a little imagination. He knew he was naïve, but he thought that somewhere in the city there must be a perfect job for him. It might take him a few weeks to find it, but he wanted to look around.

He was sure of only one thing about himself. He wanted to work, and to work hard. He'd worked hard all his life, at school, in college, and in the army. He planned to work even harder at his job. He wanted to work and to make money. That might not be the most idealistic of dreams, he knew, but he was serious about it. If he took over the family company when he was forty-five or fifty, he might become rich by default, but that wasn't the way he wanted it. Any money he made he wanted to earn himself.

"Now, of course," Mrs. Chalmers went on, "there will come a day in the future when Mr. Chalmers will step down. Not that that day is close at hand yet, but it will some day come about. The war has tired him, as it has all businessmen." She stopped and fixed Charlie with her eyes. "I sometimes wonder if you boys who were in uniform stopped to think about the people who worked long and hard hours making the things you used to win the war. Did you ever realize that every piece of equipment you used was made by

46

some one individual back at home? That hours of planning, designing, and just plain work went into its manufacture?"

Charlie had thought about this just once. Early in the war he had been issued a new canteen cover. Some girl had inked in her name, address, and phone number on the inside. "Hello, Soldier," she wrote, "call me when you get to Rochester." He still had her name in his address book.

"Things here," Mrs. Chalmers continued, her voice showing a trace of smugness, "are not like they are around Boston. We do not believe in nepotism in this city. That's why our industry is still here and still flourishing. You will have to prove yourself to Mr. Chalmers, just as he had to prove himself to my father. Not that I doubt for a single instant that you can do the work, and do it well. Just about any well-educated and intelligent person can make a good executive.

"But we will not stand for any absentee management at The Hadley Company. We believe in no long-distance calls to the Riviera. Our family tradition is one of plodding, Charles. We are plodders," she repeated, as though admitting it made it not so. "We work, and we work hard, and let the future take care of itself. My, my," she exclaimed, laughing. "Here I am giving you a sermon, and I certainly had no intention of doing that." She took a deep breath and plunged ahead. "Mr. Chalmers and I have talked this all over in some detail. At The Hadley Company you will be treated just as any other employee. I'm sure you can see the fairness of it."

"I certainly can," he answered.

She still hadn't offered him the job, and he therefore had had no chance to refuse.

"It must be plain by now," she continued, relaxing a little, "that we'd all like you to become a part of our tradition in this family. We are not trying to influence your decision, but all of us, Mr. Chalmers, Lucy, and I myself, would like very much to have you work for The Hadley Company."

He said, "I certainly appreciate this, Mrs. Chalmers."

"Then I can take it that this means you'll accept?"

"Not yet," he answered, hoping to soften the blow. "I plan to spend a week or more looking around for a job that I really can be enthusiastic about. I think I have certain abilities, and I want a job that I really can be excited about."

As he was speaking, the smile disappeared from Mrs. Chalmers' face.

"Then you mean that you would not feel enthusiastic about working for The Hadley Company?"

"I really didn't mean that at all," he answered. He wished Lucy were with him. The last thing he wanted was another scene with Mrs. Chalmers.

"Well, just what do you mean?" she asked.

"I just don't want to be rushed into things. I want to investigate as many jobs as possible before I choose."

"I see," she answered coldly. She stood up and started for the hall.

"After the wonderful way you've treated me," he said hastily, "I feel pretty ashamed about this."

"Ashamed," she echoed. "My dear boy, no one ever need feel ashamed in this family. Why should you feel ashamed? I assume you have good and proper reasons why you wish to turn this job down, reasons that apparently you don't choose to discuss with me. That is your perfect right, Charles. We can consider the whole matter closed, unless you yourself someday decide to reopen it." She continued on out into the hall, singing gaily.

"There seems to be something about me that your mother doesn't like," Charlie reported to Lucy a few minutes later, when he joined her in the nursery.

"Now what happened?" Lucy asked uneasily.

He sat on the edge of the bed.

"It's not that I'm not grateful. I know she offered me a wonderful opportunity. I just want to look around first."

Lucy didn't answer.

"I suppose I'm a silly idealist," he continued. "I've always had the idea of one day owning my own business. I can't help but think that if I commit myself right at the start to an old-established firm, I'll be more or less trapped for the rest of my life. What do you think?"

Lucy was splashing water on Lydia.

"Look at her," she exclaimed. "Isn't she cute?"

Charlie glanced at his daughter absently.

"Do you agree?" he asked.

She took Lydia out of the water and started to dry her with a towel.

"You ought to start getting better acquainted with your daughter," she said. "Would you like to help dress her?"

It was at that moment that Charlie knew what it was he had felt like since he'd arrived home two weeks before. He was a replacement that had been sent forward to join a veteran, combat-hardened division. Everyone but him seemed to know exactly what was going on.

"For God's sake," he shouted harshly, "will you kindly listen to me and answer my question? I'm asking for advice, Lucy. I need your advice. Would you rather I did this all by myself, or will you talk it over with me?"

"You don't have to shout at me, Charlie."

"I'm sorry," he said quickly, afraid she was going to burst into tears. "I didn't mean to shout. I'm upset about this. I know your mother is trying to be nice to me. I just feel trapped, that's all."

"But that's utterly silly," Lucy answered cheerfully. "That's exactly what we don't want you to feel. Didn't Mother insist that the decision must be your own?"

He nodded.

"And that's exactly the way I feel. If you feel trapped, it's just your imagination. No one is trying to trap you. It's just you feeling that way."

"Can I ask you a question?"

"Of course you can, darling."

"You would like me to work for The Hadley Company, wouldn't you?"

48

"All right," she replied calmly. "Yes, I would. And it has nothing to do with Mother or anyone else. I think you'll like working for the Company, just the way my father has liked working for the Company. Furthermore, I think you'll do a good job, and you'll end up having a life that we both like. As far as I am concerned that's what matters most. All right, so I'm dull," she added quietly. "But I honestly think all this talk about going out on your own and starting a little company is just so much nonsense. The happiest people I know are men like my father. Just because people fit themselves into an existing pattern doesn't mean they don't lead just as interesting lives as the people who strike out all by themselves into thin air. Yes, I hope you work for The Hadley Company, and I'm thinking of your future as well as my own."

"I still think I'll look around first," he answered.

"Fine, darling. Wonderful. Look around all you like, and if you find something better I'll be just as delighted as you. Don't get the notion that I'm putting any pressure on you. As far as I'm concerned you don't have to work at all, if you don't want to."

"You know I want to work," he answered shortly.

"How would you feel if The Hadley Company had nothing to do with my family?" she asked. "Wouldn't you jump at the job Mother offered you?"

"I probably would."

She nodded, and tossed Lydia toward the ceiling.

"If you're going somewhere," she called after him when he started toward the stairs, "take the car. The keys are in it."

ten

IT WAS EXACTLY ELEVEN BY THE OLD STATE HOUSE CLOCK WHEN HE REACHED the center of the city. Not much had changed during the years he had been away. There were a few new stores around the old green, and a few different signs. As always, the same prosperous river of people was moving north along Main Street toward the department stores. This was a good city, he decided as he walked down Prospect Street toward the old Wadsworth barn. Why was it such a success? he wondered. What was the source of its solidity? Tradition? It boasted of none, except that no night club had ever showed a profit here. How could you best describe its inhabitants? Two hundred thousand souls who knew they would never be President? Still, it was a good city, and he liked it.

Just inside the iron fence that surrounded the Wadsworth barn there was a large horse chestnut tree. Years before, when his aunt had taken him with her on her shopping trips, she would leave him here to gather the chestnuts. This vacant lot, he thought, with its grass and weeds and the ancient barn, was the only real museum left in the entire city. He could almost smell the horses of a hundred years ago and hear the drone of the August flies. Somehow the place had survived, an accidental monument to an age of elegance and leisure, now surrounded completely by steel girders and stone. It couldn't last. The lot, after all, was vacant. It was not being used. What did it matter that a thousand people a day passed it, paused a moment, and came away refreshed? On the books it showed as a tax loss. If a specific, constructive purpose could not be ascribed to it by the city fathers, it must be torn down, removed, cleaned up, made tidy, and if possible turned into a parking lot. If archaeologists troubled themselves to dig anywhere in this city ten thousand years from now, they would find nothing.

Nor was this getting him a job, he realized. He walked west toward Main Street and stopped on the corner, looking across to the Pearl Street Bank. Banks were on a list he had made. There was insurance, there were investments, and there were banks. He decided to start with the Pearl Street Bank.

Inside, the building was gloomy and damp. Three huge cut-glass chandeliers hung down from the ceiling. The floor was marble, polished and worn by seventy-five years of shuffling feet. A row of glass-topped tables divided the main lobby, and along the walls, on either side, were rows of wire tellers' cages. The place was hushed and quiet, like a church. The people who were waiting in line near the tellers' windows spoke in whispers, nervous and ill at ease, as though the bank did them a favor by accepting their money.

Charlie walked to a polished wooden railing off to the right of the main door. Behind the railing was a single polished desk. Behind the desk a sallow, middle-aged man sat staring at a sheaf of papers that he had removed from a wire basket labeled "In." A small polished sign on his desk warned people that they were addressing Mr. Rowan.

"Yes," Mr. Rowan said abruptly, when it was obvious that Charlie was loitering.

"Who would I talk with about applying for a job?" he asked, wondering if by saying this much he had already committed himself forever, for life, to this cold, impersonal building. Mr. Rowan looked at him with invisible eyes behind a pair of rimless glasses. He neither smiled nor frowned, his face impassive, as though he were hiding his inner thoughts or masking the fact that he had none. He touched a button on his desk and lifted his phone. A moment later he put the phone down.

"Mr. Ballard," he said, "is out. He is our personnel manager. He would be the man for you to see. I can tell you, however, that your chances right now are extremely slim. I assume you've had previous banking experience."

"None," Charlie answered. Then he smiled, hoping to thaw Mr. Rowan a little. "I bounced a check once and got to know banking procedures pretty well."

Mr. Rowan looked grim, and said, "I see."

This was no place to be funny, Charlie decided.

"Your name?" Mr. Rowan asked, his pencil poised.

"Charles Webb."

"Very well, Mr. Webb. I suggest you wait over there." He pointed to a marble bench covered with polished leather cushions. "When Mr. Ballard returns to his office I'll let you know."

Charlie took his place on the bench. It reminded him of his induction into the army four years before. He had sat two hours in a drafty gymnasium, waiting to take his physical exam. That time, however, he had been stripped to his shorts. At least Mr. Rowan allowed him to keep on his clothes.

It was the only time in his life he had observed closely the inside of a bank. It was really incredible, he thought, how little he knew about banking. What happened to the money, he wondered, once the teller's hand closed over it? Everyone seemed to know exactly what he was doing. Over the wire cages, on a horseshoe-shaped balcony that hung from the ceiling, there were rows of desks behind which more men like Mr. Rowan sat reading and shuffling papers. Now and then a uniformed messenger holding a sheet of paper glided along the balcony disappearing through a metal door at the end of the building. It was doubtless behind this metal door, Charlie realized, where the real business of banking took place. The tellers and the lines of people at the wire cages were merely a necessary overhead. The money was made behind the metal door.

Charlie had already decided his interview with Mr. Ballard would be a mere formality, that he wouldn't work in this bank or, in fact, any bank, when he became aware of a familiar face in one of the teller's cages. He was stunned. It was Danny Girard, a college classmate. Danny had been a fabulous figure on the campus at New Haven. Talented, handsome, and charming, he had skimmed through college with ease, winning his letter at football and missing Phi Beta Kappa by only a point or two. He had been just about everything at college that Charlie had not been and wished he was. Danny had written and directed two successful dramatic productions, and college had been rife with rumors that both of the shows were going to move to Broadway. In a student body filled with cynicism, Danny Girard had been one boy that his classmates respected, liked, and envied. They saw him another Cole Porter in a few years. They saw his name on the best-seller list of the New York *Times*. They saw him governor, senator, even President. When he left college in the middle of his senior year to fly a navy plane, they saw him diving a hero's death into a flaming ocean. They saw him just about everywhere but in a wire cage in a bank counting out one-dollar bills, which was what he was doing when Charlie came up to his window.

Danny had put on a little weight, mostly around his neck and face. He was still handsome, but he looked soft and stale. At college he had gone in for colorful tweeds, but he was now wearing a severe dark suit and horn-rimmed glasses.

"Danny," Charlie shouted incredulously, "what are you doing here?"

"Ninety-eight, ninety-nine, one hundred," Danny answered, stacking the bills neatly, wrapping an elastic around them, and tossing the bundle into a metal drawer. "Hi," he said, his eyes registering on Charlie. "Earning my daily bread. What in hell do you think I'm doing?"

"I just didn't expect—"

51

"To find me in a bank?"

"Hardly. I figured you for Broadway, politics, the State Department——"

"Or the White House?"

"At least," Charlie answered.

"Well, I'm in the Pearl Street Bank. Incidentally, what are *you* doing here?"

Charlie hesitated, embarrassed. "Frankly, I'm looking for a job."

"Ha. Those who live in glass houses."

They stood for a moment, gazing at each other silently. Danny glanced at his watch.

"You eaten?"

"Not yet."

"It's a little early, but since my own father-in-law runs the joint I guess I can skip out before twelve. How about the club?"

"Wonderful," Charlie answered, extremely pleased.

Danny slid his window shut and locked it. Then carefully and deliberately he swept his counter clean, putting pencils, pads, and even paper clips into a drawer, which he locked. Finally he locked the rear door of his cage. Times changed, and people changed with them, Charlie thought. At college Danny's room had resembled a dump. Open day or night, it had been filled with books, dirty clothing, empty glasses, and half-empty bottles. On the week ends it had been filled with girls. His cage in the bank, however, was as neat and as sterile as a new dollar bill.

"Let's go," he said when he joined Charlie in the lobby. "I'll tell you the whole sad story while we eat."

They were early. They chose a table against the wall. A few older men stood at the bar, men who had reached the stage of their business careers that allowed them to leave their offices at will.

"So what's a man going to do?" Danny asked, shrugging philosophically. He was sucking an olive he had removed from his Martini. "I got home about five months ago, after four years on an aircraft carrier. I was trained for absolutely nothing, I had married Louise Wray in '43 on a leave, and when I came home I had Louise and two kids waiting for me. The Old Buck—that's Louise's father—had taken my navy pay and invested it in stocks. They did pretty well for me. I had over six thousand when I got back. Louise lived with her family, kids and all. They were wonderful about it. Anyway, Louise was plenty fed up when I finally showed up. She was crazy to get a house. Not that I blame her," he added quickly, "but I just wanted to wait a while. I didn't want to be rushed into anything." Danny removed the olive pit from his mouth and deposited it in his empty Martini glass. "I had this crazy idea about starting a theater when I got back from the war. I dreamed about it all the time I was stuck on the carrier. I figured on getting a few New York tryouts to come up here, and perhaps put on a few local productions of my own. Strictly feet planted in mid-air stuff." He smiled ruefully. "You should have seen the reaction when I dropped this idea in front of the Old

Buck. It was as though I had told him I planned to invest my money in a space ship.

"Don't get me wrong. Mr. Wray is a great guy, but he's not exactly a gambler by instinct. He didn't build up the Pearl Street Bank by investing his funds in art or the theater. He nailed me one night and grilled me like a poor sucker who was applying for a loan, which as a matter of fact maybe I was. I was planning to hit him for a few thousand to buy my theater. Anyway, he said, one, no theater has ever lasted long in this city, and two, even if it did last it wouldn't show a profit. Three, he said that with a wife and two children I had a hell of a lot of gall even to think about the theater. And four, if I was thinking about applying to him for a loan I'd better try another bank."

"How about New York?" Charlie asked. The club was filling up.

"Oh sure, New York. The big chance and the mad rat race. Louise didn't want any part of New York, and she didn't want to live in one of those commuter towns. As a matter of fact," Danny added, as though the thought had just occurred to him, "as a matter of fact, Louise didn't want to live anywhere but right here."

"How was she about your theater idea?"

Danny shrugged. "How can I put it? She was cheerful and she was patient. Very, very patient. 'The decision must be all yours, Danny boy. Don't let me discourage you. I'm with you one hundred per cent no matter *what* you do.' You know how they can be."

Charlie nodded thoughtfully.

"Anyway," Danny continued, "when the chips were finally down I discovered something nasty about myself. I discovered that I didn't have the guts to do what I thought I wanted to do. So I bought Louise her home with my six thousand dollars, and I went to work in her father's bank, and the funny thing," he added, hitting the table with his fist, "the funny thing is that I'm damn glad I did. I'm happy as hell in the bank. Louise is happy as hell with her house. The Old Buck is happy. We're all happy." He paused. "It's a nasty shock to find out you're yellow, but once the shock wears off there are many compensating features, such as a steady salary, three squares a day, and a secure future for the rest of my life. Incidentally, Louise is pregnant again."

"Wonderful, Danny."

"Yes, wonderful. I even find I am a good father. I like the little bastards. We want five or six. If I behave myself and resist the temptation to dip into the till, I'll probably be running the bank by the time I'm fifty. This banking business is fascinating." He leaned across the table toward Charlie, his face suddenly intent. "I mean it. It is. It's changing fast. We're planning to branch out into the suburbs, and there's talk round about branch banks where people can drive right up and make their deposits without even getting out of their cars. Right now we're organizing a public relations department. Get this," he said, laughing. "When Mr. Wray learned I was going into the bank with him, he took me aside and said, 'My boy, I've heard you wrote plays while you were in college. Well, don't get the idea that creative talent like that will go to waste in a bank. We'll need copy for radio advertising and for newspaper advertising.'"

"Are you writing it?"

"Sure I am. Have you noticed the slogan on the buses around town?"

"Is that yours?"

"Right. Excuse me a moment, will you, Charlie." Danny stood up. "I see Joe Partridge, and I've got to deliver a message to him from Louise. We're having a few people in for dinner next Saturday night."

Danny drifted away, and Charlie ate alone for a while. The conversation had depressed him. If Danny, with his wealth of natural talent, had found it necessary to retreat into a bank, what hope was there for a person like himself? At least Danny had had a dream. He had nothing. He was merely wandering about trying to find out what jobs were available.

The bar was now crowded, and almost all the tables were taken. There were three distinct age groups in the room.

First, there were the older men from fifty to seventy years old—solid, well-dressed, contented-looking people, Charlie thought. These older men appeared vigorous and alert, as though their lives in business had brought them a great deal of satisfaction and happiness.

Then there was the middle group, the pre-heart-attack age, from forty to fifty, most of them a little too fat, with flushed faces, as though they drank more than their health warranted. They stood about in groups, talking business, their faces glowing.

Finally, there was the younger crowd like himself, in their late twenties or early thirties, veterans of nothing but the war, all of them just fighting for a start.

Here we all are, Charlie thought sadly, like a flock of sheep. The school and college bull sessions where such confident words were spoken about charting new paths—all that was now forgotten. Not one of us had what it takes to be different, he decided. Dreams were cheap, but guts were rare.

But then, was it so important to be different? What was wrong with the men in this room? Were they George Babbitts? In fact, did Babbitt exist anywhere? Had Sinclair Lewis really held up a mirror, or had he merely engineered a vicious smear?

He was aroused from his thoughts by a hand gripping his shoulder and a strident, penetrating voice inches from his ear.

"Hello, you old war hero. Welcome home."

It was Woodchuck Wallin, Charles W. Wallin, "Woodchuck" since the fifth grade at school. The origin of his nickname had been lost with the years. He didn't look like a woodchuck, being tall and lean, with a long neck and a large Adam's apple. Nor did he act like a woodchuck. Woodchuck Wallin had never hibernated in his life. He acted more like a beaver than a 'chuck. In his twenty-eight years he had never once stopped working. No one had noticed him during his early years of school. He was just there. At college, however, he had begun to make his presence felt. He managed the varsity

54

football team, he ran the student laundry, and in his senior year he started a new project, an insurance agency. By midyear he had sold policies to over half the class. Charlie had been one of his salesmen. He had quit when he discovered that Woodchuck was making most of the money while he was making most of the sales.

Woodchuck's stated ambition in the college yearbook had been a classic of truthful simplicity. He planned to sell insurance, he said, and he hoped to retire at forty with a million dollars. At twenty-eight, with twelve years still to go, he seemed to be well ahead of his schedule. He had his own agency, with over a dozen people working for him. His formula had been simple. Hard work and dodging the draft.

Charlie had never forgiven Woodchuck since the day Pearl Harbor was bombed. Up until then nearly everyone in college had been trying to figure out some way of getting out of the draft. It was the thing to do. The FBI, the State Department, a course in engineering, even marriage if nothing else was possible. But when the bombs fell on Pearl Harbor, all that had been instantly forgotten. The country was at war, and that was that. But not for Woodchuck, however.

Charlie had been in his room when President Roosevelt made the formal declaration of war. Halfway through the speech Woodchuck snapped off the radio. He then rolled up his trousers leg.

"Take a look at this," he said.

Charlie could see nothing unusual.

"All right, listen, then," Woodchuck twisted his kneecap. There was a slight grinding sound, as though a piece of sand had become lodged in a hinge.

"That little cartilage will be worth just about a million dollars to me. When you lucky stiffs come back from the war you'll all be asking me for work."

Woodchuck Wallin had never made the slightest attempt to deny he was dodging the draft. To his friends he admitted it frankly. He also admitted to everyone but his draft board that his knee was completely sound. All during the war he sold insurance. He also put out a monthly newsletter to his entire "list," as he called his friends. He called it "Chips from the Woodchuck." It was filled with information about who was fighting where and how things were going. He also kept people up to date on life at home as a civilian—the long hours he spent as an air-raid warden, how hard it was to get space on planes, and the nuisance of gas rationing. "You service men are getting all the breaks," he wrote in 1944.

"I see you've given up your cane," Charlie said, grinning at the Woodchuck in spite of himself.

"Haven't needed it since VJ Day," Woodchuck answered, grinning right back at him.

Like other able-bodied young men who walked the civilian streets during the war, Woodchuck had found it necessary to advertise his disability to avoid constant embarrassing questions. Just as some had worn eye patches or hearing aids, he had bought himself a large black cane. With the surrender of the Japanese the cane had gone into the closet.

"What's new besides all your money?" Charlie asked.

"Not a thing. How's Lucy?"

"Fine."

"You just have the one baby?"

"That's all."

"You called her Lydia, didn't you?"

Charlie nodded. Woodchuck never missed a thing.

"You're a slacker." He winked at Charlie. "I've got two. A boy and a girl."

"You were using them while the rest of us were getting them shot off." Charlie tried to make his voice sound cold, but it was difficult. In spite of his loathing for Woodchuck Wallin, it was hard not to like him.

"You bet I was using them," Woodchuck answered, delighted. "And when you see my wife you'll know why."

Charlie didn't answer.

"So what are your plans, Charlie?" Woodchuck's voice became confidential.

"I'm out looking for a job."

"Anything particular in mind?"

"Frankly, no."

Woodchuck looked at him intently for a moment. Then he squeezed Charlie's shoulder. "Work's pretty tough right now. That is, *good* jobs. If there's anything I can do to help, don't hesitate." He drifted away, and Charlie soon saw him with his hand on another shoulder.

When Danny Girard returned he said, "Did I see you talking with Woodchuck Wallin?"

Charlie nodded.

"There," Danny said respectfully, "is a one-man whirlwind. I can tell you off the record, as a banker, that he's plenty solvent."

Charlie said nothing.

"I also happen to know that in a day or so he's going to get Junior Man of the Year."

"What in Christ's name is Junior Man of the Year?" Charlie asked.

"That's the Chamber's annual award."

"What do you have to be to win it?"

"The outstanding junior citizen in the city."

Charlie thought a moment. Then he said, "Balls."

"I know what you mean, but these things don't hurt the Woodchuck's business."

"Balls," Charlie repeated.

They walked back to the bank together. Charlie left Danny at the main door.

"Don't let me urge you one way or the other," Danny said, "but I'll be glad to take you up to the old man right now. I happen to know he's looking for people like you to train for these branch offices we're going to open up. I can just about guarantee he'll give you a job."

"I guess not," Charlie answered. "This is my first day. I think I'll keep looking around."

Danny shrugged. "Maybe I don't blame you." He looked a little sad. "Well, back to the old cage. See you around." He pushed on through the swinging door.

When Danny was gone, Charlie stood for a while on the sidewalk. Not only did he not wish to work for the Pearl Street Bank; he had decided he wouldn't work for any bank. He took his notebook out of his pocket and drew a heavy line through the word "Banks." Then he walked down Gold Street, toward the park.

On the corner, a block below Main, he saw a Negro polishing a brass name plate. "Baird and Company," he read. "Members of the New York Stock Exchange." He knew even less about the brokerage business than about banking. There seemed to be something slightly mysterious about it. Brokers seldom became well known. Their profession didn't lead them, as did the law, into larger and wider fields, politics and the realm of public service. Why was this? he wondered. It could be that selling stocks was so interesting brokers never felt the need for fame. He started toward the entrance of the small brick building.

The walls of Baird and Company were decorated with English hunting prints, and the light green paint was dusty and faded. Light globes hung in a row down a long hall, the bottoms black with dead flies. If Mr. Baird made money, Charlie thought, he must take it all home with him. Very little of it was being spent on the office.

A woman sitting at a desk just inside the entrance glanced at him expectantly.

"I'm Mrs. Arnold," she said. "Can I help you?" She wore a tweed suit and dark-rimmed glasses. She seemed to be more than a mere secretary.

"I'm looking for a job," he said hesitating in the doorway.

"Come in. Come in," she answered cheerfully. "What sort of a job?"

"Selling," he answered.

"I see." She reached for a pad. "What's your name?"

"Charlie Webb."

"Any experience, Mr. Webb?"

"None."

"What have you done before this?"

"I've been in the army for four years."

"Yes, of course," she answered. "I keep forgetting all you young men have been off in the war. Were you born in the city, Mr. Webb?"

He nodded.

"Would I know of your family?"

"I doubt it. My aunt ran a dress shop for a few years."

"Oh, yes. Ruth's, wasn't it?"

"Yes."

"What makes you think you'd like to sell investments?" she asked.

Did you have to have a reason for wanting a job? he wondered. Perhaps he didn't want to sell investments. This place seemed just as dreary as the bank. He heard a ticker machine rattling at the far end of the building, and phones were buzzing.

"I want to sell," he answered.

"Well, that's a good reason, Mr. Webb. Wait here a moment. I'll find out if Mr. Baird can see you."

When Mrs. Arnold had gone, Charlie felt a sudden surge of panic. Was he hunting a job, he wondered, or choosing his jail? Perhaps before committing himself to a brokerage house he should glance about at the inmates. He walked a few steps down the hall and peered in through a doorway marked "Trading Dept." An elderly man stood by the ticker, the tape trailing out through his fingers, falling away into a wire basket. It appeared that he had recently suffered a stroke or had never recovered from an old one. His skin was the color of wet concrete, and the right side of his body was partially paralyzed. His right eyelid drooped, and the cheek sagged. With his good left eye, however, he was watching the quotations, and all parts of his body that weren't paralyzed looked happy and at peace with the world.

"Now that's strange," Mrs. Arnold said to herself when she returned to find Charlie gone. She stepped toward the street and looked down the sidewalk. Then she shrugged and walked once again to Mr. Baird's office.

"He just left." She looked past Mr. Baird and pointed out the office window. "There he is over there in the park."

"Did you get his name?"

She glanced at her pad. "Charles Webb. His aunt ran a dress shop here in the city a few years ago."

It was the dress shop, not the name, that registered with Fred Baird.

"Oh, my God," he said, glancing toward the heavens. "Get me Lowell Chalmers at The Hadley Company." When his phone rang he picked it up and said, "Lowell, this is Fred. A damn funny thing just now happened here in the office." He paused. "No. No. Not that bad. It was your son-in-law Charlie. He came in here looking for work, and apparently my Mrs. Arnold scared him away."

Out at her own desk, Mrs. Arnold, who was listening in on her extension, cut the connection with a gesture of impatience. How was she supposed to know he was a member of the family? And what was she supposed to do? Tie the young man down with a rope?

eleven

On Wednesday afternoon, when he returned to the house, Charlie found Lucy in the bedroom examining her dinner dresses.

"I didn't know you knew Charles Wallin, darling." She looked at him respectfully.

"Woodchuck? Sure. Why?"

"Lila Wallin called me about an hour ago. They want us to come for dinner."

"Tonight?"

Lucy nodded.

"I wonder what he wants," Charlie said thoughtfully.

"Us for dinner, apparently. Lila said to make it informal. That there would be just the four of us."

"You accepted?"

"We had nothing else to do."

Something was in the wind, Charlie decided. One thing he was sure of, he'd starve before he'd accept a handout from Woodchuck.

"Mr. Wallin is really quite a person, Charlie. He received all sorts of citations during the war for his work with the air-raid system around here. And someone told me he would probably be selected——"

"I know," he interrupted. "Junior Man of the Year."

"You needn't be so scornful. For someone our age he's doing terribly well."

"Remind me to congratulate him tonight."

"You poor darling, you're tired," Lucy said, hugging him affectionately. "How did the job hunting go today?"

"Lousy."

"Do you want to tell me about it?"

"Not particularly."

Until they left for the Wallins', Lucy spoke only of cheerful things.

On the way out in the car she said, "Where did you meet Mr. Wallin?"

"For God's sake stop calling him Mr. Wallin. His name is Woodchuck, and I roomed with the bastard for a year at college."

"You really are tired, aren't you?"

Charlie didn't answer.

"What's so terrible about him?"

"He's a draft dodger."

"I thought that's what you'd say."

"Well, it's a fact."

Lucy paused a moment gathering her thoughts.

"I don't quite know how to say this," she began, "but I'm going to say it anyway. You will admit that the war is over, won't you?"

"Of course it's over. What are you getting at?"

"For some reason you seem bitter about people who didn't do exactly what you did during the war. I happen to know something about Mr. Wallin."

"Woodchuck," he interrupted.

"I happen to know that Mr. Wallin did a tremendous amount for the war effort, even though perhaps he didn't join the army or the navy. He did such a good job with the air-raid wardens that he was even called to a conference in Washington about it. We were held up as a model city during the war.

People came from all over the country to see how we were organized. That was Mr. Wallin's doing."

"Woodchuck," Charlie repeated.

"And I'm also sure that Mr. Wallin would have joined the army or the navy if they would have taken him."

"His name is Woodchuck, and you're wrong. Some of the people my age who got out of the war deserved to. They really did have things wrong with them. And some of them did do more to help win the war than the men in uniform. But not Woodchuck Wallin. He sold insurance, and that's *all* he did. If he helped with the air-raid system, it was just to sell insurance. Look around you," he said harshly. "Look at our friends. Every single one of us who spent the last four or five years in the army is just floundering around the way I am. But the people our age who got out of going to war for one reason or another are riding high. Don't get me wrong. I'm going to forget about the war, but I'm not going to forget about the people who didn't help win it."

"I suggest you join the American Legion," she said angrily.

"I plan to."

"You might organize a committee to black-list everyone who didn't wear a uniform."

"I'll tell you one thing," he answered coldly. "I'll never do a draft dodger a favor."

The Wallins lived on Orchard Road. The driveway, a wide ribbon of smooth macadam, curved in through an old field of apple trees. The grounds had been recently landscaped, and the lawn, over an acre of it in all, was bright green from a heavy application of fertilizer. The planting about the house had been planned by an expert—large yew bushes, rhododendron, and laurel, arranged in clumps. Cost obviously had been incidental. The garage doors had been left open. Inside were two new cars, their chrome bumpers gleaming in the darkness.

The house itself was new, low, and modern, with a flat roof. It faced to the east, with the entire city spread out below it, six miles away. Fifty thousand dollars, Charlie thought to himself. Perhaps sixty. This was the house a man saved a lifetime to build. The Woodchuck had it when he was twenty-eight. And there was no odor of mortgage here. It all looked planned, finished, and paid for.

In the driveway, near the front door, there was a child's sock, damp and dirty. Lucy picked it up and put it in her evening bag. A colored maid answered the doorbell.

"Come right in," she said, her accent from the Deep South. "Mis' Wallin is expectin' you."

Everything in the house was new. Woodchuck Wallin had no family to give him their antique castoffs. Almost the entire east wall of the living room was glass. At the far end of the room, on a raised fieldstone platform, there was a fireplace, a copper cap over it, an inverted funnel drawing smoke out through the ceiling. There were moroccan leather hassocks, steel chairs with

60

foam rubber cushions, a glass-topped table, and a thick, heavy carpet from wall to wall. The Woodchuck had done it well, Charlie admitted to himself grudgingly. If he had built his house to advertise his wealth, he had done it tastefully. In one corner of the room there was a bar with rows of gleaming glasses, bottles, and a small dish filled with olives.

"Hi Ho, Webbs," Woodchuck shouted, striding in from the hall. He was dressed in tweeds and a bow tie. "Lila will be right along. That last lock of hair, you know. I'm Charles Wallin, Lucy." He took one of her hands in both of his. "The so-called boss of this monstrosity. What do you think, Charlie?"

"Wow!"

"Wow is right. But Lila wanted it, and what Lila wants, she gets. Shall we wait for her, or shall we drink our Martini now? Let's drink now," he said, answering his own question.

They were all sitting by the fireplace when Lila Wallin came in. When he saw her, Charlie jumped up as though he had been burned. He knew he had to do something besides just sit and stare with his mouth open. Lila was tall. At least five feet eight. Her hair was jet black. She walked slowly across the room, smiling enigmatically, her shoulders back, her head balanced carefully, as though she were carrying a book on it. Her skin, much of which was showing, was the color of cream, and her eyes were deep blue. If the setting—the house and the grounds—was regal, Lila Wallin was the queen.

"I'm always so happy to meet friends of my husband," she purred as she shook hands.

Her accent was difficult to place. Southern, Charlie decided, but still not genuine South. Something Lila Wallin had affected, he thought as he listened to her talking with Lucy. Of one thing he was certain. Lila Wallin was not local.

"As I was saying just a moment ago," Charlie whispered to Woodchuck, glancing at Lila as he spoke, "wow!"

Woodchuck grinned like a small boy.

"Where did you get her?" Charlie asked.

"Charlie wants to know where I got you," Woodchuck shouted across the room, interrupting his wife's conversation with Lucy.

"Yes, where did you find her?" Lucy asked, her tone one of awe.

"Don't you dare tell that silly old story again," Lila giggled, her voice sounding natural for the first time.

"Where did you find her?" Charlie persisted.

Woodchuck stood up and drained his cocktail glass. He was the picture of confidence and success.

"Well," he began, "once upon a time, back in 1943 to be exact, I found myself down in Texas on business. It just so happened it was the week end of the Cotton Bowl game." He paused, still grinning. "Now it also happened that one of my clients had given me a ticket, and having nothing better to do I went out to the stadium early, in plenty of time to watch that little old ceremony they call the crowning of the Cotton Bowl Queen."

"You're not Miss Cotton Bowl?" Lucy gasped, staring at Lila.

"Yes, ma'am," Woodchuck answered. "She is, or she was. Miss Cotton Bowl of 1943."

"That's absolutely fabulous," Lucy gasped again. "I've never known a Miss Anything."

"Well, you know one now," Woodchuck said. "I took one look and I knew I had to have her. So I made my plan of attack, and two weeks later she was mine."

"I thought he was some kind of nut at first," Lila giggled. Her accent had gone completely to pieces. She was now pure Texas. "He kept on pesterin' me and pesterin' me until I just had to give in."

"I sold myself just like an insurance policy," Woodchuck interrupted. "Honey, I said, I'm offering you a lifetime annuity, with no premiums. You just come and live with little old Woodchuck, and all your little old worries will be over."

"I really did think he was a nut," Lila giggled.

"Miss Cotton Bowl," Charlie muttered. Where had he been in 1943? he wondered. Fighting mosquitoes in the swamps of Georgia.

"Yes, sir," Woodchuck shouted. "Miss Cotton Bowl of 1943 and Mrs. Orchard Road of 1945. And she's given me two little extra dividends. A boy and a girl. Both of them pretty, like her."

"Which reminds me," Lucy interrupted, obviously trying to break the spell. "I found this in the driveway." She dove into her pocketbook and extracted the dirty sock.

Lila held it by the toe, her face averted, as though it were a dead fish. She then rang for the maid and turned the sock over to her.

After dinner, Charlie and Woodchuck left their wives in the living room and sat talking in Woodchuck's study.

"Take one. They're free," Woodchuck said, offering Charlie a cigar.

The cigars were so beautifully packed it seemed a shame to open them. Each one was wrapped in gold paper, and under the paper there was a sheath of fragrant cedar. The tobacco smelled good enough to eat.

"I suppose you import these direct from Havana."

"I don't get them at the corner drugstore, if that's what you mean."

"You've got it made, haven't you, Woodchuck?"

"I don't get you, boy," Woodchuck answered grinning. He sat leaning back in his chair, his feet on his desk, an aromatic blue cloud of cigar smoke drifting toward the ceiling.

"You're a son-of-a-bitch, but you've got it made."

Woodchuck's grin increased in size. "Of course I kind of wish my leg had been sound. You boys had a lot of fun in the war. It was pretty tough to be a 4F sitting at home."

"My heart bleeds."

"Yes, sir, there were plenty of times I envied you boys with your medals and your uniforms, traveling all over the world on Uncle Samuel. You must have had some wonderful experiences."

"Drop dead," Charlie answered, smiling in spite of himself.

Woodchuck stood up and walked to a small fireplace at the end of the room. He stood facing Charlie, his back against the mantelpiece.

"So how's it going?" he asked.

"Not too good. So far I've just been making the rounds. Banks, brokers, insurance. Maybe I've been too fussy, but I haven't seen much that I like yet."

"Fussy, hell," Woodchuck answered vehemently, pointing a finger at Charlie. "You're being smart. Let me tell you what happens to a guy like you in these old mossback firms. You'll work like hell for thirty years, and the day they elect the great-grandson of the founder president, they'll hand you a fifteen-dollar watch for faithful service. To Charles Webb, in recognition of his loyalty to the Conservative Bank and Trust Company. That stuff is enough to gag a maggot, and this city is shot rotten with it."

Charlie stared enviously across the room. It was hard to believe that, less than five years before, he and Woodchuck had been college students together. Wallin now made him feel inferior, as though he should be standing at attention. In the business world Woodchuck Wallin was now a colonel, and he, Charlie, was just a raw recruit.

"Remember we used to talk about that in college," Woodchuck continued. "If you don't start something of your own, you end up nowhere. The only way you get to the top of one of these established companies is to make a pile of money and then buy them out."

"You'd know more about that than I do," Charlie answered. "Of course there's always The Hadley Company. Lucy's family controls it, and they're anxious for me to go to work there."

Woodchuck smiled patiently. "How much do you know about The Hadley Company?"

"Not a hell of a lot."

"That's no company. It's just a family graveyard."

"I hear it's always paid its dividends."

"You really don't know much about The Hadley Company, do you, Charlie? Sure it's paid dividends. Five per cent. But they get their dividends out of a two-million-dollar portfolio of stocks. That's no factory. It's just one big trust fund."

"How do you know so much about it?" Charlie asked.

"Because it's part of my business to know about things like that." He walked to his desk and spoke confidentially. "The Hadley Company has a book value of a little over two million dollars, but the plant is worth just about nothing. They haven't spent a nickel out there in twenty years. If you get involved with a setup like that, you'll end up out in the cold."

"At least I'd be head of it," Charlie answered.

"The head of what? The head of nothing. They damn near sold out about four years ago, Charlie, and they'll really sell out if they get a decent offer. We had it all set, and it would have gone through except for——"

"What do you mean, *we?*" Charlie interrupted. "Were you in on it?"

"Strictly a commission," Woodchuck answered with exaggerated modesty. "I don't need to bore you with the details, but take my word for it, your wife's family wanted to sell out four years ago, and they'll sell out yet. Didn't they warn you about that?"

"I didn't hear a thing about it."

"You can't trust anyone these days," Woodchuck answered sadly. "Not even your own wife's family."

"Which still leaves me nowhere," Charlie muttered.

"Charlie," Woodchuck said, pointing the cigar at him, "I want you to team up with me."

Charlie had been expecting this.

"You wouldn't be feeling sorry for the returning war hero, would you?"

"Hell, no. I'm not sorry for anyone. I want you to come in with me because you're the kind of person I can use. Listen," he said when Charlie started to speak. "I'm just getting rolling these days. I can use salesmen. Real salesmen, the kind who'll beat the brush all day, seven days a week. I can hire dozens of the tweed wearers around here, but I don't want any part of them. I want the black shoes working for me. Guys who don't have summer places, who never play golf unless it's to make a sale. I want guys who want to make money like I do. I want salesmen who worship money."

He paused. "This is a rich town. It's just one big ripe plum waiting to be plucked. If you don't believe it, just look at my place. I didn't inherit this from any Goddam family. I paid for it myself, and I'm going to pay for a lot more before I'm through. I'm making money, Charlie. And you can make money too, if you don't get yourself bogged down in some old rotten company full of cousins and sons. You come in with me, and we'll make one hell of a team." He paused watching Charlie closely. "I'm not doing you a favor. You'll be doing me the favor. I need guys like you." He grinned. "Anyway, I like you. Sure, sure, I know you hate my guts. I'll bet you told yourself two hundred times that you'd starve before you'd let Woodchuck do you a favor. Am I right?"

"I might have thought something like that," Charlie admitted. Woodchuck was clever. He was beginning to like him.

"So I'm a bastard," Woodchuck continued. "I know it, and I don't care. Call me whatever you want, and you'll be right. But come on in with me. When you're a millionaire, you won't care what I am."

"As a salesman?" Charlie asked. He was tempted. He felt his loathing of Woodchuck Wallin dissolving. Woodchuck was offering him just the opportunity he was looking for. He'd hate himself for accepting, yet he'd be foolish not to.

"Sure, you'll start off as a salesman. You'll have to get the feel of it just the way I did. But don't think you'll be a salesman for long. I've got twelve people working for me now, and before long I'll have fifty. I'm talking part-

64

nership, boy. And off the record, you may end up with the whole business in ten years because I don't plan to stay with it forever."

"Oh?" Charlie said.

"Hell no. I plan to branch out into other things."

"Such as what?"

"Politics, for instance."

Charlie laughed. "Well, well, Governor Woodchuck."

"Well, why not?"

"The American Legion will ram you with a bayonet."

"Oh, balls. Politics is just like anything else. People back a man who gets things done, and I get things done."

"But how about your knee? Would that stand up under the rigors of a hard political campaign?"

"It's a funny thing about this knee of mine," Woodchuck answered. "It felt perfectly all right the minute you guys won the war." He grinned shamelessly.

Woodchuck's offer was still hanging unanswered. Charlie glanced around the room. There were pictures of Lila all over the walls.

"That is some wife you landed yourself," he said.

"You like her?"

"Did you think I wouldn't?"

Charlie was watching Woodchuck when he answered. For the first time a shadow of uncertainty came into Woodchuck's eyes. For a moment he looked worried, almost frightened.

"Tell me something, Charlie. Does Lucy cry?"

"What do you mean, cry?" he asked, surprised.

"Cry. Does Lucy cry?"

"Never," Charlie lied brazenly.

"Then, brother, you're lucky. Lila cries all the time."

"What's she cry about?"

"Damn near everything. When I first brought her north I was only just getting started. We rented an apartment off Woodruff Drive. It was a nice little place, but Lila hated it. She didn't want to rent. She wanted to own. So I got her a house on Quaker Lane. She hated that too. It was just like everyone else, and she didn't want to be like everyone else. She had to have a big house on the top of a hill. Damn near drove me nuts. I couldn't afford it. Every night she'd start crying about how she just had to have a big house so she could entertain. So I built this place for her last year."

"She must be happy now."

Woodchuck tipped back his head and looked at the ceiling.

"Happy. Christ Almighty. It's worse now. Worse. Now she says we don't have any friends. What good is a big house, she says, if we don't have any friends?"

Charlie grinned. "How about the Chamber of Commerce, Woodchuck? I hear they plan to elect you Junior Man of the Year. Aren't they all your friends?"

Woodchuck looked mean for a moment, and Charlie knew he had finally reached him.

"There must be a few other patriotic young men like you in the city," he persisted. "I should think you'd be very popular with them."

"We're talking about Lila. Not me," Woodchuck answered sourly. "Do you know what she really wants?"

"Let me guess. A castle?"

Woodchuck shook his head.

"No," he said. "She wants to be a member of the Garden Club."

Charlie burst out laughing. "Lila likes to dig in the dirt?"

"Hell no. She can't stand dirt. She just wants to be a member of the Garden Club."

It had all started to jell in Charlie's mind. Suddenly he no longer envied Woodchuck Wallin.

"Then why doesn't she join it?" he asked.

"Because you don't do it that way. The Garden Club isn't like the National Geographic Society. You have to be asked."

"Gee, Woodchuck," Charlie said innocently, "with all your money, I should think you'd bribe someone."

"Look, stuff it, will you, Charlie."

"Isn't there another garden club?"

"Sure, there's another club. They call it Flower and Bower, and Lila doesn't like it because it isn't *the* Garden Club. She doesn't want to join *a* garden club. She wants to be a member of *the* Garden Club."

"It looks like you bit off more than you can chew with Miss Cotton Bowl."

"Maybe I did," he admitted. "I oversold myself down there in Texas. I told Lila how I really was somebody back up here, and she believed me. How I knew all the best people and stuff like that. Hell," he said angrily, "Lila's nothing where she came from. Nobody decent ever goes into one of those Miss Whatsit contests. She figured me for a ticket to high society, and now I can't even get her into the Garden Club."

"What a dirty shame," Charlie answered.

"You'd think so too if you had a wife soaking her pillow every night."

Charlie then adopted a thoughtful expression. "You know," he said, "I just happened to think that Lucy is a member of the Garden Club. Maybe that's why she never cries."

"As a matter of fact, Charlie, your mother-in-law helped found the Club back in 1914."

"You've really done some research on this, haven't you?"

"I sure have, and brother, how I wish I could get Lila into that damn club." When Charlie didn't rise to the bait, he added, "All it would take is one of the younger members to put up her name. It's just a formality."

"Someone like Lucy, you mean?"

"She could do it if she wanted to."

Now that it was all in the open, Charlie felt completely relaxed.

66

"In other words," he said, "this is a package deal you're offering me. You give me a job in your agency, and I get Lila into the Garden Club."

"Jesus, you're crude, Charlie. I'm offering you a job with no strings attached. As far as the Garden Club is concerned, if you can help me, I'll appreciate it."

"No dice," Charlie answered. He snubbed out his cigar.

"Suit yourself. You're passing up a good opportunity."

"Let's go join our wives," Charlie answered.

Woodchuck walked into the living room, his arm around Charlie's waist. "What are you two gals talking about?" he asked cheerily. "Us, I hope."

"Gardens," Lucy answered. "Lila wants to meet Mother, Charlie. She's just crazy to learn about what plants to grow up north."

Woodchuck winced.

"I hate to break up a wonderful evening," Charlie said, "but Woodchuck has a busy day tomorrow, and so do I."

A few minutes later they all walked out to the car.

"I really envy you this house," Lucy said, as she shook hands with Lila.

"And so do I," Charlie added. Then he turned toward Lila. "You better stick pretty close to this husband of yours," he said. "It looks to me like he can get you just about anything you want."

twelve

WHILE THEY WERE AT THE WALLINS IT HAD STARTED TO RAIN. LUCY'S CAR was showing its age. There was a tear in the canvas top, and water dripped onto the floor from a leak over the dashboard.

"Do you wish you had married someone like Lila?" Lucy asked when they turned into the avenue.

"Now that's a silly question."

"Do you?" she repeated.

He thought a moment. "No," he answered firmly, "I don't."

"Does that mean you're glad you married me?"

She slid across the seat and tucked her arm through his.

"Yes, it means I'm glad I married you."

"Why?"

"Must I give reasons?"

"I'm pinning you down."

"Well, of course you're not as pretty as Lila."

"She is absolutely gorgeous," Lucy admitted.

"And you were never elected Miss Cotton Bowl."

Lucy giggled.

"Or Miss Salad Bowl, or Miss Rose Bowl."

"I've never been elected anything," Lucy said mournfully, rubbing her cheek against his shoulder.

"You're wrong," he answered. "You were elected to the Garden Club."

"What are you talking about?"

"It's all just part of the discussion I had with Woodchuck tonight."

Lucy considered his answer a moment. "I thought probably you two were talking about jobs."

"We were."

"Did he offer you one?" she asked casually.

"Yes."

"A good job?"

"The answer to a returning service man's dream."

"Then you accepted?"

"No."

"Why not?"

He hesitated a moment. "Are you prepared for a shock?"

"I guess so."

"Woodchuck offered me a job in his agency, with a chance for a future partnership. There was just one hitch. I was supposed to have you put Lila up for membership in the Garden Club."

Lucy gasped. "But that's positively the most awful thing I've ever heard, Charlie. It just isn't done that way. We're more than just a group of women who like to garden. We're——"

"I know what you are," he interrupted. "You don't have to interpret yourself."

"Girls like Lila belong in Flower and Bower. It's more—I don't know how to explain it."

"You mean Flower and Bower somehow just misses." He was grinning.

"It isn't that at all. There are probably some very nice people in Flower and Bower. But they're the high-powered crowd. They feel they have to *do* things. We're sort of shabby and relaxed."

"Like well-rotted manure?"

"Well, yes," Lucy answered, delighted with his description. "That's exactly what we are."

When he parked the car in the Chalmers' garage and snapped off the lights, Lucy held onto his arm.

"Don't go in yet. I want to talk about something."

"About what?"

"About us. You. Me. Things."

"What about us, you, me, and things?"

"When do you think you will get a job?"

"A month, a year, ten years."

"I'm serious, Charlie."

"So am I."

"Look at me," she answered, turning his head around with her hands. "I think we're going to have another baby."

68

"Oh, my God," he said, letting his head fall back against the seat. "Oh, my God," he repeated.

"I'm sorry, Charlie." She was close to tears.

"Darling," he said quickly, "I don't mean it that way." He held her close. "I'm glad we're going to have another baby. I want lots of babies. But it's all just falling down on me like a net."

"But it's falling down on me too."

"I know. I know," he whispered. "And you want to get set somewhere. You want life to be organized."

"Yes," she sobbed, her voice catching. "I'm sorry, Charlie."

He took a deep breath and looked out into the darkness of the garage. "Don't cry, Lucy. Please don't cry."

"I'm sorry," she whimpered. "I'm all wound up."

"I'll get a job tomorrow."

"But where?"

"At The Hadley Company, if they still want me."

"You won't be sorry, Charlie." She hugged him fiercely. "You'll be happy out there. And if you're not, and want to leave after a while, I won't say a word."

"All right," he answered. "I'll go out tomorrow. Now let's not talk about it any more."

She kissed him, and they walked on into the house.

"I suppose before long I'll have to be helping you upstairs," he said when they were walking through the hallway. "I missed all that business the last time."

"Oh, poof," she answered, bouncing up the stairs like an eight-year-old. "I thrive when I'm pregnant. You'll see."

It was just after nine o'clock when Charlie drove into Hadley the next morning. The factory was the first thing he saw, ten acres of dirty brick buildings with patched tar-paper roofs. The factory had been built along both banks of the river, the two halves joined by a long brick span suspended out over the dam. It was all old and decrepit, and covered with a century of coal smoke and soot.

He stopped the car and gazed out the window. The valley reminded him of Italy. The river wound between steep hillsides, and small houses were dug back into the land, with orchards and vineyards and family gardens. Most of the town was clustered near the factory and up along the banks of the Company reservoir. Make the mountains a little higher, Charlie thought, and build the houses of stone, and he could be back in Italy. All that was missing was the smell of burning charcoal and the braying of donkeys.

He could see that it had once been a practical place to establish a factory. The dam had been laid across the river at the narrowest spot in the valley, flooding the land at least three miles to the north, forming a reservoir of power. A railroad spur ran into the town from the south, following the edge of an old, overgrown canal, now empty and dry. One glance, and the history of Hadley was obvious. As the factory had grown, so had the town. As it had declined, the town declined with it.

He drove down the main street toward the river. There was a row of stores, a drugstore, a cafeteria, and a hardware store facing a small rectangular green. At the end of the green there were a church and a parsonage, both in need of paint. There were a fire house and the town hall, both buildings stained red. There was also a library, a neat square of brick, with white trim and a flagpole. Someone loved the Hadley Library, Charlie decided. It was the only building in town in good repair.

A dozen cars were parked near the factory. The river was high; a cloud of mist was rising from below the spillway, blowing up against the brick span that hung over the dam. There was an open sewer drain along the brick wall of the span, oozing yellow liquid down into the river below. As he sat in the car Charlie could hear the sound of machine presses working in one of the factory buildings, a steady, rhythmic pounding that shook the earth.

He walked across the factory yard toward a small brick building marked "Office." Just outside the door the brown steps were worn hollow from a century of use. Inside he found an elderly woman sitting at a typewriter. She continued to type, not bothering to look up at him, her fingers moving slowly, as though she had never mastered the mysteries of a mechanical writing machine. The reception room was cold. The woman wore a heavy knitted sweater and long woolen stockings.

"Yes," she said, finally looking up at him.

"I would like to see Mr. Chalmers."

"Salesman?" she asked, returning to her typewriter.

"I'm Mr. Chalmers' son-in-law."

"Oh, I see." She made a pencil mark on a piece of paper and walked toward the rear of the office.

"Come on in, Charlie," Mr. Chalmers shouted a moment later, leaning through his office door. "Mrs. Fleck, this is my son-in-law, Charlie. Mrs. Fleck runs my office for me, Charlie. She's the boss around here."

Mrs. Fleck returned to her typewriter, smiling wanly, as though what Mr. Chalmers said was hardly a joke.

"She's making out the pay roll," Mr. Chalmers whispered significantly, as he closed his office door. "She hates to be disturbed. Did she try to throw you out of the office?"

"I told her I was your son-in-law."

Mr. Chalmers sat at his desk. "You'll have to forgive the heat situation around here. We have the hardest time getting anyone to keep the boilers operating. The whole factory was stone cold this morning." He was wearing his topcoat and a scarf.

Mr. Chalmers' office could have been moved intact to a museum. The floor was teakwood, and walls were paneled in oak, and every piece of furniture in the room was an antique—the cherry desk, two grandfather clocks, and a set of matched wooden chairs.

"The first Mr. Hadley made that," Mr. Chalmers said when he noticed

70

Charlie admiring one of the clocks. "He was a blacksmith, you know, and an inventor as well."

"And an artist too." Charlie said admiringly.

"Yes, he was a number of things," Mr. Chalmers answered. "One of those fortunate combinations. Jack-of-all-trades, and master of most of them too. He even made the original plates which printed all these old advertising flyers." Mr. Chalmers pointed to the walls of the office. "I had them framed. I thought they made wonderful decoration, and of course they have historical interest as well."

Charlie walked along the wall, examining the posters. They were the sort that a century before had been nailed on the sides of barns.

"For Want of a Hadley Nail the Horse was Lost," he read, looking at the picture of a magnificent work horse pulling a plow across the field. In smaller print was written, "The Hadley Company also makes the plow."

"That used to be our trade-mark years ago," Mr. Chalmers explained. "For Want of a Hadley Nail. That phrase was famous all over New England in the old days. We've let it drop, since we don't make nails these days. Here's one of my favorites," he added, pointing to the largest poster of all.

A Union soldier with rifle and bayonet was charging across a battlefield. Under him was written, "We helped tame the South with Hadley bayonets." Below was another picture of the same man guiding a plow across a Western prairie. "And now we've pounded our bayonets into plowshares, and The Hadley Plow is taming the West."

"Old Mr. Hadley was quite a man," Mr. Chalmers said. "He started out with a horse and buggy, traveling up through New England and upstate New York, selling his horseshoe nails. Little by little he branched out into more things. Knives, axes, shovels, plows. There's a collection of all the things the company ever made at the Hadley Library. You ought to look at it some time."

"I will," Charlie answered, sitting across from Mr. Chalmers at the desk.

"So, my boy, what brings you out this way?" Mr. Chalmers asked.

"I'd like a job," Charlie answered bluntly.

Mr. Chalmers took a deep breath, and sighed. "I see." He walked across his office to the window. "So you think you'd like to work for The Hadley Company?"

"Yes, sir."

It was the moment Lowell Chalmers had been dreading. How, he wondered, without baring his own soul, would he be able to make it clear to his son-in-law that this was no longer the place for a young man.

"Charlie," he started, turning about, "I think you're making a mistake." He paused. "I suppose that's a funny thing for me to say. Wait a moment. Before you answer, stand over here next to me and look out this window. What do you see?" he asked, when Charlie had joined him.

"Maybe I don't know what you mean, Mr. Chalmers."

"Do we look like a thriving factory out here? Be honest about it. You won't hurt my feelings."

"Not particularly."

"We aren't. We're suffering from a disease known as senility. No, that's not really it," he said, interrupting himself. "The main trouble out here has been me. I've never had the temperament to run a factory the way it should be run." He moved back to his desk. "You know, I've been thinking about you lately, Charlie. You're in almost the same position I was in, forty years ago. You've married a girl who knows exactly what she wants out of life. When I married Mrs. Chalmers she knew exactly what she wanted, too. I really didn't want to work out here. I thought I wanted to teach school. I like books, you know. I thought I wanted to spend my life among books. I really didn't want to work in a factory at all."

Charlie was both fascinated and embarrassed as he listened to Mr. Chalmers. In his home on Lawn Street his father-in-law seemed vague and distant, neither happy nor the opposite, but living in a world of his own, on a plateau above the passions of the world. Now suddenly he was completely human, and as he listened, Charlie started to feel sorry for him.

"When I came out here it was supposed to be temporary," Mr. Chalmers continued. "I'd try it out, I thought, just while I got my feet on the ground. That was forty-one years ago. And I'm still here. So if you are thinking of a temporary job out here, don't. Jobs have a way of becoming permanent. I don't know exactly how to explain it. Did you ever see a Marx Brothers movie," he asked suddenly, "where Chico is playing a piano, on and on, on and on, until someone asks him why he doesn't stop, and he says he can't stop because he passed the end of the piece and has to keep going until he gets to the beginning again? That's what happens with jobs. You get past the end, and you have to keep going."

Mrs. Fleck had stopped her typing, and the office was quiet.

"You should decide on one thing first, before you take any job. Decide what you are yourself, and then find a job to fit your own personality. It takes a basically simple personality to run a factory. You have to like money, and I never gave a damn about money. You have to want to be important, and I never gave a damn about that either. In a way you must have a desire to be a little king, and consider your factory your own personal kingdom." He smiled ruefully. "One thing you can't be is a philosopher. You have to love action whether it makes sense or not. Lucy has been putting the pressure on you, hasn't she?" he asked suddenly.

"A little."

"I suspect Mrs. Chalmers didn't tell you the facts about this company. We nearly sold out a few years ago, and if another opportunity comes up, and things continue to go badly with us here, we may sell out the next time. Has anyone ever discussed our family finances with you?"

"I never felt it was any of my business."

"You'll find it gets to be your business. Little by little you'll find that your whole life revolves around the legacy that the Hadleys left behind. This factory is just a small part of it. It's really become the tail of the dog. But if the tail ever starts to wag the dog, you'll find the family will cut it off." He snapped his fingers. "Just like that. Families around here are sentimental about houses and trees and old rose bushes, but they are not sentimental about money. If this factory ever threatens the trust fund that Mrs. Chalmers' father and grandfather and great-grandfather built up, The Hadley Company will be sold at once."

"I'd still like to work here," Charlie answered.

"You don't want to think about it a while longer?"

"No."

"Your mind's made up?"

"It wasn't when I stepped into your office, but it is now."

Mr. Chalmers looked surprised. "Then my little discourse had precisely the opposite effect from what I hoped."

"If you have a job here for me, I want it."

Mr. Chalmers stepped to his office door. "Have Ralph Henry step into my office, Mrs. Fleck." He turned back to Charlie. "Ralph Henry is the plant foreman," he said. "I'll turn you over to him."

thirteen

"RALPH," MR. CHALMERS SAID WHEN THE FOREMAN ENTERED THE OFFICE, "this is my son-in-law, Charlie Webb. My daughter Lucy's husband. He wants to go to work for us out here."

Ralph Henry merely nodded, his eyes flicking over to Charlie, then back to Mr. Chalmers again. He was in his sixties, a barrel-chested man, with pale bluish-white skin. His clothing was soaked with oil and grease. His left hand had once been crushed. The two middle fingers were missing, and there was scar tissue from his wrist to the tips of the three fingers that remained. He was completely bald. The skin over his skull was reddish brown, as though it had once been badly burned, and his eyes had a curious lack of luster, like bits of jello that had gone stale. He looked tough, ugly, and mean.

"Where do you want him?" he asked Mr. Chalmers, his voice flat and impersonal, as though Charlie were a new machine.

"I leave it completely up to you, Ralph," Mr. Chalmers answered. "You know I don't interfere with the running of the shop."

"When's he starting?"

"I forgot to ask you that, Charlie, didn't I? Would you like a few more days to get ready?"

"I'm ready now," Charlie answered.

"He's ready now," Mr. Chalmers repeated, as though Charlie spoke a language the foreman couldn't understand.

73

"He isn't dressed for it," Ralph Henry answered, looking scornfully at Charlie's white shirt and necktie.

"Perhaps one of the boys in the shop can lend him some work clothes." Mr. Henry turned on his heel and started toward the office door.

"You're meant to follow him," Mr. Chalmers whispered, patting Charlie on the shoulder. "Good luck. I'll see you tonight at dinner."

"College boy?" Ralph Henry asked scornfully, as Charlie followed him across the factory yard toward the main shop.

"I'm afraid I am," Charlie answered.

"I don't have too much use for college boys. I ain't never seen one yet that's got the guts to go with the sheepskin."

Charlie smiled. He knew Ralph Henry's type. The regular army was filled with them, sergeants long on experience but short on education, whose favorite sport was hazing a young lieutenant just out of officers' school. Even the expression was the same, the mixture of pity and scorn, and the curl to the lip as though the air smelled faintly bad. The foreman's uniform might be different, but his attitude was the same.

"We've had one or two other college boys out here. The minute they saw a little dirt and found they had to work, they headed into the city for a job with an insurance company. I expect you'll do the same thing."

Charlie said nothing. The foreman was just testing him, hoping he'd blow up and make a fool of himself. At least he had learned something in the army that was useful.

"Now, Mister Webb," Ralph Henry said, "being a college boy, you probably have some particular job in mind. Shall I have some of my boys build you a special office, with your name on the door?" He stopped walking and stood looking at Charlie, his hands on his hips. "You just tell me what you want, and I'll see if I can help you."

"I'm just out here to learn the business," Charlie answered.

"You mean you think there's something about this place that you don't already know?"

"You've got your mind all made up on me, haven't you?" Charlie said, still smiling.

The foreman continued staring at him. "I give you two months out here. No more. You don't look tough enough to me."

"Why don't we make a bet on that? I'll bet you one day's pay." When Mr. Henry didn't answer, he said, "Well, is it a bet?"

"It's a bet," he answered. "I'll probably take it out of your severance pay." He turned and walked away. "Come on. I got just the job for you. It's just the right place for you to learn the business."

"Shoveling coal!" Lucy shouted, when late that afternoon Charlie dragged himself up the stairs to their room. "I don't believe it."

"I didn't get these driving the car." He showed her his blistered hands.

"Did my father put you to work shoveling coal?" she asked angrily.

"Your father had nothing to do with it. Ralph Henry, the foreman, runs the factory, and he was the one who gave me the job. Now, if you'll excuse me, I think I'll take a bath."

"I just won't have you shoveling coal," Lucy announced when he came out of the shower. "I simply will not have it."

"Take your complaint to Ralph Henry," he answered grimly.

"I'm going right this instant to my father. It's utterly ridiculous."

Charlie took her by the shoulders and sat her firmly on the bed.

"From this moment on," he said, his face inches from hers, "you will let me run my own affairs. Is that clear?"

"Charlie," she gasped.

"I mean it. I don't want you meddling in my job."

"But I'm only trying to help you."

"I don't want that kind of help. If you really want to help, get something for my hands, and then let me take care of things out at The Hadley Company my own way."

"But it isn't fair what they're doing to you. I feel simply awful about it."

"You wanted me to work at The Hadley Company, and I'm working there. Now leave me alone. I've been through things like this before, and I know what I'm doing. Is that clear?"

She stared at him for a moment. Then she said, "I'll get you something for your hands."

"I'm terribly pleased," Mrs. Chalmers trilled happily, taking Charlie's hand in hers as he came down the stairs for dinner. She looked as though she might kiss him, and he drew back a few inches. "Terribly, terribly pleased," she repeated in lieu of the kiss. "I'm glad you're working for our Company, Charlie."

"So am I, Mrs. Chalmers."

"We're all going to celebrate with a Martini. Mr. Chalmers is out mixing it now." She led him by the hand into the living room.

"To another generation at The Hadley Company," Mrs. Chalmers said a few minutes later, raising her Martini high in the air.

"I second that," Mr. Chalmers replied with less enthusiasm.

Lucy took Charlie's arm affectionately and said, "Hurrah."

"And now that we're all together," Mrs. Chalmers continued, "the time has come for me to bring up what I consider an extremely important subject. It seems to me that Charlie should start calling us something beside Mr. and Mrs. Chalmers. Don't you agree, Lowell?"

Lowell Chalmers looked indecisive and said nothing.

"What did you call my mother, Lowell?"

"I don't recall, my dear."

"Of course you do. Didn't you call her Mother H?"

"Possibly I did," he replied, looking uneasy, as though the memory brought him no joy.

"How would that be, Charlie?"

"Mother H?" Charlie asked blankly.

"Not Mother H, you silly boy. Mother C. C for Chalmers. Your Charlie does have a wicked sense of humor, Lucy. How would that be, Charlie?"

"If you say so," he answered glumly.

"Let me hear how it sounds."

"Mother C," he muttered, feeling ill.

"And now Charlie should call you something beside Mr. Chalmers, Lowell. What do you suggest?"

"I don't feel strongly one way or the other, Lydia."

"He might, of course, call you Father C."

"What am I?" he asked scornfully. "A priest?"

"That's true. That wouldn't be quite right, would it? How about Dad?"

"Great Caesar's ghost. Not at the plant, please."

"Now there's a thought." She seized on his words. "What do the men call you at the plant?"

"I hardly know, my dear."

"But you must know. You've been out there nearly forty years."

"Over forty years," he corrected.

"What do they call Mr. Chalmers at the plant?" she asked, turning to Charlie.

"I've only been out there one day," he answered evasively.

"Come on," she insisted. "What do they call Mr. Chalmers?"

"L.C.," he answered glibly. As far as he knew everyone at the plant called Mr. Chalmers Mr. Chalmers.

"L.C.," Mrs. Chalmers repeated, mouthing the words, testing them for sound. "L.C. I think that would be rather cute."

"Extremely cute," Lowell Chalmers answered uncomfortably.

"Then it's all set. Mother C and L.C. Are you satisfied, Lucy?"

She nodded. "I was going to talk to Charlie about it, anyway."

Lowell Chalmers sighed. "Must we, Lydia?"

"Must we what, Lowell?"

"Must we make life so complicated?"

"Complicated?" she echoed. "But, you silly boy, that's exactly what I'm not doing. I'm doing my best to simplify life." She took Charlie's arm and started walking toward the dining room, singing the chorus from the "Wedding March." "Ta tum ta tum, Ta tum ta tum." Then she giggled and said, "I haven't felt so gay in years."

The next morning at breakfast, as Lydia Chalmers pinned the daily carnation on her husband's lapel, she smiled at Charlie across the table.

"And what's your favorite color?" she asked. "I've never thought to ask you."

"Red, Mrs. Chalmers," he answered.

"No. No. No," she said, pointing her finger at him. "Not Mrs. Chalmers. Remember."

"Red, Mother C," he mumbled, a mouthful of soft-boiled egg going flat in his mouth.

76

"That's much better. Red. Let me see. Here we are." She pulled a red carnation out of the centerpiece and pinned it on his overalls. "Now hurry along, you two boys, or you'll be late for work."

"I usually throw mine out just about here," Mr. Chalmers said five minutes later when they were driving past Bishop's Corner.

Charlie looked blank.

"These damn flowers," he muttered angrily. "I've never worn one out to the factory yet." He lowered the car window and snapped the flower out into the wind. Charlie did the same.

They drove for two miles in silence.

"How would you like to do me a favor?" Mr. Chalmers asked.

"Of course."

"Please don't call me L.C."

"I wasn't planning to."

"Mrs. Chalmers means well on these things, but there's a strain of the coy in her, and when a woman is coy you can't cure it."

They drove another mile without speaking.

"I wish I didn't have to call Mrs. Chalmers Mother C," Charlie said finally.

Mr. Chalmers sighed sympathetically but said nothing.

"It makes me squirm," Charlie persisted.

"I know. I called old Mrs. Hadley Mother H right up to the bitter end."

"You think I'd better do it then?"

Mr. Chalmers looked thoughtful. "I suggest you ease off gradually. She might not notice it that way."

"She called me on it this morning."

"I know. I know. I heard her. I wish I could help you, but I can't."

They had reached the ridge of low mountains west of the city when Mr. Chalmers spoke again.

"Do you know what is, for me, the best time of the day?"

Charlie waited.

"It's these mornings when I drive out alone to the factory."

"I'm about to get a car of my own, if that's what you mean."

Mr. Chalmers smiled.

"It doesn't look as though I had to be diplomatic with you, does it?"

Charlie shook his head. "No, sir. You don't have to be diplomatic with me."

"You must think I'm a pretty stuffy individual. I guess I am." Mr. Chalmers slowed his car and looked off to the west and the north, at the miles of blue-green hills and mountains. "I love it," he sighed. "It's peaceful, and it's always the same, day after day, year after year."

They said nothing more then until they had reached the factory.

"I understand Ralph Henry has you shoveling coal and doing general clean-up work."

"That's right."

"When I first started, I shoveled coal and picked up the scrap too. I did it for almost eighteen months. Did you know that?"

"Mr. Henry said it was a company tradition."

"What do you think of Ralph Henry?" Mr. Chalmers asked as he parked his car by the dam.

"I've met the type before."

It was not the answer Mr. Chalmers expected. He glanced at Charlie in surprise.

"I thought he might rattle you. He has that effect on me."

"He doesn't bother me. The army was filled with sergeants just like him. They scared me when I first got out of officers' school. Then one day I realized they were even more afraid of me."

"Ralph Henry scared of you!" Mr Chalmers laughed.

"If he isn't now, he will be soon."

"I've been out here forty-one years, and he still isn't afraid of me."

"We'll see," Charlie answered, stepping out of the car and starting across the yard toward the boiler room.

fourteen

THE FOLLOWING SUNDAY, AS THEY WERE ALL FINISHING THEIR DINNER, MRS. Chalmers said casually, "Lucy and I learned something yesterday which should interest you, Charlie."

"Oh," he answered. "What was that, Mother C?" It was only the fifth time he had addressed her as Mother C. On all other occasions he had been able to avoid calling her by any name whatsoever.

"One of our old and very dear friends is Joe Pritchard. You may have heard of him?"

"Haven't I seen his name on signs all over the city?"

Mrs. Chalmers nodded. "Mr. Pritchard has a real estate agency. Just about the best in the city, wouldn't you say, Lowell?"

"Joe does very well for himself," Mr. Chalmers admitted, leaving the table and disappearing toward his study.

"Anyway," Mrs. Chalmers continued when Mr. Chalmers was gone, "almost a month ago I just happened to meet Mr. Pritchard downtown, and I mentioned to him that I might just know of a young married couple who just might one day be looking for a house." She giggled.

"Mr. Pritchard called us yesterday," Lucy said, picking up the thread where her mother had dropped it. "He's found us an absolutely darling house on Highcliffe Road."

"You didn't buy it, I hope."

"Of course we didn't buy it, Charlie," Mrs. Chalmers answered. "That would be up to you. But we did go see it, Lucy and I. And we think it's perfect."

78

"I'm sure it is," Charlie answered. "But I've already found something else. I've been doing a little research on it before I broke the news to Lucy."

"Oh-ho," Mrs. Chalmers said. "Your Charlie has been keeping secrets from us, Lucy."

"Where is it?" Lucy asked.

"In Hadley."

The two women were silent.

"Hadley?" Lucy repeated.

"Did you say Hadley?" Mrs. Chalmers echoed.

He nodded. "It's just south of the factory along the old turnpike. I think it used to be an inn once. It's not in the best of condition, but we can fix it up."

"Dear me," Mrs. Chalmers gasped. "I think I know that awful old place. You aren't serious about this, Charlie?"

"I've never been more serious about anything in my life."

"But my dear Charlie, have you considered the fact that Hadley is exactly eighteen miles from nowhere? That it is utterly isolated from good schools and from all Lucy's friends."

"The schools are all right out there, and I think Lucy will see just as much of her good friends when she's eighteen miles away as she will with them across the street. But that's not what I was thinking about, anyway."

"I gather it wasn't," Mrs. Chalmers answered.

"Why Hadley?" Lucy asked in an incredulous voice.

Charlie leaned forward over the table. "I've worked at the factory just about a week, and I've decided that I like it out there. Frankly, I wasn't sure I would, but I do."

Mrs. Chalmers winked at Lucy. "Of course, we just knew you would. This hardly comes as a surprise to us."

"And because I like working for The Hadley Company, I've decided I want to live in Hadley. I think some member of this family ought to live in Hadley."

"So that's it," Mrs. Chalmers answered, obviously relieved. "Your Charlie is a romanticist, Lucy. How charming!"

"It isn't romanticism," Charlie answered. "I feel I'm being quite practical. I want to identify myself with the town where I work. Do you remember the discussion you had with me two weeks ago, Mrs. Chalmers? You said this family had never believed in absentee ownership. Well, I don't believe in it, either. I want to work at The Hadley Company, and I feel quite strongly that Lucy and I should be residents of the town. No one in this family has lived out there in over fifty years."

"My dear boy," Mrs. Chalmers replied patiently, "I was born out there."

"I know you were. You left to move in here when you were eleven years old. That still makes it over fifty years ago."

Mrs. Chalmers' laugh was brittle.

"What was this research you did, Charlie? On my age?"

"I read a book at the Hadley Library, on the Hadley family. Mr. Chalmers wrote it."

"I see," she said stiffly. "But what we're trying to discuss here is a home for Lucy's growing family."

"Hadley will be a fine place to bring up children."

"Will be?" Lucy shouted. "Do you mean it's all set and I haven't even seen the place you're talking about?"

Mrs. Chalmers snapped her fingers. "Why don't we all run out this afternoon?" She walked quickly out into the hallway. "Lowell," she called, "come along. We're all going out to Hadley."

"Good Lord, what for?" he shouted from his study. "Don't Charlie and I see enough of that place during the week?"

"Charlie apparently doesn't think so," Mrs. Chalmers announced, winking again at Lucy. "He even thinks he wants to live out there."

It was a gray, raw, November day, and being Sunday, Joseph's day off, Mrs. Chalmers drove the Packard herself. It took her just under an hour to negotiate the eighteen miles to Hadley.

Those charged with traffic safety tended to look at the problem from the wrong angle, Charlie thought grimly as he sat in the back seat watching Mrs. Chalmers drive. Speed wasn't necessarily the only crime on the highways. The opposite of speed could be just as murderous. Mrs. Chalmers had never had an accident in her entire driving career, and because of this she assumed she was a good driver. But how many accidents has she caused in her lifetime? he wondered. One hundred? Two hundred? A thousand?

She had one standard signal, which covered everything from right or left turns to grinding, sudden stops—a limp arm hanging out the window, with a slight flutter of the fingers. When someone passed her she'd say, "Look at that fool go." When the traffic piled up behind her, a long line of frustrated, horn-blowing, wildly enraged motorists, she'd say, "Stupid fools. Why don't they go by?"

Occasionally a driver did manage to get by, hurling obscenities out an open window as he passed. If young Hot Rods had become an American menace, it was time the authorities recognized an even worse problem, the elderly Cold Rods like Mrs. Chalmers.

"And this is your dream house, Charlie?" Mrs. Chalmers said when she stopped the Packard at the side of the road.

"It's in bad shape," he admitted. "It will take some money and some work, but when it's fixed up it will be wonderful."

The inn was boarded up. It was set off the road on a small knoll, and the barn and open sheds that had once housed the carriages and the horses had burned, leaving only the foundations. Every window was broken, and where the main chimney showed above the roof, the bricks were broken and crumbling. Behind the inn, a small stream trickled through an open field and flowed on down to the river two hundred yards away.

"It has possibilities, I think," Mr. Chalmers said kindly. "I've often admired that little brook over there. It could be dammed into a pool and stocked for fishing."

"The whole place is far worse than I remembered," Mrs. Chalmers said coldly.

"What do you think?" Charlie asked Lucy.

"You can't be serious about this, Charlie."

"I thought I was. Let's get out and look around. Wouldn't you even like to see the inside?"

"Wasn't there a murder here once, Lowell?" Mrs. Chalmers asked, not stirring from her seat.

"I really don't know, my dear."

"Yes, I'm sure of it. The whole place had an extremely bad reputation at one time. I remember my mother and father whispering things about it."

"But we couldn't possibly have this place ready to live in for over a year," Lucy exclaimed.

"I realize that," Charlie answered. "In the meantime we could rent a place back in the town."

No one spoke for a moment.

"I do see something I like," Mrs. Chalmers finally said. "That old stone drinking trough over there. I've always wanted one like that for our terrace, Lowell."

"I spotted that too, Lydia. I'm sure it could be moved."

"Could you get some of the men at the factory to load it on a truck?"

"You'd have to buy it first," Charlie interrupted.

"Naturally," Mrs. Chalmers answered. "Who would we have to see about it, Lowell?"

"Me," Charlie answered. "I've agreed to buy the place by paying up the back taxes. I just about own it right now, including ten acres of land."

"Dear God!" Lucy gasped. Then she said, "Oh, Charlie! We just can't!"

"You mean you wouldn't be happy here?"

"You know I'd be happy anywhere with you, but not here. It's too awful!"

"I'm sorry. I thought you might like it. I thought in five or ten years we might have a wonderful place out here."

"Did you really buy it?"

"I said I would. It amounts to the same thing."

"You leave Charlie alone," Mr. Chalmers said suddenly. "Maybe he's got himself a good investment. Perhaps they'll want to widen the road someday." Then he added, "Tell us what you agreed to pay for it, Charlie. I'm sure Mrs. Chalmers and I would be willing to pay that much for the trough."

"No you don't," Lucy shouted, laughing. "Charlie and I own the trough. We might decide to put it on *our* terrace if we buy the house on Highcliffe Road. Could we stop by there, Mother, when we get back in the city?"

"Of course we can, darling. Of course we can." She started the Packard and turned it around in the middle of the road.

Highcliffe Road was near the golf course, one of three streets in a new development known as Overton Heights. The tract had originally been a swamp, and the builder, faced with standing water six months of the year and realizing he would have to spend a fortune for fill, had merely given the streets lofty, dry-sounding names, and had then equipped the cellar of each house with a sump pump.

"Aren't you going to get out?" Lucy asked, when Charlie sat watching Mr. and Mrs. Chalmers heading up the sidewalk toward the front door.

"I know what's inside. Seven rooms, copper plumbing, a modern kitchen, light green walls, and a den."

"Don't be angry with me," Lucy said, turning his face toward hers. "It's just what I want. It really is."

"It's exactly like everyone else."

"But darling, what's so terrible about that? And who is this 'everyone else?' Danny and Louise Girard are just down the street. And the Robinsons are over there. You say 'everyone else' as though they're somebody awful, but they're all our friends."

"I'd like to ask you something," he said. "What is our eventual plan about a home?"

"I haven't really thought that far ahead."

"But this is only the first move, isn't it? Won't we eventually turn this place in for something a little bigger and a little better, as though it were a car?"

"It isn't like that at all."

"But it is like that. I hate the thought of spending a few years here and then moving on somewhere else. I'd like to buy a home, not a house."

"But I'll make it a home. You'll see. You don't know what I can do with a place like this."

"I don't like it," he answered sullenly. "If you want it, I'll live here. But I don't like it."

"Just come look at it." She hesitated, looking at him imploringly. "Please, Charlie."

"You'll be happy here, Lucy?"

"I will, darling. I promise you."

She pulled him out onto the sidewalk and ran ahead of him toward the front door.

fifteen

FOR THE FIRST TIME IN A NUMBER OF YEARS, THE CHALMERS WERE ABLE TO gather together their entire family for Christmas. Polly, with a new haircut, arrived by train from New York late Christmas Eve. Anne and her husband Clyde, after driving most of the night from Philadelphia, arrived at the house at eight o'clock Christmas morning. At ten, when the first present was torn open, the gathering included Mr. and Mrs. Chalmers, their three daughters, their two sons-in-law, and their grandchild Lydia.

Little Lydia's pile of presents was immense. The Chalmers had never felt that an orgy of spending on one day each year represented the true Christmas spirit. Also, being a family that had everything, the gifts they presented to each other were everyday necessities rather than once-in-a-lifetime luxuries. For instance, Charlie received six cakes of soap, a pair of socks, and a carton of cigarettes. From Lucy, according to agreement, he received nothing. With a new house to equip, she felt it more sensible to spend their money on something they both needed, such as an automatic washing machine or a new laundry reel for the back yard. A grandchild, however, was a new experience for all the Chalmers, and for her it seemed permissible to relax the usual rules of modest Christmas giving.

From Mr. Chalmers she received one share of Hadley Company stock, worth two hundred and forty-five dollars at the closing of the local market the previous Friday. Mr. Chalmers merely mentioned to Lucy and Charlie that the share had been registered in Lydia's name, and that he would keep it in his safe deposit vault until they had rented one of their own. He also took the opportunity to suggest to Charlie that it was time he too rented a vault, not only for Lydia's single share of stock but also for Lucy's four hundred shares, which he had been keeping for her ever since it was left to her by her Grandfather Hadley.

It was the first time Charlie had known how much Hadley stock Lucy owned. Some quick mental figuring as he was talking with Mr. Chalmers made clear that, assuming Grandfather Hadley had left equal shares to Lucy, Polly, and Anne, the three Chalmers girls controlled nearly ten per cent of the company. The first chance he got, he decided, he'd look over the holdings of the other stockholders to find out how control of the company was divided.

Mrs. Chalmers gave Lydia two dozen spoons, antique heirlooms which, as she explained to Lucy, should not be used. In addition she gave Lucy a check for one hundred dollars, which was to be used as Lucy saw fit, as long as it wasn't for groceries. She didn't mind being remembered for a clothes reel, she said, or a scatter rug in the upstairs hall, or even a second telephone in the bedroom, but she deplored the habit of the young who tended to spend their Christmas money paying last month's food bills.

Polly gave Lydia two new dresses, and Anne and Clyde presented her with a Bible, a beautiful thing with a soft leather binding and thin pages that were nearly transparent. There were also scores of other presents for Lydia from as many relatives, Chase and Hadley, including six antique wooden chairs which Charlie estimated would need at least fifty dollars' worth of repair before they were usable.

Lucy, with her usual efficiency, allowed her daughter a single look at each present, and then gathered them all into a pile near the piano, along with the cards, to make her post-Christmas task of thank-you notes an easier one. Christmas in the Chalmers family, Charlie decided, was hardly a day when members of the family gave presents to those they loved, but more of a partial estate settlement. Many things changed hands, but little cash was involved.

Aunt Ruth sent Lydia a new dress from Florida. She had also sent the Chalmers a basket of oranges.

Just before dinner Lydia collapsed in exhausted tears. Lucy scooped her off the floor and started toward the hall and the crib upstairs.

"Let me take her up," Charlie said, intercepting her.

"I'd better do it," Lucy answered. "I'm afraid she needs changing."

"I'd really like to put her to bed," Charlie insisted.

"She'll just scream."

"I can stand it."

"You don't know what you're getting into."

"Let me find out."

He took Lydia out of Lucy's arms and climbed up the stairs, carrying his daughter delicately, as though she were fragile and might break. Polly was standing in the upstairs hallway, watching him, smiling with amused scorn.

"Behold the domesticated male."

Polly seemed determined to make her two sisters look like bumpkins. She was wearing a green cocktail dress, her arms and shoulders bare, a long string of pearls looped twice around her neck.

"Open the door for me," he said. "I don't want to drop her."

"Do I smell something faintly bad, or is that my imagination?" Polly asked, following him into the nursery.

"Stand well back," Charlie said, as he started to strip his daughter. "We wouldn't want to soil Aunt Polly's lovely new dress, would we, Lydia?"

"I want to make a confession," Polly said as she watched Charlie fumble with pins and diapers. "I've never been in on this operation before."

"That makes two of us. Oh, God," he muttered, when the extent of Lydia's problems became dramatically evident. "Perhaps we had better call Lucy."

"Oh, hell," Polly answered, pushing him aside. "We ought to be able to figure it out just by using a little common sense."

"And raw courage," Charlie added, grinning. He walked toward the bathroom. "Lucy sometimes dunks her in the wash basin. I'll draw some hot water."

"How do you know if it's too hot?" Polly asked a moment later, coming up behind him, holding the naked Lydia carefully away from her dress.

"God only knows. Dip her in. If she howls we'll add more cold."

Lydia had stopped crying. Six months old and no longer merely an animated lump, she was staring at her Aunt Polly with fascinated wonder.

"You know," Polly said thoughtfully, sloshing water on Lydia's pink body, "she looks like you, Charlie. She really does. Help me hold her. She's as slippery as an eel."

"Do you think we could stick her back in the crib without diapers?"

Polly shook her head. "That's one thing I do know. You've got to have diapers and rubber pants." She patted Lydia dry with a towel, becoming more and more efficient as she gained confidence.

84

"You did it," Charlie said two minutes later, when Lydia was lying in her crib, dry, clean, and again clothed in diapers. "I'd almost swear you must have five or six of your own."

"She's rather cute," Polly said thoughtfully, staring down into the crib.

"I think so too," Charlie answered, turning away, hiding a sudden tear that he didn't want Polly to see. "Did you ruin your dress?"

"It will dry."

Polly walked out into the hall and went on down the stairs.

Christmas dinner was over at three. They all went into the living room, where Mr. Chalmers had built a fire, and sat talking for a while until Mrs. Chalmers suddenly announced she wished her daughters to play some music.

"Oh, no, Mother," Polly shouted. "Let's not ruin everything."

"Oh, yes," Mrs. Chalmers answered firmly. "Run upstairs and get your other cello, Polly, and bring down Lucy's violin."

She walked to the piano, raised the top, and set a metronome next to the music stand.

The only thing the three Chalmers girls possessed in common, Charlie decided, as he listened to them play for the next half-hour, was a lack of talent. All of them played woodenly, without spirit, Lucy looking embarrassed, as though she knew it was hopeless, Polly bored, as though she didn't care, and Anne with grim determination, as though she still hadn't given up trying.

It was the first time he had seen anything more than a picture of Anne. She was thirty-three and already quite gray. A short, plump girl, she had a nervous habit of blinking, as though there constantly were something in her eyes. There were deep lines between her eyebrows, put there by a constant frown. She was wearing a brown woolen dress and low-heeled shoes.

After a while Charlie slipped away and walked to the kitchen. The turkey had been dry, and he wanted a glass of water. He lingered in the pantry, listening to the music coming down the long hallway.

He must be growing up, he thought. For the first time since he'd come home from the army, he felt contented. He was glad he was married, he was glad he had a daughter, and he was glad he had a house of his own. Earlier, just the thought of all this had merely depressed him. Even Lydia, his own daughter, had seemed like part of a female conspiracy to force him into a life he didn't want.

He had thought of it as he and Polly had put Lydia in her crib. Lydia was his. He had a daughter. He would soon have another. Perhaps a son. Someday there would be a tree in his living room, and the family Christmas would be at his house. It would be his turkey that the family ate, and his children who came back with their wives and their husbands. Then it would be his grandchildren who gave Christmas its real meaning.

The sight of Anne had sobered him. She was proof that if you tried to make life complicated, you suffered for it. Christmas must be no day of rejoicing for her, he thought, but rather the loneliest day of the year. What good was a career, or success, or being interesting, or different, if on Christmas morning there was no child under the tree? Christmas was a day of individual reckoning. No matter what you were all the rest of the year, with no child at Christmas you were a pauper.

The pantry door opened, and Anne's husband Clyde came into the kitchen. He grinned sheepishly when he saw Charlie.

"I just slipped out for a drink of water."

"It's the turkey," Charlie answered.

Clyde filled a glass at the sink; then he wandered across the kitchen and stood near a window, melting holes in the frost on a windowpane.

He looked younger than Anne, a tall, thin, boyish individual, with narrow shoulders and a scrawny neck. He wore his hair long. The back of it curled out over his clerical collar, and on the sides it covered the tops of his ears. His dark blue suit was shiny and unpressed, and there were knots in his shoelaces. If he hadn't been a member of the clergy, his appearance would have shouted but one thing. Failure.

"Do you like working in Philadelphia?" Charlie asked.

"That's a question I never ask myself," Clyde answered. "My work is there, therefore I must live there." He seemed stiff and on the defensive.

"I hear you and Anne do wonderful work."

"I wonder who you heard that from?" Clyde asked, still making holes in the frost. "Not someone in the Chalmers family, I'm sure."

His animosity was obvious. How did one talk to a minister? Charlie wondered. The usual question, "How's business?" would not only be meaningless but also blasphemous. As far as he could see, he and Clyde had just one thing in common. They had both married into the Chalmers family. In order to carry on a conversation, that wasn't enough.

"What actually do you and Anne do down there?" Charlie asked.

"I knew that would be your next question. What is your answer when people ask you what you do?"

"I tell them I work for The Hadley Company."

"And that satisfies them?"

"It seems to."

"You're fortunate. I don't have such a convenient answer."

The hell with him, Charlie thought. He was Anne's project. Not his. Anne was the member of the family who liked to adopt strays. Not him. He must be a terrible minister. Clyde seemed filled with bitterness, not love and charity.

"It's cold out," Charlie said.

"It seems to be."

"When are you driving back?"

"Anne decides things like that."

Anne probably did all the driving too, Charlie thought. Clyde Harbert made him uneasy.

"Oh-ho," Mr. Chalmers shouted, pushing through the pantry door. "I thought I'd find you two deserters out here." Mr. Chalmers was the picture

86

of Christmas good will. His skin was bright pink, and he glowed with contentment. "Let's all have a drink," he said, heading for the icebox.

"Is the noise over in there?" Charlie asked, thankful he was no longer alone with Clyde.

"That noise, as you call it," Mr. Chalmers laughed, "cost me just over four thousand dollars. You'll find out someday when you start getting the bills from the music school."

"Nothing for me, thank you," Clyde said as Mr. Chalmers dropped ice into three glasses.

"Nonsense. Let's all have a drink. It will do us good."

"Anne and I don't drink," Clyde persisted.

"But Anne isn't here." Mr. Chalmers handed Clyde a glass.

Clyde said nothing and looked grim. It was growing dark outside. The heat had come on in the kitchen, the pipes were creaking.

"It's nice to have a family around you at Christmas," Mr. Chalmers said, beaming contentedly into his whisky glass. "Even if they do insist on playing that terrible music." He grinned. "That's what life is. Family and children. Nothing else matters. Don't you agree?" he asked, turning to Clyde. "You're the philosopher in the family."

Clyde poked at the ice in his glass and didn't reply. He hadn't tasted the drink.

Mr. Chalmers leaned forward over the kitchen table and waited until Clyde looked at him.

"Clyde," he began, "Mrs. Chalmers has asked me to bring up something about you and Anne that is worrying us both a great deal." He paused and looked embarrassed.

"I guess I'd better go on back into the living room," Charlie said uneasily.

"Sit down. Sit down," Mr. Chalmers insisted. "What I have to say to Clyde isn't private. We're all one family here. It's about Anne. Both Mrs. Chalmers and I think she looks worn out and exhausted."

"Anne works hard," Clyde answered stiffly.

"That has always been your answer when we bring up this subject. We wonder if it isn't the type of work that she's doing which tires her, rather than the amount of work. Lucy works hard, but she seems to thrive on it. Right, Charlie?"

"Lucy is pretty tough."

"Now we don't deny that you and Anne are doing a fine thing down there in the slums, Clyde. But you've both been at it now for almost eight years. Isn't it time you got out among some of your own people? Isn't it time you passed this mission of yours, or whatever you call it, over to someone younger? I'm speaking as a father. I'm worried about my daughter Anne. If you won't consider her, Mrs. Chalmers and I have to."

"Anne does what she wants to do," Clyde answered coldly.

"But isn't it time you persuaded her that she needs a change?" Mr. Chalmers said, setting his jaw. "Why on earth don't you get yourself a small church somewhere? Get out among some normal people for a change. You and Anne are beginning to look as though you were born in the slums. Enough is enough. You've done your part. You've lived with those people for eight years. Isn't it time you made a break?"

"Why don't you discuss this with Anne?" Clyde asked. He was sitting on the edge of his chair, his face pale.

"I am discussing it with you," Mr. Chalmers answered evenly. "And I would like your answer."

Clyde pushed himself up from the table and stood glaring at Mr. Chalmers for a moment, his fist doubled up, as though he wanted to smash it against his father-in-law's mouth. Then he turned and walked out of the kitchen, slamming the pantry door back against the glass cabinets, rattling the chinaware.

Mr. Chalmers stared at Charlie in astonishment.

"Did I say something that warranted that burst of temperament?"

"Clyde's a little on edge about something."

Mr. Chalmers added more whisky to his glass. "Dammit, I've never liked that boy," he muttered. "Excuse me for saying so, but it's the truth. I wish to high heaven Anne had never gotten involved with him. Anne is sweet, good, and kind, and I think she felt sorry for him. That's always been her only trouble. She feels sorry for people."

"Wasn't it Anne's idea to start this project in the slums?" Charlie asked quietly.

"Good Lord, what difference does it make whose idea it was? It's a terrible idea, no matter who thought of it."

"What do they do?"

"That's just it. No one knows. I'm not sure they do anything. They just bought this old building, and all kinds of riffraff hang around it accepting handouts. Clyde seems to have this idea that to be a good minister he not only must teach what Christ taught, but that he must also live like Christ lived."

"I can see how a minister might believe that," Charlie answered.

"My dear boy, Christ wasn't married. And if he were, I'm quite certain that his wife would have looked just as haggard as Anne does."

"Why *don't* you discuss this with Anne, as Clyde suggested?"

Mr. Chalmers looked annoyed. "You don't know Anne. She's a hard girl to discuss anything with." He sighed wearily. "Why can't things go smoothly? Why do my children have to get themselves in messes like this?"

Mrs. Chalmers burst into the kitchen.

"Anne and Clyde are leaving," she announced angrily. "What were you and Clyde fighting about?"

"Me fighting with Clyde? That's utterly ridiculous, Lydia."

"Clyde stormed back into the living room and whispered something to Anne. They're on their way out to their car."

"Why can't that boy settle down?" Mr. Chalmers asked wearily, following his wife out of the kitchen. "I was hoping they'd stay on here over New Year's."

88

Charlie was sipping a fresh drink when Polly lazed into the kitchen.

"What's this, a solitary drunk?" she asked. "Is my horrid little family too much for you?"

"Join me," he answered, pushing the bottle toward her.

"How about this one?" she asked, pointing at Clyde's untouched glass. She sniffed it, and added more whisky.

"Polly," Charlie said. "I was just wondering why you all bothered to come back here."

"A good question. A damn good question. Ask me again when you're driving me down to the station."

"Am I driving you to the station?"

"Will you?"

"With pleasure."

She glanced at him over the top of her glass. "What did go on between Clyde and my father?"

"Your father was suggesting to Clyde that he stop acting like Jesus Christ and start earning a living."

"I say amen to that."

"He was worried about the way Anne looks."

"If you ask me, she's heading for a crack-up."

Charlie rose and moved to the window. The holes that Clyde had melted through the frost had frozen over again.

"Why does everyone blame Clyde for the way Anne looks?" he asked. "What was Anne like before she was married?"

"Just the same, only younger," Polly answered, laughing.

Charlie nodded.

"I've never had any family of my own, and I'm just beginning to learn what a mutual protection society a family can be. If you ask me, I think it's Anne who's making a mess out of Clyde's life. All this business about not wanting children."

"Who told you that?" Polly asked, embarrassed.

"Lucy. She told me all sorts of things before we were married. If you ask me, Anne's the freak in the Harbert family, not Clyde. Any woman who doesn't want children is a freak."

"I suppose you don't think it's possible for a woman to be normal without children."

"Frankly, I don't. Women were put on earth to get married and raise children. The minute they start to complicate things with careers and hair-shirt operations like missions in Philadelphia, they run into trouble."

"Well, for God's sake," Polly asked angrily, "what would you have us all do? Spend our entire lives dunking babies in wash basins? There must be more to life than that."

"Not for anything less than a genius. Anyone can be an eccentric, provided they have an independent income, but it takes talent to be a genius, and I don't think this family has any."

"Are you talking about me now?" Polly asked, looking at him thoughtfully.

He didn't answer. Lucy walked into the kitchen.

"If you plan to catch the six o'clock, Pol, we have to go right now. I've got to feed Lydia."

"Your husband," Polly answered sweetly, "has volunteered to drive me down to the station."

Lucy glanced toward Charlie questioningly.

"If it's all right with you," Charlie said.

"I'd like to be back at our house by seven," she answered, her voice crisp and efficient. "So don't linger along the way. Polly has a fetish for missing trains, particularly when there's a man with her."

"Flattery will get you nowhere," Polly said, draining her glass. She stood up. "Let's go, Charlie. I've been waiting all day to get you away from your wife."

"Poor Lucy," she said when they started down Lawn Street. "Here she has you all signed, sealed, and delivered, and still she's jealous."

Charlie just grinned. Polly was wearing her fur coat buttoned up under her chin, her mouth a dark red shadow against the whiteness of her skin.

"She ought to be grateful to me," Polly continued. "Wasn't it me you came to see that afternoon?"

"How did you know that?"

"Lucy told me months after your wedding. She's an honest, straightforward type."

"It's true," he admitted. "You were one of my big dreams. I thought that if there could be a perfect girl in the world, you must be it."

"That's very sweet of you, Charlie."

"When the army was bouncing me around from camp to camp, whenever I'd meet some new girl I'd end up comparing her to you, and then usually I'd never want to see her again."

"Charlie," Polly said suddenly. Then she said nothing more.

"Charlie, what?"

"Why on earth did you marry Lucy? Did you love her?"

"If I tell you the truth, you'll probably never speak to me again."

"Why did you?"

"I liked what she was. I liked the idea of marrying into a family like yours. It's something you probably can't understand."

"You liked what we were?" she asked, astonished. "I've always *hated* what we were. No, that's not exactly it," she added, correcting herself. "What we were just bored me. That's why I got out."

The city was cold and dark. Charlie drove slowly, making the two-mile trip to the station last as long as he could. Polly slid across the seat and curled her legs up under her, leaning her shoulder against his.

"You're ahead of schedule, aren't you?" she asked.

"Of what schedule?"

"Don't be coy. You remember the discussion we had at your wedding. The seven-room house, the two cars, the job in the family business, and the wife who runs you as though she owns you."

Charlie didn't answer.

"Even if I had been home that afternoon, Charlie, and even if you had asked me to marry you, I wouldn't have. I want a man who can think for himself. I want someone who will beat me."

"Ho hum."

"Ho hum, what?"

"I'm sure you said the same thing when you were in your sophomore year at college."

"That doesn't mean I was wrong."

"You ought to grow up, Polly."

"Me? Grow up? I did grow up, and that's why I left this place."

"Why don't you look at yourself in a mirror when you get back to New York, and admit what you are?"

"What I am?" she echoed. "Well, what am I?"

"I'd say you were a failure. You were born with your beauty and not much else. If you didn't have a chunk of Hadley Company stock in your name, you would have come crawling home long ago, willing and anxious to get dull along with the rest of us. You don't have any talent. Why don't you admit it? If you had, someone would have discovered it by now. You're twenty-six, and still kidding yourself."

She moved away from him and put her feet on the floor.

"I was enjoying your company up until now."

"You can criticize your sisters, but you can't take it yourself. I was thinking about you when we were putting Lydia to bed. Lucy and I will eat you someday. You have this romantic, little-girl notion about a noble savage who will drag you off to his cave and make you his wife. You think that just because Lucy is pushing me around a little bit now, she's going to do it forever. I know what I want, and I'm going to get it. I'll make you a little bet." He turned and looked at her. "Ten years from now I'll be running your entire family. You just watch. The whole family will be revolving around me, including Lucy."

He stopped the car by the station.

"Thank you, and good-by," Polly said coldly. She stepped out onto the platform and walked away. She had forgotten her suitcase. Charlie ran after her.

"You forgot this."

"So I did," she answered. She looked stunned.

"Can I tell you something?" he asked.

"Haven't you told me enough already?"

"Children and a family can be very pleasant," he said.

"People just bury themselves with children," she answered bitterly.

"No matter how you live, Polly, you'll get buried long before you die."

She patted his arm and smiled at him wanly.

"Run along home to your poor, dear, dull Lucy. I'm sure she has some cold turkey waiting for you." She took her suitcase and walked toward the station. "I'll see you next Christmas, Charlie."

sixteen

EACH MORNING IT WAS RALPH HENRY'S POLICY TO WANDER ABOUT THE PLANT for an hour or so talking with the men in the various departments. During the winter months, with his woolen mackinaw, his knitted hat, and his gray-white complexion, he looked like a cadaver trying to stay warm. His last stop each morning was the powerhouse, where he'd pause for a talk with Charlie.

"There's one thing about coal," he said one morning in February, "it warms you twice. Once when you shovel it, and again when it burns."

He grinned, waiting for Charlie to react. Then he removed his hat and rubbed his hairless scalp with the palm of his hand.

"I suppose the first thing you'll do when you move up to the front office is install an oil system out here. Then you can just sit up there in your nice comfortable chair and jiggle a thermostat."

This interlude in the powerhouse each morning, the sight of the heir apparent of The Hadley Company covered with coal dust, was quite obviously the high point of the foreman's day. Charlie slammed shut the furnace door and leaned his shovel against the wall. Then he started to remove his overalls. After four months, he thought, it might be time to make his first move.

"Have you got a minute to talk, Mr. Henry?" He stepped out of his overalls and hung them on a nail.

"You going somewhere?" the foreman asked, watching him.

"That will depend on you. I'm quitting as janitor."

Mr. Henry grinned and sat on a bench next to the wall.

"I've been expecting it."

"You have everything pretty well figured out, don't you?" Charlie said sarcastically.

"It looks like I had you figured out, don't it?"

"You've got everything all figured out except one thing, and that's how you're going to stop this factory from going under. You can run the men and the machines, but you're not much good when it comes to business."

The foreman just stared at him for a moment. Then he said, "If you got something to say to me, you better get it off your mind."

"I just want to ask you one question. How much longer do you give this place out here?"

"What are you getting at?" The foreman's voice was nasty. "If you want to quit, then quit. I don't need no lecture."

"You need something. Everybody out here keeps telling me what a wonderful man you are. How you came here when you were fourteen years old and got to be foreman when you were twenty-five. If you're so good, why is it that so many of your buildings are empty? Why are you down to seventy-five men? This place is failing, and you haven't got the guts to admit it."

"Goddam it," the foreman shouted, half-rising from the bench, "it don't make no difference to me who you are. No man talks to me that way."

"I didn't think you'd listen to me," Charlie answered. "Things are in a mess out here, but you don't dare think about it." He walked toward the powerhouse door. "All right, I'll quit right now. I won't even bother to tell you what I think of your operation out here. You've been hoping I'd quit all along, anyway."

"I ain't scared of you or anybody else," the foreman shouted, moving in front of him. "If you got something to say, say it."

"All right then, sit down," Charlie said. He waited. Ralph Henry stared at him for a moment, then moved back to the bench.

"The minute you saw me four months ago, you had me pegged for another member of the family who was looking for a soft job. I suppose you think I want to write poetry or paint pictures. I guess you think you're the only one who really likes this factory." Charlie moved back to the center of the room and folded his arms across his chest. Four months of shoveling coal and picking up scrap metal had put fifteen pounds of muscle on his arms and shoulders. He was healthier and stronger than he had ever been in his life.

"I've got news for you," he continued. "I like this place too. I like this factory, and I want to run it someday. I don't want to run your end of it, but I want to run the business end of it. I thought that after a while you'd see I wasn't scared to work. I was hoping you'd even get to like me. The men in the shop told me that you like anyone who likes this factory. I didn't think I'd have to tell you that. I hoped you'd see it for yourself. If you figure me for another Lowell Chalmers, you're wrong. I don't want the family to give me that office up here. I want to take it away from them."

"I'm listening," the foreman said when Charlie paused.

"I can do something out here that needs doing, and I don't mean operating the powerhouse or a machine. I think I can do what old Mr. Hadley used to do. I think I can sell. If somebody doesn't start getting some new business out here, this factory will fail."

"We pay dividends regular," the foreman answered, looking uneasy for the first time.

"You don't earn them. You and your broken-down old machines don't earn a cent of dividends. They come from selling water power, and from the interest the company gets from the cash Mr. Hadley earned fifty years ago. The family could sell this factory tomorrow, and they wouldn't feel it. In fact they'd be better off if they did sell out tomorrow. Every day this place goes downhill that much more. In another year or two it won't be worth anything."

"Goddam it," the foreman shouted, "what can I do? I'm not running the place. It's him up there." He jerked his thumb toward the front office. "I'm just the foreman out here."

"Do you want the factory to fail? Is that what you want to happen?"

"Want it to fail?" the foreman shouted. "If they sell out here, they'll find me floating in the river."

"Then why don't you do something about it?"

"What can I do, Charlie?"

It was the first time the foreman had called him by his given name.

"You can start by giving me credit for liking this place as much as you do. I like working here. I want to run the factory someday, and I mean the way it ought to be run. You won't find me sitting in an office all day. I'll go out selling the way Mr. Hadley did. How do I prove that to you, Ralph? How do I get it through your head that I'm not like Mr. Chalmers?"

The foreman started to smile.

"I guess you proved that to me already," he answered. "He worked in here for eighteen months, shoveling coal, just like you."

"I know all about that. But that doesn't mean I'll do it for eighteen months."

"He ever tell you who got him out of here, Charlie?"

Charlie shook his head.

"Lydia. Lydia come out here and started screaming to her father. We could hear her all the way back in the shop. You take my Lowell away from the coal pile, she shouts. You give my Lowell a better job." The foreman stood up and started rubbing his hands together. "Right then we all knew we'd have trouble when he took over the front office. When a man has to have his wife doing his fighting for him, he's no damn good. So you want to sell, Charlie? Is that what you have in mind?"

"Not right away. I want you to teach me your end of the business first. I want to go through all the operations in the plant, so when I go out selling I'll know what we can make."

"Goddam it, we can make anything. We got machines and men. That's what I always told Old Mr. Hadley. He'd ask, Ralph, can we make this, or can we make that? And I'd tell him we can make anything if we get the order. Like the bayonets we made for the war back in '17. Old Mr. Hadley sends me a telegram from Washington. Can we make bayonets, he asks. I sent him a telegram back. Get the order, I said. And he got the order, and we made bayonets. Five million of them."

The foreman opened the furnace door, spit into the burning coal, and slammed the door shut again.

"Do you know what he done in your war, Charlie? Nothing. That's what he done. The only new business we got out here was when they come begging us to help out. Every factory was booming everywhere, but not us. He sits up there writing his memories or something. Him and his goddam library, and his goddam antiques, and his goddam summer place at that goddam Island."

"All I want is a chance," Charlie said quietly.

The foreman smashed his fist against his palm.

"All right, I'll give you a chance. I'd like to see this old place really rattling like it did once. When Old Mr. Hadley was running things I used to get out here at five in the morning, and he'd be up there in his office an hour ahead of me. He liked to work. He died right out here in the yard when he was eighty-eight years old. He didn't worry none about the stockholders. When he wanted to do something, he did it. When he wanted someone from back in the shop he'd open the window and shout. We'd hear his voice over the noise of the grinding wheels. And the old-timers around here then used to tell me both his father and his grandfather was just like him. And then *he* comes along." Again the foreman jerked his thumb toward the front office. "And then we get him and his antiques, and his summer place, and his library. I'll tell you something, Charlie. Old Mr. Hadley made a mistake when he moved into the city. I went to school with Lydia." He smiled fondly. "She was just like her father when she lived out here. Tough, hard, and mean."

"She still is," Charlie said, grinning.

"But the city done something to her. She's gone fancy in that big place Old Mr. Hadley built in there. She forgot about this town out here. She forgot about where all her money came from. If she stayed out here she'd love this place just like Old Mr. Hadley loved it. If she could see it every day, and if she could see it going downhill like it is, she'd of got someone in to run it. She'd of let that Lowell of hers go write his memories somewhere else, and kept the factory going." He looked at Charlie. "I figured maybe you were going to live out here."

Charlie shrugged. "Lucy likes the city life."

"Some of us was hoping you'd move the family back out here. When Jim Hartry up at the town hall told me you bought the old River Inn property, I figured that's what you had in mind."

"Lucy likes the city life," Charlie repeated.

Ralph Henry had filled his pipe. He opened the furnace door, lifted out a small coal with the shovel, and set it on top of his pipe.

"Lydia ever tell you I asked her to marry me?"

"You?" Charlie exclaimed, sorry he had laughed when he saw the foreman's expression.

"Old Mr. Hadley tried to get me to go to some fancy college. He told me he'd pay my way. I couldn't see it. I used to work here after school, and I didn't figure I needed no college education. When Lydia turned me down I knew I'd made a mistake. I was good enough to take her out walking in the woods, but when she wanted a husband, she picked *him*. Him and his college degree."

"No wonder you don't like college boys," Charlie said.

Ralph Henry shook his head. "They ain't all like him. Once in a while you get a good one. Like you." He grinned. "I've just been waiting for you to hit me over the head with your shovel. If you didn't get mad at me, I didn't want you out here anyway. That Lowell there, he's always been scared of me. You think I give you a hard time. You should of seen what I did to him." He grinned. "I give him eighteen months of hell until Lydia come out here and gets him moved up to the office."

95

"Just give me a chance," Charlie said evenly.

Ralph Henry held out his hand.

"I hope you got no hard feelings against me, Charlie."

"Not as long as you pay up your bet," Charlie answered, smiling. "I've been out here four months. Didn't you bet me a day's pay I wouldn't last that long?"

The foreman reached for his wallet. "How much do you make a day?"

"Fifteen dollars," Charlie answered, starting to grin.

The foreman laughed. It was the first time Charlie had seen him look happy since he'd worked at the factory.

"Take my whole damn wallet," he said. "It looks like we've been getting you too cheap."

When the plant closed at five, Charlie found Mr. Chalmers waiting by his car.

"I have some good news for you," he said. "Ralph Henry seems to think it's time we stepped you up. You'll start tomorrow morning in the stamping room."

"That is good news, Mr. Chalmers."

"I hoped you'd be pleased. Ralph and I discussed you at some length today. It was his thought, and naturally I heartily agree, that it was time you saw more of our operation out here. Ralph plans to move you from one department to another. I'm just explaining this to you so you'll know what's going on."

"I appreciate this," Charlie answered.

"You're happy out here, aren't you?"

"Yes, I am."

Mr. Chalmers looked thoughtful. "You'll find that working for a small company like this has its advantages. There's something about carrying on a family tradition that can't be computed in dollars and cents. It's one of life's intangibles."

"I feel that way strongly myself," Charlie answered.

"And don't worry. We're keeping our eyes on you. Ralph told me he thought The Hadley Company was lucky to get you, and I agree."

"Thank you," Charlie answered.

When he arrived home he found Lucy in the kitchen.

"I've got a new job at the factory."

"Oh, good," she answered. "What?"

"Stamping room."

"That doesn't sound too glamorous. Is it?"

"I'm pleased with it."

She put her arms around his neck and kissed him affectionately on the cheek. "You're not sorry you're working out there now, are you?"

"I'm happy as hell."

96

"I knew you would be." She kissed him again. "Be a dear and set the table, would you? I've got to give Lydia a bath."

seventeen

THEIR SECOND BABY, ANOTHER GIRL, WAS BORN IN JULY. THEY NAMED IT Roswell, after Roswell Hadley, Lucy's great-aunt, who next to Mrs. Chalmers was the largest single stockholder in The Hadley Company. There was more at stake in the choice of the name than either Charlie's or Lucy's individual preference. Aunt Roswell was in her late eighties. It was generally hoped that one day she might die.

Lucy spent all of August with her mother down at the Island. Charlie joined her for a week, and also commuted on the week ends. Lucy and the children came home after Labor Day.

Then one afternoon in mid-October when he returned from the factory, Charlie said, "I'd like to talk with you a little bit about my job."

"Don't tell me you have another new one? You poor darling, you just get set, and they move you to some other department."

"I mean about my job in general."

He was giving Roswell her bottle. Lucy sat across the room combing Lydia's hair. Next to her on the couch a kitchen timer ticked noisily. Green beans were cooking on the stove.

"What about your job in general?" she asked.

"I'm not planning to do it just yet, but probably next spring I'll be going out selling for the Company."

"What does that mean?" She glanced at him warily.

"It means I'll be a salesman."

"Is that good or bad?"

"It might be bad for you. At least until you get used to it. But it will be good for the Company. That's why I'm going to do it."

"You mean you'll be staying away nights?" Lucy asked, the truth of what he was telling her beginning to register.

"Probably three or four nights a week at first."

"And who," she said angrily, "dreamed up this wild idea?"

"I suppose I did. But it's no wild idea. There hasn't been a single representative from The Hadley Company out selling for over twenty years. Not since your grandfather died."

"How interesting," Lucy answered scornfully. "What do you want me to say? How delighted I'll be to be left alone with one child a year and a half, and another two months old?"

"I'm just warning you about it. I thought you might want to get help with the house."

"But I don't want a maid complicating my life. We've been all through that before. The house isn't set up for it."

"All right," he answered. "But I'm just warning you that I won't be around as much as I am now. You won't be able to count on me to feed bottles and wash dishes. I don't object to doing it," he added quickly. "But when I go out selling, I just won't be here."

"Is this whole thing just your personal brainstorm?"

"It has to be done, and I'm the only one who can do it."

"Then you haven't discussed it with my father?"

"Not yet. I don't plan to start until next spring. I'm just letting you know in advance."

"But what on earth makes you think you have to do it?"

"Because we need new products out there, and we have to make more of an effort to sell what we make now. The Hadley Company is dying by inches."

"Here we go on that again," Lucy said. The timer alarm sounded. "I'll go put the beans on simmer. When you finish with Ros, toss her in her crib." She walked briskly out of the room, pulling Lydia along with her.

He felt more at ease with Roswell than he ever had with Lydia. He had watched her grow, and he had paced the hospital waiting room while she was born. Part of it was Roswell's personality too, he thought. Lydia was high-strung and nervous. Like her Aunt Anne, he occasionally thought. But Roswell was an easy child. He watched her suck greedily until the bottle was empty. She was nearly asleep in his arms when Lucy returned from the kitchen.

"She finish it?"

"Every drop."

"You're a pig," Lucy said, scooping the baby off his lap. "I'll put her to bed, and then we can eat. You might go on out to the kitchen and supervise Lydia. She makes a terrible mess with her food when she's alone. Also check the beans. I may have put them on low instead of simmer."

For the next two minutes Charlie stuffed a mixture of strained meat and vegetables into Lydia's tightly closed mouth. Now and then she knocked away the spoon, spilling food on the kitchen floor. Finally he opened the kitchen door and whistled. The Littlehales' boxer shot through the shrubbery and slid across the floor, mopping the linoleum with his tongue. Charlie then put Lydia into her play pen and started to set the table. The phone rang just as he noticed the beans boiling over.

"Get it, will you," Lucy shrieked from upstairs. "I'm changing Roswell."

He turned off the stove and headed for the phone. The moment he left the kitchen Lydia started to howl.

It was Terry Goddard.

Charlie said, "Hold it a minute, Terry. All hell has broken loose around here."

He returned to the kitchen, hooked an arm around Lydia, and carried her with him to the phone.

"O.K. Hello again, Terry. Things are now under control."

98

"Did I call at a bad time in the Webb household?"

"Things are always bad in the Webb household. Did you want to speak with Lucy?"

"Not particularly," she answered. "You'll do."

Terry Goddard had married Lucy's second cousin Newell. She was from Denver, a lithe blonde with a flat Western accent and an unashamed preference for husbands. As a family duty Lucy had entertained her just once. Terry had spent much of the evening sitting on the piano, surrounded by men, singing army songs. She had never been back.

"I'm giving a little party next Friday," Terry said. "Want you and Lucy to come."

"Sounds great," Charlie answered. "We'll be there."

"Nothing special. Just the usual boring little dinner. But no games. I promise you."

"We'll be there," Charlie repeated.

There was a pause.

"How are things, Charlie?"

She sounded as though she really wanted to know. That must be Terry's charm, he thought. When Lucy's Garden Club friends called, they were as impersonal as an answering service. They delivered their message and hung up, nervous lest someone might think they were flirting.

"Things are all right," he answered. Lydia slid out of his arm and sprawled on the floor.

"Do I hear something screaming?"

"Just my daughter Lydia."

"What did you do to her?"

"Dropped her. Hold on a minute." He leaned over and glanced at Lydia's cheek. She had gouged it on his belt buckle on the way to the floor. "She'll live," he said, returning to Terry.

"What did you call the new one?"

"Roswell."

"Veddy fancy."

"After an aunt. We hope to inherit a half-million dollars."

He could say that to Terry. Newell, her husband, had just inherited a quarter-million himself.

Terry laughed. "Friday," she said. "Sevenish. Looking forward to seeing you. Good-by." She hung up.

He put Lydia back into her play pen and wiped the blood from her cheek. While he was out of the kitchen the Littlehales' boxer had pried off the lid from the garbage can, and yesterday's salad was smeared over the floor. Charlie found a piece of stale salami in the icebox and threw it out the kitchen door. The boxer dove after it.

"Who turned off the stove?" Lucy asked, when she returned to the kitchen.

"I did. The beans were boiling over."

"I thought I said to put them on simmer."

"You did, but the phone rang. I was busy."

"Who called?" Lucy asked, turning on the stove again.

"Terry Goddard."

"Ugh. What did she want?"

"Dinner next Friday. I said we'd go."

"Ugh," Lucy said again.

"What's the matter with that?"

"Nothing. I was looking at the floor. Who spilled the salad?"

"The Littlehales' boxer. He was cleaning up after Lydia."

"Next Friday," Lucy asked thoughtfully, scraping the salad up with her fingers.

"Yes."

"We're going to the Stewarts."

"Ugh," he said gloomily. Helen Stewart was seven months pregnant, and the state secretary of the League of Women Voters.

"Put Lydia to bed for me, would you?" Lucy said. "And try to be quiet. Roswell's already asleep."

A few moments later Lucy shouted up the stairs, "Are you coming? Everything's getting cold."

"I'm having trouble with the pins," he shouted back at her. Roswell stirred in her crib and started to whimper.

"Honestly," Lucy said angrily, sprinting up the stairs. "I would think by now you could do at least some of this."

Both the children were still crying upstairs when Charlie and Lucy started to eat.

"Peaceful here," Charlie said.

"I hear it all the time," Lucy answered, her voice catching.

"I know you do," he said quickly, terrified that she too was about to cry. "Let me clean up tonight, Lucy. When we're through, you go on into the living room and read."

"It's like this all day," Lucy said, not listening to him. "All day, every day, day after day."

"I know."

They ate the rest of the meal in silence.

"I'm afraid that wasn't much of a supper, darling," Lucy said, coming around behind him and rubbing her cheek against his. "Come on, let's wash up together. It goes much faster when we do it together."

When they were washing the dishes he said, "We didn't really finish our discussion about my job. About my going out during the week selling."

"But I thought it was all settled," Lucy answered cheerfully. "You apparently feel you must do this thing, and what right do I have to stop you? You always do what you want, and I'm sure you will this time."

When they had finished in the kitchen Lucy went on up to the bedroom. She worried him. He hadn't expected her to give in that easily. When he had first mentioned it, before supper, she was ready to argue about it. Now she seemed resigned. She must, he decided, be near the breaking point.

He climbed the stairs to the bedroom.

Lucy was sitting up in bed, dressed in her nightgown, reading.

"I love you," he said, sitting next to her.

"That's nice of you." She closed her book and put her glasses on the table.

"You're a wonderful wife, and I'm very happy."

"I try to be a good wife, Charlie."

"I have a feeling you're mad at me."

"Of course I'm not mad at you." She reached for his hand and squeezed it. "I'm never mad at you."

"You're working terribly hard, Lucy, and I'm working hard. We're both pretty tired. Our life will smooth out little by little. Things are a mess right now."

"Stop worrying," she answered, squeezing his hand again. "Stop worrying about me. I'll get along. Go on down to your den. I put a new lamp down there for you. I think it's just what you wanted."

He went on down to the cellar. Beyond her winter clothesline and her ironing board, Lucy had cleared out a corner and told him he could use it for a den. At first he hadn't been convinced he needed or wanted a den, at least not one with a damp concrete floor and an exposed sewer pipe running at head height along the ceiling. But with the addition of a comfortable reading chair, a table for his business magazines, and now a decent lamp, he found it far more pleasant to live in the cellar than in the living room. The living room had become too much an annex of the nursery, and it was difficult to concentrate on business affairs when sitting on a couch or chair that smelled faintly of vomit.

Lydia Chalmers was at work in her sewing room the next morning when she heard Lucy call to her from the bottom of the stairs.

"I'm up here, darling," she answered, speaking through a mouthful of pins.

While she waited she heard Lucy's steps, firm and vigorous, coming up the stairs. One would hardly guess, she thought, that Roswell, the new baby, was scarcely a month and a half old. Customs and habits changed. In her day, provided one could afford it, doctors insisted on weeks and weeks of rest after the birth of a child. Stairs were regarded with horror. The doctors of Lucy's generation, however, took the opposite view. No longer was childbirth an event, but merely an interruption of the daily tasks. Bring back the servant once more, Lydia thought, and get rid of electronics, and doctors would once again advise new mothers to spend more of their time resting.

"You're looking rather chipper," she said when Lucy came into the room. "Sit for a moment and catch your breath."

Lucy lit a cigarette and looked vaguely about the room for an ash tray.

"I'm afraid you'll have to use that metal wastebasket over there," her mother said. "People don't usually smoke in my sewing room."

Lucy dragged the basket toward her chair.

"Can I talk to you, Mother?"

"You know you can always talk with me."

"About something serious, I mean?"

"It can't be too serious, I hope."

"It's about Charlie."

Lydia felt a slight tingle in her scalp. "Oh," she asked, "is he beating you?"

"Please, Mother."

"Well then, what about Charlie? Doesn't he like the new baby?"

"He seems to adore her. It's about his job at the factory."

"I see," Lydia answered, the tingle in her scalp becoming more pronounced. "I hope you're not going to tell me he doesn't like his job. Your father tells me he seems quite happy."

"Did Father mention anything about sending Charlie out on the road selling?"

"On the road? On what road, darling?"

"Did Father say he planned to make a traveling salesman out of Charlie?"

"I've never heard a single word about it. I don't think The Hadley Company has salesmen. Another organization handles all that for them."

"Then he didn't mention it?" Lucy persisted.

"I wish you'd come right out and tell me what you're getting at," Lydia Chalmers said gently. "You and I have never had to beat around the bush with each other like this."

"Charlie," Lucy said angrily, "announced to me last night that sometime next spring he plans to spend most of his time away from home."

"Doing what?" Lydia asked incredulously.

"Selling. I just wanted to be sure this wasn't Father's idea. I don't want to interfere with Father's business, so I thought I'd better check with you first."

"But how utterly ridiculous, Lucy. Of course it isn't your father's idea. He would have talked something like that over with me, and he hasn't said a word about it."

"Charlie insists the Company needs salesmen," Lucy said.

"*Charlie* insists?" her mother said haughtily. "Who is Charlie? The last thing I knew, he was still sweeping floors and shoveling coal."

"I think he's some kind of an assistant to Mr. Henry now."

"Indeed. Is he? Nevertheless I don't believe he's in any position to decide what the Company needs and doesn't need."

"He keeps saying that the Company is going downhill. That there won't even be a Company before long unless someone does something about it."

"That's not even worthy of discussion, Lucy. Excuse me for saying it, but your Charlie ought to have his ears boxed."

The room was quiet for a moment.

"There's another thing too, Mother. Maybe I'm just being selfish about this." She hesitated.

"About what, darling? I'm sure you're not being selfish at all."

"Do you think Charlie ought to leave me completely alone? It would mean that I'd have to cope with everything all by myself. I could do it," she added quickly, "but do you honestly think it would be fair of him to make me do it? Our generation lives a different sort of life. You just can't get any servants, and no one has them. Husbands have to be around to help with things. It sounds terrible when I put it that way. It's not that I'm trying to make a servant out of him, but our generation simply has to share the jobs around the house or they don't get done."

"Of course some husbands do have to be away from home, Lucy."

"I know. But the whole idea of our having Charlie work where he is working was so he could be home. That's why I've always admired the way you and father have lived. I think you managed things perfectly, and I just hope I can do half as well with my life."

"That's terribly sweet of you, Lucy." Lydia was touched.

"I really think Charlie plans to go through with this, Mother," Lucy said, getting the conversation back on the track. "I just wanted to get your advice about it before I did anything."

"I think the simple solution would be for me to say a word to your father about it."

"Would you?" Lucy asked eagerly. "The last thing I want to do is to interfere in The Hadley Company. I know I have to keep my nose out of it. But if you could help me it would be wonderful."

"I think I can handle it quite gracefully, darling."

"You won't mention that I had anything to do with it? I know Charlie would be furious."

"Perhaps," Lydia Chalmers said sweetly, "I don't fear your husband's violent temper quite as much as you do. I can't quite rid myself of the feeling that your Charlie ought to consider himself an extremely fortunate young man."

Lydia was waiting for her husband Lowell when he returned from the factory. She met him in the hallway and pinned a fresh flower in his buttonhole.

"Have a good day?" she asked cheerfully.

"The usual," he answered.

"Can we talk about something?" she asked, following him into the study.

"I suppose so," he answered. He made it a policy to be unenthusiastic when Lydia interrupted his evening reading hour.

"Would you like a little sherry?"

"I think not," he answered, settling into his chair and glancing at the headlines.

"Could you put your paper aside for a moment?"

He let it slide to the floor.

"I heard something rather fantastic about our Charlie today, Lowell."

"What's he done now?"

"Lucy seemed to think you were sending him out sometime next spring as a traveling salesman."

"What's this, Lydia?"

"That was my reaction. Then you know nothing about it?"

"Absolutely nothing."

"Then it isn't true?"

"If it were, wouldn't I know about it?"

"You don't think it's something he might be planning to do without even consulting you?"

"Well, good Lord, who's running the plant, Lydia? Charlie, or me?"

"I honestly believe it would be a disaster for poor Lucy if Charlie were made to leave home."

"You tell Lucy that Charlie isn't going anywhere. And if he does go somewhere, it will be me who decides it. Not him."

He reached for his paper and resumed his reading. When Lydia was gone, he removed the flower from his buttonhole and placed it in an empty vase he kept handy for the purpose.

eighteen

SIX MONTHS LATER, THE FOLLOWING APRIL, WHEN WORD CAME TO HIM FROM Mrs. Fleck that Charlie wanted to see him, Lowell Chalmers thought the interview would concern money. He had completely forgotten Lydia's warning of the previous fall.

"Come in, come in," he shouted when Charlie knocked on the office door. "Wonderful morning, isn't it? I've just been sitting here at my desk gazing out on the river. You can just feel the whole world springing to life."

"Yes, sir," Charlie answered, without much interest. Mr. Chalmers' desk was littered with sheets of paper and old books. "You're not working on a novel, are you?" he asked.

"Oh, good Lord, no. Nothing as ambitious as that. It's just this history of the Hadley Canal I promised Miss Oldershaw at the library." He rose from his desk and looked at Charlie intently. "It's a fascinating subject. Would you believe it, this little stretch of canal that runs past our factory here was once planned as a link in a vast network of inland waterways. Our ancestors had large dreams."

Charlie nodded. "I'd like very much to read it when you finish it. I enjoyed your other three books."

"Have you really read my things?" Mr. Chalmers asked, obviously pleased. "Yes, I have."

He had found Mr. Chalmers' books displayed in the Hadley Library. There were three of them in all—*The Annals of Hadley*; *The Hadley Family, Then and Now*; and a short literary essay entitled *George Borrow, Artist or Poseur*.

"And do you think I show talent for a young man of sixty-five?"

"You certainly write well," Charlie answered.

Mr. Chalmers made a gesture of impatience.

"Yes. Yes. I write well. People have been telling me that all my life." He poked a pencil through his desk blotter. "But not one soul," he said, "at least not one whose judgment I respect, has ever told me I possess talent."

"But have you ever tried to prove it one way or the other?" Charlie asked.

"Just what do you mean by that?"

"These books you've written," Charlie continued. "Couldn't just about any well-educated person have written them, assuming he had the leisure time and the means to have them privately published?"

"Well, I suppose so," Mr. Chalmers answered, raising his eyebrows in surprise.

"Isn't there anything in your life that has meant more to you than George Borrow, or *The Hadley Family, Then and Now*?"

"Well, of course there is," Mr. Chalmers answered, annoyed. "In my lifetime I've done a great deal of thinking on a great variety of subjects."

"Then why not write what you think?" Charlie persisted. "Anyone can collect facts. All that requires is patience. If you're really curious whether you have talent or not, why not try to make sense out of your thoughts? Isn't that the real test?"

Lowell Chalmers flushed angrily.

"Never before have I ever been called a coward to my face. And so gracefully," he added.

"I'm sorry," Charlie apologized hastily. "I didn't really mean to——"

"That's quite all right," Mr. Chalmers interrupted. "You happen to be quite right. I would like very much to sit down some day and expose a few of my thoughts."

"Then why not do it?" Charlie asked.

"Because, my dear boy . . . well, the point is, you don't understand what you're asking me to do. If I wrote about my own life and the way I've lived it, I would have to express opinions about those who have shared it with me —my wife, my friends, my own children." He looked at Charlie in agony. "What emerged might horrify them. They would feel that I had stabbed them in the back." He shook his head sadly. "I don't have it in me to be that cruel."

"But everyone thinks cruel things about their friends, Mr. Chalmers."

"Ah, yes," he answered. "Everyone does. But not everyone writes it down." He gazed wistfully out the window, as though the subject fascinated him. "I've been tempted," he admitted. "Oh, how tempted I've been at times. But so far any temptation I've had has never been as strong as my fear of what people would say. My fear of what people would say," he repeated, smiling to himself. "No man ever does what he wants to do if he fears what people will say."

The office was quiet for a moment.

"Now then," Lowell Chalmers said, abruptly changing the mood, "I gather you wish to talk to me about something."

"Yes, sir. About my job."

"And what about your job?"

Charlie would want more money. Lowell Chalmers was certain of it. There was in his son-in-law what seemed to him a certain element of greed.

Since he'd started at the factory, Charlie had already had two raises in pay. That in itself wouldn't have bothered Lowell Chalmers. It was the fact that his son-in-law had asked for the raises that had disturbed him. He was now making close to five thousand dollars a year. Lowell had searched his conscience that morning while he waited for Charlie to appear in his office. He had decided he'd been generous enough. Two raises in eighteen months was sufficient. He himself took only twelve thousand dollars in salary. His total income from The Hadley Company was far greater because of the income from his and Lydia's stock, but his salary was a small one. This was something Charlie must learn. The Hadley Company was not a gold mine. It had a responsibility to its stockholders.

Lowell decided to air the whole matter.

"I hardly know where to start on this," Charlie said.

"That shouldn't be difficult. Just tell me what's on your mind."

"I seem to have reached a dead end in The Hadley Company. I suppose that's what I really want to say."

It was not what Lowell Chalmers expected. Was Charlie about to leave the Company? he wondered.

"I'm afraid I don't understand."

"I've gone through all the departments, from the powerhouse to the shipping room. I feel I know the whole operation pretty well. But where can I go from here?"

"There's always my job," Mr. Chalmers said, an edge coming into his voice. "Let me go on," he added, when Charlie started to speak. "I think I know what's at the bottom of all this. You want more money. Why don't you and I discuss what we think the policy ought to be about your salary? You're making nearly five thousand dollars a year. That's not a great deal of money, but I think you'll find it compares favorably with what your friends are making elsewhere. I think we have been generous with you. Let me continue, please," he said as Charlie tried to interrupt. "As members of the family we can't raise our salaries out here just because we'd like to. I'd like to pay you one hundred thousand dollars a year. But you've got to earn it, and I'm sure you'll admit that you aren't. Do you see my point?"

"I don't want more salary this time," Charlie answered. "I was about to suggest that you pay me less."

"What's that?" Lowell Chalmers asked sharply.

"I want you to cut my salary in half. I want half my present salary, and a commission."

"Ah ha," Lowell Chalmers said thoughtfully. "Then you must be planning to sell something."

"Yes, sir. I'd like you to send me out as a salesman for the Company."

Lowell Chalmers nodded.

"I now begin to see what all this is about. My dear boy The Hadley Company doesn't have salesmen. We don't need them."

"I think we do need them," Charlie answered quietly.

"I guess you don't fully realize how our business operates," Mr. Chalmers continued. "When a company is as old and as well established in a specialized market as we are, we don't need salesmen. Our name has already been spread far and wide. Our old customers would no more be without Hadley knives than they would be without sales clerks. We deal through two wholesale houses, Charlie. They handle all the actual selling for us. Experience has proven to us that this is the only practical way for us to do business."

"Perhaps if we developed a sales organization of our own we might show a profit for a change."

Mr. Chalmers flushed. "I'd like to remind you," he said, "that we haven't missed a dividend out here in over eighty-five years."

"I know all about that, but none of it comes from the operation of this plant. You sell water power to some of the other factories along the river. You collect rent from real estate both here in Hadley and down the river. You pay your dividends from that, and from the money that you have invested in the portfolio of stocks. If this factory had to stand alone, it would fail tomorrow."

Lowell Chalmers' face had turned a bright red. "Aren't you taking advantage of your position as my son-in-law?" he asked.

"I'm sorry," Charlie answered. "I don't seem to have the knack of being tactful about a subject I feel strongly about."

"And what is this subject you feel so strongly about?"

"I want to sell," Charlie answered. He waited until Mr. Chalmers looked at him. "I'm offering to take a cut in salary. I don't want to keep working out here unless we can make this company show a profit on its actual operation. You warned me when I first talked with you that someday the Company might be sold. I want to prevent that. I think I can double our business in two years." As he spoke Charlie gained confidence. "I want to visit every store that sells our knives," he continued, "and every store that doesn't sell our knives. We make the best knives in the world. Mrs. Chalmers said that when she first suggested I work here. She was right. We do. But if we make the best knives in the world, why in hell don't more people know about it? What are these wholesalers doing?" he said angrily. "Nothing? From the orders we get, that's what it looks like to me. If I'm wrong, if I can't sell more than they do, then I'll look for a job somewhere else. But I'd like a chance to show you what I can do."

"Charlie, Charlie, Charlie," Mr. Chalmers said, starting to smile. It was a crisis he'd have to handle carefully. A single careless word, and he'd lose his son-in-law altogether. "I appreciate your frankness, but you're being naïve. We have a long-standing gentlemen's agreement with our wholesalers. They have their own salesmen. It would be highly unethical for us to send one of our own men into their territory. You would run into conflicts. Also, since you've been frank with me, I'll return the compliment. Am I the head of this company, or are you?"

"You are, of course," Charlie answered.

"Then you don't think an idea of this sort should come from me?"

"What difference does it make who it comes from, as long as the idea has merit? I've been talking this over with Mr. Henry for over a year. He's behind me completely. Even Mrs. Fleck, your secretary, has been working in her spare time on a list of every store we've ever dealt with. I have my routes all worked out, and I'm all set to go. All I need is your permission. I hope you'll give it to me. As far as conflicts with these wholesalers and their salesmen, I suggest we write them and tell them what we're doing. If they don't like it, then I suggest we drop them completely. They couldn't do much less for us than they've been doing for the last few years anyway. And I don't think they will drop us. I think they'll wake up and do a better job for us."

"Could I get a word in here, Charlie?" Mr. Chalmers asked, still smiling. "There's one element that you apparently haven't even considered. That's your wife, Lucy. How will she get along with you away during the week?"

"I don't think Lucy has anything to do with it," Charlie answered coldly. "We're talking about business, and not my personal life."

"The two are interwoven. What sort of life would you be giving Lucy?"

"She could come with me if she wants to."

Mr. Chalmers laughed. "With two small children?"

"Good Lord," Charlie said angrily. "Other men go on the road, and their wives survive."

"Charlie," Mr. Chalmers said patiently, "I'm going to compromise with you. I'm not going to tell you no, and I'm not going to say yes. As far as your going out right away, the answer is no. But perhaps in a year or so, if conditions seem ripe, we'll consider the whole thing again. Will that suit you?"

"No, sir, it won't," Charlie answered promptly. "I don't think this company will last more than a year or so unless someone goes out selling and looking for new products right now."

"Then my answer is no," Mr. Chalmers said, his jaw set. "I've given you my reasons, and we won't discuss it any further."

"Then I'm afraid I'll have to hand in my resignation, Mr. Chalmers."

Mr. Chalmers walked toward Charlie and put his hand on his arm. "Of course I won't accept it. We like the work you're doing out here. We want you to stay with us. I wouldn't allow you to leave us even if you wanted to. And I don't think you do. Let's drop this for the time being." He walked back to his desk. "You expressed an interest in my manuscript on the Hadley Canal. I'd be happy to let you read it before it goes off to the printers. How would it be if I dropped it off at your house some evening soon?"

Charlie looked at him for a moment without answering. Then he said, "Thank you, Mr. Chalmers. I'd enjoy reading your manuscript very much." He left the office.

"How did it go?" Ralph Henry asked him. He had been waiting out in the factory yard.

"The answer was no."

The foreman swore. "Did he let you explain what you wanted to do?"

"The answer was still no."

"What do you plan to do now?"

"I told him I'd quit."

"Are you going to?"

"I haven't yet made up my mind."

Henry rubbed his scalp for a moment. "Wait here for me," he said. Then he turned and walked rapidly toward the office door.

"Why, Lowell," Lydia Chalmers exclaimed, when she found her husband sitting alone in his study at one o'clock that afternoon. "What on earth brings you home at this hour? Is something wrong?"

"I'm afraid a number of things are wrong," he answered wearily.

"At the plant?"

"At the plant."

She walked across the study and perched herself on a straight wooden chair, her hands folded in her lap, her lips a thin, worried line.

"Would you care to discuss it with me?"

"I'd like to discuss it with someone," he answered. "That much I know." He gazed out the window for a moment. It had clouded over during the morning, and a warm spring drizzle had started to fall. "Do you remember our conversation last fall about Charlie going out selling?"

"Quite clearly," she answered.

"Charlie asked me about it today, and I told him no. I told him that in a few years we might consider it again, but for the present the answer was no. I was friendly about it, but also quite firm."

Lydia nodded impatiently.

"I suppose he was angry," Lowell continued. "He talked about leaving the Company, but I don't think he really meant it. I think he left my office resigned to the fact that I had said no."

"It sounds to me as though you handled our son-in-law extremely well," Lydia answered.

"I thought so myself. But two minutes after Charlie was gone, Ralph Henry burst into my office. He said that if I didn't allow Charlie to do what he wanted to do that he'd quit, and every man out there would quit with him. He said some nasty things about me, Lydia. Things that hurt deeply."

"Such as what?" Lydia asked, her face suddenly pale.

"He said I was the one who should quit. That I should go write my books somewhere else. That as a businessman I was no good, Lydia. That's exactly what he said. That I was no good."

"How foolish of Ralph," Lydia answered with icy calm. "I hope you allowed *him* to resign."

"But I couldn't, Lydia. I honestly think every man would have walked off the job with him."

"Then what did you do?"

"What could I do? I called Charlie back into my office and told him I had reconsidered. Starting next Monday, he's going out as a salesman."

"I see," Lydia answered. "I realize that you probably don't need any advice from me, but my suggestion now would be for you to reconsider once more. Let Ralph Henry quit if he feels he must. But I don't think he will. He's bluffing, Lowell. It's just simple blackmail."

"Lydia, listen to me, I've been thinking over this whole business. What's wrong with letting the boy go out? A lot of things Charlie said to me make sense. Perhaps he *can* increase our business. Perhaps we *do* need a sales organization of our own. Our business has been slipping badly. Maybe he can do something about it."

She shook her head. "It's a matter of principle," she answered. "Whether Charlie should go out selling or not is beside the point. You've allowed him to push you around. You've been bluffed into something. This is all Charlie will need. From this moment on he'll do exactly as he pleases out there, and you won't dare stop him."

"But what else can I do?"

"You can call Ralph Henry this instant and tell him his resignation is accepted. Throw it right back in his face."

"And the whole plant will close with him."

"I don't believe it will. I think it will all blow over."

"I just can't face it," he said wearily. "I'm just not good at this sort of thing." He pressed his hands against his forehead. "Why do these things have to come up in the first place?"

"Because our son-in-law Charlie is determined to have his own way. That's why. That's the nub of it right there, Lowell. He wants to run things."

"I'm just not up to fights like this, Lydia. They tear me completely to pieces. Why don't we just let the boy do what he wants to do? He talks about doubling our business. Let's allow him to go out and see how hard it is. He's full of confidence now. Perhaps he won't be so confident in a few months."

"It's a matter of principle," Lydia repeated sharply. "Either we stay in control of The Hadley Company, or we don't."

"He even offered to take a fifty per cent reduction in salary, Lydia. He wants desperately to sell."

"All in good time, Lowell. When he sells, we must be the ones to decide. Not him."

He sighed. "I just wish there were some other way of handling it. How about Lucy? Can't she make him see reason?"

"The way to handle it is for you to call Ralph Henry this instant."

"I can't do it," he repeated. "I just can't face it. You don't know what it's like to have someone shouting insults at you right in your own office. I'm just not up to things like this. If you want to call Ralph Henry, then do it, but I simply can't cope with it."

Lydia sat quietly for a moment, thinking. Then she stood, patted her husband on the head, and walked toward the hallway.

"Be of good cheer," she said. "Perhaps I can find a solution for you."

She climbed the stairs and walked rapidly to her sewing room. Then she sat by her phone, drumming her fingers on the table. Finally she dialed a number.

"It's your mother, darling. You weren't taking a nap, I hope." She paused. "You poor dear. I'm terribly sorry. I wouldn't have disturbed you for the world except that your poor father has just returned from the factory as upset as I've ever seen him in his entire life." Again she paused. "Oh, heavens no. His health is fine. It's about your Charlie." She bit off each word sharply. "Apparently, from what I can gather, your Charlie has made an extremely ugly scene out there today."

Again she paused, listening. "Yes, it's about that business you warned me about last fall. Charlie stormed into your father's office today, shouting and yelling, demanding that he be allowed to do exactly as he wishes. I gather he hurled a number of nasty insults at your poor father. Really a most disgraceful exhibition, darling."

She paused. "What could he do? After all, Charlie is a member of our family. He's your husband, darling. If he hadn't been, your father would have thrown him out of his office in one minute flat." She listened a moment. "Yes, of course he gave him his way. With Charlie practically out of his mind with rage, what else could he do? He hoped you could make him see reason. The point is, Lucy, it boils down to a matter of principle. That is what your father says, and I agree completely. Whether or not Charlie should go out selling right now has nothing to do with it. Your father is running the Company, not your Charlie. I hope I'm being fair, darling. I realize you will catch the brunt of this thing, but your Charlie has some personality traits which are far from pleasant. I think we both realized that the day when he came back from the war. He likes to run things, and he has no feeling about what it's like to be a member of a family." She paused.

"He does, Lucy. He insists on his own way in everything, and he doesn't care a fig for anyone else." Lydia dropped her voice and spoke feelingly for a moment. "And I like him, darling. I like him very much indeed. But someone just has to teach him a few manners. That's the crux of the matter right there. If he gets away with it this time, you can be certain that from this moment on he'll do exactly as he wishes in everything."

When she had stopped talking with Lucy, Lydia walked to the window. Below, down on the terrace, Lowell was standing in the rain. Lydia rapped angrily on the windowpane. When Lowell turned around and looked up at her, she pointed toward the terrace door. He didn't move. She pushed open the window.

"It's raining," she called. "Aren't you being rather foolish standing out there getting wet?"

"I'm enjoying the sensation," he answered.

"Whether you enjoy it or not, I suggest you consider who it is that takes care of you when you get sick."

His shoulders drooped wearily. Then he turned and walked into the house.

It started at ten o'clock, just as they were going to bed. As he emerged from the bathroom, dressed in his pajamas, Charlie glanced at Lucy and said casually, "I have some news about my job."

"Oh," she answered, equally casual. "Father give you another raise?"

"Not exactly." He moved to the bureau and fumbled in the sock drawer, finding a pair for the morning. "That was a good meal you cooked tonight, Lucy."

"Meaning my meals aren't usually good?" she asked.

"No. Just meaning it was a good meal."

He could sense it in the air. His wife was spoiling for a fight. She had been reading in bed. She closed her book and put it on the bed table.

"What's the news about your job?"

Charlie crossed the room, carrying the socks, and found a stack of clean diapers on the chair next to his side of the bed. He scooped it up and looked about the room for a place to put them. Lucy had been washing and ironing all day, and the room was cluttered with laundry. He placed the diapers on the top of his bureau, next to a mound of towels and sheets.

"As of Monday," he said, "I'll be doing what I discussed with you last fall."

Lucy rolled onto her side and fumbled for a cigarette. She lit it with the lighter on the bedside table.

"I must have forgotten what it was we discussed last fall." She exhaled a lungful of smoke toward the ceiling.

"About my going out selling for the Company."

"Oh yes," she said. "That's right. We did talk about it, didn't we?"

He nodded, standing by the window, listening to the rain drip off the eaves. If there was to be an argument, he preferred to be on his feet. Rest, if it came at all, could come later.

"Is that your only news?" she asked.

"I just thought you'd be interested."

"Oh, I am," she answered sarcastically. "Thank you so much for letting me know." She rolled on her side again and crushed out her cigarette. Then she snapped off the light. "Shall we say good-by now, or do you want to wait until Monday?" When he didn't answer she slid down under the covers. "If you have no objection, I think I'll go to sleep."

He stood in the darkness for a while, listening to the familiar sounds of the house. The electric clock in the thermostat was humming, and across the hall he could hear Lydia stirring restlessly in her sleep. The window was open. A cool breeze blew in on his legs.

After a while he moved across the room and sat on the chair. The evening was far from over. He knew Lucy better than that. She was no more asleep than he was. How would she start it? he wondered. Would the light suddenly go on, and would he be face to face with cold fury, or would she merely start to cry? It wouldn't make too much difference, he decided. His mind was made up. Nothing she could do or say would change it.

When he heard the smothered moan coming from Lucy's side of the bed, he thought calmly that she hadn't cried in over a year. Would it affect him

112

the same way it had at first? he wondered. Tears were frightening. He could listen unmoved as strangers cried, other peoples' wives and other peoples' children, but his own wife's tears were like a hand squeezing blood out of some internal organ. It must be guilt, he thought. Somehow, he himself must be to blame.

Perhaps he should burst into tears himself. That would make quite a scene. He smiled. Lucy crying, him crying, the noise waking up Lydia and Roswell. They could all make an evening of it. He stood up and turned on the light.

Lucy was lying on her back. Her face was red, and her cheeks were already streaked with tears. Was this an essential part of every marriage? he wondered. If it was, how long could he stand it? It was hard to feel quite the same about a woman once you had made her cry. He moved to the foot of the bed and grabbed the bedposts.

"Are you ready to discuss it?" he asked coldly. "Or shall I just let you cry?"

Lucy rolled onto her stomach and clutched her pillow with her arms.

"All right," he said. "I'll just let you cry."

He walked to the bureau and took out a sweater. The cellar would be cold.

"If you want me," he said, "I'll be reading." He started for the door.

"Charlie," she sobbed, her voice catching. She was leaning on one elbow, her eyes swollen. "I mean very little to you, don't I?"

"You mean a great deal to me," he answered.

"You don't love me at all."

"Of course I love you," he answered.

What surprised him about himself was his own voice. It was calm and quiet, as though it belonged to another person. He wanted to scream at her, to lift her off the bed and fling her against a wall.

"Of course I love you," he repeated.

"How can you?" she sobbed, "when you always do exactly as you want to. You never care a thing about my feelings in anything."

Only once before in his life, he thought, had he ever felt exactly as he did at this moment. During the war in Italy an artillery shell had landed less than ten feet from where he was standing. It had stunned him for an instant. When he came to, he had crawled into the shell crater and had stared at the blue Italian sky, wondering what he was doing there.

"Do you want a divorce?" he asked, his voice flat and cold.

"Charlie," she gasped, a note of panic in her voice.

"Well, that's what we're working up to, isn't it? If I'm so terrible to live with, why keep on with it?"

"Charlie," she gasped again.

"I mean it," he said harshly. "Let's be honest for a change. We've been working up to this, haven't we?" He pointed a finger at her. "If you start crying again, I'll walk out on you, Lucy. I mean it. I'm sick of your tears." He paused, watching her. He heard no sound of crying. "You tell me I never do anything you want me to do. Since I've been home, that's all I have done.

Every single important decision we've made has been your decision. I'm living where you wanted to live. I'm working where you wanted me to work. We see the people you want to see. We live your life from start to finish. Everything you've wanted, you have. You've been running things, and you know it."

He hesitated again, watching her. She had covered her face with her hands. "And now we're at the bottom of it all. We're talking about something that really matters to me. You're meddling into my job, and I won't have it. You will not turn me into putty like your father. And that's what he is. He's weak, and your mother squeezes him this way and that. I'm not putty, and you are not going to push me around. I'm sick of it."

"You've thought all this out, haven't you?" Her voice had changed. It was now as cold as ice.

"Yes, I have. You married me. You're my wife. It's time you broke away from your mother."

"What's my mother got to do with this? Why must we drag her into everything?"

"Because she's mixed up in everything. She's a meddler. She likes to run things. Let her run her husband, but not me. I can run my own affairs."

"And you plan to leave me at home to shift for myself?"

"If you insist on putting it that way, yes."

"Then my feelings do mean nothing to you."

"Not on the subject of my job. I'd be glad to have you help me, but I won't have any more meddling from either you or your mother."

"But my mother knows nothing about this."

"Stop lying to me," he said quietly. "She knows all about it. You went over and discussed it with her last fall. I could tell by the way your father reacted today. Then he left the office early today, and I'm sure he told your mother what happened out there. I suppose she called you. I don't like it, Lucy."

"Then it's my turn to ask you if you want a divorce?"

"No, I don't. I liked you when I married you, and I can like you again. But I don't like you right now. If you want to dominate some man, you picked the wrong husband. If you really knew how pathetic your father is, Lucy, and what an unhappy life he leads, you wouldn't be so anxious to do the same thing to me. Your mother runs him."

"You really hate her, don't you?"

He shook his head. "I don't hate her, but someday she'd better watch out. I might lose control of myself and kick her in the teeth."

"Mother was right," Lucy said icily. "She said that someone would have to teach you some manners."

"Then you *have* discussed all this with her?"

"Let's drop it," Lucy answered. "You plan to live your own life, and there's no point in discussing it further."

"No," he answered. "Let's say just one more thing. Thanks to you and your mother, The Hadley Company nearly folded today. When your father turned me down, I told Ralph Henry I was thinking of quitting. He went in to your father and said if I quit, he'd quit, and he'd take every man off with him. He meant it. He wasn't bluffing. You and your mother nearly fixed things for good out there. You'd better stay out of our business from now on. The stockholders' meeting is the place for you and your mother to complain. Leave us alone the rest of the time." He left the bedroom and went down the stairs.

He sat at the kitchen table for a while, listening to the rain dripping in the gutter pipes outside. In the distance he could hear the cars on the avenue, their tires whining on the wet pavement. He was hungry. He opened the icebox door and found a cube of stale cheese and a quart of milk. Also the icebox light was burned out. He put the cheese and the milk on the table, and reached over a mound of salad and yesterday's meat to remove the dead bulb. His elbow nudged over a fresh bottle of cream, soaking his pajama bottoms and spreading a film of cream over the kitchen floor. When the icebox light was working again, he mopped up the kitchen floor and rinsed out his pajamas in the kitchen sink. Then he sat damp and cold, eating cheese and drinking milk.

The house seemed much too quiet. Since March, water had been leaking into the cellar, and he knew the sump pump should be working. From March to June it flicked on and off, every forty-five seconds, as regular as a pulse, dimming the lights, its hum audible through the kitchen floor. When he had finished the milk, he opened the cellar door and peered down the stairs. The cellar floor was flooded with at least an inch of water.

It must be a fuse, he decided, fumbling about in a kitchen drawer where Lucy kept the new ones. A moment later he waded across the cellar floor, throwing off the main switch before he replaced the burned-out fuse. He stood for a moment ankle deep in water, listening to the water gushing through the pump, his feet numb with cold.

Finally he climbed back up the cellar stairs and walked to the living room. He stretched out on the couch, covering himself with pillows, shivering and miserable.

This fight with Lucy, he knew, had been building up for a long time, since he'd come back from the army a year and a half before. It wasn't really that she was trying to run him, he thought. There was nothing mean or calculating about Lucy. She knew what brought her happiness in her life, and she saw no reason why the pattern should be disturbed. A life that consisted of nothing but children, sump pumps, burned-out fuses, and mopping the kitchen floor, with an office and a job for the husband, and the Garden Club for the wife, could be a very pleasant one. Tulips to plant in season, the lawn to mow, the golf course, a place on an island. Eventually there could be retirement, grandchildren, a workshop in the cellar, or water colors of sand dunes.

It was surprising, he thought, how important The Hadley Company had become in his life. After resisting the pressure to work for the family company, he now was determined that it must survive. When he'd first met Lucy, when he'd first stepped into the Lawn Street house, he thought it was just money that kept a family together. But money, he'd learned, made no difference at all. The families that survived were those who kept whatever it was that had made them a family in the first place. Without The Hadley Company, the Chalmers and their cousins and their aunts would be nothing, just people living comfortable, contented lives until they died. The Company was the magnet that held them together.

This was important to him, he decided. It must have been this that attracted him to Lucy in the first place. He liked the idea of being part of a family, and he was determined to be the head of it someday. Perhaps his portrait would hang in a hallway, and his great-grandchildren would be able to say casually, "Oh yes, he was quite a man, in his own small way."

It was also a personal matter, he decided. If he didn't set a goal for himself—some goal, any goal—eventually would come a day of reckoning when he'd have to face himself, as Mr. Chalmers would, and admit to himself that he was a coward, and that it all had been a waste of time. He'd never be famous, or even well known, but at least some descendant might bless him for not being soft.

Upstairs Roswell had started to cry. He listened for a while. When he heard Lucy cross the hall, he left the couch and climbed the stairs. He found Lucy holding Roswell in her arms, rocking her.

"What's her trouble?" he asked.

"I just changed her," Lucy answered. "It can't be that."

"She's probably hungry. I'll go warm up a bottle."

He fed Roswell the bottle himself. He loved his children at night. They smelled of sleep and contentment. By day, no matter how young they were, they asserted themselves, warning that they would eventually rebel and go their own way. But at night they were babies, innocent and warm.

"You like Ros, don't you?" Lucy asked. She was sitting across the room, watching him. She was pale.

"I love all my family. You, Lydia, and Roswell. I love you all more than anything in the whole world."

"I love my family too, Charlie."

He nodded. "I know you do."

Roswell finally sighed and fell asleep in his arms. He put her back in the crib, and Lucy tucked a blanket around her.

"Now what?" she whispered, facing him.

"I was hoping you'd invite me back to bed."

"I was hoping you would think things over downstairs."

"I did," he answered. "You can let me do what I think is best for our family in my own way, or you can return to your mother. I mean this, Lucy."

She reached for his hand. Her fingers were cold.

"Promise me one——"

"I'll promise you nothing," he interrupted. "Nothing except a husband

116

who is doing what he thinks ought to be done. Now do we go back to bed, or don't we?"

"Yes, we go back to bed," she whispered, leading him across the hall.

"Incidentally," he said, "I was fixing the light in the icebox, and I spilled the cream."

"It doesn't matter," she answered crawling into bed, hugging him, her whole body cold. "We can eat eggs for breakfast and put milk in our coffee."

"I also drank all the milk."

"It doesn't matter," she repeated, hugging him fiercely, both of them shivering. "And thank you for fixing the light."

nineteen

IT WAS RAINING. THE THUNDERSTORM HAD MOVED ON TO THE EAST, LEAVING behind it a steady downpour. Steam had collected on the windshield of Charlie's car, and he drove slowly, peering out along the headlight beams. When he saw a neon sign ahead, he slowed and pulled off the road into the parking lot. Then he sat looking at the café for a moment, wondering if it were the sort of place he wanted. It was after nine o'clock, and he was tired. He needed a good meal before he found a motel for the night.

"Eva's," the neon sign read. "We like Truckers." The outside of the café looked like thousands of others, cinder blocks painted white, a tar-paper roof, the flickering sign, and the gravel parking lot littered with paper. Finally he stepped out of his car and ran across the parking lot, dodging the puddles, his shoulders hunched against the rain.

Inside, the café smelled of frying fat and grease. There was a counter with a row of stools, and the usual stainless steel coffee urns. There were cigarette- and gum-vending machines, toothpicks, straws, mustard and catsup bottles, and a juke box. There were also two booths along one wall. A plump middle-aged woman was wiping the counter with a damp rag.

"Howdy," she said. "I'm Eva. Wet enough for you?"

He nodded. When it was cold, they asked you if it was cold enough. When it was hot, was it hot enough. When it rained, was it wet enough.

"Can I get something to eat?"

"You just made it," she answered. "I was closing up for the night."

He walked to the counter and handed her a dollar bill.

"I have to make a phone call first. I'll need some telephone change."

She punched the cash register and slid the silver across the counter toward him. When he walked to the phone booth, she moved around the counter and looked out the café door, into the parking lot.

The circuits were busy. It took the operator nearly two minutes to put through his call. While he waited, Charlie leaned against the phone booth door and watched the small rubber fan above his head.

It had been a week since he'd called Lucy, and more than two weeks since he'd last seen her. He hadn't planned to be away that long. In the last fifteen months, since he'd first started out selling for the Company, he'd missed only two week ends at home, even though more than once it had meant a good deal of extra driving.

"I feel guilty when I don't get home on the week ends," he had told her once, after driving all night from Buffalo.

"Don't," she had replied. "If you want to stay away, you stay away." And she had then added, "Don't you ever say, when you stop traveling around all over the place, that you had to give it up because your wife insisted on it. When you give it up, if you ever do, it's going to be your decision and not mine."

What had he accomplished in the last fifteen months? he wondered as he waited for the sound of Lucy's voice at the other end of the line. In some ways, quite a bit. In other ways, nothing. He had improved the Company's business. A single look at the balance sheet would prove that. He'd visited every hardware store that sold Hadley knives, and a lot of stores that didn't sell Hadley knives. The Hadley Company had less than five hundred outlets when he had first started out, and now they had over eight hundred. There were two new girls with Mrs. Fleck back in Mr. Chalmers' office handling mail. That was another change he had made. It was the start toward a sales department. Then, completely by chance, he had opened up an entirely new field for The Hadley Company.

Six months before, he'd met a man in a Rochester hotel who was traveling about checking the kitchen equipment in a chain of thirty hotels. From him he had received an order for a thousand dollars' worth of heavy-duty kitchen knives. It wasn't a large order, but it had led to more. He'd gone to New York and visited the buying offices for every hotel chain in the country. In all, he'd obtained nearly twenty thousand dollars' worth of business that way. The profit from this alone had more than paid for his salary. As a salesman he had been successful, but he still had not accomplished what he had set out to do. He had nearly doubled The Hadley Company's business in fifteen months, but as yet he had found nothing new for the company to make.

One thing he was certain of after fifteen months of visiting stores. The Hadley Company had to enter a new field. That was the way all the old companies had managed to survive. If something they had been making for years became outmoded by something new, they bought out the new patents and started making that. They might have started out making scythes, but they were now making mowing machines; or if they made their first million building wagons, they were now making millions more building automobiles. To survive, a company had to gamble, to try to foresee the future. If they couldn't make a new product themselves, they had to buy out a company that could. After fifteen months he had improved The Hadley Company's old business, but the future looked just about the same as it had when he started out. He had prolonged the factory's life, but he hadn't cured its disease.

"Your party is on the line," the operator said, interrupting his thoughts.
"Hi," he said, "it's Charlie. You weren't asleep, I hope."

The phone had rung just as Lucy had dropped off to sleep. She stumbled out into the hall and fumbled in the darkness for the light switch. Who, she wondered, could be calling at this hour? Certainly not her mother. She had finally trained her mother not to call in the afternoon, nor after nine at night. She heard the hum of the long-distance wires.

Then Charlie said, "Hi. You weren't asleep, I hope."

"Charlie?"

He laughed. "Who were you expecting? I just called to find out how you were."

"Where are you?"

"In a café just east of Cleveland."

"When are you coming home?"

"I'm on my way right now."

They were quiet a moment until he asked, "What are you doing?"

"Sitting in the hall without a stitch on. It's hot here. Simply awful."

"We're having a rainstorm."

Again he was quiet. Lucy could feel the wicker seat of the chair pressing into her bare legs. Her skin was sticky and warm.

"Are you awake, Lucy?" he asked.

"More or less."

"I had an idea. How about you hopping a plane tomorrow and coming out here? We could take a few days off together, and work our way back east in my car. Bring your golf clubs and mine. We'll play a few courses together."

"How could I?" she asked. "How about the children?"

"Won't your mother take them for a few days?"

"She's down at the Island."

"Couldn't you find some woman to come in?"

"Just like that?"

"Well, hell," he answered, "bring the kids along too. We can swing up through northern New England and make a real trip out of it. I'm about due for my vacation, anyway."

"That's hardly my idea of a vacation," she answered. "Anyway, Mother is expecting me down with her for the month of August."

"I wish you'd do it," he insisted. "We've never taken a trip anywhere together."

"Charlie," she answered firmly, now thoroughly awake, "I can't. Think of my end of things for a change."

"All right," he answered, giving up. "I was just feeling lonely for my family."

"Then come home."

"I'm on my way."

He hesitated a moment.

"What did you do today?"

"The usual things," she answered. "Fed the children, washed dishes, hung out the laundry. Nothing new except the washing machine exploded."

"Exploded?"

"The door flew open, and about a thousand gallons of water poured out onto the floor. It took me a whole hour to mop it up."

"Maybe we need a new machine."

"It's just the door," she answered. "It needs someone to fix the catch. I'm helpless about things like that."

"I'll do it when I get home."

"Do you think you'll be here by Friday?"

"I probably will."

"I thought we might have a few people in for dinner. Eight or ten. Would you mind?"

"Why should I mind?"

"You always seem so exhausted when you get back from one of your trips."

The operator interrupted, warning them that their time was up.

"Dinner sounds fine," he said hastily. "I'll be home Friday."

Lucy heard the wires hum for an instant. Then she hung up and reached for a cigarette. When she lit it, her body looked paper white in the glow from the match. At least this was one advantage of living alone, she thought. With Charlie away, she could walk about the house naked whenever she felt like it.

Down the hall she heard Lydia stirring restlessly in her sleep. She opened the nursery door and looked inside. Lydia was awake, staring at the ceiling, her body drenched with perspiration.

Lucy went into the bathroom and filled a bowl with cool water. For the next five minutes she bathed Lydia with a washcloth, blowing on her damp skin to cool her.

"Your father just called on the telephone," she said. "He's on his way home."

She put Lydia back in her bed and kissed her bare stomach, making her laugh. Roswell woke up and pulled herself up in her crib.

"Now I suppose you want a bath too," Lucy said to her younger daughter. She got a fresh bowl of water and sponged Roswell's neck and back.

Her children were growing up. Lydia was almost three and a half, and Roswell nearly two. Would they like each other, she wondered, when they were older? Probably not. They would be just as different as she, Anne, and Polly had been.

"You two terrible creatures go to sleep," she commanded fondly as she left their room. "I want no more nonsense out of you."

She loved her children as much as she loved life itself. How could a woman exist without babies? she wondered.

Instead of going back to her bedroom, Lucy went down the stairs to the kitchen. She was thirsty. She opened the icebox door, the cold air spilling down against her bare legs. The ginger ale was all gone. She poked about among plastic bags filled with lettuce and cheese, looking for a stray bottle. There was nothing except a jar of peanut butter and another jar of mayonnaise.

She wrenched an ice tray loose and carried it to the sink. That was another advantage in having a husband away, she thought. If she felt like drinking a glass of ice-cold sherry at eleven o'clock at night, she could do it without offering an explanation. She carried the sherry back up the stairs to her bedroom.

Charlie, she thought, had sounded disappointed when she told him she couldn't meet him in Cleveland. She probably could have met him if she'd wanted to. He'd certainly been after her steadily enough, during the past year, urging her to go with him on his trips, calling it a vacation for both of them. He didn't seem to understand that to look at miles and miles of open road, and then see some city like Albany, or Rochester, or Buffalo, or Cleveland at the end of it, was her idea of nothing.

She liked it at home, and she really didn't have much fun anywhere else. If she occasionally needed a change, she got that down at the Island. She lived a life she liked, and there seemed no particular reason to change it. Charlie ought to be thankful that she did like her home. Some wives were always whining to be taken places. It was probably dull of her, but she'd be perfectly contented never to go anywhere the rest of her life. It all didn't make sense, she thought. Philosophers urged people to seek peace of mind through inward contentment and satisfaction. Well, she was contented, and she was satisfied, and all that made her was dull. To be interesting and exciting, it appeared that one must be slightly neurotic. I like my home, she said to herself, and I like my life. There is no reason to disturb it.

She leaned back against the headboard of her bed and glanced about her room. It had changed, with Charlie away so much of the time. It was as though she had reverted to adolescence. Most of the books in the house were piled here and there about the floor, on tables, or on the top of Charlie's half of the bed. She had brought the radio upstairs and set it up on the bed table. Damp, washed stockings hung from a curtain rod, drying in an open window. Her dress and slip lay across the back of a chair, and three pairs of her shoes were under her bed. There was an empty ginger ale bottle on the window sill, and a glass half full of melted ice water. This is my true personality, she thought. Remove a man even temporarily from my life, and I become lazy. My bedroom, instead of a neat, efficient cog in the machine that people call a home, becomes a sanctuary where a woman can do as she wishes, including lying naked and alone on the top of her bed, sipping ice-cold sherry at eleven o'clock at night.

She raised a bare leg and examined it in the glow that came from the street. Was there anyone who thought she was pretty? she wondered. She raised her other leg, and then lowered them both slowly onto the bed, feeling her stomach muscles harden. Was this all there was to marriage? If it was, there could be nothing so overrated in the whole world. She squirmed upward again, draining the last of the sherry, letting the final frigid drops linger at the base of her tongue.

Did she smell good? she wondered. Did Charlie enjoy making love to her? Probably not. For every time love was interesting, it was ten times a chore. Her mother had packed a book in with her wedding things when she and Charlie had been married. She had read it after Charlie left her to go overseas. From it she had learned just one thing. To be competent in bed, a woman had to train like an athlete and sleep late in the morning. Events all conspired to make physical love in marriage difficult—familiarity, fatigue, children, meals to cook, washing machines that exploded, a cellar that flooded four months of the year.

She heard a burst of laughter come through the open bedroom window. Across the street the Robinsons were having a party. She could be there, she thought, if Charlie were home. There were probably all sorts of parties that she could go to if her husband were something besides a wandering salesman.

She rolled off her bed and walked to the window. Her skin tingled. What would the reaction be at Ed Robinson's party, she wondered, if suddenly she were to appear on the terrace with nothing on? Would the men be entranced or merely embarrassed? Through the window she noticed Ed escorting a couple out the front walk to the street. She stood motionless, feeling the warm breeze on her bare skin. Could they see her? she wondered. Suddenly she hoped they could. It was part of the dream she'd been having lately, where she was always naked, and some man, or men, were making love to her. No specific man that she knew or had ever seen before, but a demon lover that came only in dreams.

Ed Robinson disappeared back into his house, and the street was quiet again. She walked over to her bed and turned on the radio.

"Here we go into inning number eleven," a familiar voice said, "with the score Boston two, and Chicago two."

There were always baseball games, Lucy thought. Somehow or other she had become quite interested in baseball during the last year. It gave her a choice of something to do in the afternoons—either a nap or a baseball game on the radio. She turned the volume low and lay on her back, listening. People were laughing again at the Robinsons'.

The woman was still wiping the counter when Charlie left the phone booth. He took a menu from the rack and headed for a booth at the far end of the café. The woman followed him, carrying a glass of water.

"Wet enough for you?" she asked again. Then she said, "I guess I asked you that before. We got a special on vegetable soup tonight."

After eating in hundreds of cafés during the past fifteen months, Charlie had become wary of specials. He said, "I'd like some kind of steak, and two or three rolls if you have them."

"Coffee?"

"Milk."

122

"Coffee will keep you awake if you're planning to drive on east tonight."

She must be the curious type, Charlie decided. She probably played games with herself to relieve the boredom, trying to guess what her customers were, where they came from, and where they were going.

"Milk," he repeated.

The woman shrugged and moved back toward the kitchen.

There was the usual selection in the juke box, western, hillbilly, and jazz. He put in a quarter and punched three keys. He didn't care much what music he listened to. He liked it all, slow, sweet, fast, or sentimental. Jazz was something you could count on wherever you were.

While he listened to the music, he walked to a window and stood watching the rain. What would remain of all this in ten thousand years? he wondered. A few roads, piles of rubble that once were cities, traces of rust here and there that were now automobiles, and drifting sand?

Was there a time in every civilization, he wondered, when they who lived in it knew they had been born in a wonderful age? Could the Romans of Caesar's time have considered themselves any more fortunate than the Americans of today? You could feel it as you drove about the country. America had no real problems any more. It was all a success, one large, smoothly functioning machine. The cities were prosperous, the farms endlessly fertile, the people well fed, and the children well educated. The dreams of the pioneers had come true. They had lived and died believing in the future, and now the future was at hand.

When he saw the steak being put on the table he moved away from the window.

"You live anywhere near New York?" the woman asked him, lingering by the booth.

"Fairly near," he answered, buttering a roll.

"How far?"

"A hundred miles or so. Why?"

"I just wondered." She walked back to the kitchen, and a moment later he heard her talking with someone behind the door. She reappeared carrying a dish of limp green beans. "You some kind of a salesman?" she asked, lingering again.

He nodded, cutting the steak.

"I figured that when I heard you put in the call to your wife."

She was more than curious, he decided. She was inquisitive.

"You have children?"

"Yes, I do," he answered, putting down his fork, staring at her.

"I suppose you think I'm nosy."

"That's all right. What else would you like to know? My wife's name is Lucy, and I have two daughters, Lydia and Roswell."

She nodded, watching him.

"Can I give you anything else?" she asked.

Peace, he thought. Peace and quiet, so he could listen to the juke box.

"I guess that's all until dessert," he answered.

She turned and walked away. Again he heard her talking to someone in the kitchen.

She probably typed him as a lonely salesman, he thought. Probably most of the men who came into the café were crazy to talk. He was just as lonely as everyone else, but he'd found it never did much good to talk with people he'd never see again. He wished Lucy would go on some of his trips with him. If he could get her away from home for a week or so, if he could be with her driving along a highway, or in a hotel in some city neither of them had ever seen before, it would be easier to make her see why he wanted to do something with his life. The whole country was a vast flood tide. You could sense it when you moved around. If Lucy would just once join him on a trip, she might understand why he hated the thought of becoming marooned in a stagnant backwash for the rest of his life.

"How's the steak?" the woman asked him, moving toward the booth.

"Very good."

She paused. "Could I sit down a moment?"

"Sure," he answered, surprised.

She sat opposite him, leaning her elbows on the table. Her eyes were pale blue, the only color visible in her plump round face.

"I got a favor I'd like to ask you," she said. "I got someone back in the kitchen who wants to get to New York."

The other voice Charlie had heard a few moments before had been that of a girl. He said nothing.

"She's just a kid. No more than nineteen. A good kid."

"They always are," he answered quietly.

"She isn't what you think. She's from a farm near here. I gave her a job because she was broke. She's no tramp. She could be my own daughter, the way I feel about her."

"If you're about to ask me to give her a ride, the answer is no," Charlie said. "There are laws about things like that, and anyway I'm not interested."

"She'll be no trouble to you. She's got enough money to buy her own food. She just needs a ride."

"How about truckers? They are always willing to lend a nineteen-year-old girl a hand."

"I don't want this girl to have nothing to do with no trucker."

"I wish I could help you," Charlie answered, "but I can't. I don't pick up hitchhikers. Particularly girls."

"Maybe if you see this girl you'll change your mind."

He hesitated. He did want to see her. If he didn't, she'd haunt him for months. His thoughts would be full of a girl he'd never seen, a girl who was just a voice behind a kitchen door at Eva's Café, ten miles east of Cleveland.

"Even if I do see her I'll tell her just what I've told you already," he answered.

The woman stood up and walked rapidly toward the kitchen. Charlie waited, a slight prickle along his spine.

124

Thank God she was ugly, he thought, when the kitchen door opened and the girl walked toward him. She was as thin and as straight as a stick, her figure neither bad nor good, but nonexistent. She was wearing a dark skirt and a blouse stained with grease from a frying pan.

"Eva said you wanted to see me," she said, standing next to the table. She was terrified.

"What do you want to go to New York for?" he asked. The side zipper on her skirt was broken. She had gathered it with two safety pins, and through the gap Charlie could see bare flesh.

"I just want to get a job."

"New York is filled with girls who just want jobs. You've got a job here."

It might be fun, he thought, to take a girl like this in hand. What a difference fifty dollars could make in her appearance. A new pair of shoes, a dress, and perhaps a sweater. She'd look well in a sweater, particularly if she washed her hair. Underneath the kitchen smoke her hair looked blond. She also had nice eyes, large and frightened, like a doe.

"I can't take you with me," he said. "I'd like to, but I can't."

"I don't want anything except a ride. You won't have to pay for my food or anything like that."

"I know," he answered. "What's your name?"

"Arlene."

It was the devil, he thought. A devil named Arlene was standing next to him in Eva's Café. The devil in a ripped skirt, and smelling of kitchen grease.

"Go on home," he said harshly. "Go on home and marry the boy next door. You'll be much better off that way."

"I want to go to New York."

"I won't take you. You know damn well I'd like to, but I won't."

She seemed less frightened now.

"Eva said she thought I could trust you."

"You can't trust me any more than you can trust the truckers."

She smiled, waiting. When he hesitated, she said, "I don't mind. I just want a ride." She spoke quietly, as though she didn't want Eva to hear her.

"Take this," he said, handing the girl a five-dollar bill. "Pay my bill with it and keep the change. Then go buy yourself a new skirt."

He stood up and walked quickly toward the café door. Outside, the rain had nearly stopped. He ran back across the parking lot and slid behind the wheel of his car. Suddenly he felt completely exhausted. He started the motor and backed his car around. Then he gunned it out onto the main road. With luck, he thought, he'd be home in time for Lucy's dinner party on Friday night.

twenty

HE ARRIVED BACK AT THE FACTORY AT ONE O'CLOCK ON FRIDAY. AS ALWAYS when he returned from one of his trips, Mrs. Fleck looked as though she wanted to throw her arms around him.

"I just knew you'd be here today," she said, beaming at him. "And we have some news for you, for a change."

"Good news, I hope."

"I'll call Mr. Chalmers," she said. "He's up at the library working on one of his manuscripts."

"Do you think I'm important enough to disturb his writing?" he asked, grinning.

"As far as I'm concerned," she answered, looking at him with frank approval, "you're important enough to disturb William Shakespeare. Go on into his office and sit down," she commanded, waving her hand. "I'll get him right over."

While he waited in Mr. Chalmers' office, he called Lucy.

"Thank God you're back," she told him. "Eight people are coming tonight, and I was just beginning to worry about what I'd do without a husband. We need gin, Charlie. Pick up a bottle on your way home."

Mr. Chalmers walked into the office, holding out his hand.

"Welcome home," he shouted. His face was bright red from two recent weeks at the Island. "I was beginning to think you'd gotten lost."

"I ran into something I thought worth investigating. It took time."

"From the looks of it, it must be in there," Mr. Chalmers answered, glancing curiously at Charlie's brief case.

"In a way, it is."

"Well, open it up. Let's have a look."

"I'd like Ralph Henry to see it too, if that's all right with you."

"Certainly," Mr. Chalmers answered. He walked to his office door and asked Mrs. Fleck to call the foreman. Then he closed the office door. "While we're waiting, Charlie, I'd like to talk with you privately about a personal matter." He walked back to his desk and sat on a corner of it. "It's about your wife Lucy. Mrs. Chalmers and I are getting worried about her."

"Is something wrong with her?" Charlie asked.

Mr. Chalmers just looked at him for a moment. Then he said, "Dammit, I know you well enough and I respect you enough to come right out with it. When are you going to give that girl of ours a vacation?"

"I called her earlier this week. I tried to get her to join me in Cleveland."

"Cleveland?" Mr. Chalmers asked angrily. "Who ever heard of a vacation in Cleveland?"

"Every time I go out on one of my trips I try to get her to go along with me."

"Do you think that's the kind of a life Lucy would like? Listen, Charlie, you've been at this selling now for almost a year and a half. You promised to double our business, and you have. We're all proud of what you've done. But isn't it time you eased up? Rest on your oars for a spell. You haven't taken any time off in over a year."

"I will when I get things organized."

"Why don't you run down to the Island with Lucy when she goes off next week to join her mother? Take the whole month of August down there. All work and no play makes Jack a dull boy. Or don't you like it at the Island?"

Charlie shrugged.

"Or is it because you don't like living with Mrs. Chalmers? I know what it's like. Mrs. Chalmers and I stayed with her parents for years, and I wasn't too fond of that either. If that's what's bothering you, you can stay at the Retreat. That's our camp. You can live your own life out there."

"That isn't it," Charlie answered.

"Then what is it?"

"Frankly, Mr. Chalmers," Charlie answered, "that island of yours bores me. Once I get there I can't find anything to do."

"Nothing to do?" Mr. Chalmers echoed in astonishment. "Good Lord, you can fish and swim, and play golf, and sail, and read. Nothing to do?" he repeated. "You're the first person I've ever heard say that. That island is part of our life, Charlie. We love it down there. Lucy loves it. We all hope you'll love it someday. I don't know what you've got in mind after this trip, but for Lucy's sake I wish you'd spend a month down there. As Mrs. Chalmers says, it's hardly fair to leave her alone so much of the time."

"She leaves me alone too," Charlie answered evenly. "If she wants me to go with her on her trips, why doesn't she go with me on mine?"

Mr. Chalmers looked at him sadly. "You can be rather unreasonable at times. You're being unreasonable right now."

"Maybe I am. But I set out to work at this job of mine, and that's what I'm going to do. If Lucy wants to help me, fine. If she wants to spend her summers on an island, that's up to her. Someday I hope to take a lot of time off. But not now. I've got too many things to do."

Ralph Henry came into the office.

"How are you, Ralph?" Charlie asked, smiling at him.

"Busy, that's how I am. You tell him about Chicago?" he asked Mr. Chalmers.

"Chicago?" Mr. Chalmers asked blankly.

"Sears Roebuck," Mrs. Fleck shouted in from the outer office.

"Oh, by Jove, that's right," Mr. Chalmers answered, snapping his fingers. He moved around his desk and sat on his chair. "Two days ago, right out of the blue and without any warning, a young man walked in here and asked if we could make a knife like this." Mr. Chalmers fumbled in his desk drawer.

"Like this," he repeated, handing Charlie a small wooden-handled kitchen knife. "I called Ralph. Ralph took one look and said he could."

"It was one of the hardware buyers from Sears Roebuck," Mrs. Fleck shouted.

"He give us an order for ten thousand," Ralph Henry added, winking at Charlie. "Said if they go that's only the beginning."

"What do you think of that, Charlie?" Mr. Chalmers asked proudly.

"Shall we tell him?" Charlie asked the foreman, smiling.

"Tell me what?" Mr. Chalmers said.

"I had Ralph make me up two or three of these knives six months ago. I thought it would be a good way for us to get into the mass market. This man from Sears Roebuck was probably named Hendrick. Is that right?"

"Then this was your doing?"

"Whose doing did you think it was?" Ralph Henry asked angrily. He turned to Charlie. "How did you work it?"

"I went out to Chicago two weeks ago. That's why I've been away so long. I just went into their buying offices and showed them everything we could make, including bayonets. That's all there was to it. So he took the kitchen knife. Can you make ten thousand of them, Ralph?"

The foreman swore. "Why do you think I'm so busy? I'm really tooling up on this thing. I figure this little knife of yours is going to go like hot cakes, and in another year we'll be making millions of them. I'm getting ready for it."

"Who's going to sell these millions?" Charlie asked, laughing.

"You are," the foreman answered calmly. "I'm going to make them, and you're going to sell them."

"Good work, Charlie," Mr. Chalmers said. "I had no idea you were behind all this. I thought this man Hendrick coming in here was just one of those things."

"Hendrick probably came back here just to look over the factory. Sears Roebuck doesn't tie up with a company without checking the operation first. Maybe they'll get somebody else to make them cheaper."

Mrs. Fleck came into the office, obviously able to restrain herself no longer.

"I told Mr. Hendrick," she said, "that if he was thinking of price alone he was in the wrong place. I told him The Hadley Company was old before Mr. Sears or Mr. Roebuck was even born."

Charlie roared with laughter. "You mean he didn't scare you with all that money, Mrs. Fleck."

"I could tell he liked what we made. If he hadn't been interested, why would he come all the way East? When I was through with that man from Chicago, he didn't do any more talking about price." She went back to her desk.

"Well now," Mr. Chalmers said, when the office was quiet, "what's your surprise for us, Charlie?"

"This," Charlie answered, opening his brief case and taking out a strip of steel.

Ralph Henry reached for it. "What is it?" he asked.

"It's a blade for a rotary lawn mower. It's rough. It has to be sharpened and bored."

"Looks easy," the foreman replied. "How many?" He grinned.

"Fifty."

"Just fifty?" Mr. Chalmers asked, obviously disappointed.

"That's right. Just fifty. But that's not what I want to talk about." Charlie walked the length of the office and sat on a window sill. "Ever since I've been traveling around I've been looking for some way of getting into another branch of this business. In the old days, the company used to make shovels and axes and plows. We gave all that up, and didn't pick up any new things to make."

"Lawn mowers?" Mr. Chalmers asked sarcastically.

"No, not lawn mowers," Charlie answered. "The company which wants us to make this blade for them makes all kinds of industrial blades and knives. At least that's what their business is. They don't have much of a business because no one's been pushing it. In fact, they're just about to go under."

"I'm afraid I don't follow all this," Mr. Chalmers said.

"They have a building with about fifty thousand dollars' worth of machinery in it. There's just about six men in all working in the plant. They only have one good customer. They make blades for one of the big farm machinery companies. They can't really expand because they need capital."

"How do we fit into this picture?" Mr. Chalmers asked.

"I'd like The Hadley Company to buy them out. I think they'd sell out at an appraisal price which wouldn't be much over a hundred thousand dollars at the most. Probably less. I talked it over with the man who owns the place. He seemed interested. He'd keep right on working there, and we'd do his selling for him. I'd do his selling for him. My feeling is that the two operations would fit in nicely together. We might lose money on it for a year or so. If worst came to worst, we could move the business back here, but I think we should operate both plants for a while to see how it went."

"How could you possibly do all this selling alone?" Mr. Chalmers asked.

"I couldn't, and I don't intend to. I think it's time we hired some other salesmen. I have some ideas on that too."

"Slow down here," Mr. Chalmers ordered, waving his hand. "One thing at a time. More salesmen, yes. I think that's a good idea. I realize that you've been carrying altogether too much of a load. I don't know how we'll find these salesmen, but I agree that we should hire them."

"I can find them," Charlie answered.

"But buying out another company?" Mr. Chalmers shook his head. "That is another matter. First of all I'd have to discuss the matter with the directors, and then it naturally would have to be approved by all the stockholders. You're talking about a capital investment here."

"I didn't expect we'd decide it today," Charlie answered. "But I'd like to

129

take Mr. Henry with me in a week or so to look the place over. I need some professional advice. It looked good to me, but I might be wrong."

"That would be up to Ralph, of course," Mr. Chalmers answered.

"I thought we'd fly out at company expense," Charlie said, grinning. "We could do it on a week end. I'd hate to take Ralph off the Sears Roebuck job."

"Perhaps we all ought to go," Mr. Chalmers said. "But not now. Let's do one thing at a time. First let's see about hiring some more sales personnel. I meant it," he added, when Charlie started to interrupt. "One thing at a time. I'd have to discuss this other matter with our directors before I made any move on it. There wouldn't be much point in it if they were lukewarm about it. Some of our directors are pretty big stockholders in the Company."

"That's fair enough," Charlie answered. "In the meantime, with your permission, I'll go ahead with some new sales personnel."

"You can't get going on that too soon to suit me," Mr. Chalmers answered. "I leave it completely up to you."

When he got out of Mr. Chalmers' office, Charlie stood for a while talking with Ralph Henry out in the Company yard.

"You'll like the man who runs this little shop out in Cleveland," Charlie said. "He's no businessman, but he knows how to make things."

"Chalmers didn't seem to like the idea of buying him out."

"He'll mull it over for a year or so, and that's all right with me. They're failing out there anyway, and a year from now we'll be able to buy them out for just about nothing. In the meantime we may have to handle a few small jobs like these lawn-mower knives just to keep them going." Charlie grinned. "What I really wanted out of Mr. Chalmers was permission to hire salesmen. I'm getting a little tired of calling on hardware stores."

Mr. Henry nodded. Then he tapped Charlie on the chest with the end of the lawn-mower blade.

"I got no more time to waste standing here gabbing with you," he said. "You handle things up front, and I'll handle them out back. You do the thinking, and I'll do the work." He grinned and walked toward the main shop.

Ralph Henry looked younger these days, Charlie thought. There was color in his cheeks, and he had even bought himself a new pair of overalls.

twenty-one

THE GIRARDS WERE THE FIRST TO ARRIVE, AND LOUISE WAS UNMISTAKABLY pregnant.

"Oh, good Lord, not again," Charlie said grinning at Danny.

"Quantity, not quality, is the Girard family motto," Danny answered.

130

"Is this three?"

"Four," Louise answered, mildly surprised that anyone might be unaware of it. She passed Charlie in the hall and headed out toward the kitchen to help Lucy. Louise had completely oriented herself to what appeared to be her main purpose in life, bearing children. Her hair was pulled back over her head in a severe knot, and she wore low heeled shoes and a cotton maternity dress.

"You're a brave, brave man, Danny," Charlie said, walking with him into the living room. "What will it be? A Martini, or something you mix yourself?"

"Nothing. I'm not drinking for the duration."

"Duration of what?"

"Our pregnancy," Danny answered. "Louise is having her usual minor troubles, and since she isn't supposed to drink I decided I wouldn't either."

"How damn dull."

Danny took the remark in good spirit. "I've become a dull fellow, or haven't you noticed?"

He was wearing a pair of gray flannels, a dark blue coat, and a red and black vest. There was a noticeable ring of flesh hanging out over his belt line, and a pendulum of fat under his chin. All that remained of his college buoyancy was his eyes. They were still bright blue and enthusiastic.

"So what's new in the knife business?" he asked, dropping a half-dozen peanuts into his mouth.

Charlie didn't have a chance to answer. The doorbell rang, and Lucy yelled from the kitchen, "Get it, will you, darling."

"Mein Host," Ed Robinson roared heartily as he came in the front door. He seized Charlie's hand. Ed had gone to Dartmouth and had never recovered from it. His clothing ran heavily to green. At Hanover he had majored in German, thinking in vague terms about a career in the State Department. However, he had ended up as a broker, and now used his German only at cocktail parties. "Greetings, Herr Banker," he said, advancing toward Danny.

If Louise Girard had been obviously pregnant, Mary Robinson was embarrassingly so. She patted Charlie's hand and said, "Hi." Then she aimed herself at the living room couch and sank into it with a sigh, as though she might never rise again. Without looking at her, Ed dropped a pillow behind her back and handed her a highball.

The last couple, the Butlers, arrived at seven-thirty. Lucy was sorry for the Butlers because no one ever saw them anywhere. Ben was in charge of a large IBM machine at an insurance company, but beyond that had never been able to explain what it was he did for a living. His hobby was taking pictures of flowers in the summer and snowflakes in the winter. According to Betty, his wife, he spent most of his time at home in a darkroom. He was wearing a yellow checked vest and a bow tie.

Lucy's bond with the Butlers was through the Garden Club. She and Betty had taken a course in flower arranging together. Betty was older, in her late thirties, her hair completely gray. She was pregnant with her fourth and final child.

"Looks like Lucy has gathered a gay group of wives," Charlie muttered to Ed Robinson as he was pouring him a second cocktail. "Lucy seems to be the only one here still eating for herself alone."

"How do you know she is?" Ed roared, reaching out and grabbing Lucy's arm, pulling her against his shoulder, and squeezing her in his best cocktail party style. "You've been away, Mein Host. How do you know Lucy doesn't have a friend?"

Lucy giggled. "Well, I don't, and I'm not. Not even a little bit."

"I'll bet it's Charlie's fault and not yours." He kept his arm around her.

Lucy seemed to like it, Charlie noticed with surprise. He looked at his wife closely for a moment. She was getting pretty, he decided. Lucy's looks were improving with the years. She was wearing a lavender dress, and her body was firm and vigorous.

For the next half-hour Charlie wandered about the room with the cocktail shaker, hearing only fragments of conversation. Danny and Ben Butler were talking about football, Ed Robinson was telling Lucy about the new drier he and Mary had recently bought, and the three pregnant wives were lined up on the couch comparing notes about their doctors.

"What I like about Larry Foster," Mary Robinson said as Charlie filled her glass only half full on her request, "is that he tells you what's what. None of this damn beating around the bush. If you're gaining too much weight, he tells you. He's tough, and I like that."

"But he's got the coldest hands," Louise giggled.

"And so has Doctor Werner," Betty Butler put in, shaking her head when Charlie held the shaker poised over her glass. "I wish I had nerve enough to tell him to wear gloves."

"Can I get in on this conclave of virgins?" Charlie asked. No matter what their background, their breeding, or their upbringing, wives' conversation tended to become earthy by the time they were carrying their third child.

The women hooted at him, and Mary Robinson said, "Run along, you mere man. Go talk business with someone."

"Mein Host," Ed Robinson roared at him from across the room, where he was still talking with Lucy. "I would have a few words with you. Don't run away," he said to Lucy, his arm enclosing her bare shoulders. "H'm," he mused, "mighty firm flesh around here."

Ed was a little high. His face was flushed under his tan, and he exuded warmth and a faint aroma of talcum powder.

"Last Wednesday night," he said, "we had a small select gathering at our house. Incidentally, Lucy, why didn't you come on over? You wouldn't have minded, would you, Charlie?"

"I wanted to," Lucy answered. "But who wants a single woman?"

"Who wants a single woman?" Ed repeated. "I love single women." He squeezed her shoulder again, winking at Charlie.

Did Lucy like this, Charlie wondered? He suspected that if a man had treated her like this at a party three or four years before, she would have either slapped him or burst into tears.

"To continue," Ed said, "at eleven o'clock or thereabouts, I was escorting the Chadwicks down my front walk to their car. As is my wont, I just happened to glance across the street at your house. And what did I see in the bedroom window but——"

Lucy twisted away from his arm and put her hand over his mouth.

"Let's eat, everyone," she shouted. She walked toward the kitchen. Ed grinned after her like a small boy.

"What did you see?" Charlie asked, smiling wanly.

"I've got him worried," Ed called after Lucy as he headed for the food. "We'll teach him to leave you at home alone."

They ate in the living room, plates balanced on knees, a community salad bowl on the floor.

"I just don't see how you do it," Mary Robinson said admiringly to Lucy. "Everything so hot and good like this. Parties at our house are always such terrible brawls."

"Why, Mary, you give simply marvelous parties," Lucy protested.

"She means the food is always a mess," Ed put in. "People come to our house to drink. We make our money on the bar."

"No, seriously, Ed," Mary insisted, turning to her husband, "why can't we do something quiet and nice like this just once in a while?"

"Because Ed isn't the quiet and nice type," Lucy said, rescuing the conversation from what appeared to be a subject of Robinson marital friction. She started toward the kitchen. "The coffee must be hot by now. I'll go get it." On her way by she plucked at Charlie's sleeve. "Go up and check Lydia, will you, darling. I think she's having a nightmare."

The wives carried their coffee upstairs. It was a custom Lucy believed worth maintaining, that of the men and women splitting up after dinner, even though it meant the wives must retreat to a bedroom on the second floor, along with a dirty shirt and a pair of afternoon socks that had not been kicked into the closet. The day of the drawing room was past, but the spirit lingered on.

With Danny Girard and Ben Butler deep in the mysteries of Ben's IBM machine, Ed Robinson led Charlie out into the front hall.

"I promise you I don't make it a habit of talking business at parties," he said, backing Charlie against the hall radiator, "and if I'm making a nuisance of myself just say so. But does anyone in particular handle your investments for you?" Ed had lost his cocktail flush, and his eyes were burning with a stockbroker's zeal.

"What investments?" Charlie hedged. "Lucy's the capitalist in our family. I'm just a working man."

"I hope you're not insurance poor," Ed answered, laughing easily. "Or do you have all your millions tied up in cash?"

"What money I have is in the bank, if that's what you mean."

"At one and a half per cent?"

"Two, to be exact, but safe from the raids of wolves like you."

"Seriously, Charlie, the only damn reason why I bring this up is that we're both salesmen, and neither of us tries to sell anything we don't believe in. A case came up just the other day in the office. My father had this customer who lost her husband back in the '20s. She had three small children. She had less than ten thousand dollars of insurance money when her husband died, and my old man invested it for her. Let me tell you what happened," Ed said hurriedly, when Charlie tried to interrupt. "No, she didn't lose everything in the depression, if that's what you were going to say. He invested it all in local companies for her. I mean, my God, what's more solid than companies right around here, where you know the management, when you know——"

"What happened to the widow's ten thousand dollars?" Charlie asked.

"I'll tell you," Ed answered. "Thanks to the stocks my father bought her, she sent every damn one of her children through college. She bought herself a house. She drives a new car every other year. And get this. Get this, Charlie," he repeated, tapping his host on the chest, "if she sold out today she'd have over thirty thousand dollars in cash." Ed looked triumphant. "Show me the insurance jockey who can equal that kind of a record."

Charlie thought a moment. Then he said, "You give me an idea at that, Ed. I do have a little money in the bank. I might give you an order for some stock."

"Oh hell, Charlie. Don't get me wrong. I wasn't trying to make a sale tonight. We're here to enjoy ourselves and all that sort of thing. But I'd like a chance to set up a program for you. I could drop over here some night and go over the whole thing with you."

"I have a program," Charlie answered. "I'll give you a standing order to buy all the Hadley stock that shows up on the market."

"There isn't much of that around, old man. You ought to know. It's tightly held."

"If anything shows up, you buy it for me," Charlie said. "I have confidence in the management."

"Lucy's father?" Ed asked, tipping his head toward the stairs.

Charlie grinned at him. Then he said, "Let's go rescue Danny from Ben's business machine."

"You never did tell me how you like selling knives," Danny said, when he and Charlie were standing by the fireplace.

"Well Danny, I like it," Charlie answered.

Danny was smoking a metal-stemmed pipe filled with strongly aromatic tobacco. He looked glazed and well fed.

"They tell me you're traveling all around, making like a brush salesman."

"Dammit," Charlie answered, "I'm just doing what needed doing out there twenty years ago. It's fascinating, Danny. It really is. I like to sell, and I can already see results. We'll show a genuine profit out there this year. That's what I'm trying to do. Make the Company stand on its own feet."

Danny Girard had started to smile.

"You find that amusing?" Charlie asked, annoyed.

"I was just recalling your expression when we ate together in the club a few years back, and I was waxing inspirational about banking. You thought I'd lost my grip."

"O.K., O.K.," Charlie answered embarrassed. "So I'm just a bush-league businessman like everyone else around here."

They were silent a moment.

Then Danny said, "Incidentally, I've been writing a couple of songs."

"Wonderful," Charlie exclaimed, genuinely enthusiastic. "I hope you'll send them off to some publisher in New York."

"Oh, hell no," Danny answered. "They're just for the Junior League."

Charlie said, "Oh," unable to think of anything else to say.

"At least it keeps my hand in."

"Your hand in what?" Louise Girard asked, advancing toward Danny and linking her arm through his. "We've got to run, sweetie. I promised the children we'd *do* something with them tomorrow."

"We've got to go too, Ed," Mary Robinson said, following Louise into the room.

"Don't go," Lucy wailed. "It's not even eleven o'clock."

Ed patted Lucy's bare back, allowing his hand to linger.

"Leave when the party is going strong, I always say." He gave Lucy's back a final pat. "If ever you get sick of Charlie, just let me know."

"Marvelous casserole," Betty Butler said as she joined the procession out the front door.

"I didn't get a chance to talk with you much tonight," Ben Butler said as he shook hands with Charlie. "We'll have you over to our house soon."

"Do that," Charlie answered without enthusiasm. Ben Butler, he thought, would be far more interesting if he could take his IBM machine with him and demonstrate. It was small wonder the Butlers were never seen anywhere.

When Charlie was climbing the stairs behind Lucy, she said, "I think everyone had a good time tonight, don't you?"

"They said they did."

"I suppose it wasn't exactly an original party, but you can't be original all the time."

"It's pretty difficult," he agreed.

When they were in the bedroom Lucy said, "I heard something absolutely fantastic from Mary tonight. Lila Wallin is getting a *divorce* from Wood-chuck."

"Well, what do you know!" Charlie exclaimed.

"I was completely stunned when Mary told me. I said they had seemed utterly devoted when we ate dinner with them a few years ago."

"I suppose Lila got pretty bored around here. What's she going to do? Did Mary know?"

"The word seems to be that she's marrying some advertising executive from New York." Lucy paused a moment. "Where would she meet someone like a New York advertising man?"

"In New York, I suppose. Where else?"

"I wouldn't trade a life in New York for the one we have here for a million dollars, would you?"

"I doubt if the problem will ever come up," he answered, checking his socks to see if he could wear them the following day.

When they were in bed, Lucy said, "Can I ask you a silly question?"

"I suppose so."

"Do you think any of our friends ever have affairs?"

"That is a silly question."

"Do you?" she persisted.

She slid nearer to him and reached for his hand, putting it under her cheek.

"I doubt it very much," he answered.

"Why not?"

"For one thing, all the women are pregnant."

Lucy giggled. "How about when they aren't pregnant?"

He shook his head. "This isn't a favorable environment for affairs. This is a breeding ground, not a playground." Then he said, "I meant to tell you this afternoon when I came home, I won't be away quite so much of the time from now on. We're going to hire a couple of other salesmen. When I get them organized I'll be home a lot more."

"That will be pleasant," she answered. "I hope you're not doing it just for me."

"I'm not. I'll still be leaving once in a while, but not every week. Incidentally, what was all this business about Ed looking across the street the other night?"

"You know Ed," she answered. "He was just a little high."

"He must have seen something."

"I probably left some stockings hanging in the window."

"He certainly made a big thing out of it."

They were quiet for a moment. Then Lucy said, "I'd like another baby, Charlie."

"Did all those pregnant women make you feel guilty?"

"No. I just think I need a baby."

"Need one?"

"Uh hum," she said nodding. "Need one."

"Whatever you say," he answered. "You're in charge of the baby department."

She reached for one of his ears, pulled his face around, and kissed him.

twenty-two

"As usual, the prince is playing his old man's game," joe pritchard said with affectionate scorn as he, Lowell Chalmers, and Fred Baird started off on their first threesome of the new golfing year. Joe had fortified himself with two quick drinks in the locker room, and by the time they had all reached the second tee his face showed the effects of it, flushed with alcohol and good will. Joe had been a halfback at Yale in 1908, and now in 1950, forty-two years later, he still had an appearance of fitness, even though much of his weight had slipped down to his waistline. He was wearing a dark blue sweater which looked well with his silver-gray hair. "Down the middle Lowell," he sneered. "What in hell would you ever do if you landed in a trap? Kick it out with your foot?"

"Don't let this bucket of guts rattle you," Fred Baird said, putting his arm around Lowell's shoulders. "If Joe can't beat you with his clubs, he'll do it with his mouth."

Fred looked as dignified on the golf course as he did in his brokerage office. He was wearing gray flannels, and a white shirt and a necktie. The necktie was dark blue.

"It's my honor, I believe, gentlemen," Lowell said, unperturbed by the horseplay. He teed up his ball and drove it slightly over two hundred yards straight down the middle of the second fairway.

Joe Pritchard couldn't rattle him. At least not on a golf course. Not a man lived who could rattle him on a golf course. Why did he love this game so much? Lowell wondered as he walked off the second tee and headed toward his ball. It wasn't the beauty of a golf course, although he did like the sight of hundreds of acres of rolling grass and greenery. However, his whole life was full of spacious lawn and large trees, and golf filled no lack in this direction. Nor was it the exercise. He managed to get plenty of exercise all year long, either by walking about the town of Hadley during his long lunch hours or wandering up the beach when he went to the Island. Golf, he thought, meant something quite different to him, something unique, that he alone could understand.

A golf course was one place where good things seemed to happen to him. It had started back in 1907, when he'd been an alternate on the Yale team. One of the regular members of the team was sick, and he'd been called upon to play a match against Harvard. He'd won it. He could still recall every detail of that match even though nearly forty-three years had passed—every stroke, every lie, and every mistake his opponent had made. Then it had happened again in 1916, when he won the club championship. He broke seventy-five on his final round for one of the three times he'd ever done it in his life. That had been another event in his sixty-three years he wasn't likely to forget.

As he had grown older his game had changed rather than deteriorated. He had gradually given up all thought of overpowering the course, and instead had learned how to outwit it. He had become adept at placing each shot in a strategic spot, as though he were playing outdoor pool, and if he had three-putted on more than two greens in the last twenty years, he couldn't remember it. He no longer played in tournaments or entered the club championship, believing his day for that was long since past, but he never embarked on a round of golf with his good friends Joe Pritchard and Fred Baird without just one thought in mind. He was out to beat them.

That might be what he loved about golf, he thought. If everything else he did bore the mark of a man who shunned competition, on the golf course he played to win. Each new eighteen holes was a fresh challenge, a clean slate. Every time he stood on the first tee, a brand-new ball gleaming white against the green sod, he could indulge himself in the dream that this might be the perfect day, with no missed shots, no unlucky breaks, and no mistakes in judgment. By the time you were over sixty, he knew, a man had long since given up thinking about perfection in the way he lived, or had lived, or should have lived. But in eighteen holes of golf, perfection was still possible. It would always be possible until he was too weary to walk around the course. It was a great game, Lowell Chalmers thought to himself as he stroked his second shot easily and watched it roll dead, ten feet from the pin.

"Say, grandfather," Joe Pritchard said as they were crossing the avenue toward the third tee, "isn't your daughter Lucy about to have another child? Seems to me Helen mentioned it to me this morning."

"I believe she is," Lowell answered casually, as though he wasn't too much concerned. He was writing down the three scores. They had made their standard ten-dollar bet, he and Joe giving Fred one stroke a nine. Joe would play good golf on the first nine, but would start to fade on the back side, when he felt the need of a drink.

"Say now, isn't he the casual grandfather?" Joe said, winking at Fred. He turned back to Lowell. "They tell me you're going to kill yourself if it's another girl."

"It's my honor again," Lowell answered. "Unless one of you gentlemen beat my birdie three."

He played the next seven holes in four over par, finishing out the nine in forty. Joe had a forty-one, and Fred a forty-four.

"Want your scores, gentlemen?" Lowell asked when they waited on the tenth tee. "I'm one up on Joe and three up on Fred. Anybody care to see the card?"

"You'll fold on this side," Joe said sourly.

Lowell considered the statement for a moment.

"Would anyone like to place an additional ten-dollar bet that I won't break eighty for the eighteen?"

"Make it a hundred," Joe answered, nudging Fred.

"One hundred it is," Lowell answered without hesitation. "One hundred apiece, I presume."

"What goes on here?" Joe shouted. In nearly forty years of playing golf together he had never known Lowell to bet more than ten dollars on anything. "Is Hadley going to declare an extra?"

"Yes or no?" Lowell asked. "Is the bet on or off?"

"You doddering old fool, it's on," Joe answered. "You probably won't break ninety."

"We'll see," Lowell answered. On the tenth hole, he drove two hundred and twenty yards down the middle of the fairway, and a few moments later sank a twenty-foot putt for his par.

He played the eleventh, twelfth, thirteenth, fourteenth, and fifteenth in even par, not missing a stroke. He stopped talking to Joe and Fred, concentrating on his game harder than he had ever concentrated before in his life. This, he knew, was going to be his day.

As he pitched an approach shot dead to the sixteenth pin, he started toying with an idea. If Lucy's boy, his first grandson, was born by the time he arrived at the clubhouse that afternoon, he might call the newspaper and dictate a birth notice. He knew Owen Griffith, the editor, and Owen, he thought, would recognize a good story when he saw one. Tomorrow morning, somewhere in the paper a small headline would read, "L. C. Chalmers breaks eighty. Daughter gives birth to a grandson." Lydia would surely be horrified, but he didn't care. This would be one time in his life he'd do something without consulting her.

That Lucy was going to have a boy he had never doubted for an instant. He was certain of it now, and he was certain of it when Charlie had first told him Lucy was expecting her third child.

"If it's a boy," Charlie had said, "we plan to call him Lowell, after you. If it's a girl——"

Lowell had interrupted him fiercely. "None of this 'if it's a girl' stuff. It's going to be a boy, and that's all there is to it."

He and Charlie had been sitting in the office. He closed the door so Mrs. Fleck wouldn't listen in.

"I'm going to admit something to you, Charlie," he said, "that even now I don't like to think about. Mrs. Chalmers and I were married four whole years before we had our first child. Children seem to come easily for you and Lucy, and you'll never know what it's like to not have them. But Mrs. Chalmers and I waited four years. When Anne was born we considered ourselves so lucky to have a baby that we didn't even think about whether we wanted a boy or not. We just wanted a child, and finally we had one. Then we waited another three years, and when Lucy arrived, again we were grateful. But when Polly was born—I'm ashamed of myself for this," he said, "but I'll tell you, because it's true. When Polly was born I almost couldn't bear to look at her. Of course I soon loved her very much. But at first I couldn't forgive her for not being a boy. I wanted a boy. Lord, how I wanted a boy!

Girls are fine. They are a lot of fun for a father when they're young. But the minute they turn into the other sex, they're gone. You can't reach them. You'll know what I mean someday. They don't ask you for advice, and if they did, you couldn't give it to them anyway. Being a father with three girls is almost as lonely as being a father with no children at all."

"I'm fairly neutral on the subject," Charlie answered.

"Don't talk rot," Mr. Chalmers said angrily. "We have plenty of girls in this family. We want a boy." He smiled. "So you plan to name him after me?"

"Yes, sir."

"Well, I like that. I'll be proud to have a grandson named after me."

As he walked toward the eighteenth green, after having put his second shot forty feet from the pin, Lowell had a second idea. He'd take the two hundred dollars he was about to collect from Joe Pritchard and Fred Baird and start a bank account for young Lowell Chalmers Webb. Then he'd add another eight hundred to it and make it an even thousand. And he'd see that a little Hadley stock was registered in young Lowell's name. Young Lowell, he repeated to himself. That had a nice ring to it. This would be one grandson who never doubted for a single instant that he was wanted in this world.

Things, he thought happily, were going well. Charlie had pushed the Company ahead more in four years than he had in forty years. There would be a few surprises in the annual statement this year. Life was going well no matter how you looked at it.

"You're away," Fred Baird said when they reached the eighteenth green.

"Now let me see," Lowell said. "Unless I'm mistaken, if I take two putts I have a seventy-nine. You gentlemen might as well get your wallets out right now."

"We pay off when we see the ball in the cup," Joe Pritchard replied. Lowell Chalmers never three-putted, and he knew it.

Lowell sank on one knee and started to examine the green. Between his ball and the cup he could see nothing which would cause any trouble. It was for him a standard putt, a little roll to the right, then a level run with the cup at the center. There was nothing unusual about the grass either. It was all even and growing straight. He walked slowly toward the cup, looking for tiny holes he might have missed. This was one time he didn't plan to take three putts.

At that moment Tommy, the bar steward, came out of the clubhouse and walked rapidly across the terrace. "I've got a phone message for you, Mr. Chalmers," he shouted. "Mrs. Chalmers called in about a half-hour ago."

"Leave him alone, Tommy," Joe Pritchard yelled. "We want no excuses when he misses the next two putts."

"Mrs. Chalmers told me to give him this message the minute he came in." There was a broad grin on Tommy's face. "She said he'd want to know about it right away."

Lowell Chalmers took the slip of paper Tommy handed him, but didn't look at it. He folded it carefully and put it into his shirt pocket.

Then he said, "Move aside. I'm going to sink this putt. There's a good deal riding on it."

Once again he lined up the ball. Since he had been disturbed he'd have to start all over again. For the first time in his life Lowell Chalmers knew he was superstitious. There was far more than a mere two hundred dollars riding on this putt. There was a grandson as well. This was the omen he had been waiting for. If he sank his next putt, he knew the message that Tommy had given him would be good. If he missed, it would be bad.

Joe Pritchard and Fred Baird sat down at the edge of the green. Over the years they had become used to Lowell's slowness on the greens. It was as much a part of his game as his straight drives and deadly approaching.

"You don't have a pack of cards, do you, Fred?" Joe Pritchard asked, grinning.

"Now, then," Lowell said out loud, speaking to himself more than to anyone else. He drew back his putter and let it swing through like a pendulum, keeping his eye on the spot where the ball had rested. He didn't look up until the ball had nearly reached the cup. He watched it roll closer and closer, slowing just where it was meant to slow, moving an inch to the right at the last minute, just as he knew it would move. For just an instant the ball hesitated on the lip of the cup, and then disappeared.

Lowell straightened up, raised both his arms toward the sky, and roared with laughter. Then he reached into his pocket for the slip of paper.

As he read the note his hand started to shake. Then his face turned an ashen gray. Finally he whirled about on the green, his spikes slicing into the turf, and hurled his putter toward the caddy house. It smashed against the side. Then he walked toward the clubhouse, a picture of weary defeat.

"What the hell?" Fred Baird asked.

Joe shrugged. "Looks like another girl. Let's go have a drink."

Fred nodded and scooped up his ball.

Charlie had been sitting in the hospital waiting room when he saw Larry Foster step out of the elevator. Larry looked exhausted, as though he hadn't slept an uninterrupted eight hours in over a year. For him the dream of all obstetricians had come true. He had become fashionable. He was driving himself cruelly, day and night, all summer long, his skin gray and his eyes dark with fatigue, his sole reward an income he dared discuss only with the collector of internal revenue. Like a professional athlete, he knew his good years were limited. There would be time enough to repair his health when his own generation was no longer producing babies.

"Another nice little girl," he said, smiling at Charlie compassionately. Larry had four children of his own, two boys and two girls.

Charlie drew in a deep breath and sighed.

"What trite thing do I say now?"

Larry didn't answer. He took Charlie's elbow and led him outside into the hall.

"I'll go into this with Lucy later, in more detail, but I don't think you'll have any more, old man. It looks like this one will be your last."

"Is Lucy all right?" Charlie asked.

"She's fine. Not a thing to worry about in the world. I'll tell you all about it when we have another look in a month or so. I just thought I ought to warn you."

"But she is all right, Larry?"

"She's fine," he repeated. Then he backed away toward the elevator. The hospital loud-speaker was paging him. "Gotta go, old man. I got two more probables and one definite for sure before midnight." He smiled the thin smile of a busy doctor, and disappeared.

Mrs. Hodges met Charlie at the door when he returned from the hospital. She was a garrulous widow of sixty who went from one Highcliffe Road household to another, scheduled far in advance the moment all danger of miscarriage was past. She lived only for newborn babies and gossip, and her conversation consisted mainly of platitudes.

"Well, Mr. Webb?" she asked, her face registering anticipation.

"Girl," he answered.

Her expression changed into one of vague, professional disappointment. To her, the sex of the child mattered little. Boy or girl, her work for the next two weeks would be roughly the same. However, fifteen years' experience with fathers had taught her that it was best to look disappointed whenever the new baby was a girl.

"Mrs. Webb is all right?"

"She's fine," Charlie answered. He started toward the stairs.

"Well, it's like I always tell my new fathers," Mrs. Hodges said, following him. "It isn't for us to question God's will. He has the whole world to worry about, not just your family or mine. We should all give thanks that he allows us to *have* children. That's what I always tell my fathers when they . . ."

Charlie ceased to listen. Lucy had left a long list of friends to call, including her mother at the top of the list.

"It's another girl, Mrs. Chalmers."

"That's just wonderful, Charlie," Mrs. Chalmers trilled. "But you see I knew it already." She giggled. "I had Lucy instruct Doctor Foster to call me the instant he knew the good news." She hesitated a moment. "Have you and Lucy discussed possible names for the baby?"

"What would you think of Darleene?" Charlie asked.

"Darleene?" Mrs. Chalmers replied, obviously horror-struck. "Is there a Darleene in your family?"

"I was just thinking it was time we lifted ourselves out of this rut in names. Why must these family names be passed along from one generation to another like antiques? Why don't we try to be a little more fashionable?"

"Fashionable?" Mrs. Chalmers echoed. She had about as much interest in fashion as she did in horse racing.

"Why not a name with a little zip to it? Like Debra, or Fawn?"

"Zip?" Mrs. Chalmers repeated. "Fawn? You're thinking of naming your daughter Fawn?"

Charlie laughed. He had tortured his mother-in-law long enough.

"I am going to call her Ruth," he said. "After my aunt. Is that all right with you?"

He hung up. He still had fifteen more calls to make, including one to Florida, to his aunt.

"You've received the good news I hope, Lowell," Mrs. Chalmers said the instant her husband came in the front door.

"I have received the news," he answered, the word "good" conspicuously absent. He stumbled slightly as he walked across the hall. As he passed through the study doorway he struck his shoulder on the jamb. Then he aimed himself at his chair.

"Have you been drinking, dear one?"

"Yes, dear one, I have been drinking. In fact, dear one, I believe I might possibly be a little drunk."

Mrs. Chalmers looked tolerant, and lingered in the study doorway.

"I had the oddest conversation with our son-in-law about names. Did you discuss it with him at all?"

"Charlie promised to name my grandson after me," he answered.

Lydia giggled. Then she walked to her husband and placed her hand on his head, rubbing his bald spot affectionately. "You're terribly disappointed, aren't you, Lowell?"

"Aren't you, my dear?"

"Not at all," she answered promptly. "What we all really wanted was a healthy baby, wasn't it?"

"I would have preferred," Lowell answered, enunciating each word with meticulous, drunken care, "I would have preferred," he repeated, "a healthy boy."

twenty-three

ONE EVENING EARLY THE FOLLOWING DECEMBER LUCY RETURNED FROM THE hall telephone with her face wrinkled into what Charlie knew was her "Aunt-Roswell" expression.

"For you, dear," she said, waving him toward the telephone. "Aunt Roswell."

"What does she want now?"

"Don't ask me. Shall I tell her you're out?"

"What will I tell her if she wants us for dinner again?" he asked, as he walked toward the hall.

"That the children have leprosy," Lucy answered.

"Seriously, Lucy."

"Think of something. Anything. But don't say yes."

He settled himself at the hall table, arranging cigarettes, matches, ash tray, and a pad and pencil for ticktacktoe. Telephone conversations with Aunt Roswell Hadley were apt to consume a great deal of time.

Had he adopted Aunt Roswell, Charlie wondered, or had she adopted him? Originally he had merely felt sorry for her, and had insisted that Lucy ask her for dinner at Highcliffe Road. At first he had been unable to understand Mrs. Chalmers' apparent cruelty to the one surviving member of the family who bore the Hadley name.

Eighty-eight years old, one hundred and three pounds of selfish arrogance, she lived alone in a dusty apartment on Woodbridge Circle, amid a clutter of Hadley antiques and African violet plants. She could have been in Alaska for all the Chalmers saw of her. Once each year, officially and with considerable fanfare, Mrs. Chalmers would ask her to dinner, either Christmas or Thanksgiving. At eleven in the morning Joseph and the Packard would be dispatched to collect her, and at three in the afternoon she would be returned. Four hours of entertainment each year took care of any vague feelings of guilt Mrs. Chalmers might have. For the rest of the year Aunt Roswell lived only to water her plants, to fight with her landlord, and to keep her checkbook in balance.

"What's the harm in being decent to her?" Charlie had asked when Lucy balked at inviting her to dinner.

"You'll see," Lucy had answered. "She'll get her hands on you, and you won't have a moment's peace. She *uses* people."

Lucy had been right. In an idle moment Charlie had once figured up what Aunt Roswell Hadley would owe him if, over the last four years, he had charged her a dollar an hour for his time. It came to well over two hundred dollars. When a faucet leaked in her apartment, she called him instead of a plumber. When her closet door stuck, he was asked to plane it down. Whenever she needed a ride to a greenhouse, she called him instead of a taxi. Whenever she fought with her landlord, it had become Charlie's job to explain to the long-suffering man that Miss Hadley was eighty-eight years old, that she had spent most of those years alone, that if she claimed that someone were peeking into her bedroom window at night, the whole matter could be solved by installing a Venetian blind and sending him the bill. The bill had arrived, and shortly thereafter a call from Aunt Roswell asking him to drop over to show her how to operate a newfangled blind that her landlord had forced on her.

"The more you do for her the less she'll appreciate it," Lucy had warned. "She'll never thank you. She'll never give you one damn thing in return."

That wasn't strictly accurate. In 1949 she had given him an African violet plant, which had died.

He lifted the telephone receiver and shouted, "Hello, Aunt Roswell. How are you tonight?"

"I'm fine thank you, Charles," she answered in her querulous monotone.

No one in the family was sure whether Aunt Roswell was really deaf or merely enjoyed having people shouting at her.

"Drop a coin on the sidewalk, and she'll hear it two blocks away," Mrs. Chalmers once said. "But ask her to do you a favor, and she's stone deaf."

"I hope we see you at our meeting tomorrow afternoon," Charlie shouted. "Our annual meeting."

"That's what I'm calling about, Charles."

He waited. All conversations with her were punctuated by long moments of silence.

"The meeting is at two, I presume?"

"Yes, it is, Aunt Roswell," he shouted. He knew now that she was about to ask him to drive her out. He decided to make her say it.

"They don't have bus service to Hadley, do they, Charles?"

"I'm afraid they don't, Aunt Roswell."

"I know in the old days the trolleys used to run out there. I suppose they don't any more, do they?"

There hadn't been a trolley operating from the city in nearly fifteen years, and Aunt Roswell knew it.

"I'm afraid not, Aunt Roswell."

"It's so difficult to get a taxi this season of the year. And they charge such exorbitant rates."

He waited.

"Would it be too much trouble for you to drive me out, Charles? I could be ready at one."

That she was concerned about any trouble she might cause him he knew was a mere formality. She had been causing someone in the family trouble for every one of her eighty-eight years.

"Why should you drive her out?" Lucy asked angrily when he returned to the living room.

"She says she can't afford a cab."

"Oh, pish, posh," Lucy exploded. "She could buy every taxi in the city."

No doubt she could at that, Charlie thought the next afternoon as he was driving Aunt Roswell to Hadley. Computing her net worth at the present market value of Hadley stock, she could raise well over a million dollars if ever she had to. However, it seemed unlikely that she'd ever have to, her only extravagance being African violets. Deaf, crippled with arthritis, her gray skin hanging in loose wrinkles, she might live forever, he thought, like a cricket that has escaped the first freeze. Her eyes were as bright as black diamonds, a warning to anyone foolish enough to test her that behind them was a brain still as sharp as a needle.

"Shall I tell you in advance what we hope to discuss out here today?" he asked.

"I hope you cleaned up the factory yard as I suggested at last year's meeting, Charles."

"We have, Aunt Roswell. We sold enough scrap metal to pay for the whole job."

She would approve of that, he knew. She still wore a hat she had purchased for her brother's funeral nearly twenty years before, and she had bought herself her grave marker during the depression, when prices were low. It was stored in the Hadley warehouse.

"Our business is well up over last year," Charlie began, "and we've increased our work force to over a hundred. We've reopened the span, the building that extends out over——"

"I know the span very well," she snapped at him. "I discussed the plans with my brother when he built it in 1910."

"Anyway," Charlie continued, grinning, "our business is up, and our profits are also up. For the first time in over ten years we can pay a small dividend out of our current earnings, instead of interest from our cash reserves."

"Then you plan to issue an extra dividend?" she asked.

"Well, no," he answered. "In fact we plan to spend it all on expansion. I've been urging Mr. Chalmers for over a year to consider buying out a small company in Cleveland, Ohio——"

"I know where Cleveland is," she snapped again. "I went there many times with my father before the turn of the century."

Charlie smiled again. Aunt Roswell was as harmless as a rattlesnake.

"We hope to branch out into another field. You probably know I've been spending most of my time during the last two years or so traveling about, trying to increase our business. I've also been looking for ways for The Hadley Company to diversify. In order to prosper these days, manufacturing companies have to——"

"You needn't lecture me on business practices, Charles. Just tell me what this plant in Cleveland makes."

"They make all variety of industrial steel blades for other manufacturing companies. The bulk of their business in the past has come from the makers of farm machinery. My feeling is that with our capital behind them, and some increased sales effort on our part, it can become extremely profitable."

"Will you move the operation back here to Hadley?" Aunt Roswell asked.

"We don't plan to. They have a new building out there, and all our buildings are old. We operate efficiently up to a point, but someday we'll have to rebuild completely. Until we get a new factory back here, it seems wise to keep them going out there."

He had spoken of rebuilding casually, expecting a reaction. Aunt Roswell merely nodded, her eyes partially closed. She said nothing more until they reached Hadley.

When they came in sight of the factory she said, "That's a nice fence you put up, Charles. My brother always used to say that to be prosperous a factory must look prosperous."

"Does that apply to people and their clothing?" he asked glancing at her. Her coat had last been in style in 1910.

146

"Just because you've given me a ride out to Hadley doesn't mean you can insult me," she snapped.

"Someone has to insult you, Aunt Roswell, or you'd be wearing that coat for another twenty years. Why don't you go downtown tomorrow and buy a new one? You can afford it."

He stopped the car by the dam and walked around to open the door.

"I'd offer to help you across the street if I thought you'd accept."

"And why shouldn't I accept?" she asked.

"I'm told you hit Boy Scouts with your cane."

"Run along," she said, delighted. "I'm sure you have things to do. I'll meet you here after the meeting, and if it isn't too much trouble, you can run me back into the city."

He was the only member of the family who wasn't afraid of her, he thought as he crossed the street to the office. Mr. Chalmers treated her like a dangerous child—a child because she was so old, and dangerous because she owned thirty per cent of The Hadley Company. Mrs. Chalmers pretended to ignore her, but couldn't, since Aunt Roswell had been someone she couldn't subdue. The three girls, Lucy, Anne, and Polly, sent her birthday cards, not out of sentiment, but in respect for Aunt Roswell's will, a document she had always guarded as carefully as her virginity. Was she the cripple she seemed to be? he wondered, as he watched her cross the street, bent double, using her cane as a third leg, never having less than two points on the ground at all times; or was she the fraud he suspected, hoping to enlist the sympathies of the unwary who might feel sorry for her? When she reached the office steps, she hesitated, glancing about to be sure no one was watching her. Then she negotiated the steps with comparative ease, without even using the cane.

"Well, well," Charlie said when he stepped into Mr. Chalmers' office and found Ed Robinson sitting along with nearly a dozen other stockholders. "I thought I noticed your name on our list."

"If you're going to make this old clinker of a company go places," Ed answered, "I'm here for the ride."

From the front of the office, Mr. Chalmers motioned to Charlie with his finger.

"I'm glad you're here," he whispered. "I've been delaying things until Miss Hadley arrived."

"I drove her out," Charlie answered.

"Has that old nuisance been bothering you?" Mr. Chalmers asked angrily. "She has no right to ask you to do things like that." Then he said, "I'm going to call on you for most of the talking today."

"You're not expecting any trouble, are you?"

"Who knows which way Aunt Roswell will jump? She's given me fits in the past."

Mr. Chalmers called the meeting to order by tapping his desk with a silver-plated bayonet.

"It's indeed a pleasant surprise to see a few new faces out here," he began. "In the past our annual meetings were, shall we say, intimate family gatherings."

There was a ripple of polite laughter in the room. Mrs. Fleck, her pencil poised, was sitting at a card table, waiting to make a shorthand note of anything she felt significant. Over the heads of the stockholders, the view out the office window was bleak and gray. The reservoir was frozen, and the spillway over the dam was coated with a foot of bluish-white ice reaching down to the rocks below. In the distance, the low mountains looked deserted and cold.

"I even see a broker, Mr. Robinson, at our meeting," Mr. Chalmers continued. "Has there been activity on Wall Street with our stock, Mr. Robinson?"

"Just like Standard Oil of New Jersey," Ed Robinson answered, laughing.

"Well now, that's just fine," Mr. Chalmers answered, reaching for his copy of the annual report. He had spent the entire month of November composing it, working over each paragraph, each sentence, each word as though it were a document of state, a treaty with a hostile foreign power. "Why don't we all glance at the report that has been passed out among you, while I read some of the more important sections out loud."

While he listened to Mr. Chalmers read, Charlie glanced about the office at the stockholders. Aunt Roswell, with her thirty per cent, was sitting in the front row, holding her hearing aid at arm's length as though it were an exposure meter. Behind her were the two elderly Chase sisters, the remains of what Mrs. Chalmers called "the other side of the family." Her grandmother had been a Chase. Annual meetings for Emily and Deborah Chase were merely an outing, a way of exercising their chauffeur. From the meeting they would go to an antique shop or to a tearoom. They seldom spoke unless spoken to, and, having no need of more money, were inclined to agree with whatever was suggested and with whoever was the last to speak.

Fred Baird was present both as a director and as a stockholder. He would also speak for his clients. If he had any objections to the expansion plans, Charlie knew he would have made them known to Mr. Chalmers at the directors' meeting. Houghton Wray was at the back of the room. A director in at least a dozen companies, he would say nothing unless it concerned borrowing money. The annual stockholders' meetings of The Hadley Company gave him nothing but an annual chest cold. He wore his topcoat, and he sat near the radiator.

Mr. Chalmers had finished reading the report.

"You will observe," he said, a note of pride creeping into his voice, "that we had a large increase in our net income this year. This has been most gratifying."

"What are you going to do with it?" a nasal voice asked from the back of the room.

"Is that you, Ledyard?" Mr. Chalmers asked, smiling indulgently.

"How much of a Christmas present are you going to give your poor workmen out here?"

148

"Who is that man?" Aunt Roswell hissed at Charlie, her voice echoing out into the room.

"Mr. Pittman," Charlie whispered.

Ledyard Pittman was a distant cousin and had inherited his Hadley stock. Originally a member of a good family, he had drifted into newspaper work and was therefore considered to be a member of the lunatic fringe.

"How many shares does he own?" Aunt Roswell hissed again.

"Five," Charlie answered.

Aunt Roswell's scornful sniff sent another ripple of laughter through the room. Ledyard Pittman allowed his question to remain unanswered.

"I will now turn the meeting over to my son-in-law," Mr. Chalmers said. "It will be his task to tell us of the Company's future plans."

As he spoke, Charlie addressed his remarks only to Aunt Roswell's hearing aid. No one else in the room much mattered, as far as he could see.

"As you may know," he began, "over two years ago Mr. Chalmers decided to send me out as a salesman for our Company. He felt that the time had come for our Company to follow along with the tradition that built the Company originally." He paused and glanced about the room. Ledyard Pittman looked bored. Houghton Wray's mind seemed to be elsewhere. Mrs. Fleck was busy taking notes. Emily and Deborah Chase were looking at the posters on the office walls, and Fred Baird was making some pencil computations on the back of his annual report. Only Ed Robinson and Aunt Roswell were paying strict attention.

"The old saying about build a better mousetrap and the world beats a path to your door is a lie," Charlie continued. "The first Mr. Hadley invented a better horseshoe nail, but he beat a path to the world's door. He went out selling it, or else we wouldn't be sitting here today. I think my efforts have been fairly satisfactory. Our balance sheet shows that. We are now training two additional salesmen, and hope soon to have a complete sales force. One thing the first Mr. Hadley did was to be constantly on the lookout for new things to make. Nowadays they call it diversification. He started making plows because he spent so much of his time with farmers. He started making Hadley knives when he found no one else in this country was making a good knife. By the time his grandson was running the Company there was no more business in nails, and very little in plows, and our knives had become our mainstay."

Charlie paused again. Out the window he could see the Chase sisters' chauffeur standing on the dam, breaking a hole through the ice with a stick. While he hesitated, Aunt Roswell turned off her hearing aid and settled back into her chair.

With Aunt Roswell no longer listening, Charlie relaxed. He quickly outlined the plan for taking over the plant in Cleveland, discussing what they made and how he hoped it would fit into The Hadley Company's operation.

"It's our thought," he finished, "that this new division will eventually be quite profitable."

"Are you going to move it back here?" Ed Robinson shouted from the back of the room.

"No, we aren't," Charlie answered. He saw Aunt Roswell turn on her hearing aid again. "Which makes me want to add one thing more," he continued. "It's my hope that in a few years we'll all be sitting in this room talking about building a new factory right here in Hadley. It's certainly something we need."

"Thank you, Charlie," Mr. Chalmers broke in smoothly. "All of us have been extremely interested in your remarks. Gentlemen, I know some of you have businesses you must attend to back in the city, and I think we can put this matter to a vote. The management and the directors naturally have discussed this thing, and we are in favor. Do we have any objection?"

"No objections," Aunt Roswell snapped, struggling to her feet. "I move we adjourn." As far as she was concerned, the meeting was over.

As the stockholders filed out of the room, Mr. Chalmers grasped Charlie's elbow.

"Did you tell Aunt Roswell you'd drive her back into the city?"

"Yes, sir, I did."

"Dammit," he exclaimed, "if that old woman is pestering you, I'm going to have Mrs. Chalmers put a stop to it. Aunt Roswell can make your life miserable if you let her. She used to bother me with her outlandish requests."

Ed Robinson was waiting outside in the Company yard.

"Got a minute?" he asked.

"No more than a minute. What's on your mind?"

"First let me say that I like this." Ed patted the annual report. "And I know who did it. You."

Charlie shrugged. "It didn't take much to improve things out here."

"I used to tell my customers to stay away from Hadley stock like the plague. The only way I thought they'd ever get their money out would be by a forced sale."

"There won't be any forced sale around here," Charlie said grimly.

"Not if you continue to show these figures. But what I wanted to talk about, Charlie, was the way Mr. Baird is handling your reserves. You're not getting the mileage out of that chunk of cash you should. I'd like the chance to go over a few ideas with you if you——"

Charlie pointed to his car. "Can't now," he said. "I promised one of our stockholders a ride back into the city."

"I'm a stockholder too," Ed answered, grinning. "How about a ride for me?"

"When you own thirty per cent of our stock," Charlie answered, "I'll carry you on my shoulders."

At nine o'clock that evening the telephone rang again. It was Aunt Roswell.

"Now what?" Lucy asked, when Charlie returned to the living room.

"She wants me to drive her into the city tomorrow afternoon."

"What for?" Lucy asked incredulously.

"To buy a new coat."

"This is too much," Lucy exploded, getting to her feet. "I'm going to call Mother right this instant and have her put a stop to this business."

Charlie stepped in front of her.

"Go sit down," he ordered gently. "You let me handle your Aunt Roswell my own way."

"But years ago she used to do this to my father. She drove him absolutely wild."

"She doesn't drive me wild. I like her."

"You like her!" Lucy echoed. "You *like* Aunt Roswell?"

"I like her," he repeated. "She's just about my favorite member of your family."

twenty-four

UNTIL MARY ROBINSON BECAME AN ORGANIC GARDENER, ED ROBINSON HAD the best lawn on Highcliffe Road. Each year, openly and without shame, he had applied four hundred pounds of Vigoro, two hundred pounds in the spring and another two hundred in the fall. Because of it, the sod had been dark green, velvet soft, and completely free of weeds. Then one day Mary became organic, and within two years Ed's lawn was ruined.

First, the flow of chemical fertilizer was stopped, and under Mary's direction Ed constructed a compost pile in the back yard. Next, she made arrangements with her neighbors for Ed to collect their weeds, leaves, grass clippings, stumps, and even garbage. "If it will rot, I want it," she told everyone. She bought two bales of hay from a farmer, ordered two pounds of angleworms through the mail from California, added a gallon of Quik Rot, and stirred scientifically for one year. When she felt it had worked enough—when, like wine, she felt her compost pile was mellow—she had Ed fork it all out onto the lawn. As a result he soon had an interesting collection of weeds and very little else—fox tail, chickweed, Canadian thistle, poverty grass, pusley, and millions of dandelions. Also worm casts by the hundreds.

"I keep hoping it's just a stage she's going through," Ed complained more than once to Charlie. "Like Lucy and her flower arranging."

Flower arranging had become a hobby with Lucy soon after Charlie had returned from the war, and Lucy had become active in the Garden Club. Gradually it had become more than a hobby, and in 1951, when she won a first prize at the flower show, it became her religion. No longer did carrot tops or outside cabbage leaves go into the garbage can. They were placed in pots and kept fresh for weeks on end, on the chance that they might be useful as background or filler material. Charlie had once discovered six limp potatoes sprouting in the sump hole. Thinking that Lydia must have been playing a makeshift game of cellar basketball with the sump hole the goal, he had gathered the potatoes, sprouts and all, and run them through the disposal. When Lucy found out about it she had flown at him in a rage. These potato sprouts were to have been the accent in an arrangement of vegetables.

In March, 1952, two weeks before the annual flower show, Lucy sat herself next to Charlie on the living room couch and said, "Do you think there are any pussy willows in bloom on that land we own out in Hadley?"

"So it's *our* land now? I thought it was just mine."

"Your land, our land, do you think there are pussy willows in bloom yet?"

"There may be. Why?"

"I was just wondering."

"You never wonder without a reason. Flower arrangement?"

"In a way."

"Pick all you want," he said, returning to his paper. "Just don't tear them up by the roots."

"Actually," she continued, "we need more than just pussy willows."

He put his paper aside again. "We?"

"The Arrangement Committee."

"Look," he said gently, "start at the beginning of this thing."

"It's just that our committee promised to enter a March garden in the Flower Show."

"What in the world is a March garden?"

Lucy looked vague. "That's the trouble. Now that we've promised to do it, none of us really know what's expected of us."

"Whose suggestion was it?"

"Mine."

"Then you must have had something specific in mind when you thought of it."

"I did, more or less."

He waited.

"They've given us a whole section," Lucy continued. "My idea was to have a background of birch and whatever else we could find that has color all the year. Then I thought some sort of trickle of water flowing along in front. You can do that with pipes and things. Then along the water I was thinking of pussy willows and benzoin and things like that."

"Skunk cabbage?"

"This is serious, Charlie. The Flower Show is in two weeks, and there are only four of us to do the whole thing."

"And the honor of the Garden Club is at stake, no doubt."

"We don't want to make fools of ourselves, if that's what you mean."

"All right," he answered. "Why don't we plan an outing for Saturday afternoon? I'll watch the children, and you and your committee can go rape the countryside."

They went out in three cars. Kay Bemis took her oldest boy, Robin, age eight, who was supposed to be company for Lydia. However, the moment he saw the river he wandered off alone, leaving Lydia to play with Roswell. Charlie put Ruth, who was in the toddler stage, at the bottom of a cellar hole, where she could amuse herself with a pile of ashes, broken glass, and rusty nails. Lucy and the Arrangement Committee climbed the hillside, armed with clippers, trowels, rope, and a shovel. Charlie sat on the remains of an old inn doorstep and gazed down at the river.

It was a warm day. The river was running high, filled with the melting spring snow. On the opposite bank there was the first trace of red in the soft maples, and the moss on the stones had lost the dead look of winter.

A half-mile away, up the valley, he could see the top of the Company chimney, and the black, dirty roofs of the factory buildings. Now and then he stood up to check Lydia and Roswell. They were building a dam across the brook, both of them soaked to their knees. Once, when he glanced down into the cellar hole, he found Ruth chewing on the neck of a broken bottle.

"Drop it," he ordered sternly, pointing, as though she were a puppy. "Out. That's right. Spit it out."

When Ruth started to cry, the bottle neck fell to the ground.

After a while Kay Bemis passed him on her way to the car. She was carrying an armload of ferns.

"Why so pensive?" she shouted at him.

"Just peaceful," he answered. "Come join me."

"I will when I unload. I'm dying for a cigarette."

They sat talking for a while, watching the river. Kay was an ugly girl. "Poor thing, she looks like her father," was the way even her own mother described her. Her father, "Toad" Richardson, was the president of an insurance company. Kay had joined the Red Cross during the war, "to get out of her rut," as she said, and also to look for a husband. She had returned with Dave Bemis, a Californian, who had gone into the insurance business. They lived now on Southcliffe Road, two streets down in Overton Heights.

Suddenly Kay said, "Dave envies you, Charlie."

"Good Lord, why?" he asked, surprised.

"Because you're doing what you want to do."

"Am I?"

"Aren't you?"

Behind them Ruth was crying. Charlie lifted her out of the cellar hole and aimed her toward her two sisters. "Go find Lydia," he said, pointing toward the brook. Then he shouted, "Lydia, I'm sending Ruthie over there. See that she doesn't drown."

Again he sat next to Kay on the doorstep.

"Aren't you doing what you want to do?" she asked.

"I suppose I am." Then he added with conviction, "Yes, of course I am."

"And that's why Dave envies you."

Neither of them spoke for a moment.

Then Charlie smiled and said, "I was just remembering how I felt when I came back from the war. I didn't have the slightest notion of what I really wanted to do. Lucy and her mother more or less pushed me into The Hadley Company, and now I like it."

"I suppose we pushed Dave into insurance too," Kay said thoughtfully. "My father always liked it. I thought Dave would too."

"But I've really gotten interested in that old pile of bricks over there," Charlie said, pointing up the river. "Lucy's ancestors worked damned hard to build that place. I think everyone in the family has forgotten how hard they did work."

"Doesn't Mr. Chalmers work hard?" Kay asked.

"He hasn't been allowed to."

"Dave says that no one is supposed to work very hard around here."

"And he's right. You ought to know. The two cardinal sins here are not working at all and working too hard. Husbands are expected to be available at all times, when needed. When they aren't needed, they may go put in their time at their office." He glanced at Kay. "What's Dave want to do?" he asked.

"He says he'd like to sell something he can touch, and he wants a job where he can move around a little bit."

"He ought to come see me," Charlie said casually. "We've just bought out a small factory in Cleveland. We are hoping to train someone to take charge out there."

"Well, why don't you ask him?" Kay answered, equally casual.

"He'd have to move to Cleveland."

"Meaning that I'd have to move to Cleveland?"

He nodded. "And if you're like Lucy, you like it right here."

"Even *Cleveland* couldn't be worse than living here with a bored husband."

"I'm serious now, Kay. I'll ask Dave about this if you think he'd be interested."

"I know he'd be interested, so don't ask him unless you want him, because he'll take the job."

Lucy and the rest of the committee were heading down the hill, hauling armloads of birch trees and brush.

"Do me a favor," Kay said quietly. "Promise me you won't tell Dave I had anything to do with this."

"I won't say a word."

"In fact," Kay said, standing up, "when he breaks the news to me I'll probably put up one hell of a fight. Cleveland," she muttered, moving off toward her car. "The last thing I ever wanted to be was a pioneer." Then she turned about and said, "But ask Dave, will you, Charlie? In case I've forgotten to mention it, you'll be getting a wonderful man."

A week later, on Sunday night, Lucy returned from a phone call and said, "A crisis has arisen."

"Flower Show again?"

She nodded. "Mother just called. She's offered to sit for our children for the first two nights if we will do her a favor."

154

Charlie adopted an expression of wary patience.

"I thought *I* had agreed to sit for the children."

"You did, but now we need you somewhere else."

"You mean your mother needs me somewhere else."

Lucy nodded. "She's entered a table of house plants for the first two nights. Some of them are simply beautiful."

He waited.

"They'll be on a table near the main entrance."

"I know what's coming," Charlie muttered.

"You do?"

"I am about to be made a plant sitter."

"Oh, darling, would you? It would help Mother out of a terrible jam."

"Danny Girard sat last year for his mother-in-law's yucca tree. Why can't you women sit for your own plants?"

"It isn't dignified. People might think we were trying to sell them."

"Then why not string a rope around the table, with a sign, 'Do Not Touch,' or something like that? 'Trespassers will be prosecuted.'"

"They do have ropes, but you've no idea how vicious some people are when it comes to plants. They go around snipping off leaves and taking cuttings. You really have to guard things."

Charlie sighed. "All right. I'll do it. How about a stool? Danny said he got flat feet last year."

Monday night at the Flower Show passed without incident as far as Charlie was concerned, except his neck stiffened in the continuous blasts of cold March air that swept into the armory through the main entrance. Out of the thousands that shuffled past in the sawdust, laden with folders and free packets of Burpee zinnia seeds, a grand total of seven stopped to look at Mrs. Chalmers' plants. Six of them passed on without comment. The seventh, an elderly woman who carried a notebook, asked him the names of the plants. When he said he didn't know, she moved on to another exhibit, a large tank of tropical fish, which always attracted a crowd. There were no leaf snippers, no stem pinchers, and no blossom smellers, three types Lucy had warned him about.

On Tuesday night Kay Bemis arrived with Dave.

"How'd she get you in here?" Charlie asked, laughing.

Dave made a face. "Kay arrived home last night and said if you were gentleman enough to sit for your mother-in-law's plants, I could at least look at her flower arrangement."

"Have you had to arrest anyone yet?" Kay asked.

"People stay away from this table in droves," he answered. "Send Dave back here when you're through with him, Kay. I can use a little company."

"O.K.," she answered cheerily. "I'll only keep him a minute."

She pulled Dave toward the line of flower arrangements, talking steadily as she passed each one, gesticulating with her hands. Dave smiled with cynical amusement, like a carpenter at the Museum of Modern Art.

In all, Charlie had seen Dave Bemis only five or six times, and always at parties. If you knew he was from California, the signs were obvious. There was a bland handsomeness about him, his skin permanently tanned. Also he was openly friendly, as though just because he liked people he therefore assumed they would like him. After all, Charlie thought, that was what a salesman needed, a personality that could make friends quickly. From what he could see of Dave Bemis, he looked good.

During the week he had mentioned to Mr. Chalmers that he was thinking of hiring Dave.

"Is that the one who married one of the Richardson girls?" Mr. Chalmers asked.

Charlie nodded.

"I leave it all up to you, Charlie. I know the Richardsons quite well, of course. They're good solid people. He's from California, you say?" Mr. Chalmers looked vaguely concerned.

"Fresno."

"Still, I don't think anyone in the Richardson family would marry anyone they hadn't checked on pretty thoroughly in advance. If you want us to take him on, go to it. You're in charge of our sales department."

"I've done my duty," Dave said when he returned without Kay. Then he grinned and said, "What do you do if someone reaches out like this and makes a pass at a leaf?" He leaned over the rope and reached for one of Mrs. Chalmers' white African violets.

"On your way, brother," Charlie snarled at him, "or I'll knock your teeth in."

An old woman who had stopped at the table gasped with surprise.

"It's all right, madam," Charlie said, bowing. "He's a friend of mine. Duck under the rope, Dave. Where did you leave Kay?"

"Down with Lucy at their exhibit. The girls take this stuff pretty seriously, don't they?"

"You can't kid a Catholic or a flower arranger," Charlie answered.

The armory had filled with people. It had turned cold outside, and the pale winter complexions and the dark winter clothing made the mass of color in the displays seem even brighter. At the other end of the hall a department store was putting on a fashion show. A knot of teen-agers were whistling at the models as they passed across a stage. The air smelled of cigarette smoke and damp earth.

"When you've seen one of these shows, you've seen all of them," Charlie said. "It's just a stunt to sell more garden supplies."

Dave was sniffing one of Mrs. Chalmers' orchid plants.

"Kay and I bought some liquid fertilizer here last year," he said. "The folder that came with it said it would revolutionize gardening. We poured it on some pansies, and they grew three feet tall but never put out blossoms."

They were quiet for a moment.

"How are things in the insurance business?" Charlie asked.

"The same as they always are. Secure."

"Is that good or bad?"

"Neither. Just dull."

"I gather you don't like it?"

"I'm told I'll get used to it. They say you get numb."

Charlie moved to the far corner of the table, his back to the hall.

"We've just bought out a small shop in Cleveland," he said. "We think it has quite a future."

"Cleveland," Dave said thoughtfully.

Charlie nodded. "It's not much of a plant yet. Just a warehouse, a small plant, and ten acres of land near a railroad siding."

"Are you going out there to run it yourself?"

"No. We figure on training someone for a while and then putting him in charge."

"I suppose you have your man all picked out?"

"Not yet. We're just looking around."

Dave laughed. "If I wasn't sure Kay would blow her top, I'd ask you to look me over."

"Well," Charlie said quietly, "how about it?"

"Are you serious?"

"I've never been more serious in my life. You'd have to go to work with us out in Hadley for a few months. We'd send you through our factory to give you an idea of what we do. Then you'd have to be a salesman for a while. You could go out with me on some of my trips. I'm planning to set up displays in most of the hardware shows. You could help me with that. Then if things worked out, we'd put you in Cleveland, where you'd be pretty much on your own. It would mean a lot of time away from your wife."

"Kay is going to blow her top," Dave said grimly. "We are about to have one turbulent scene."

"Wives get used to not having a husband home all the time. Lucy has."

"Kay likes the stable life. You don't know her the way I do."

"Everyone who likes the city likes the stable life. But if Kay thinks you really want to do this, she'll go along. She'll have to," he added. "Just tell her you're going to do it, no matter what she thinks or says."

"Dammit," Dave said, "I'll talk it over with Kay and let you know tomorrow."

"What would your answer be if I asked you to say yes or no right now?"

"Are you asking me to say yes or no right now?" Dave asked, startled.

"Of course not. You might not like what you see of our factory, or you might not like the pay we offer you. But I'm just curious as to how you feel about it."

"I'd say yes, Charlie. Just like that."

"Come on out tomorrow. I'll show you around. If you like it, you can go home and tell Kay you have a new job."

They were interrupted by a shriek from Lucy at the other end of the table.

"Charlie," she shouted, "look at Mother's Clivia plant."

"What's the matter with it?" he asked blankly. The plant looked all right to him.

"About two seconds ago I saw one of those filthy little high-school boys running out a side exit with a beautiful Clivia blossom. And look," Lucy wailed, "he must have sliced it off right here." She pointed to a bleeding stem.

"Oh, brother," Dave Bemis muttered. "You've got troubles, boss."

"Run along," Charlie said. "I'll see you tomorrow at the factory."

"The least you could do is take your job seriously," Lucy said angrily. She was near tears. "Mother will be wild."

"I'll break the bad news to your mother myself," Charlie said when they were turning in Highcliffe Road. "There's no point in your taking any blame for it."

"She'll be simply fit to be tied," Lucy said miserably. "This was the first time she'd ever had a Clivia in bloom for the show."

They found Mrs. Chalmers seated alone at the kitchen table. She looked ill, or as though she had recently recovered from an illness, her face pale, her expression grave. She had heated herself a cup of soup.

"Sit down, children. Something rather serious happened here tonight."

"Is something wrong, Mother?" Lucy asked immediately frightened.

"It's all right now, darling. It could have been a good deal worse than it was. I shudder to think what might have happened if I hadn't gone upstairs when I did."

"Good Lord, what, Mother?" Lucy shouted.

"I did exactly as you asked me to, Lucy. At seven I drew the girls a bath. Not too deep. I remembered your instructions precisely. I also put all three of them into the tub together. I suppose that might have been careless of me, but I remember our old nurse Alma used to do that with you three in the old days." Mrs. Chalmers sipped her soup. "I'm still quaking when I think what might have happened."

"What did happen?" Charlie asked impatiently.

"I'm telling you, Charles," she answered. "At least I'm trying to. I placed Lydia in charge. It seemed to me that at her age she should be perfectly capable of helping her two sisters with their bath."

"She is," Lucy interrupted, "as long as you keep your eye on her."

"I'm afraid that's what I didn't do," Mrs. Chalmers continued. "They seemed to be getting along so well I went on downstairs to make some telephone calls. I'm up to my ears in this frightful hospital drive, and I've been given a long list of names to call before next week. I thought, what better time to make my calls." She paused, again sipping her soup.

"What happened upstairs?" Charlie asked.

"I first noticed that it seemed quiet," Mrs. Chalmers said. "You know how with children you begin to wonder what they're doing when they suddenly are quiet. I didn't think much about it at first. They had been so happy together in the tub when I left them. That little minx Roswell had soaped the back of the tub, and she and Lydia were sliding down into the water, just like two happy little otters."

"If you're just going to say that water leaked through the bathroom floor," Lucy interrupted, "that will be nothing new."

"I'm afraid not, darling. I'm afraid what I'm going to tell you is that I am not a responsible baby sitter. It seems that Lydia and Roswell have a game they like to play. It's called Lifeguard."

"Lifeguard?" Lucy echoed blankly, looking at Charlie.

"Yes. Lifeguard," Mrs. Chalmers repeated. "Did Lydia, by any chance, see someone being rescued down at the beach last summer, Lucy?"

"Not that I know of."

"Well, she seemed to know a great deal about the proper procedure, including artificial respiration."

"Good God," Charlie muttered.

"Yes, Charles. Good God. When I arrived back in the bathroom Lydia was kneeling on little Ruthie, giving her artificial respiration. And I must say she seemed to need it," Mrs. Chalmers continued. "Apparently, Lydia had first held Ruthie face down in the water, in order to drown her. Then when she decided she was sufficiently drowned, she rescued her. That's what she kept telling me. That she was rescuing her from the water."

"Is she still out?" Charlie shouted.

"Of course not," Mrs. Chalmers answered stiffly, as though it were a stupid question. "I held her up for a moment by her ankles, and the water drained out of her. She came around almost instantly. But I must say the whole thing has given me a horrible fright."

"Is Ruthie all right now, Mother?"

"Perfectly, darling. She went to sleep just like a little lamb. But I'm afraid I'm just not a proper baby sitter. The next time you'll simply have to hire someone who is trained for these things."

In the silence that followed Charlie said, "I suppose now is my chance to break my bad news to you, Mother Chalmers."

"Bad news for me too, Charles?"

"I'm afraid so."

"If you're about to tell me that no one admired my plants, I assure you I'm quite used to that."

"I'm afraid someone did admire your plants. At least one of them."

"Tell her," Lucy said grimly.

"Tell me what?" Mrs. Chalmers said, her eyebrows raised.

"Someone sliced off the blossom on your Clivia plant, Mother Chalmers."

Mrs. Chalmers glanced at Lucy. "Your husband is joking, Lucy."

"I'm afraid he isn't, Mother."

"My Clivia plant?" She turned back to Charlie. "But weren't you right there? Didn't you see it happening? Couldn't you stop it?"

"I was there, Mother Chalmers, but I'm afraid I was talking to a friend of mine."

"My Clivia plant?" Mrs. Chalmers repeated. "Someone cut off the blossom?"

"I'm sorry, Mother Chalmers."

159

Mrs. Chalmers turned again to Lucy.

"Is he sorry or not?" she asked.

"Of course he is, Mother."

Mrs. Chalmers stood up and moved toward the hall to get her coat. As she was leaving through the front door, she said, "Thank you, Charles. I appreciate your help tonight." Her voice could have cut glass.

"You're welcome, Mother Chalmers," Charlie answered. "And we appreciate yours."

"It might have been worse," Charlie told Lucy when they were turning off the lights.

"I hardly see how. Mother's been nursing that plant for one whole year, trying to get it to blossom in time for the show."

"I meant about Ruthie," he answered. "Lydia might really have drowned her."

twenty-five

BY THE TIME LYDIA HAD GONE THROUGH THREE GRADES OF PUBLIC SCHOOL SHE had picked up a number of bad habits. Jews had seeped into the Overton Heights development, and by the time she was eight years old Lydia had quite a distinct Jewish accent. Neither Lucy nor Mrs. Chalmers were particularly amused by this, nor were they horrified, both of them feeling certain that in due time Lydia would outgrow it, that her English would return to normal the moment she learned the significance of the word "accent." In fact they almost thought it cute of Lydia when she came home from school talking about her "wint-teh" coat, and when Lydia's class spent a week studying birds, the phrase "paint-ted bunt-ting" became quite a by-word in the family. "And how is my little paint-ted bunt-ting today?" Mrs. Chalmers would ask her oldest granddaughter when they all went over to the Lawn Street house for Sunday dinner.

Then there was also minor consternation because Lydia referred to her schoolmates as "girl friends" or "boy friends." Family pressure was brought to bear on these matters, and Lydia became quite conscious of it, doing her best to keep her accent and her language pure. Like any normally intelligent child she split her language into two separate dialects. One she used with her girl friends and her boy friends. The other she spoke at home. From nine to three each day her speech was an American alloy. With her parents and her grandparents she did her eight-year-old best to keep it pure English gold.

However, everything came to a crisis one Sunday noon just as Mr. Chalmers bowed his head to say grace. Lydia chose that moment to cross herself.

"What were you doing?" Mrs. Chalmers asked in frosty surprise, the instant Mr. Chalmers was through.

"Yes, what were you doing?" Lucy echoed.

"What *was* she doing?" Charlie asked, springing to the defense of Lydia, who was looking both embarrassed and trapped.

"What were you doing?" Mrs. Chalmers repeated. "I mean this business?" She made a series of gyrations with her right hand and arm.

"Practicing," Lydia answered, lowering her head.

"Practicing what, darling?" Lucy asked.

"Come now, let's not frighten the poor child to death," Mr. Chalmers put in. "You had an itch, didn't you, Lydia?"

"Be quiet, Lowell," Mrs. Chalmers said. "What were you practicing, Lydia?"

"Everyone does that before they pray," Lydia answered miserably.

"I see," Mrs. Chalmers answered precisely. "Look at me, darling." She waited. "Everyone does not do it before they pray. *We* do not do it before *we* pray."

"Everyone at school does it, Grandmother Chalmers."

"I hardly think that everyone at school does do it," Mrs. Chalmers answered. "How about all your little Jewish friends? Do they do it?"

Lydia nodded.

"Come now, Lydia. Do they?"

"If they don't, Danny O'Niel socks them."

The dining room was silent for a moment. Then Mrs. Chalmers said, "Are you serious, child? Does this little Irish boy force all of you to cross yourselves?"

"If we don't, he hits us," Lydia answered. "He's real tough." Then she added proudly, "He's my boy friend."

"Let it go, Mother," Lucy said meaningfully. "Let's talk about it after dinner."

"Yes, do let's talk about it after dinner," Mrs. Chalmers said grimly, starting to cut her meat.

Sunday dinners at the Chalmers' had always followed the same pattern. Charlie considered it all a part of church. Church ruined the first part of the day, and dinner at the Chalmers' ruined the rest. He, Lucy, and the children would arrive at the Chalmers' at twelve-fifteen, all of them a little mean from boredom and hunger. Mr. Chalmers would offer them a drink. Mrs. Chalmers would say, "Dear me, Lowell. On Sunday?" He would retreat gracefully. It was a mere ritual with him, to prove that he, at least, was not stuffy. Then after a hectic half-hour, with the children snapping and snarling at each other and the older people wishing they dared, dinner would finally be announced, and they would eat—Ruthie and Roswell in the kitchen, Lydia, from the time she was seven, at the main table.

Dinner would be over at two. Mr. Chalmers would drift away silently to his study, and Lucy, after putting the children upstairs for their rests, would sit in the living room with her mother for their weekly gossip review. In exchange for the news of her generation, Mrs. Chalmers would offer Lucy certain choice tidbits from hers. If Lucy told her mother that someone had seen Petie Osborn dining with his secretary, Mrs. Chalmers would tell Lucy that Petie Osborn Senior had been just the same in his younger days, that Dodie Osborn hadn't even been able to trust him with the maids.

Gradually Lucy would become sleepy and would put her head onto her mother's lap. Here they would stay until nearly four, mother and daughter, talking, or catching forty winks, as Mrs. Chalmers called it, since she never took naps. Naps to her were immoral, a mere form of escape, like alcohol or opium. It was permissible to become sick, but not tired. You could take forty winks on a Sunday afternoon, but never a nap.

The house on Lawn Street cast a spell over Lucy. The moment she stepped through the door, Charlie would lose her. Again she'd be a daughter and no longer a wife. Lucy and her mother shared certain pet phrases together, words that to them meant volumes and to him nothing. "Around and around she goes," Mrs. Chalmers would giggle, and Lucy would smile, remembering some secret from her childhood, some episode of Chalmers history. "Your poor Charlie doesn't know what we two are talking about, does he?" Mrs. Chalmers would say, twisting a lock of Lucy's hair gently in her fingers. He didn't, nor did they ever enlighten him. When Lucy returned to Lawn Street, she crawled back into her mother's womb, and Charlie would be cut loose to walk alone in the garden.

On the Sunday that Lydia crossed herself, however, there were no forty winks in the living room after dinner. Lucy and her mother were both sitting wide awake, on two separate Windsor chairs.

"So the time has finally arrived," Lucy said by way of her opening remark.

"Charlie's noble experiment is over," Mrs. Chalmers added, smiling at Charlie with nothing but good will.

"Miss Nickols, here we come," Charlie muttered grimly.

"Yes, Miss Nickols, we are coming," Lucy said firmly. "We should have started her there."

"Good Lord, just because at eight years of age she's fallen in love with someone named Danny O'Niel. Isn't it better to have her get it out of her system at eight instead of eighteen?"

Mrs. Chalmers, obviously pleased to have Charlie on the defensive, said gently, "Didn't you once tell Lucy that you used to linger outside Miss Nickols on your way home from public school? I thought you admired all the little girls who went there."

"I envied them," he corrected.

"All right, you envied them. Don't you want your little girls to grow up being envied?"

"No, I don't," he said angrily. "I want them to grow up feeling at home in this mess we call America."

"Charlie's getting pompous," Lucy said wearily. "I feel completely at home in this mess you call America, and I never went to public school in my life. Did I, Mother?"

"She didn't, Charlie, and Lucy is one of the best-adjusted young ladies I know."

"Certainly she is. As long as she can eat Sunday dinner every week with her family. As long as she is surrounded and protected by her circle of old friends. As long as she doesn't have to move one inch from her own little puddle."

"We're getting off the subject," Mrs. Chalmers prompted. "I'd like to tell you, Charlie, what's been happening right here on Lawn Street. Do you know the Addison place?"

He nodded. "I know. It's going to become a nunnery or something."

"And they've bought the land on the opposite corner to put up a parochial school."

"I know. I know. I know," Charlie answered impatiently. "I don't like it any more than you do. But the solution isn't to put our children in our own parochial schools."

"What *is* he talking about?" Mrs. Chalmers asked, turning to Lucy.

"Charlie just doesn't like Miss Nickols," Lucy answered. "We've been through all this before."

"I do like Miss Nickols," he insisted. "But it honestly seems to me as though the whole educational system is breaking down around here. The Catholics are yanking their children out of the public schools. We're yanking our children out of the public schools, and I suppose before long the Jews will be doing the same thing. It's against everything I believe in."

"A very wise man once said to me," Mrs. Chalmers told them calmly, "to experiment with yourself, if you must, but not with your children."

"This is all just sheer snobbery," Charlie answered. "The Catholics are snobs with their parochial schools, and we're snobs with our Miss Nickols. Someday it's going to tear this country apart."

"Charlie, Charlie, Charlie," Mrs. Chalmers said, laughing.

"It will," he insisted. "Within Lucy's and my lifetime you'll see a mean, ugly fight about this thing we're talking about. What's it going to be? A public school system for everyone, or parochial schools for everyone? The thing's building up, and I hate to help it along."

"In the meantime," Mrs. Chalmers said, "your Lydia comes home crossing herself."

He sighed. "I don't like it any more than you do, Mrs. Chalmers. I just wish the Catholics could confine their religion to their churches, but I guess they can't."

"Charlie," Lucy said, waiting until he looked at her. "Please let's send her to Miss Nickols."

"All right," he answered, "we'll send her to Miss Nickols, but I hate it."

Because he'd capitulated too easily, Mrs. Chalmers said, "I must say I don't like it either. The problem was nowhere near so acute in our generation. We had these people, but we didn't have to live with them as closely as you do now." She turned to Lucy. "What did a Catholic mean to you when you were young?" she asked.

"Did I know any, Mother?"

"Of course you did, darling. Think."

"You mean the maids?"

"Exactly." She turned back to Charlie. "You see, thirty years ago we had a built-in safeguard. It doesn't exist today. You say the word 'Catholic' to your daughter Lydia, and she thinks of a rather charming little Irish boy named Danny O'Niel. I'm sure he is charming," she added. "They always are at that age."

Charlie stood up. "If no one minds," he said, "I think I'll go for a walk."

"Roswell too?" Lucy asked, following him out into the hall.

"Roswell too?" he echoed.

She nodded. "She'll be starting in the first grade next year."

"Dammit, no," he said angrily. "Not in the first grade."

"All right," she agreed quickly, afraid that he might change his mind about Lydia. "And Charlie, I really agree with you about schools and things, but what can you do?"

"Nothing," he said wearily. "Nothing."

He walked on up the stairs to collect Lydia and Roswell for the Sunday walk on the golf course. Lydia was beginning to show an interest in the game.

twenty-six

WHEN DAVE BEMIS MOVED OUT TO CLEVELAND IN JUNE OF 1953, DRIVING OUT with Kay and their two children, he left a year-old Irish setter named Brian with Charlie. The agreement was that Charlie would keep the dog for the summer, until Kay got set in their new house. Then when Dave came East in the late summer for the New York hardware show, he would take the dog back to Cleveland with him. Lucy was far from pleased.

"I can think of one reason right off the bat," she said when Charlie brought Brian home with him. "I hate dogs."

"I was thinking of the children," he answered. "I thought this would be a fairly good way of trying a dog out. I've noticed that almost everyone on the street has a dog."

"Exactly," she answered. "Everyone does have a dog. Did you hear what happened to the Robinsons' Scotty last week? It came home completely torn to shreds by the Littlehales' new boxer. Ed has a fifty-dollar bill from the vet."

"Brian looks like he can take care of himself," Charlie answered, smoothing the hair on the top of the setter's head. "I hate to have the girls growing up afraid of dogs."

"We never had one."

"Look, Lucy," he said, "Brian stays for the summer. If you must know the truth, I was thinking of myself. Brian will be good company, and when you and the children are away at the Island it gets lonely around here."

Lucy's expression softened. "You poor darling," she said. "Are you really lonely without us?"

"Sometimes."

"Then come with us. The Hadley Company will never miss you."

"I can't, and you know it. With Dave gone, I've got to break in another new salesman."

"I don't see how Brian will fit in with that."

"I'll take him with me."

She patted Charlie's head. "Have your dog if you must," she said cheerfully, "but I never thought I'd play second fiddle to an Irish setter."

Charlie returned from his first selling trip of the summer on a hot, muggy evening at the end of June. He parked his car in the driveway and let Brian out onto the lawn.

"You run around a while," he said to the dog. "I'll go up and take a shower."

After three weeks with him, Charlie had begun to think of Brian as a human being. During the days when he was driving from one city to another, the setter had sat on the front seat next to him or leaned out the window, his ears flapping like two small red flags. When they stopped for the night in motels Brian had given him an excuse to get some exercise. They'd gone for a swim in the Hudson River and climbed a mountain in upstate New York. It was going to be quite a loss, he knew, when Dave Bemis finally claimed his dog at the end of the summer.

Charlie went on into the house, opening the windows and the doors. The rooms smelled musty and stale. First he'd take his shower. Then he'd call Lucy and tell her he wouldn't be down over the week end. He'd been away from the factory for two weeks, and work had piled up on his desk. He planned to spend Saturday morning, when the plant was quiet, cleaning it up.

There were those, he knew, who commuted every week end to a summer place, no matter how far away it was. But week-end commuters, he had observed, followed a pattern. They were more interested in sailing, sun tan, and golf than they were in their jobs, even though they claimed it was their wife and their children they were driving to see.

As he was soaping himself in the shower his loneliness hit him for the first time. An empty house, he thought, was misery when you'd been away for two weeks. As you grew older loneliness was apt to increase. When you were in your twenties, you were sure that the next day or the next week something interesting would happen. But by the time you were thirty-five you could predict things. You knew what you'd be doing the next day, the next month, and even the next year.

The last two weeks had been successful. The new salesman was just out of college. If the boy liked the work and made good at it, Charlie planned to send him on out to Dave in Cleveland.

When he'd driven into Hadley at noon that day and had passed the hardware store, he'd noticed a row of new lawn mowers out on the sidewalk. Jim Hartry, the proprietor, was tying on the price tags. Charlie had stopped his car and had shouted at him.

"Those look like the mowers we make the blades for, Mr. Hartry."

Jim Hartry was a short, squat man with a tobacco stain on his lower lip. Besides running his hardware store, he was the town's first selectman and also the head of the Republican Town Committee. He wore a blue denim jacket and a hat that had been given to him by a grain company.

"What's good for the factory," he said, waving toward the river, "is good for me."

"How are they selling?" Charlie asked.

"Pretty good. People seem to like 'em."

He wandered over to Charlie's car and leaned his elbows against the open window.

"Got a minute, Mr. Webb?"

Charlie grinned at him. "Since you're a Republican, Jim, you can call me Charlie."

"That answers me one question I was going to put to you. You never can tell these days when a young fella like you might be one of them eggheads."

"Not me," Charlie answered. "What's on your mind?"

"Politics," Jim Hartry answered, turning his head slightly and ejecting a stream of brown tobacco juice into the gutter. "You acquainted with George Ames?"

"I've heard of him. Doesn't he have a farm up the river?"

Jim Hartry nodded. "He's also our man at the State Capitol. We've been sending him up there for twenty years. Fine man. There ain't no man better than George Ames, only he's getting kinda old."

"Come on in and sit down," Charlie said, curious. Jim Hartry slid onto the seat.

"I'll come right out with it, Charlie. Some of us out here have been wondering whether maybe you would be interested in going up to the State Capitol." He grinned. "Big money in it. Six hundred dollars a year."

"You forgot two things," Charlie answered. "First of all, I've already got a job that keeps me plenty busy."

"The busier a man is, the more he can do," Jim Hartry answered, as though he had been expecting such an answer.

"The other thing you forget is that I don't even live out here."

"You own property. Ralph Henry down to your factory told me a few years back you was figuring on building down there sometime."

"Sometime, perhaps, but not right away." Then he added, "I'll be honest about it, Jim. I'd like to go to the State Capitol. But to move out here right now would take some doing."

"Wife doing?"

Charlie nodded. "Lucy's life pretty much revolves around the city."

Jim Hartry looked thoughtful for a moment. Then he spat out the car window.

166

"It was my grandfather," he said, wiping his lower lip with the sleeve of his jacket, "who started your wife's great-great-grandfather on his way to Washington. I had kind of a notion I'd start you down the same road. Only I don't want you when you're old, because by that time I'll be dead myself. I've been looking around for a candidate like you for twenty years. I'll tell you something, Charlie," he continued, "there's a lot of Democrats down there in your factory, and they's the ones that's been telling me I ought to run you."

"What do they want to do?" Charlie asked, laughing. "Get me away from the factory?"

"You're the best thing that's happened to this town in thirty years, since Old Mr. Hadley died, and there ain't nobody in this whole town who don't know it."

"Well, thanks," Charlie answered, touched. "And I'll think about this business because I'm tempted."

Jim Hartry stepped out of the car. "Don't wait too long. Old George Ames might take a notion to die up there in the Capitol."

Charlie had been thinking about his talk with Jim Hartry all the rest of the day.

After he was finished with his shower, he lay on the bed for a while. When he had been in college, he had often thought about a political career. The beginning of most politicians' careers always seemed to be mysterious. How did they get their first political office? he wondered. Once a foot was on the bottom rung of the ladder, to climb it seemed comparatively easy. But where did the ladder start? He had learned the answer that afternoon. Political careers started in the minds of men like Jim Hartry, who chewed tobacco and ran the hardware store in Hadley.

He rolled off the bed and slipped into a pair of army suntans. His thirty-two-inch army trousers fitted a little tight, but the top button still met the buttonhole.

He walked out into the upstairs hall and opened the phone book. Lucy had written the number on a slip of paper and clipped it inside the cover. Just as he reached for the telephone, it rang.

It must be Mr. Chalmers, he thought, inviting him over for a late supper at the Lawn Street house.

"Hi," he said, when he lifted the receiver.

"Hi, yourself," a woman's voice answered. "Do you own a dog?"

"Oh, Lord," Charlie said. "What's he done?"

"This is Terry Goddard, Charlie."

"That's a relief," he answered. "I thought you might be a police matron."

"Your dog is sitting on my back porch howling. Listen." After a moment of silence, she said, "Do you hear him?"

"Vaguely. Throw something at him, Terry, and tell him to go back to 37 Highcliffe Road. Tell him it's a white house with dark green blinds."

"He won't budge, Charlie."

"Did you feed him? I hope not."

"Not a speck."

"Then he'll come back. He's hungry."

"I doubt it very much. I think he thinks he's found something more interesting than food."

"Such as what?" he asked, by now curious. He hadn't seen Terry Goddard in almost a year.

"It's a slightly sordid subject," she answered. "When you come over to get him, you'll find out for yourself."

The Goddards lived on Centercliffe Road, one street down. Their house, like all the others in the development, was a seven-room colonial with a wood shingle roof. It was at the end of the street, in a grove of pin oak trees.

There were at least six other dogs on the Goddards' lawn, including the Robinsons' Scotty and the Littlehales' boxer. They lay in a silent ring, now and then raising their heads to sniff the air and howl. Brian was on the Goddards' back porch, standing on his hind legs, scratching the kitchen door and barking.

"What goes on?" he asked Terry when she peered through a one-inch crack in the door. "Are you and Newell running a kennel?"

"Dogs just seem to like us," she answered with exaggerated innocence.

Charlie had brought a length of clothesline. He tied it to Brian's collar and looped it about his wrist. Terry opened the door and stepped out onto the porch. She was wearing shorts and a man's white shirt. She was barefooted, and there was bright red nail polish on her toenails.

Terry had changed since Charlie first met her. When Newell brought her back from Denver there had been a sparkle about her. When she entered a room conversation was apt to stop for an instant, then start up again as the men drifted away from whomever they were talking to, particularly their own wives, and headed toward Terry. Her skin had been brown and smooth, her body flat and hard, and her movements graceful, like a female leopard.

Now, however, she looked beaten down and bored. She had gained weight, most of it around her neck and chin, and her hair was dirty. It hung in a careless pony tail down the back of her shirt, gathered together with an elastic. She could use a bath, Charlie thought. Her skin looked sticky, coated with two-day perspiration.

"I've been mopping the kitchen all day," she said, interpreting his expression. "I'm filthy dirty."

"You and Newell must have a female dog around here somewhere," he said, nodding toward the lawn. The collection of dogs was moving closer, enticed by the open door.

"We do. She's down in the cellar in the laundry room. Newell's away with the car or I'd take her to a kennel."

"Where did Newell go with the car?" he asked, lingering.

"Fayetteville, Kansas," she answered casually, as though it were the most natural place in the world for a husband to be.

"What in hell is he doing out there?"

"Seeing some of his radio pals." When Charlie looked blank, Terry added,

168

"He talks to these people at night on his radio. Newell's a ham. I think that's the phrase."

"And you stay at home and entertain dogs?"

"And read, and sleep, and mop the kitchen floor." She moved to the porch railing and sat clasping one knee. There was nothing wrong with Terry's figure that a little exercise wouldn't cure, Charlie thought as he watched her.

"I just had a thought," he said. "I could run your dog out to a kennel if you'd like me to. I have nothing else to do. Lucy's away."

"Would you really, Charlie?"

"I'd be glad to," he answered. Then he looked at her steadily for a moment. "How about you?" he asked. "I'll take you out to dinner."

"Couldn't possibly," she answered, meeting his gaze.

He walked toward her. She straightened out one leg and put a bare foot against his knee, stopping him three feet away.

"Couldn't possibly," she repeated. "Those things just aren't done around here."

"If Newell is foolish enough to leave you at home alone, he should be punished."

"I could have gone with him," she answered. "Fayetteville, Kansas just wasn't my idea of heaven in late June."

"Have dinner with me, Terry."

"We shouldn't, you know, Charlie. Overton Heights has ten thousand eyes."

"I'll be back in twenty minutes," he said. "Wear something purple or blue. I think of you wearing that color."

He pulled Brian along toward his car, not giving Terry a chance to answer. He was back twenty minutes later.

"I'm here," he shouted up the stairs.

"Mix yourself a drink. I'll be another minute or two."

He walked into the Goddard living room and sat on the couch. The room was cold and bare, the walls a pastel green, the ceiling white, and the curtains a pale yellow. Everything in the room looked new and unused; even the fireplace bricks were still unmarked by fire. The room shouted the fact that there were no children in the Goddard household. There were no scars, no scratches, no tears or stains, and no crayon marks on the walls.

"So," Terry said, coming into the room from the hall, "here I am all ready to give the neighbors something to talk about."

She was wearing a dark blue summer dress and red shoes. She had also washed her hair. It hung off the side of her head in strands, still heavy and damp.

"Better wet than dirty," she said. "And it will dry. Do you mind?"

"It just makes it obvious how good looking you really are," he answered.

She started toward the front door. Then she stopped and said, "Oh, I almost forgot Beth."

"Beth?"

"The cause of all this. She's down in the laundry room. I'll go get her."

169

When they were driving west out of the city Charlie said, "Can I ask you a question? Why don't you have your dog spayed?"

Terry was ready with an answer. "Because," she said, "I thought that one sterile female in our house was enough."

Had his question been thoughtless, Charlie wondered, or had Terry's answer been unnecessary? She left him with nothing to say.

"Ask a foolish question and get a foolish answer," he said finally.

"We should have her spayed," Terry admitted. "Newell wants to. But I enjoy the spectacle of hundreds of dogs descending on me twice a year. If I'm feeling lonely I merely venture out, select a dog like a big red setter, read who owns him on his name tag, place a phone call, and presto, I have company."

After they put Beth in a kennel Charlie said, "Have you ever eaten at an inn called The Stage, on the Albany Turnpike?"

"Newell takes me nowhere," Terry answered. "Sounds divine. Let's go."

"It's twenty-five miles from here."

"Twenty-five miles, ninety-five miles. Who cares?"

After they had driven for a while, Terry said, "Will Lucy be annoyed with you when you tell her you took me out to dinner?"

"I don't plan to tell her," he answered.

"Then let's get our signals straight. We don't mention this to anyone. Am I right?"

"That seems sensible to me."

"I just wondered what your policy was on these things."

"I have no policy, Terry. You happen to be the first wife I've ever taken out to dinner other than my own."

"Well, that's nice," she answered. "I thought perhaps you had Brian trained to go sit on the back porches of lonely wives."

The Stage had once been a coach stop on the route from Boston to Albany. It was a large white inn, with a long row of sheds leading out to a sagging barn. Charlie liked it because it wasn't cute. The bar was just a bar, with no clever signs and sayings on the walls and no *New Yorker* cartoons on the napkins. They didn't sell hand weavings from North Carolina, or maple syrup from Vermont, or souvenirs from downtown New York. The owner of The Stage assumed his customers came to eat and drink. The floors and the walls were pine, wide boards curled with age and stained with time and smoke.

"Let's sit out on the terrace," Charlie said, leading Terry on through the dining room and the bar. "We can order a steak and have a drink or two while we wait."

"Lead on," she answered promptly.

It was a welcome relief from dinner out with Lucy. Lucy liked to weigh all things before she made a decision—where they should sit, which table and which chair at the table she should choose, which plate, which drink, and above all else which entry on the menu.

"They make a drink here called the Coachman. I don't know what's in it, but it's excellent."

"I'll take one," Terry answered.

"Are you always this agreeable?"

"I was wondering if you were always this competent."

"Only with another man's wife."

"Probably I'm only this agreeable with another woman's husband," she answered.

There were two tables on the terrace, both of them under an apple tree. Just before dark a jet passed high overhead, with the sun, which had long since disappeared behind the mountains to the west, reflected from the plane's vapor trail, a twenty-mile-long ribbon of white hanging in the atmosphere.

"Now where do you think he's going?" Terry asked, gazing at the sky.

"Who knows? Wherever it is, he's in a terrible hurry to get there."

When they had finished their dinner they sat quietly, lulled into contentment by two cocktails, a steak, and a bottle of wine. The first crickets of the season were singing in the grass beyond the terrace, and two dogs were barking in the distance.

"Does Lucy leave you alone often?"

"In the summer. She likes the ocean."

"And you don't?"

"I don't have the interest or the time."

A green apple the size of a marble bounced onto the table from the tree above. Both Terry and Charlie reached for it, their hands meeting, the apple rolling onto the ground.

"So," Terry said, making no attempt to remove her hand from his. "Tell me what your problem is."

"Problem? I have no problem."

"You must. If you didn't have a problem, you wouldn't be here with me."

"Whatever it is, it isn't anything that you can solve."

"Well, what is it? I collect men's problems."

He hesitated a moment, thinking; then he said, "I suppose my problem is that there are no problems. I married into a family that has everything. Money, leisure, education, friends, and children. Starting tomorrow, I could spend the rest of my life lying in the sun, and life would go on just like a pleasant dream. We have no excessive virtue, no vices that we can't control. We don't have mistresses in New York. We don't drink too much. We don't want things, and whatever we do want we can have."

"Sounds nice," Terry answered dreamily.

"It isn't. It's awful."

"Then you must want something you don't have, Charlie."

"I suppose I do."

171

"What?"

"Oh, I suppose success. Something I get all by myself."

"Then go be a success."

"Are you laughing at me?" he asked, embarrassed. "You asked me to bare my soul, and I'm baring it."

"I'm not laughing," she answered.

He pulled her hand closer to him over the top of the table.

"I'm beginning to learn that it's a lot easier to be successful at something when you start at the bottom. When someone hands you a pleasant, contented existence on a silver platter, it takes guts to rise above it. I was offered a chance to run for political office today," he continued. "I'd like to do it very much. But it will mean I have to throw my life into an uproar for a while. I'll have to move out to Hadley. That will put Lucy's friends and her mother eighteen miles away instead of a half-block away. It will mean she has to be a lot more self-sufficient than she is now. Just because I'm slightly ambitious, her life will change too, and she won't like it. For her, life is perfect now, and she won't see why we should change it. Why fool around with paradise?"

"Paradise?" Terry said sarcastically.

"Lucy thinks it is."

"But she has everything she wants."

"Don't all the wives? Don't you?"

The moment he asked her the question he regretted it. Terry drew her hand away.

"You forget I have no children," she said quietly. "Why don't we pay the bill and start along home?"

When they were a mile from The Stage, Charlie glanced at Terry and said, "I'm sorry I got on that subject. I just didn't think."

"Don't be sorry," she answered blithely. "I was just thinking what a delightful evening this has been, and feeling sad that it had to end."

"Does it?" he asked. When she didn't answer, he said, "When is Newell coming home?"

"Next Sunday night," she answered. "And don't ask me, because I'll say no."

Centercliffe Road was dark when Charlie parked his car in front of the Goddards' house.

"The dogs have finally gone," Terry said, looking out the window.

He slid across the seat and put his chin against her back. If she had turned about he would have kissed her. She didn't move.

"Next Sunday is a long, long time away. What are you going to do in the meantime?"

"Sleep late. Eat cheese for lunch. Take a nap until three. Then ride to the A and P on my bicycle to buy more cheese."

"Is that what you're going to do tomorrow?"

172

She nodded.

"Why don't I drive you to the A and P?"

She shook her head. "I need the exercise."

"Actually, I was going to suggest that——"

"Don't suggest anything," she interrupted. "I promise you I'll say no."

"Then say no. I was going to suggest a picnic at the Chalmers' farm."

"All right. No." She opened the car door and stepped out onto the sidewalk. "Thank you for a lovely evening," she said, peering in at him through the open window. "It was a surprise, but a nice one."

"Is this the end of our affair?"

"It would seem so."

"You might see me tomorrow at the A and P. Buy a little extra cheese. Some bread, hamburger, and some beer. Enough of everything for two."

"No, and good night," she answered.

She disappeared up the front walk.

twenty-seven

AT THREE O'CLOCK THE NEXT AFTERNOON TERRY RODE ACROSS THE PARKING lot on her bicycle toward the store's main entrance. She was wearing Bermuda shorts, blue tennis shoes, and a bright red sleeveless blouse. She locked the rear wheel of her bicycle, took a cloth shopping bag from the wire basket on the handlebars, and disappeared into the throng of Saturday shoppers.

After waiting a moment, Charlie stepped out of his car, walked across the parking lot, turned the bicycle upside down on his shoulder, and carried it back to his car. He unlocked the trunk and wedged the bicycle inside, letting the trunk cover rest on top of it. Then he waited, watching the store exit.

It was a clear, hot day. The afternoon sun shimmered off the paved parking lot and reflected from the glass and stainless steel walls of the store. In twenty years, he thought, the cities with their narrow streets, their dark stone buildings, and their hopeless traffic snarls would be dead, replaced by the suburban shopping centers like this one. Here parking was no problem, and there was no need to visit the city any more. There was a drug store, a hardware store, a bookstore, a restaurant, the A and P, a florist, a hairdresser and barbershop, even a branch bank and a brokerage and insurance office. Not only was it efficient, it was beautiful, as colorful as any European fair. There were grass areas with dogwood trees and shrubbery. The color scheme had been thought out in advance, the buildings painted white, with black and gold signs and acres of glass brilliantly clean, like new diamonds. There was too much talk about what was bad in America, he thought, and too little appreciation of what was good.

When Terry emerged from the store, she merely glanced at the bicycle rack and then headed straight for his car.

"I suppose this is your idea of a joke," she said with no trace of a smile.

"It's a hobby of mine," he answered. "Stealing bicycles. This makes the fifth I've picked up this week."

"Very funny. And now that you've shown how clever you are, I would like to be on my way."

Her shopping bag was heavy. She rested it on the open window of his car.

"What did you buy?" he asked.

"Food. None of your business," she said, pulling the bag away when he tried to peer inside. "Get me my bicycle, if you don't mind."

"Get in and I'll drive you home."

"We went through all that last night," she said wearily. "And I said no."

"I hoped I could persuade you to change your mind."

"You can't."

"At least get in for a moment and we'll talk."

She shook her head. "Look, friend, that will lead inevitably to complications, and you know it."

"Naturally. That's why I suggested it."

"Half the people in the store," she said, glancing over her shoulder, "either know me or you or both of us."

"Is it illegal for two people to talk?"

"It all depends on what they talk about."

"We'll talk about the weather. Get in."

"Charlie," she said, hesitating, not finishing her sentence.

"What?"

"Let's not get involved."

"Let's," he answered. "Get in."

"Will you promise you'll drive me straight home?"

He didn't answer until she was sitting next to him.

"I'll take you home," he said, "but only to leave your bicycle. We're going on a picnic, assuming you bought some beer."

She opened her shopping bag. "Twelve cans. Enough?"

"Plenty. How about an opener?"

"It's there."

"And a bathing suit?"

"It's at the bottom of the shopping bag."

"I didn't notice it," he answered.

"You'll hardly notice it even when I have it on. Where are we going?"

"The Chalmers have a farm about fifteen miles from here. It's back in the woods. No one will know we're there."

"You were supremely confident, weren't you?"

"I was hopeful."

"Can we get something straight right from the start?" she said, turning sideways in the seat and looking at him for a moment. "I want no complications."

"There won't be any."

174

"I mean it. I enjoy your company, but that's all I plan to enjoy. I'm married to Newell and plan to stay that way."

"Fair enough."

"I want no embarrassing scenes. No wrestling matches which end up with both of us furious."

"Are you really as cold-blooded as you sound?" he asked, smiling.

"I am completely cold-blooded," she answered. "That's one thing I wish to make clear."

"All right. It's clear. But in the meantime try pretending that you're enjoying yourself as much as I am."

"What would you have me do?"

"Smile at me, for instance."

"All right." She smiled. "There. Anything else?"

He stopped the car in the Goddards' driveway. "Yes," he said. "Run upstairs and grab a sweater. It gets cool out there at night. I'll put your bicycle in the garage."

Terry started toward the front door. "Incidentally," she said, "you owe me four dollars." She handed him the sales slip. "Picnics with me come high."

A half-hour later, when Charlie led her out onto the terrace at the farmhouse, Terry said, "So this is your little hideaway."

"Not mine," he answered. "I haven't been out here in years."

He looked across the open field toward the brook in the distance. Very little had changed since he had first seen the place with Lucy. Swallows were swooping and diving overhead, and the air still smelled of dry grass and sweet fern. The house had been painted, and the long road in had been repaired. Everything else was the same.

"Mr. Chalmers' life is a series of islands," he said. "Or fortresses. But he makes the fatal error of giving his family a key. Let's go on in and open the place up. Then we can have a beer and a swim."

"Is there a place where I can change?" she asked, when they were in the house.

"Choose any room you want," he answered. "They're all empty."

Fifteen minutes later they were sitting on the bridge over the pool tossing pebbles at any empty beer can floating below them in the water.

"Why don't you buy this place from the Chalmers?" Terry asked as she opened two more cans of beer. "I'd live out here if the Goddards owned it."

"Lucy would die of loneliness. I'm away most of the time."

"All husbands are away most of the time. Newell comes back from his office at five, eats, and disappears into the cellar with his radios. I sit upstairs either watching television or reading mystery stories. He might just as well be in Siberia."

There were a few small fish in the pool, surfacing for bugs, sending out ripples toward the banks. The pool needed cleaning. The spring rains had filled it with gravel.

"I don't suppose I'd be so jealous of Newell's radios," Terry said idly, when Charlie didn't answer, "if I had a child or two to occupy me."

He hesitated a moment, then he said, "It's none of my business, but can I ask you a personal question?"

Her knees were bent over the edge of the bridge, her feet a few inches from the water. She stretched out a leg and stirred the pool with her toes.

"Go ahead and ask me."

"Is that because you can't have children, or what?"

"It would seem so. We've been trying for nearly ten years."

She let herself down toward the water, her hands gripping the wooden planks of the bridge. Then she pressed upward, the muscles in her arms and back as hard as steel. "I'll bet Lucy can't do that," she said.

"I'm not sure I can myself," he answered. He slipped over the edge of the bridge and lowered himself toward the water. When he tried to push himself upward again, nothing happened. Terry pried loose his fingers, and he dropped into the pool. She dove in after him.

They swam together the length of the pool and crawled out on the concrete dam. Then they walked up onto the grassy bank and lay on two towels, on their stomachs, face to face.

"How about doctors?" he asked. "Have you been to see one?"

"Oh, my God," she answered. "Don't mention doctors to me."

"You don't believe in them?"

"Of course I believe in them. I've seen six hundred and thirty-six of them in the last eight years. I've been poked, twisted, squeezed, photographed internally and externally, and hung by my heels from a curtain rod. Every obstetrician in the eastern half of the United States knows me intimately, and I do mean intimately."

"And what do they say?"

"That there's nothing wrong with me. And furthermore, I don't think there is."

"Then why not adopt a child?"

She sighed wearily, as though it were a question she had been asked many times before.

"Because I want a child of my own."

"Don't most people adopt children when they want them as badly as you do?"

"I want one of my own," she repeated.

A flock of starlings was flying overhead, their wings whirring as they passed, heading in toward the city for the night.

"What makes you so certain you can have one of your own?"

"Six hundred and thirty-six doctors can't be wrong." She rolled over onto her back. "And now I'd like to ask you a personal question."

"Ask away."

"How do I phrase it?" she asked herself, sitting up and gazing down at the pool. "When you were inducted into the army . . ." she hesitated. "When

176

you had your physical examination, were they interested in whether you could have children or not?"

"Good God, no," he exclaimed, laughing.

His physical exam had taken place in a high school gymnasium. He remembered it as a nightmarish afternoon. Four hundred other draftees like himself had sat about for hours dressed only in their underwear shorts, all of them clutching a warm bottle of urine with their name on it, waiting for an interview with an exhausted doctor, who would ask them if they wet their bed and then would inspect their feet. The army was interested in eyesight, ears, teeth, and blood pressure, but not in their powers of reproduction. As far as they were concerned, that was optional.

"That was one test they didn't run, Terry."

"Newell says they tested him."

"What outfit was he trying to get in? The WAC's?"

"He insists they tested him, and he also insists he came through with flying colors."

"I gather you have your doubts."

She turned and looked at him.

"He's refused to allow any of my doctors to test him."

"Then I don't blame you for being suspicious."

"Did you know Newell at college?" she asked.

"Vaguely. He went to Hotchkiss, and he had most of his friends before he got to New Haven."

"He told me once he had an illegitimate child in New Haven."

"Newell?" Charlie exclaimed incredulously. He remembered Newell Goddard at college chiefly for his clothes, an endless wardrobe of blanketlike tweeds, pink button-collar shirts, hard-soled moccasins, and expensive silk ties. He could have left Yale at any time, and only the York Street tailors would have missed him.

"He says it was some girl he met in a bar."

"A few girls got pregnant down there every year, but if Newell met her in a bar, everyone else met her in the same bar, and who knows whose fault it was? There was nothing very private about those girls."

He noticed a mosquito on Terry's shoulder. He smashed it with his hand, leaving a smear of blood on her skin.

"Let's go eat," he said. "It's getting cool."

They started back toward the city just before nine. In the darkness, and over the back roads, the trip took nearly an hour. Terry spent most of the time talking about Denver.

"Have you ever been there?" she asked.

"I flew in and out of the airport once," he answered. "It looked like a wonderful city."

"They used to say during the war that you never saw a soldier walking the streets of Denver, that all of them had places to go."

"A hospitable city?"

"Yes, and it leads to complications."

"Such as marriage?"

She nodded. "Such as. My mother just about died when I told her I'd met Newell in a hotel bar. I stole him from my best friend," she added, when Charlie didn't answer.

"Something I want to ask you, Terry. I met girls here and there about the country during the war. Some of them I might have married. But how did you girls know what you were getting? I mean, here we all were from other parts of the country, all of us looking exactly the same in our uniforms——"

"You mean how did I know Newell wasn't a shoe clerk before he joined the Air Force?"

"Exactly."

"Not that it would have made much difference," she said. "We were in love."

"Sure, I know. But you must have thought about it. At least your parents must have been curious."

Terry giggled. "Dun and Bradstreet," she said. "My father had them check Newell and his family the instant I brought him back to our house. Then too I did some checking on my own."

"How?"

"I examined the labels in his clothing."

"Army PX?"

"No, and that's what convinced me. Newell had all his uniforms tailor-made in New Haven by J. Press."

"That sounds like Newell."

"He even had some olive drab undershirts with a J. Press label. I was highly impressed."

"So love, plus J. Press undershirts, made marriage seem like a good idea."

She nodded. "And it's worked out all right. Newell and I get along well."

Highcliffe Road was quiet and empty when Charlie turned his car off the avenue.

"Are you in a hurry to get home?" he asked.

"I ought to be," she answered, not looking at him. "Why?"

"I was just thinking that you might do me a favor."

"What kind of a favor?"

He turned the car into his driveway and flicked off the lights.

"You could show me how to operate an automatic washing machine."

"You mean you don't know?" she asked incredulously. "I thought all modern husbands cooked, washed, and changed diapers."

"My room is piled high with laundry," he said. "I need someone to organize it for me."

"Doesn't Lucy have a cleaning woman?"

"I thought I might get you for nothing."

She hesitated a moment. Then she said, "Don't you really know how to work the machine, Charlie?"

178

"No, I honestly don't," he answered. "And if you show me I'll give you a glass of brandy."

She opened the car door and slid out onto the driveway. He followed her into the house through the kitchen door.

"Where's the washing machine?" she asked.

"In the cellar. But let's have the brandy first. Go on into the living room. I'll be with you in a minute."

He kept the liquor under the kitchen sink, along with Lucy's detergents and the floor wax.

"Here's to something, but I'm not sure what," Terry said a moment later when he handed her a glass. "Very very good," she added, drinking the brandy quickly. She placed the empty glass on the mantelpiece, a smear of her lipstick on the rim. "And so, off to my domestic chores," she said, starting for the stairs. "Where's your pile of laundry?"

"Upstairs. I'll be right behind you."

There were sixteen steps in all. They had reached the eighth step when Charlie stopped suddenly, his body rigid. A car had turned into his driveway, its headlights flashing through the front door, reflecting from the walls.

"Friends of yours?" Terry asked quietly.

"Don't move," he answered.

The car hesitated in the driveway for a moment. Then it backed out onto the street and started to move slowly toward the avenue.

"Just someone turning around," he said. "But perhaps I'd better close the front door."

He had joined Terry again and they had nearly reached the upstairs landing when Brian started to bark, an angry growling explosion that could mean only one thing. Someone was coming up the front walk.

"Now, goddam it, what?" he muttered, racing back down the stairs. He turned on the outside light and opened the front door. When he stepped outside and saw Mrs. Chalmers cowering against a yew bush, Brian coiled and ready to spring at her throat, his knees went weak with terror.

"Is this creature yours?" Mrs. Chalmers asked. "Lucy warned me that you'd adopted a dog."

And it was the luckiest thing I ever did, Charlie thought. If Brian never did another useful thing as long as he lived, he'd earned his keep forever tonight.

"That's just Brian, Mother Chalmers," he shouted, his face turned toward the open front door. "What are you doing back from the Island?" he shouted again, praying that Terry could hear him.

"Will you kindly do something about this vicious animal," Mrs. Chalmers said angrily.

Charlie grasped Brian by the collar and dragged him onto the front doorstep. Then he reached behind him and pulled shut the door. If he were lucky, Mrs. Chalmers wouldn't have her key. Fortunately he had locked the kitchen door. He could get in later by climbing through a window.

"I'm not used to being greeted this way at my own daughter's house," Mrs. Chalmers said, still eying Brian nervously.

"Brian's death on prowlers, Mother Chalmers. If I'd known you were coming, I would have tied him up in the garage."

"I was hardly prowling," Mrs. Chalmers answered frostily. "I've come up for a hospital meeting, and I thought I'd just drop over to see how you were making out."

"I'm making out very well, Mother Chalmers. I was just heading up for bed."

"So early?" she asked.

"I've been rather tired lately."

"You poor boy. You need a vacation. That was one of the things I wanted to talk about. Lucy gave me explicit instructions that you were to drive down this week end and spend the week with your family." She hesitated, obviously expecting to be asked inside.

"I'd ask you in," he said, "but I'm afraid the door blew shut, and it's locked. I'll climb in later through the kitchen window. And how is Lucy?" he asked cheerfully. "I was planning to call her tomorrow."

Mrs. Chalmers was fumbling in her pocketbook.

"Yes," she said, "here it is. Lucy gave me her key," she held it up triumphantly. Then she inserted it into the lock, and pushed open the door. "Lucy's fine," she said as she stepped into the front hall. "Naturally, she feels rather neglected down there all alone."

He had gone through four years of war, Charlie thought, and more than a year of actual combat, but never had he been in a tighter spot than he was at this instant. If he could just detain Mrs. Chalmers in the hall or in the living room, he might be able to bluff it through.

"First," she said brightly, "I have to get some clothes for Lucy. We've had a stretch of wet weather down there, and the poor child is desperate for dry things for the little girls."

"Can't I get them for you?" Charlie asked eagerly, moving in front of her as she started for the stairs.

"If you're like my Lowell," she answered, giggling, "you don't know where a single thing is in the entire house."

"The upstairs is a mess," Charlie said desperately.

"I promise you I won't notice a thing," she answered, stepping past him.

Charlie followed her up the stairs. His initial panic had given way to an almost uncontrollable desire to burst into wild laughter.

"All I ask is that you don't go into the bedroom," he said following her down the hall. "I haven't picked up a thing in there in weeks."

"Lucy did ask particularly for a pair of low-heeled walking shoes," Mrs. Chalmers answered, opening the bedroom door and snapping on the light. Charlie waited outside in the hall, his body numb.

"Ah, here they are," Mrs. Chalmers said from the depths of Lucy's closet. She walked back toward the hall, singing gaily. "What do you mean the room's a mess? It's as neat as a pin." She patted his arm. "Be a dear and wait for me downstairs. I have a dozen more things to collect. Do run along."

He sat in the living room, listening to Mrs. Chalmers moving about upstairs. The explosion would come at any moment, he thought, waiting, his heart pounding against his chest. How would he handle it? he wondered. It would be a mess. He remembered again that Terry Goddard's mother-in-law was Mrs. Chalmers' best friend. Then he heard Lucy's mother opening the linen closet doors. And after that the bathroom door. Next she walked through both the children's bedrooms and the guest room. The broom closet, he thought suddenly. Surely Lucy hadn't asked for a broom or a can of floor wax. Then he heard Mrs. Chalmers struggling with a door, and he knew which door it was. The broom closet door was the only one in the house that fought back. She had covered everything. He heard her coming down the stairs, still singing her gay little tune.

"Here I am with my loot," she said, dropping the bundle on the living room table. She snapped on a light and then sniffed the air suspiciously. "Have you been drinking, Charlie?"

"I had a drink," he answered coldly. "If that's what you mean."

Now that he had escaped the catastrophe that had seemed inevitable, his terror had changed into anger. What business did she have showing up at his house at nine o'clock at night without a warning? She might at least have phoned.

"Drinking alone?" Mrs. Chalmers persisted.

"If my wife leaves me alone, I have to drink alone," he answered. Mrs. Chalmers raised her eyebrows and sat on the arm of the couch.

"Well, here we are," she said cheerfully. "It's not often that you and I have a chance to have a nice little chat, is it, Charlie?"

"About what, Mother Chalmers?"

"Oh, about our Lucy. She is so terribly lonely down there, Charles. We all were so terribly disappointed that you didn't come down last week end."

"I had something to do that I felt more important."

"Are you annoyed with me?" she asked. "You seem rather on edge."

"I'm sorry," he answered. He had just noticed the two brandy glasses on the mantelpiece, one of them with an obvious stain of lipstick.

"Let me put it another way," she continued. "Do I do something that annoys you? You can be perfectly honest with me."

"I don't think I know what you mean, Mother Chalmers."

"Of course you know what I mean. Why is it that you've never allowed yourself to become one of our family? We want you to be one of us, you know. Our things are your things, and our family life should be your family life. With so little family of your own, I should think you'd welcome us."

"Perhaps I thought I was marrying Lucy instead of her mother," he answered. If Mrs. Chalmers wanted honesty, he'd give it to her.

"What on earth do you mean by that?" she asked, shocked.

"I had hoped to have a family life of my own, our own, Lucy's and mine, instead of having to fit myself into an established rut."

"Rut," she echoed.

"Rut," he repeated. "Lucy's in a rut. You're in a rut, and Mr. Chalmers is in a rut. I was hoping I could stay out of it."

Mrs. Chalmers tightened her lips. Then she forced herself to smile.

"But I think even you would agree that it's a good rut, Charles. It's a life thousands of people would be willing to trade for their own. Just a moment. Let me go on. You do have such a habit of interrupting," she said sweetly, still smiling. "I suspect you care little for tradition. What is it they say, that what man doesn't understand, he tries to destroy. That's you, you see. You don't understand our traditions, and you would like to destroy them. Isn't that true, Charlie?"

"I think I know more about your family traditions than you do yourself, Mrs. Chalmers. And let me finish," he said quickly. "You do a lot of interrupting yourself." He smiled at her as sweetly as she had smiled at him. "There used to be a tradition of work in your family. Your father worked, and his father worked, and *his* father worked. That's the tradition I think worth maintaining. Not the big house on Lawn Street or a big house on some island. I like to work, Mrs. Chalmers. I have a chance of running for political office at the next elections. Your great-grandfather went to Washington as a senator. Perhaps I might like to do the same thing. That's the tradition of your family I respect. But it will take some help from my wife, and I don't get much."

"I find your remarks rather offensive," Mrs. Chalmers answered, no longer able to control her anger. Her lips were a thin blue line.

"Perhaps I'm trying to be offensive. It's time you and I understood each other. I thought I was marrying a wife, not someone's daughter. I wish you'd stop interfering with Lucy's life and mine."

"I've heard quite enough of this," she answered, rising to her feet. "I was hoping we might have a pleasant discussion, but I certainly won't listen to your insults."

"No one ever really says what he thinks to you," he said. "And when they do, you can't take it. Anyone who doesn't agree with you, you consider offensive."

"Indeed," she said coldly. "The one thing I pride myself on is that I never do interfere with my children's lives. I am available for help and advice, but I am not a meddler."

"Let's not argue," Charlie answered, suddenly weary. "You don't like me, and you probably never will. Lucy should have married some spineless vegetable like . . ." he hesitated, unable to go on. He had wanted to say Mr. Chalmers.

"Like whom?" Mrs. Chalmers asked.

"Like Newell Goddard," Charlie answered, snatching a name out of the air. Mrs. Chalmers faced him, her expression set with determination.

"I've been putting off telling you this for a long time," she said. "I had hoped I'd never have to. But you leave me no alternative. If you will just consider the matter, I think you'll agree that just about everything you have today in this world, you owe in great measure to Mr. Chalmers' generosity and to mine. We have been generous with you. We supported your wife and child while you were away in the army. We allowed you to live with us when you returned. We saw that you obtained a job when for a while it looked as though you might be at loose ends indefinitely. And you have accepted these handouts without a word of thanks. It's been that way from the moment you returned eight years ago. Never once have I heard a word of thanks pass your lips. Not once."

"And not once has anyone ever thanked me for what I've done for your family company, Mrs. Chalmers."

"Stop it," she shouted at him, her eyes blazing.

"I won't stop it. I'm running the family company these days, and I'm running it pretty well. I've worked like hell out there, and just about everything I've accomplished has been over dead bodies. When you thank me for that, I'll thank you for your generosity." He walked to the mantelpiece and lifted off both the brandy glasses, twirling the stems between his fingers. He no longer cared what Mrs. Chalmers thought. "You and I are alike, Mrs. Chalmers. Ralph Henry told me quite a bit about you. He liked you back in the old days, when you were living in Hadley. He told me once that if you'd been a man you'd be just like your father. Your father liked to run things, and you like to run things." He smiled across the room at her. "I like to run things too. That's why you and I don't get along. I'm planning to get control of The Hadley Company someday, and you know it."

"I think we'd better say good night," Mrs. Chalmers answered. "I don't know how much you and your companion were drinking, but I would say quite a bit from the way you sound. Do come visit your wife, Charles, if you can possibly spare the time."

"I think I'll drive down tomorrow," he answered.

"Good. We'll all be delighted to see you. Good night," she said sweetly, heading for the front door.

"Don't forget the bundle of clothing, Mother Chalmers. That's what you came for, wasn't it?"

"How silly of me," she said, lifting the bundle from the table. "Good night, Charles. Your little girls will be so happy to see you. They talk about you all the time."

A moment later he ran up the stairs and stood in the hall.

"She's gone, Terry."

He didn't expect her to answer. If Mrs. Chalmers hadn't been able to find her, she wasn't in the house. He sat at the hall telephone and dialed the Goddards' number.

When Terry answered, he said, "Mrs. Houdini, I presume. How did you do it?"

"While you two were chitchatting on the front walk, I slunk down the stairs. Then when you came in, I went out. It was that simple."

He waited. Then he said, "She's gone now."

"And so am I," Terry answered.

She hung up before he could answer, and he was left sitting in the hall, the dial tone buzzing in his ear.

twenty-eight

Because she thought he would prefer it, when later that summer Charlie joined Lucy and the children for a ten-day vacation, Mrs. Chalmers insisted he stay "up island" at the place they called "Lowell's Retreat."

As a family, the Chalmers did not believe in naming things. People who installed signs at the end of their driveway, "Longview," or who drove station wagons with "Crooked Brook" stenciled on the sides, were, the Chalmers felt, in a class with those who embroidered "His" and "Hers" on their bath towels. Nevertheless, because they owned a total of four separate establishments, for the sake of clarity alone, they had found it necessary to assign certain vague titles to their houses.

First there was "Home," or "the Lawn Street House." Then there was "the Farm," sometimes called "the Pool." During the summer months, when they moved to the Island, they lived at "the Harbor House," occasionally referred to as "the Boathouse," since that was what it once had been. Finally, thirteen miles away, up island, they owned "Lowell's Retreat."

The Retreat was the only dwelling Lowell Chalmers had ever built himself. All the other houses were a part of the Hadley family when he married into it. The Retreat came about as a result of his feeling, after a few years of marriage, that he needed a place to escape, a place to be alone, to read, and to think. Therefore, in 1919, he had bought a five-hundred-acre tract of wilderness that extended from the ocean across the South Road, and inland as far as the Middle Road. Along the ocean was a quarter-mile of eroding cliff, and behind that sandy rolling hillsides, bayberry bushes, some fields of coarse grass, stone walls, and a flock of semiwild sheep which competed with the deer and the rabbits for what little edible greenery remained. He paid six dollars an acre for it, and the Island family that sold it to him considered Lowell a typical mainland fool. He even agreed to let the sheep graze free of charge, as he said he enjoyed them in his view.

During the entire summer of 1920 he had wandered about his Island empire looking for a proper site for his cabin. He finally settled on a small, grassy plateau two hundred feet back from the edge of the cliff. He then built modestly, but well, a white-cedar-shingle structure, little more than an enclosed shed, where he could sleep, read, think, admire the ocean, and glory in the seasons, the sun, the birds, the silence, and the solitude. To the south, the ocean stretched away never ending and blue, like the sky. To the north, everything he could see, he owned. To the west and east, only a few weathered gray shadows by day, and at night a few yellow flickering lights, reminded him that he wasn't alone in the world. Solitude was what he wanted, and he was happy with it.

Then in the early thirties, the rest of the Chalmers had discovered that their father's retreat had great possibilities for overnight beach picnics. The Island was developing fast. What had once been a half-day's trip over rutted, sandy roads, through farmyards and brooks, was now but an hour away from the civilized end of the Island. In order to use the Retreat, however, a few changes were made. An outhouse might be satisfactory for a man existing alone, but women needed an inside bathroom. That meant plumbing and water, and therefore a well. The original cabin became a kitchen, and two wings were added to provide sleeping space. Lowell's books gave way to kitchen crockery, his desk was moved out to make room for a stove and an icebox, a lawn was hacked out of the bayberry bushes, a garage and a pump house to house an electric generator were built, and a half-mile-long driveway was carved in from the South Road. It was during this time that "Lowell's Retreat" became gradually "the Retreat," and finally "Our Retreat."

But after a week of it Charlie had had enough. There were the beach, the ocean, the shells, the seaweed, the driftwood, the cliff, the sky, the clouds, the sun, and the birds. At night there were darkness, mosquitoes, silence, and sleep. The beach ran for miles in both directions, a gleaming white ribbon of sand, beyond it the empty ocean. All he had to look forward to each day was a flight of geese, flying low in a long, uneven V, heading for a freshwater pond for their evening meal. A quail had hatched her brood near the pump house, and warily she would lead them out onto the lawn, where they would dust themselves, dark balls of animated fuzz. Occasionally sea gulls lit on the roof of the house, digesting, spattering the shingles. During the week, Charlie had also seen six airplanes and a helicopter.

Friday afternoon, with Lucy and the children at the beach, he left the house and wandered out to the edge of the cliff. With him he carried a pistol and a box of cartridges. There were always rabbits to shoot. He sat on the cliff, blasting down at a rock in the ocean, listening to the fractured lead whine out over the water.

It was a warm July day, with a soft ocean breeze. A race was in progress, a few white sails out on the ocean. Lucy, he knew, was supremely happy here. To her the birds weren't just things that flew. They were warblers, song sparrows, towhees, and terns. The wildflowers weren't just spots of color. They were wild roses, clematis, butter and eggs, and Indian paintbrush. She'd be up early in the morning to cook breakfast. She'd then make a picnic lunch and take the children to the beach. At one-thirty she'd return for naps. At four it was the beach again for the final swim. Dinner was at seven. Then the day's dishes, the futile attempt to read, the yawns, bed, and the final silence.

There were other houses along the shore. By the Chalmers' standards it was becoming crowded, with at least one family every half-mile. Occasionally words of greeting were exchanged with other nice couples who sat by their private sand dunes, and once children and sandwiches were exchanged with a Professor Barnes and his wife. He taught botany at Harvard.

"Why don't we ask them up for cocktails?" Charlie had suggested.

"But don't you see," Lucy had explained patiently, "we just don't do that here. All of us see enough people during the winter. No parties. It's an informal rule around here." Then she had added, "I just wish you'd relax and enjoy yourself. This is heaven, if you'll only admit it. Look," she said, pointing to their three girls, sun-drenched and as tan as leather. "Isn't this the way you want them to grow up?"

He wasn't sure, he thought. He just wasn't sure. He lay on his back for a while, sighting his pistol at a cloud. Then he rolled onto his stomach and aimed at the row of sea gulls sitting on the roof of Lowell's Retreat. He was tempted. To shoot a sea gull would somehow express his mood.

He misjudged the distance, and the bullet drilled into the roof below the ridge line, splintering a dry shingle. The birds exploded off the house and flew hysterically toward the ocean. He shot at them again as they passed overhead.

"Charlie, did you shoot the house?" Lucy yelled at him, running up the path.

"I didn't realize you were back," he answered, ashamed. "I was shooting at a bird."

"But they're protected," she cried, obviously appalled. "You can be fined."

"Then fine me," he answered. "It might liven things up."

She stared at him for a moment. Then she sat next to him on the ground. "Darling, are you bored?"

"That's the understatement of the year," he answered.

"But why? I hoped you'd love it here."

"No people, Lucy. I like to do things and to see other people doing things."

"Shall I ask some friends of ours up for hamburgers tonight?"

"Friends?" he asked hopefully.

"The Lords. They live out on the South Road. I met them on the beach this morning. They have a couple visiting them."

"Bird watchers?" he asked cautiously.

"Probably. They're English."

"Cocktails?"

"I don't think Grayson Lord drinks."

"If I'm going to listen to bird talk I'm going to drink," Charlie answered, rising to his feet and pulling Lucy up after him. "I'm sorry I shot a hole in the Retreat. It just seemed like a good idea. Shall I run down to Lobstertown to get the hamburgers?"

"Do," she answered. "And if you plan to drink, get some extra ice. They have it at the Lobster."

Until the Jews came to Lobstertown, artists, tourists, and fish had been its only source of income. A collection of sagging wooden buildings built on poles out over the harbor, it was a summer haven for pleasure craft and a

186

winter haven for fishermen. There was a general store, a fish market, an art gallery, a Coast Guard station, and a cloud of sea gulls diving for minnows and garbage in the water. At the edge of the village a sign read, "You Are Now Entering Historic Lobstertown." An idle Christian teen-ager had re-written the sign to read, "You Are Now Entering Historic Tel Aviv."

The summer visitors who had been coming to the Island for years liked to cite Lobstertown as an example of what can happen to a nice place when those in charge fail to exercise due care and caution. It had all started during the early forties when the town's only inn, the Beach House, its business slack because of the war, had opened its doors to Jews. There was nothing to worry about, the old-time visitors told each other. They were the better type —artists, professional people, musicians, and writers. Liking what they found, the ease and informality of the place, these people bought property and then invited their friends. Mrs. Chalmers summed up the catastrophe that took place during the forties in Lobstertown when she said, "We didn't mind the Jews, and we still don't mind the Jews, but it's their friends and relations that have ruined the place."

"If only they'd stay off the beach," Lowell Chalmers added. "But unfortunately they know the law."

He referred to the law of public domain, which allows anyone to walk on the sand below the high-water mark. That left even the eleven-mile stretch of private ocean beach open for attack from the flanks. Whole groups of them would wander away from Lobstertown at low tide, careful to walk only on the still-damp sand, having run into more than one hostile dry-sand owner in the past. They had organized a summer theater, a concert orchestra, a recreation center for the children open to all on the Island, and the Lobster, an eating place that had once served only New England boiled dinners but now could compete with the finest restaurants in the world. Lobstertown had always been a quaint place during the summer months, and now added to its quaintness was an air of gaiety and excitement, a crowded beach swarming with children and their parents, dances on Saturday night, concerts, so much activity that the rest of the summer population of the Island was drawn to the place in spite of themselves, hoping to share in the fun.

Of all the spots on the Island he had visited, Lobstertown was the one place Charlie really liked. He drove his car out along the paved sand dune and parked at the edge of the harbor dock. The tide was going out, and the gulls had moved to the mouth of the harbor outlet, diving for the fish that were heading to sea. In the distance he could see the mainland. The sun blazed in off the calm water, white heat reflecting from the sand in shimmering waves.

Beyond, out on the public beach, a portable radio was blaring, and at least a dozen teen-agers were dancing on the sand. Out in the water twenty more were trying to sink the raft, tilting it first one way and then the other, a few of them sliding off into the water with each plunge. Men were reading newspapers, well-oiled women with dark glasses were soaking up the sun, small children, naked and brown, were digging in the beach with shovels and pails.

After a while he stepped out of his car and walked out onto the beach. He might prefer to have his children spend their summers in a place like this, he thought. It was useful to know a warbler from a bird and a cinquefoil from a wildflower, but wasn't it also important to recognize a fellow American when you saw one?

A hundred feet up the beach he noticed a young man sitting on the sand, his bare legs enclosing a portable typewriter, a pile of crumpled paper next to him, weighted down with stones. He was a handsome individual, swarthy and lean, with a thin, intense face and short black hair. He was tall, with muscular shoulders and narrow hips. He wore a pair of brief, tight-fitting, white bathing trunks. Charlie watched him for a moment, admiring his concentration. Whatever he was composing on his typewriter, he was thinking of that alone, oblivious to the rubber beach ball that was being tossed back and forth over his head by two young girls. A poet? he wondered. A writer? Was he writing lyrics for a musical comedy? It was possible to meet almost anyone these days on the public beach at Lobstertown.

He walked closer and then paused, watching, wishing he were a child so he could merely ask the man what he was writing. Suddenly the sheet of paper was ripped out of the machine, crumpled up, and tossed aside.

"What are you doing?" Charlie asked. "Writing a book on birds?"

"Birds?" the man said, gazing up blankly, not registering.

"Everyone with a typewriter on this island is writing about birds."

"What can you write about birds?"

"How they fly, fast or slow. How big they are. Where they live. What color their wings are, and how many eggs they lay."

"No kidding. Is there a market for it?"

"There seems to be."

Charlie felt himself being sized up by a pair of dark, slightly cynical eyes.

"Is that what you do? Write about birds?"

"Not me. I'm just a salesman."

"A salesman? You don't sell soap, do you?"

"I guess I'm bothering you," Charlie answered, stung by what he thought was sarcasm. He started to walk on up the beach.

"Wait a minute," the man called after him. "I just asked you that because that's what I'm writing about. Soap. I've got it on the brain."

He seemed eager for company. He held out a pack of cigarettes. "Smoke?" he asked. "They're slightly damp."

"Thanks," Charlie answered, accepting one.

"Sit down, if you haven't got somewhere to go."

"What kind of soap are you writing about?" Charlie asked, lowering himself to the sand.

"Detergents, to be exact. You staying here in Lobstertown?"

"We have a place up the beach." Charlie pointed vaguely.

"I'm Nate Taylor. I'm staying at the Beach House."

188

They were quiet a moment. A swordfishing boat was easing along the shore, its motor throttled down, heading for the harbor inlet.

"Do you like the Island?"

"It's all right. Quiet. I work better with noise."

"Detergents seems like a funny thing to write a book about."

"Book? Who said anything about a book? I'm writing copy."

"Advertising?"

Nate Taylor nodded. Then he looked at Charlie speculatively for a moment.

"Let me ask you something. When I say Ivory Soap, what's that mean to you?"

Charlie glanced at Nate Taylor in surprise. He was fascinated by this intense-looking Jew.

"It floats. Is that what you mean?"

"Right. That's what I mean. How about Palmolive?"

"The skin you love to touch."

"O.K. How about Lifebuoy?"

"B.O. and my school shower."

Nate Taylor laughed. "You pass," he said.

"What goes on?"

"I'm just trying to reassure myself about something."

Charlie settled into the sand, digging holes with his heels.

"Can I read it?" he asked, reaching for one of the crumpled pieces of paper.

"No, because it's no good. I'm reaching for a new approach, and I don't have it yet. That's why I was asking you about soap. Now I'll ask you about detergents. What's Dreft mean to you?"

Charlie thought a moment. "Not much, I guess. I know it comes in a box."

"What color box?"

Charlie shrugged. "Yellow? Blue? I don't know."

"How about All?"

"All?"

"All. What color box does that come in?"

"Red? White? I don't know."

"Wrong. It comes in a bottle. How about Swift?"

"Swift?" Charlie said blankly. "Have I ever heard of it?"

"No, you haven't, because there's no such thing. But you weren't sure, were you?"

"They all sound the same to me."

"Right," Nate Taylor said, lifting his typewriter and letting it hit the sand. "They all sound the same, and they all are the same, and that's the fault of the advertisers. With all the millions they've spent advertising detergents, not one of them has emerged with a brand concept."

"Brand concept?" Charlie repeated.

"Jargon. I mean when someone says 'Ivory,' you say, 'It Floats,' just like Pavlov's dog. And when someone says 'Lifebuoy,' you sing out 'B.O.' But when you hear the word 'Dreft,' all you think of is something vague like dishes."

"So?" Charlie asked.

"So I'm going to change all that." He grinned and lay back on the sand. "I've been handed a new account. It's a new detergent that's exactly the same as all the other detergents, no better and no worse. But I'm going to make it *seem* better and different."

"What's the name of it?"

"It doesn't have a name yet. They wanted to call it Waft, but I said I wouldn't handle it for them if they did."

"What's wrong with Waft?" Charlie asked. He hadn't enjoyed himself so much in days.

"That's been the genius of the soap people," Nate answered. "Lifebuoy. Now that's the last name you'd ever choose for a soap, isn't it? It doesn't even sound clean. But it clicked. Like Gold Dust."

"Twins," Charlie muttered, grinning.

"Name any soap, and you'll associate some advertiser's brain child with it. Detergents have missed the boat."

"Maybe you can't do it with detergents."

"They did it with cigarettes. Philip Morris."

"Milder," Charlie answered.

"Lucky Strike?"

"It's toasted."

"Ballantine Beer?"

"Mel Allen." Charlie laughed. "You win." Then he snapped his fingers, and said, "Oh, my God."

"You look like a man who just remembered he forgot something."

"I have. I bought four pounds of hamburger for a party tonight. It's back there rotting in my car." He stood up, hesitating, staring down at Nate Taylor. "Why don't you come along?" he said suddenly.

"Come along where?"

"To our house. Have dinner with us. I'd like to talk more about advertising. I'm interested in the subject."

Nate Taylor seemed about to accept. Then he said, "I just remembered. I can't. I've got a date."

"With who? Bring her along."

"It's just one of the girls who works at the Beach House. Back in New York she's in show business."

"She sounds even more interesting than you," Charlie grinned. "Bring her along."

"Well," Nate Taylor answered thoughtfully, "maybe I will."

"Do it. Do you have a car?"

"No, but Lyn has. What time, and where?"

"Do you know the South Road?"

"The main road down the island?"

Charlie nodded. "When you pass the general store here in Lobstertown, go exactly three miles and two tenths more. Drive until you see two large stone posts at the right. There's a sign there that says, 'L. C. Chalmers. Private. Keep out.' We're at the end of that road."

"But who in the world is he?" Lucy asked in dismay, when Charlie returned to Lowell's Retreat and told her to expect two more for cocktails and dinner.

"Someone I met on the Lobstertown beach. He's bringing a girl. His name is Nate Taylor, and hers is Lyn."

"Jewish?" she asked, cocking her head.

"I expect so."

"Well now, either they are or they aren't."

"Yes. Jewish," he answered, angry that he felt defiant about it.

"All right," she said quietly, looking at him as though he had lost his mind. "But I'll leave it up to you to take care of them. They're your project. Not mine."

The Lords and their house guests, the Goodenoughs, arrived promptly at six. Charlie had met Grayson Lord three days earlier on the beach. He was a tall, lean man in his late thirties, with thinning sandy hair, and light-blue eyes set deep in his head. He wore a pair of leather walking boots, tan canvas trousers, and a long-billed swordfishing cap. Binoculars hung from his neck.

"Have you met Jane?" he said casually, tipping his head, as though he could count on his wife being two paces to the rear and one to the left.

"How do you do, Mrs. Lord," Charlie said, grasping a strong, calloused hand.

"Heavens, call me Jane," she said. "I'm not quite that old."

She was older than her husband, Charlie judged. Her hair was gray, and her skin was wind-burned and rough. She wore knickers, woolen stockings, and low-heeled walking shoes. A pair of binoculars hung from her neck.

"These are the Goodenoughs," she said. "Rod and Sheela. And Rod hates to have me say this, but he is the world's foremost authority on salt-water mammals."

When Charlie looked interested but blank, Rod Goodenough said, in a brittle English accent, "Whales and seals, old boy. Is that a Martini you're carrying?"

Rod Goodenough would be all right, Charlie decided. Like Grayson Lord, he was in his late thirties, with a long haircut and an English air of being confidently wellborn.

"Excellent," he said, sipping his drink. "Sheela. Have one. I insist on it. Good for international friendship and all that sort of thing."

"Do," Lucy urged, more at ease when she saw both the Lords with a drink.

"Perhaps a little sherry," Sheela Goodenough answered. She seemed prepared to have a frightful time, dressed only to repel mosquitoes, with heavy tweeds and long stockings.

"What a magnificent view," Rod Goodenough said admiringly, gazing over the ocean, holding out his glass for a refill.

"This isn't tea, you know," Charlie said, smiling. He liked Rod Goodenough. It was so easy for the English to be loved in America, he thought. All they had to do was to admire everything and keep what they really thought to themselves.

"My dear fellow," Rod Goodenough answered, "I detest tea, and I love Martinis. And oh-ho, what have we here?"

Nate Taylor and his girl Lyn were advancing up the path from the end of the driveway. Charlie's heart sank when he saw them. He should have warned Nate what to wear. Nate was immaculate in a Palm Beach suit, pink shirt, and a necktie. He looked marvelously handsome, and equally out of place. Lyn's shoulders were bare, and her heels were nearly three inches high. She swayed when she walked, not because she tried to but because she could move no other way. She was wearing harlequin glasses with rhinestone rims and a light blue Persian shawl. When she shook hands with Lucy, Jane Lord, and Sheela Goodenough, she shone like a bit of cellophane in a bag of old wool.

"They're all yours," Lucy muttered as she passed Charlie on her way into the house.

Praise the Lord for alcohol, he thought a half-hour later. It could break down any prejudice and all barriers known to man. Nate Taylor had cornered the three wives in the house, and he was talking to them intensely about detergents, moderating a wild, friendly argument, the living room rocking with shrill feminine laughter. Even Sheela Goodenough seemed to be enjoying herself, and Jane Lord had removed her binoculars. Out on the lawn Grayson Lord and Rod Goodenough had surrounded Lyn, and were gazing at her through a pleasant Martini haze, as happy as two eight-year-olds with a single ice-cream cone. Grayson Lord had put his binoculars around her neck, and Rod Goodenough was wearing her glasses.

When Charlie drew near with his cocktail shaker, Lyn took him aside.

"Are you an American?" she whispered, her accent pure Long Island.

"I am," he answered. "Aren't you?"

"What's with that one?" she asked, pointing at Rod Goodenough.

"English."

"And that one?"

"Boston."

"He said he was an ornithologist."

"That's his profession."

She gave Charlie a look, shrugged, and returned to her admirers.

"Gray," Jane Lord shouted, bursting out of the house. "Look. There he is."

"There who is?" Grayson Lord asked, turning toward his wife with no enthusiasm.

"The marsh hawk. See. Down there. He's over that stand of oak trees."

"Some other time, old girl," Rod Goodenough said, turning Jane Lord about and aiming her back toward the house. "Your husband and I have more interesting game afoot." He giggled. "What lethal concoctions," he added, gazing at his empty glass. "One more of these, and I think I shall see a whale over that stand of oaks."

"Hawks come, and hawks go," Grayson Lord muttered, when his wife Jane was out of earshot.

Before he left with Lyn after dinner, Nate Taylor caught Charlie alone.

"I've enjoyed this," he said, his expression making it obvious he hadn't expected to.

"I'm glad," Charlie answered. "Your girl Lyn was the hit of the party."

"Not my girl," Nate answered promptly. He hesitated a moment. "I wanted to ask you and Lucy and your children for a picnic tomorrow. You just come as you are. I'll supply the food."

"Well, we might," Charlie answered. "I'll have to check with Lucy first, but I know we haven't anything else to do."

"Come on over to the beach about eleven or so. We can have a swim before we eat."

"We'll be there," Charlie answered. "Sure you don't want us to bring some food?"

Nate shook his head. "On me," he said. He shook hands, and snapped his fingers at Lyn.

"Must you drag her off, old man?" Rod Goodenough wailed. "I was just getting warmed up about whales and seals." There was silence from the direction of the three wives. "Well, I suppose you must," he added, shrugging. "When you come to England, you just come visit us, Lyn." He turned to his wife. "Darling, Lyn is coming to England."

Sheela Goodenough could think of nothing to say. The Martinis had long since worn off, and she, Jane Lord, and Lucy were discussing tweed.

The makers of gin, Charlie thought, should print a special label and paste it on the back of all bottles. "Caution!" it should read. "After Martinis, users are advised not to discuss either money or personalities." Lucy started it soon after the Lords and the Goodenoughs were gone, while she and Charlie were cleaning up the kitchen.

"I would like to make a request," she began cheerfully. "If you must pick up people on the Lobstertown beach, will you kindly refrain from asking them up here."

"She was rather pretty at that," Charlie answered sarcastically.

"Oh, stop it, Charlie. You know very well what I mean."

"No, I don't know what you mean. I thought they made the party. Without them, we would have sat around talking about marsh hawks, whales, and piping plover."

"Well, the wives all sat around talking about detergents."

"From what I observed, Nate seemed to make it fairly interesting."

"Was that his name?" Lucy answered. "I kept calling him Taylor."

He took her gently by the shoulders. "Let's not," he said. "We both have the post-Martini jitters. At least I do. Let's talk about cheerful things, or let's not talk at all."

"I want to get something off my chest," she answered.

He sighed. "All right. Say it. I defiled the sanctity of Lowell's Retreat."

"I can't say what I mean without sounding simply awful, Charlie."

"Then sound awful. I can take it."

"First of all, I know you're right, and that I'm wrong. But sometimes I don't think you'll admit that there's another side to all this too."

"Of course I'll admit it. I'm just as full of ugly thoughts as you are, only I'm trying to be more practical about it."

Lucy sat on the couch in front of the Franklin stove. The fire had burned down to a mound of warm ashes. Outside, the whippoorwills had started.

"One by one all the nice places are getting ruined," she said. "You didn't know this island in the old days, the way we did, but it was just wonderful then. When we came over in the old steamer we knew almost everyone on the boat, or if we didn't know them, they seemed like people we'd *like* to know. Now the ferry looks as though it's going out to Coney Island."

"But let's be practical about this," he answered.

"How can you be?" she answered. "We're being eaten alive. And I don't mean just here," she added. "The whole country is suddenly swarming with people. Awful people. Like locusts. We're being eaten."

He said, "Listen to me, Lucy. I think I know how you feel, and it's sad that we all can't go on living in pleasant exclusion any more, but we can't. I don't want our girls growing up believing the whole world consists only of us and our retreats. I'd like to expose them to these people you think are so awful. Let them decide for themselves which ones they like and which ones they don't, instead of condemning them as a unit. Tell me honestly," he asked, "did you like Nate Taylor?"

"What difference does it make whether——"

"Did you like him?" he repeated.

"Of course I liked him," she answered. "He was extremely good-looking and . . ." She paused.

"And what?"

"And quite fascinating. I enjoyed talking to him very much."

"I'm glad, because he's asked us all over to Lobstertown tomorrow for a picnic."

"Did you accept?"

"I knew we had nothing else to do."

"Jane Lord asked us on a bird walk."

"Did you say we'd go?"

"I didn't commit you to it, but I said I'd go. Lydia is getting quite interested in birds."

Charlie shook his head.

"I'm going to Lobstertown."

"Why?" Lucy asked quietly. "No, I mean it. Why? Why are you cultivating this Nate Taylor?"

"Perhaps I plan to use him," he answered.

"You use him," she shouted. "He'll use you."

"Maybe. I'm thinking of spending some money at the factory on advertising. Perhaps Nate Taylor is going to pick up a new account."

"Oh, Charlie, no," Lucy wailed. "He's not the type you want."

"I think he is. I want someone who isn't afraid of the market place."

"But The Hadley Company doesn't make detergents. You want a man who understands quality. Nate Taylor wouldn't know what the word 'quality' means."

"We'll see," he answered.

When he arrived at the Lobstertown beach just after eleven the next morning, Charlie saw Nate Taylor sitting alone near the stone jetty. Nate waved a pair of dark glasses at him.

"Where are Lucy and the kids?" he asked.

"They wanted to come in the worst way," Charlie lied, "but Lucy promised Jane Lord she'd go bird walking with her."

As he spoke, a slight glaze came over Nate's eyes.

"Are you sure you wouldn't rather go bird walking, too?"

"I'm here, aren't I?" He paused. "I hope you didn't break yourself buying all that food." Nate had the picnic all arranged on a beach blanket.

"It doesn't matter," he said. "We can feed the birds and the salt water mammals."

They swam out to the raft and lay in the sun. Two navy destroyers were anchored a mile offshore, their bows facing into the tide. A number of boats from the harbor were ferrying out to look at them, the calm water dotted with sails and oars.

"Had enough sun?" Nate asked after a while. "I'm getting hungry. Let's go eat."

By twelve the beach was crowded with dogs and children, all of them digging in the sand. Two buses from the other end of the island had parked behind the breakwater, and at least fifty tourists were walking along the edge of the water, pocketing shells as though they were precious stones. As they were finishing their lunch, a small naked baby stumbled over Charlie's feet, and lay weeping in the sand, forgotten by his mother, his mouth ringed with lavender soda pop.

"The Great American Public," Nate said thoughtfully. "They keep me in business."

"I never did ask you," Charlie said. "What agency are you with?"

"I have my own."

"I'm impressed," Charlie said, smiling.

"You shouldn't be. I have an office, a desk, a telephone, and a woman who does my art work and types my letters."

"No copy boys, switchboards, and account executives? I thought all New York advertising agencies were huge."

"Some of them are. But I've *tried* to stay small, and I've succeeded. That way I can handle a certain number of accounts, and handle them well."

"How did you get into advertising in the first place?" Charlie asked.

"I more or less fell into it. I worked in a radio station in New York for two years. I used to write copy for some of their accounts. I found I had a knack for it, so after the war I decided to go into it all the way."

"Do you make a living?"

"I get by. I probably could have done better if I had gone in with my father in the clothing business, but money isn't the only thing I want."

"You do want that, though, don't you?" Charlie asked.

"Sure I want it. I'd like to be a millionaire."

Nate had brought along an ice cooler filled with beer. Charlie opened a can.

"Can I ask you a professional question, Nate?"

"It might cost you money."

"Why should a company advertise?"

"So Nate Taylor can live in a style to which he is not accustomed."

"What can advertising do for a company?" Charlie persisted.

"Depends on the company. Depends on what it's trying to sell."

"Let's take a mythical company. Let's say it's been in business for over a hundred years. Let's say that for a long time it was successful, and made a lot of money without spending a nickel on advertising."

"That's an impossibility right there," Nate interrupted. "There never has been a successful company yet that didn't advertise."

"This one hasn't."

"Of course it has. It has a sign out in front, doesn't it?"

"As a matter of fact it doesn't. It blew away in the hurricane of 1938, and they've never bothered to put it up again."

"All right, no sign. But they put their name on their products, don't they?"

"They do that."

"And to be successful in the past, someone must have done some hard selling."

"They did that."

"Well, selling is advertising. Selling is the best advertising there is. In fact advertising is just a form of selling. That's why so many account executives end up as presidents of companies. In order to write good copy, you have to get the feel of a company. You can't just dream up something out of the air."

"The trouble is," Charlie said thoughtfully, "the whole idea is frightening. You hear about these fabulous amounts it costs for a one-minute commercial on radio or television, and you can't see how you'll ever get it back."

"Sometimes you don't. That's the gamble you have to take. Let's go back to this mythical company. Let's give it a name. Let's call it The Hadley Company."

"Don't tell me you've ever heard of it?" Charlie asked, surprised.

"I checked with your wife last night. It's a bad habit I have. I also bought this in the general store this morning." He fumbled in the picnic basket and took out a kitchen knife. "This is yours, isn't it?"

"Well, well," Charlie answered, pleased. "This was my own brain child. We sell those through Sears Roebuck mostly. We've made almost a million of them."

"And you're thinking of selling ten million more?"

"We'd like to."

"All right. Let's get back to your company. Tell me if I'm wrong. You really haven't tapped a national market yet. Is that right?"

"That's right. We have a couple of salesmen, and we have a lot of stores handling our knives, mostly east of Chicago."

"So you have two choices. Either you can hire about a hundred more salesmen and pay them a salary and a commission, or you can do the same thing in advertising. When some storekeeper out in California reads your ad, he's talking to one of your salesmen. Or if one of his customers comes in asking for one of your knives, he's talking to another one of your salesmen, and that's the best kind, someone who wants to buy. That's the main reason why you have to advertise these days. The country is so big you just can't cover it with salesmen, but you can cover it with advertising. Let me tell you something about these soap companies or these cosmetic companies," Nate said, warming to his theme. "All they really are is advertising. They have a little factory somewhere, and a warehouse, and the rest is all advertising—display counters in department stores, fancy bottles and containers, and a nice smell. The product they sell is always the same. The fight comes with the advertising. Like Gillette. I can buy fifty kinds of razor blades that are just as good as blue blades, and most of them cost less, but when I go into a drugstore all I can remember is Gillette. They've just smothered everyone else, and they've gotten rich in the process. Think of that," he said in awe. "Razor blades, something a man uses every day, a necessity, and one company has managed to take over almost the entire market because they're willing to spend millions on advertising. You ask what advertising can do, and there's your answer."

Charlie hesitated a moment.

"Would you consider taking on a new account?" he asked.

Nate Taylor acted as though he had been expecting the question. "You must be a fool, Charlie. Taking on an advertising agent is like marrying someone. You don't ordinarily propose after an hour on the beach together."

"I think you're the type we need."

"So what type am I?" Nate asked quietly.

"It looks like I've put my foot in it," Charlie answered, grinning.

"No, that's all right. What type do you think I am?"

"Perhaps I see you as someone who isn't crippled by so-called tradition, as we all are. The Hadley Company makes a good product, but right now we need someone who can guide us into the mass market. We've been coasting on our reputation too long."

"But why me?" Nate protested. "Not that I'm not interested in taking your money, but if I take on a job, I plan to do it my own way. I'd want you to understand that in advance."

"I just think you might see us with a fresh eye. What we take for granted you might find worthy of some inspirational copy." Charlie smiled. "I'd like you to see our factory, anyway."

"Well, frankly, I'm interested. I'm a little sick of underwear, toothpaste, and detergents."

"Why don't you drive up with me tomorrow morning?"

"You don't expect me to say no, do you?"

"I'll pick you up at quarter after five tomorrow morning, and we can take the six o'clock ferry." Charlie stood up. "Now I'm going to be rude, and go on back to the house. If I'm leaving tomorrow morning, I ought to spend a little time with my children."

Nate looked embarrassed. "Are you going to see Grayson Lord today?" he asked.

"I might. Why?"

Nate reached into a beach basket. "I bought this when I bought that knife of yours." He held up a copy of Grayson Lord's *Shore Birds of New England*. "Maybe you could get him to autograph it for me."

Charlie took the book, grinning. "You've been spending your money right and left."

"Don't worry," Nate answered. "I'm planning to get it all back."

twenty-nine

THE NEXT MORNING WHEN THEY REACHED THE CITY, INSTEAD OF GOING ON through and out to the factory, Charlie turned up Lawn Street and drove into the Chalmers' driveway.

"Don't tell me this is your plant," Nate said.

"Hardly," Charlie answered. "The Chalmers live here. I just thought you ought to see it."

The Lawn Street house had never looked better. There had been a thunderstorm the evening before, and the slate roof was still wet, steaming in the hot July sun. The whole yard looked cool and green in a dozen different shades—the ivy leaves on the stone walls, the elm and maple trees, the hemlock, pine, and the holly trees in the borders, and finally the lawn, freshly cut and smelling of drying grass.

"It looks like the Botanical Gardens," Nate said in admiration, looking out over Mrs. Chalmers' greenhouse toward the golf course.

"Let's go inside," Charlie answered. "You'll like that too."

Inside the front door, in the hall, Nate stood looking up at the family portraits, his hands clasped behind his back, his eyes critical, as though he were visiting an art gallery.

"Correct me if I'm wrong," he said. "But these aren't very good, are they?"

"That, sir," Charlie answered, laughing, "is not art. Those are ancestors."

"Ah, ancestors. About art I know a good deal. About ancestors, nothing."

Charlie led him into the living room. Nate glanced at the floor in surprise. "Is it supposed to be like that?"

"Like what?"

"All bumpy?"

"It's the summer dampness. When the heat comes in the fall, the floor lies flat again."

Nate moved to the piano and raised the keyboard cover. Then he played some fast, noisy jazz. As he listened, Charlie looked about the room nervously, half-expecting Mrs. Chalmers to emerge from the woodwork.

"Who plays?" Nate asked.

"Nobody."

"Then why the piano?"

"Piano lessons."

"Then someone must play."

"Everyone around here takes lessons, but no one plays."

Nate digested the answer for a moment. "Then why don't they get rid of it? Sell it?"

"There are grandchildren who won't play either, and a piano looks nice as part of a flower arrangement."

"But it's in tune," Nate protested. "Who tunes it?"

"They have a man come in."

"Ah, they have a man come in," he repeated, as though he liked the sound of the phrase. "Then why don't they have a man come in who can play the piano?" He ran his thumbnail up the keyboard and then covered the keys. "It's a beautiful instrument. Do they know it?"

"They know it. Everything in this house is beautiful. They may not be artists themselves, but they recognize talent in others."

From the living room they went into Mr. Chalmers' study. Nate gazed at the books in awe.

"Who reads?"

"Mr. Chalmers."

"He must be a wise man if he's read all this."

"That's his trouble. He's read too much. He also writes books."

Nate looked impressed.

"He's a writer?" he asked. "What's his first name? Have I heard of him?"

"I didn't say he was a writer. I just said he wrote books." Charlie reached over Mr. Chalmers' desk and pulled out a copy of *The Hadley Canal*. "This is one of his." He handed the book to Nate.

"There's a market for this?" Nate asked in astonishment.

"He gives them away."

"Gives?"

"Writing is his hobby. Just like knitting for a woman, only not as useful."

Nate moved to the window and stood looking out on the terrace.

"Pardon me for being crude," he said, "but how much would it cost to buy a place like this?"

"You can't buy it. What you really like about it isn't for sale. You have to inherit it, or marry into it, like I did."

Mr. Chalmers' clock struck eleven times.

"Anyone can make a lot of money," Charlie continued, "and build themselves a big house like this, but it takes about three generations to fill it with atmosphere, pianos that no one uses, floors that warp, dust and antiques. Look," he said, spreading out one of the study curtains, exposing a large gap in the material. "This curtain is one of the things that makes this room so nice. Polly Chalmers sliced that hole there when she was three years old. Every time Mr. Chalmers draws his curtains and sees the mess she made, he feels young again, remembering when Polly was three years old."

"Polly?" Nate asked.

"Lucy's younger sister. That's her picture on the desk."

Nate carried the picture to the window. It was Polly at eighteen, at the top of her backswing, lithe, strong, and full of teen-age disdain.

"Married?"

"Not yet."

"How old?"

"Nearly thirty."

"Where's she live?"

"New York."

"With all this up here she lives in New York? Why?"

"The answer is complicated," Charlie answered. "Let's go meet Mr. Chalmers out at the factory."

That Nate Taylor made Mr. Chalmers nervous was obvious. Charlie had interrupted him as he was writing his semimonthly letter to Anne and Polly, a stack of newspaper clippings arranged on his desk and his new dictating machine by his side. As was his habit during the summer months, he had moved his desk to the opposite end of his office, and the north window was open, a breeze coming in off the river and the reservoir. Mr. Chalmers had removed his suit coat. He was wearing an English shirt with removable collar and cuffs, and dark polka-dot tie.

"An advertising man, eh," he said suspiciously, as though Charlie had introduced him to a confidence man. "My son-in-law has been threatening me with this."

"Charlie was kind enough to show me your house, Mr. Chalmers," Nate answered unperturbed. "I've never seen a more beautiful place in my whole life."

"Well, now, Mr. Taylor. Do you want to buy it?" It was Mr. Chalmers' standard joke. If anyone admired his home he immediately offered it for sale.

"I'm afraid I'll have to tend to my business a while longer before I could even pay the taxes on it."

"What firm are you associated with?" Mr. Chalmers asked.

"Nate has his own firm," Charlie answered.

Mr. Chalmers rose from his desk and slipped on his coat.

"I'll be frank to say that advertising has never appealed to me, Mr. Taylor. From what I observe, most of it is much too crude for my taste."

"It needn't be, Mr. Chalmers. A good advertising agent considers himself a representative of the firm he works for. He's just another salesman."

"I suppose this advertising is an extremely expensive proposition."

"It usually is," Nate admitted. "It frequently doesn't pay unless you do spend a lot. I probably ought to tell you, Mr. Chalmers, that if I don't think I can help you, I won't even take the job. We have our own ethics in my business."

Mr. Chalmers looked skeptical. "Most advertising I see in magazines doesn't appeal to me, nor does it make me want to buy. If anything, it affects me in just the opposite manner. For instance, I would no more buy my clothing from one of these Robert Hall plain pipe rack stores than I would wear yellow shoes. Why pay for overhead? they say, and I say, why pay for advertising? I believe in the word-of-mouth method, and I mistrust people and companies who boast about their own qualities. But don't let me discourage you," he added, attempting a generous expression. "Go along with my son-in-law and look over our factory. But let me warn you that you have to convince me too, and I still write the checks out here, even though Charlie is pretty much running our operation."

"Yes, sir, I understand," Nate answered. "Would you mind if I took a picture of you sitting at your desk, Mr. Chalmers?"

"I beg your pardon?" Mr. Chalmers said, glancing at Charlie.

"Photography is a hobby of mine," Nate said. "And that's a beautiful view you have out this window here."

"Well now," Mr. Chalmers answered, "take all the pictures of my view you wish, but surely you don't need me in the picture."

"You would give the picture more meaning."

"I never realized before that my face gave any picture meaning," Mr. Chalmers answered, sitting at his desk.

Nate Taylor snapped two pictures with a small camera he had been carrying in his pocket.

"Thank you," he said. "If they turn out well, I'll send along a print."

As they started toward the office door, Mr. Chalmers said, "Can I see you for a moment, Charlie. Would you excuse us, Mr. Taylor?"

"I'll wait outside," Nate answered. He shook Mr. Chalmers' hand. I've enjoyed meeting you, sir."

"Not at all," Mr. Chalmers answered coolly.

The moment he was gone Mr. Chalmers turned to Charlie.

"That young man looks like a Jew."

"He makes no attempt to hide it."

"Don't snap at me, Charlie. I merely asked the question."

"Yes. He's a Jew."

"Where on earth did you meet him? I thought you were on a vacation."

"I met him at the Lobstertown beach."

"Well, no wonder."

"He's smart."

"Aren't they all smart?" Mr. Chalmers answered sadly. "Did you ever run into one who wasn't?" He paused, and returned to his desk. "Would you care to tell me why you've asked him here in his professional capacity? You must have some particular reason for it."

"I have. I think he might see us with a fresh eye, and I think the whole setup here, including the Lawn Street house, fascinates him. I have a feeling he might come up with something really good."

"You're sure it's not only money that fascinates him."

"Money fascinates me too, Mr. Chalmers. That's why I want to advertise. So we can make more of it."

"I have no quarrel with that," Mr. Chalmers answered. "I merely question your choice of advertising agent. I doubt if Mr. Taylor ever bought a Hadley knife in his entire life or would know what to do with one if you gave it to him. Taylor," he added sarcastically. "They do have the most incredible brass these days. I fully expect to meet one named Chalmers before long. I suppose his father was a tailor, and he just decided to change his name to Taylor. I don't trust them, Charlie, and I particularly don't trust the ones who change their names."

"You trust me, don't you?"

"Of course I trust you."

"I think I can hold my own with a Jew, or anyone else for that matter." Mr. Chalmers shrugged. "Go to it," he said, "but just remember——"

"Yes, sir, I know," Charlie interrupted. "You still sign the checks."

Charlie joined Nate out in the factory yard.

"So far, so good," he said.

"I have a suspicion your father-in-law didn't like me."

"He just doesn't trust you," Charlie answered.

"Why not?"

"As far as he is concerned you're in a sleazy business. I didn't realize you had a hobby," Charlie added, pointing to the camera. Nate had been taking pictures of the factory yard and the dam.

"I don't. But I had an idea back there in the office, and when I have an idea I try to get it on film. I find it works better than a notebook."

Charlie led the way toward the main shop.

"Now you'll meet obstacle number two," he said. "Our foreman, Ralph Henry. He won't like you either."

"What should I do or say to impress him?"

"Change your clothes, cover your face with grease, and chop off one or two fingers on both hands."

"I know the type," Nate answered grimly.

They found Mr. Henry bent over a machine. At the introduction, he merely fixed Nate Taylor with a pale blue eye, nodded, and then returned to his work.

"That was easy," Nate muttered a moment later.

"Don't look now, but he's following us," Charlie whispered. "He probably thinks you're a spy."

"I am," Nate answered. "Let's just wander around, and you answer my questions. And don't be discouraged if I ask some stupid ones. What seems important to you may not to me. I gather this is where you do your sharpening."

Charlie nodded. The main shop was filled with fine gray dust from the grinding wheels. They walked to the far end of the building and then stood watching the grinders, all of them with dust masks and goggles.

"By hand?" Nate asked incredulously.

"By hand, what?"

"You sharpen your knives by hand?"

"That's the only way you can get a really high-quality knife sharp. These men are artists."

"I heard someone shout for more water. What did he mean by that?"

"He wanted the grinding wheels to go faster. We operate by water power here."

"You're kidding, Charlie."

"Of course I'm not kidding. What do you think that dam is for, and the river?"

"But wouldn't electricity be more efficient?"

"Maybe. But the water is already here. And anyway, our grinders like the feel of water."

They climbed the narrow passageway and walked out into the span. The windows along the north side of the building were open, and Nate leaned his elbows on a window sill and gazed down toward the dam thirty feet below.

"How many factories still use water power?" he asked.

"I have no idea. They're going one by one. Like the covered bridges."

"Like the covered bridges," Nate repeated. "What about this shop you have in Cleveland?" he asked.

"We hope to build that up into something. Right now, we're making lawn-mower blades for two of the big manufacturers and not much else. Our plan is eventually to make everything that has an edge on it, and make it out of the best steel there is. In other words, we hope to end up with an integrated operation."

"O.K.," Nate said suddenly, starting back toward the passageway to the main shop. "I guess I've seen enough."

Charlie followed him, disappointed. He had feared Nate would be discouraged when he saw the factory, but he hadn't expected him to be so blunt about it.

"I suppose I wanted you to be honest," he said, when they were again out in the yard, "but you certainly have been."

Nate glanced at him. "Honest? I haven't said a word yet."

"You're not interested in us. Isn't that it?"

"I've never been more interested in anything in my life," he answered.

Charlie followed him through the factory gate and up the concrete steps to the top of the dam. The town of Hadley had placed a wooden bench near the spillway. Charlie sat next to Nate on the bench, and they both lit cigarettes, gazing out over the water to the north. Across the spillway a young boy was fishing, using a limb from a tree for a pole. Two hundred yards away, up along the bank, three more boys were swimming, swinging out over the water, dangling from the end of a long rope tied to the remains of an old railroad trestle. The air was warm, quiet, and still.

"How's the fishing in here?" Nate asked.

"It's all right for boys. The water isn't too clean."

"The skating must be good in the winter."

"That's something you didn't see, Nate. We also make skate blades. We sell them to some of the better manufacturers, and they fit their own shoes to them. Most of the good figure skating blades are ours."

Nate nodded impatiently, his eyes like black agates, glittering with excitement.

"I'll be honest with you," he began. "I've never handled an account like this before. Most of my things have been the big splashy kind. Like that detergent business I was telling you about. Hit-and-run things. Before I tell you some of the things I've been thinking, I'd like to ask you a question. What if advertising paid off for you? Could you increase your production to take care of it?"

"Someday I'd like to build a whole new factory out here," Charlie answered. "But I'd have to do it from earnings. For years this factory has really been more of a trust fund than it has a going business. I'd welcome a flood of new business, because that would force a little action."

"You're sure that in your heart you don't really love antiques, just like your father-in-law?"

"I like to sit in antique chairs," Charlie answered, laughing. "But I'd just as soon work in a new plant."

"You say you have a steady, small business right now. Why not just let it go on that way?"

"Because it isn't that simple. Either we go forward or backward, and if we go backward the Company will probably be sold out from under me. People around here are not sentimental about companies that are eating into their grandfather's trust fund."

"You'd like to take the Company over someday, wouldn't you?" Nate asked. "All right, so it's none of my business. Let me ask you something else. If you had to sum up The Hadley Company in one sentence, what would it be?"

"That's a tall order."

"What do you tell people when you're trying to sell your knives?"

"I tell them we make the best knives in the world."

"Do you believe it?"

"Yes, I do. Did you notice that small carving knife on Mr. Chalmers' desk? That came back in the mail a week or so ago. Some old woman sent it on from California. She said her grandfather brought it West with him a hundred years ago, and now it needed a new handle. Every knife we put out is just as good as that. I'm convinced that if people——"

"All right," Nate interrupted. "Now sum up the whole business in a single word."

Charlie thought a moment. "Quality," he said. "We're one of the few factories left that really believes in quality."

Nate nodded, as though what Charlie had said only confirmed what he had been thinking himself.

"Now I'll tell you one of the hazards of my business," he began. "The advertising business. Just about all the good accounts you pick up have already been ruined by someone else. You have to spend the first hundred thousand dollars trying to undo what some word butcher has chopped up before you ever saw the account." He flipped his cigarette into the river and lit another one. "The point is this," he continued. "The easy thing for me to suggest would be for you to pick out one of your products, like that kitchen knife you've been making for Sears Roebuck, and build a campaign around that. I could just about guarantee that in a year or so you'd have that knife in every hardware store and department store in the country, and you'd probably be selling them by the millions, and making quite a bit of money at it."

"Let's go," Charlie said enthusiastically.

Nate shook his head. "I'd like to try a completely different approach. If you examine the really successful advertising campaigns of the last fifty years, you'll find they all have something in common. They go at it like a good mason building a wall. They start by laying a foundation. They work on that for a long time before you ever see anything above the ground. Then when they do start laying the stones, they make sure every one of them fits. They don't just pile them up one after the other. They fit each one of them into place. And when they're through, the wall is solid. There isn't anything that can push it over. Good advertising is like that. Sure, I can spend your money and sell your knives, but I'd like to really lay some groundwork first. Expensive groundwork," he added, glancing at Charlie.

"You better be a little more specific."

"I'd like to advertise what The Hadley Company is, and what it has stood for for over a hundred years. I'd like to lay a foundation for about a year, and worry about the hard selling later. I'd like to tell this country that there is still one factory left that turns out quality things. I'd make this place a tourist attraction before I ever thought about the dollars-and-cents return. I'd like to convince people that Hadley knives were something unique, a carry-over from an age of simple colonial elegance." Nate grinned. "I'll spare you the rhetoric. But eventually, when I've put the point across that Hadley knives are the finest in the world, then I'll start surprising them with cold facts and figures, about price and where you can buy them."

"I don't think my father-in-law will buy it."

"I think I can handle your father-in-law. What I want to know is will you buy it? Let me tell you something else about advertising," Nate continued. "Most of it is just where-do-we-go-from-here stuff. They never take time to set up a definite picture of the product they're trying to sell. One year they paint it red, and the next year it's blue, but none of it really sticks because

205

they haven't plugged any continuous theme. It's like my father used to say when he was buying cloth for his business. If a salesman ever boasted, 'This material is just as good as XYZ worsted,' my father would throw the salesman out of his shop and go buy some XYZ worsted. What I'd like to happen in a few years is to have the other companies that make knives go around telling people that their knives are just as good as Hadley knives. I'd like to set you up as quality, the top. Then after we do that, we can start the hard sell."

"How will you do it?" Charlie asked.

"I'm going to think about it."

"Not too long, I hope."

"What's the rush? A month won't make any difference, will it?"

"I like to get things done."

"And I like to get things done too," Nate answered. "But this is something I'd like to do right."

"What do I do now?" Charlie asked, a little let down.

"You drive me to the station, and in a month or so I call you from New York. Then we have lunch together, on me, and I lay this thing out for you in specific detail. If you like it, you say yes. If you don't you say no."

"And if I like it, we'll still have to sell it to Mr. Chalmers."

"You leave Mr. Chalmers to me," Nate answered, walking toward Charlie's car. "Maybe I understand your father-in-law better than you do."

thirty

DURING THE YEARS OF HER MARRIAGE LUCY HAD NOT BEEN ONE TO COMPLAIN openly about her role as wife, mother, cook, and scullery maid. She knew, as did everyone else, that with emancipation and the vote the plight of women had become worse, and along with servants, small feet, and the fan, the species known as "lady" had long since disappeared from the earth. Thirty-five years before, her mother had been able to raise three healthy children, and never herself change a diaper. She had seen that her family was fed, and she had never cooked a meal. If her mother wished something to be done, she saw to it that someone did it. Lucy, however, if she felt a job worth doing, must do it herself.

Her acceptance of this state of affairs did not mean she could think of no way to improve it. She was a faithful reader of a column in the local paper called "Doctor DeWitt Says," a forum for disenchanted wives and husbands to wash their dirty linen in public. Charlie was apt to find the good doctor's pronouncements pinned to the back of his reading chair. "Husband and Wife —The Modern Team," or "Is Housework Necessarily Woman's Work?" or "Do Children Really Need A Father?" The point Lucy was making was clear.

But how, he wondered, could one be what Doctor DeWitt called a "modern father" and still earn a living? Whenever he was home, he kissed his children good night, all except Roswell, who objected to his beard. He admired their clothes, even though they all looked the same, and twice he had strained his back playing a game called rat, in which the girls beat him to death on the living room floor.

Nevertheless he knew he should be doing more. He wasn't getting to know his daughters as a modern father should. He really hadn't done much more for them than to be a living example that there was such a thing as the opposite sex. Therefore, when Nate Taylor called him late in August and suggested lunch and a conference the following day in New York, as part of an all-out effort to get to know his children better Charlie suggested to Lucy what he thought was an excellent idea.

"It really isn't as complicated as it sounds," he insisted, when he discussed the idea with her after supper. With Lydia entered that fall at Miss Nickols and in need of a physical exam, Lucy had returned early from the Island. "We'll take the eight o'clock train," he continued, "and make a day of it in New York. I have just one thing to do down there, lunch with Nate Taylor, and perhaps an hour or so with him in his office. The rest of the time Lydia, Roswell, and I can visit the zoo or the Empire State Building. Things like that."

"And leave me home?" Lucy asked.

"I thought you'd welcome a day away from them. Naturally you can go if you want to."

"Certainly I'd like to go to New York, but not with the children."

"The whole point of this is for me to be with my children for a day."

She snorted. "How would you possibly handle them when you were having your conference with Nate Taylor? What do you have to see him about, anyway?"

"Business," he answered vaguely. "And don't worry about the girls. I'll figure out ways to amuse them."

"Well," she asked, "do you want me to go, or don't you?"

"Of course I do."

"All right. I'll call Mother."

She started to the phone.

"Why call your mother?" he yelled after her.

"To see if she'll sit for Ruthie."

"Couldn't we just get an ordinary sitter?" he asked warily.

"Not on such short notice. Don't worry. Mother is much better with children than she used to be."

Lucy returned a moment later.

"Mother's come up with a marvelous idea. She's going along with us. Joseph can drive us all down in the new Chrysler. She thought the train sounded hideous, and I agree."

"How about Ruthie?"

"We can leave her with Elsa."

"Oh, damn," Charlie said bitterly. "I want to see my children, not your mother."

"You can be so casual about something like this, Charlie," Lucy answered hotly. "You have no idea what it means to get the children dressed, fed, and loaded onto a train at eight o'clock in the morning. Mother isn't trying to horn in. She's just trying to do me a favor."

"Let's drop the whole idea," he said. "I'll go on down alone."

"You will not, because it's all arranged. Joseph will be here at seven-thirty tomorrow morning."

Lucy headed toward the kitchen and shouted out into the back yard.

"Lydia and Roswell! Come on in. You've all got to have baths."

There was an immediate shout of protest from the back yard.

"We had baths last night," Lydia shrieked.

"I know it, and it makes no difference. You're going to New York with Grandmother tomorrow, and I want you to be clean."

Promptly at eight the next morning Mrs. Chalmers, Joseph, and the Chrysler arrived at Highcliffe Road. Mrs. Chalmers was bubbling with enthusiasm.

"Darlings," she said when they were out of the city, on the parkway heading south to New York, "we are in absolute luck."

Lucy was dispensing the first of her boxes of raisins to Lydia and Roswell. On all long trips, she allotted one box per child every thirty miles. In addition, her pocketbook always contained a surprise for good behavior, to be awarded at the end of the journey, usually chocolate bars.

"Why are we in luck, Mother Chalmers?" Charlie asked warily.

"After Lucy called last night I sat for a half-hour wracking my brains trying to think of something that would be fun to do today."

"We're going to the zoo," Lydia interrupted.

"We can always visit a zoo," Mrs. Chalmers answered. "I decided that today we must do something special."

"Not the United Nations, Mother Chalmers."

She turned on Charlie angrily. "No, not the United Nations. But I might add, since you brought the subject up, that it's exactly this attitude of yours, this cynical smugness, that makes world peace so——"

"Please," Lucy implored. "Let's not get started on that this early in the morning."

Mrs. Chalmers settled back against the seat and lapsed into an angry silence.

"We're going to the zoo with Daddy," Roswell shouted, taking advantage of the lull in the conversation. She waved her arms and sprayed raisins onto the car floor.

"Hush," Lucy ordered, "and pick up those raisins. Every last one of them. And you help her, Lydia."

"Me?" Lydia shouted, outraged. "Why should I pick up *her* raisins?"

"Because I told you to. What would you like to do in New York?" she asked, turning again to her mother.

"I hardly think Charles really cares, darling."

"Of course I care, Mother Chalmers."

She leaned forward again, her smile returning.

"Do you remember me speaking of my friend Clara Armitage, Lucy?"

Lucy looked vague.

"She's a friend from my Dobbs Ferry school days. I called her last night, and by a stroke of sheer good fortune she's in New York. She insisted that we all come to lunch and spend the afternoon with her."

"That lets me out, of course," Charlie answered. "I have a business appointment."

"Indeed," Mrs. Chalmers said. "My understanding was that this was to be a family excursion."

As Charlie took a deep breath, Lucy's elbow drove hard into his ribs.

"Would all of us enjoy Mrs. Armitage, Mother? I mean, the children and all?"

"My dear, she lives in absolutely the most fabulous house on Fifth Avenue. It's the sort of place that not one person in a million ever sees— What *are* you doing?" she asked, interrupting herself, glancing at Lydia in alarm.

"Mother said to pick up Roswell's raisins."

"But with your hands, child. Not with your teeth."

"Lydia's eating my raisins," Roswell wailed, bursting into tears.

"Stop it, both of you," Lucy shouted. "Listen to me, children. Lydia, Roswell, listen to me. We are going to a civilized city today, and I want you to act like civilized human beings. Is that clear?"

"I don't want to go to a civilized city," Roswell sobbed. "I want to go to the zoo with Daddy."

"Charlie," Lucy said grimly, "will you please discipline them? This was to be my day off."

He lifted Roswell onto his lap and pointed out the car window.

"Let's see who can count the most animals along the road. Whoever wins gets a dime."

"That old game," Lydia said scornfully. Then she screamed, "I see a white horse."

Roswell leaped off Charlie's lap and landed on Mrs. Chalmers' feet. "Where?" she shouted, her raisins again spilling onto the floor.

"A good time will be had by all," Charlie muttered. "See what I have, kids. Gum."

Mrs. Chalmers looked at him darkly.

"I will not have Clara Armitage seeing my grandchildren chewing gum."

"Mother Chalmers," Charlie answered firmly, "we still have another seventy-five miles to go. I promise you all gum will be disposed of the moment we see the Hudson River and Riverside Drive." He handed a stick to each of his daughters and bit off half a stick for himself. It was going to be a long, long day.

New York was hot, the late-August sun burning through a haze of smog. They left the parkway and headed across town through the park. Already the patches of grass were crowded with men lying in the shade, newspapers covering their faces. Joseph turned the car uptown when they reached Fifth Avenue, and stopped on the corner of Eighty-fourth Street.

"We'll see you at five, Joseph," Mrs. Chalmers said. "You'll be all right, won't you, alone in New York? I might suggest a few things for you to do. There's the Botanical Gardens, and of course Radio City. Do try to do something worthwhile, won't you Joseph?"

He said, "Very good, Mrs. Chalmers," and eased the Chrysler away from the curb. Joseph, Charlie suspected, would head uptown to Yankee Stadium. There was an autographed picture of Mickey Mantle under the sun visor of the car.

The Armitage mansion was a large square of brownstone surrounded by a high black iron fence. With the neighboring buildings crowding close in around it, what once had been a lawn and garden was now bare ground, shaded to death and smothered with soot. Near the street entrance there were an empty pool and a marble figure. The main door was made of bronze, thick and heavy, as though it guarded the entrance to a bank.

Before she pressed the bell Mrs. Chalmers gathered Lydia and Roswell close to her, and tilted their chins back until they looked at her.

"I want you to listen to me," she said quietly. "Try to understand what I tell you even though it may be difficult. You are about to see something that few people in the world have ever seen. This is one of the original Fifth Avenue mansions. It's a part of the history of our country. When you're as old as I am you will be able to tell your grandchildren that you saw part of a bygone era. Today it is still standing. Soon it will be gone. I want you to remember this experience. Is that clear, Lydia and Roswell?"

"Is this the zoo?" Lydia asked, glancing at her father.

"Hush," Lucy answered. "Listen to what your grandmother is telling you."

"I have to go wee," Roswell said, squirming.

"I knew we should have stopped on the parkway," Lucy said grimly.

Mrs. Chalmers squared her shoulders, glanced at Lucy, Charlie, and the two girls, and pressed the bell. Then she whispered, "This door looks Italian. Do you suppose it could possibly be a Ghiberti?"

If so, Ghiberti must have fitted it with a Yale lock, Charlie thought as he watched the door open.

An elderly white-haired butler peered at them, his expression one of well-trained scorn. "Yes," he said frigidly.

Mrs. Chalmers giggled. "Aren't you Forbes?" she asked.

"Yes, madam."

"We are friends of Mrs. Armitage. I think she is expecting us."

"Your name, madam?"

"I am Mrs. Lowell Chalmers, and this is part of my family."

"I see," Forbes answered. "I'll ask if Mrs. Armitage is in." He left them standing in the entranceway as he disappeared inside.

"Isn't he marvelous?" Mrs. Chalmers whispered. "Right out of a bygone era."

A moment later they were ushered into a downstairs lobby, a bare room with a stone mosaic floor, furnished only with a table, a telephone, and an elevator door.

"If you please, madam," Forbes said, nodding toward the elevator.

"I have to go wee," Roswell whispered in the darkness, as the elevator shuddered upward.

"Hush," Lucy hissed.

"But I do, Mommie."

"I know you do, darling, and so do I. We'll find a bathroom in a minute."

"Isn't this marvelous?" Mrs. Chalmers whispered. "This must be one of the earliest elevators ever made."

Forbes made three separate passes at the fourth-floor landing, first overshooting it by two feet, then dropping below it by two feet, bracketing it, and finally compromising to his own satisfaction.

"Well done," Mrs. Chalmers giggled.

"I beg your pardon, madam?" Forbes said, his hand on the elevator door.

"You operate your elevator like an expert."

"I don't believe I understand you, madam."

"That's all right," Charlie said. "Just let us out." The elevator was swaying at the end of its cable.

"Miss Crosby, Mrs. Armitage's secretary, will be right along," Forbes said as he opened the elevator door. He closed it behind them and sank out of sight, the elevator cables whining with the load.

They were standing in a hallway that ran the entire width of the building. At each end was a small round window.

"What now, Mother?" Lucy whispered.

"I have to go to the bathroom too," Lydia said.

"Look, kids," Charlie answered. "We all have to go to the bathroom. Just hold your water."

"Charlie," Lucy warned, but she giggled.

"I haven't felt like this since I toured the Pentagon," Charlie muttered.

"Hush, children," Mrs. Chalmers said. Steps were echoing down the hallway.

"Ah, Mrs. Chambers," Miss Crosby said. "Mrs. Armitage is expecting you."

"Chalmers," Mrs. Chalmers answered giddily.

Miss Crosby was a short, dark little woman in her mid-fifties, with flat heels, a flannel skirt, and ink-stained fingers. Her skin was paper white, as though she hadn't been out in the sunlight for years. Her eyes flicked over the children and back to Mrs. Chalmers again.

"You had a pleasant journey, I hope. Follow me, please. Mrs. Armitage is planning to eat her breakfast in the library. She'll join you there in a minute."

"I do hope we are not completely discumbobulating Clara's entire day," Mrs. Chalmers answered, following Miss Crosby down the hallway.

"Not at all, Mrs. Chambers. She was only too happy to rearrange her schedule. I know she's looking forward to seeing you."

"Chalmers," Charlie said firmly. He'd met the Miss Crosby type before, usually as generals' aides in the war. Their position carried with it the privilege of arrogance.

"It doesn't really matter," Mrs. Chalmers whispered. "Isn't this marvelous? We could be in another world."

"I have to go wee," Roswell announced in a loud, clear voice.

"Do you possibly have a bathroom?" Lucy asked desperately.

"Yes, of course," Miss Crosby answered crisply. When she reached the end of the hall, she glanced at the children in the light, possibly to decide which bathroom suited them. Then she said, "You'll find one right here. Will you need towels?"

"I hope not," Lucy answered, wrenching open the door and pulling the children in after her.

Charlie and Mrs. Chalmers followed Miss Crosby into the library. It was a small octagonal room that opened out onto an interior courtyard. Books lined the walls from the floor to the ceiling. A cut-glass light fixture hung from the ceiling by a bronze chain, and there was an Italian fireplace with an iron grill, and some old, well-worn chairs. The morning newspapers were arranged on a lowboy next to the couch.

"Mrs. Armitage will be with you in a moment," Miss Crosby said, her mouth assuming the position of a smile as she backed out of the room.

"What does Mr. Armitage do?" Charlie asked, when Miss Crosby was gone.

"The poor soul is dead," Mrs. Chalmers whispered. Then she leaned close to his ear. "Suicide. Don't mention his name."

"I mean, what business was he in?"

Mrs. Chalmers looked thoughtful. "Armitage Worsted sticks in my mind. Could that be it?"

Charlie reached for the New York *Times* and turned to the financial page. He found Armitage Worsted between Armco Steel and Armour and Company. It was listed at eighty-two bid, eighty-four asked, and paid four dollars a year plus an extra.

"You're right," he said. "Armitage Worsted."

At that moment the library door opened and Mrs. Armitage came in. Despite her dressing gown, she took charge the moment she appeared. She was tall and lean, with a receding chin and deep-set eyes. It was her teeth, however, which gave her character. The dentists of her childhood had quite obviously put aside their instruments and admitted defeat. The teeth lay bare like a quarry on the side of a mountain. She advanced toward Mrs. Chalmers, both her hands outstretched.

"Lydia, Lydia, Lydia. My dear, how are you? What is it? Thirty years?"

"Nearly, Clara. Perhaps even longer." Mrs. Chalmers held onto Clara Armitage's hands, gazing at her in rapt admiration.

It was the first time Charlie had ever seen Mrs. Chalmers in awe of anyone. But of course, he thought, this was Fifth Avenue, not Lawn Street. Mrs. Chalmers had been outranked.

Mrs. Armitage turned toward him and said, "And this must be your son-in-law."

"Yes, this is our Charlie, Clara. My daughter Lucy's husband."

"Do you have a last name, Charlie?" she asked him.

"Webb, Mrs. Armitage."

Lucy came in then, with Lydia and Roswell clinging to her dress.

"And you must be Lucy," Mrs. Armitage cried. "And these two cute little things are your daughters."

"Shake hands," Mrs. Chalmers hissed as she smiled.

For the last fifty miles along the parkway, Lucy and Mrs. Chalmers had been coaching Lydia and Roswell on how they should greet Mrs. Armitage. Every detail of the meeting had been covered except one. No one had mentioned Mrs. Armitage's teeth. Both Lydia and Roswell had expected to meet a woman, not what appeared to be a large beaver. They stared fascinated at the teeth, their mouths open, their hands hanging limply at their sides.

"What a wonderful family, Lydia," Mrs. Armitage said, breaking the spell. She seated herself on the couch and pressed a buzzer. "I'm ringing for my breakfast," she explained. "Now you have two other daughters, Lydia. Where are they, and what are they doing?" Her tone indicated a good filing system on the part of her secretary, rather than any genuine interest in the Chalmers family.

"My Anne, the oldest," Mrs. Chalmers said, "married a minister. They live in Philadelphia. Polly still isn't married, and is here somewhere in New York."

"Aunt Polly is trying to be an actress," Lydia volunteered, anxious to join in the conversation now that the horror of formal introductions were over. "She isn't, though."

"Really," Mrs. Armitage answered. "One of my daughters married an actor. That's Jane," she added, at Mrs. Chalmers' look of surprise. "She always had weird taste in friends. Do sit down, everyone. Wouldn't you all like some more breakfast after your long trip down?"

"When do we go to the zoo?" Lydia whispered to her mother.

"Hush," Lucy whispered back at her.

When Mrs. Armitage's breakfast arrived, rolled into the library by a young colored girl, Mrs. Armitage dipped two lumps of sugar into her coffee cup, and handed one each to Lydia and Roswell.

"You do allow your girls to taste coffee, I trust, Lucy?"

Mrs. Chalmers giggled. "You know the younger generation, Clara. They have no rules whatsoever. I'm allowed to have my say on only one thing. We still don't allow gum in our family. How about the rest of your brood, Clara? Mrs. Armitage has six children," she added, glancing at Charlie.

"My brood? Let me see. They're difficult to keep track of. I told you about Jane with her actor. Sue ended up married to a boy from Chicago. He packs meat or some such. She hates it, but naturally she has to put up with it. Then Audrey, poor girl, married a Spaniard."

"How fascinating," Lucy exclaimed.

Mrs. Armitage pointed a piece of toast at Lucy. "Don't ever let one of your girls involve themselves in an international marriage," she said. "European girls, yes, but the men, no. Of course Audrey, poor thing, was struck with the glamour of it all. I assume you're not Spanish," she said with a smile, turning toward Charlie, who had been taking no part in the conversation.

Mrs. Chalmers laughed. "Dear me, no. Our Charlie couldn't be more American. How about your boys, Clara?"

"My boys? Let me see. There's Maxwell, Junior. He's out in Los Angeles losing every cent he owns in real estate. He's been married more than twice, I'm afraid. We'd all give up on him if he weren't so completely charming. Then there's Bardwell. He has the Maine place. He fancies himself a farmer, and he also writes."

"How simply marvelous," Lucy said. "What sort of thing does he write?"

Mrs. Armitage waved her hand. "He refused to let any of us even peek at it. Novels, I suppose. What do people write in Maine if it isn't novels? That makes five of my children. Oh yes, there's Roger." She looked grim. "We used to call him Jolly Roger because he was always so humorless. Jolly Roger is running the mills. He thinks only of business twenty-four hours a day, and he's without doubt the dullest individual in the entire world. He flies all over the country in his plane with his battery of secretaries, and the only time any of us see him is when he needs our signature. I detest businessmen," she said airily. "Are you a businessman, Charlie?"

"I'm afraid he is," Mrs. Chalmers interrupted.

"What things do you do, Charlie?"

"He's with us, Clara. Charlie came in with us after the war."

Lydia plucked her mother's sleeve. "Now?" she whispered.

"What *does* the child want?" Mrs. Armitage asked. "Another lump of sugar?"

"I'm afraid they have an absolute fixation about seeing a zoo," Mrs. Chalmers replied.

"Don't you two girls see enough wild animals up there in the country?"

"We live in a city," Lydia answered, outraged.

"And you'd like to see a zoo?"

Both girls said, "Yes," in unison.

Mrs. Armitage pressed another buzzer. When Miss Crosby entered the library, she said, "Susanne, would you ring up my daughter Audrey's floor, and see if Consuelo would like to take her Juan and these two little things to the zoo."

"Is Audrey living here?" Mrs. Chalmers asked, when Miss Crosby had backed out of the room.

"Yes, poor thing, she is here," Mrs. Armitage answered. "I told you," she added, "that European men are simply impossible. Even actors make better husbands."

The creaking of the elevator could be heard through the library wall, and a moment later a thin, dark-eyed boy entered the library and stared sullenly at his grandmother.

214

"Lydia and Roswell, this is little Juan. You run along with him upstairs, and his nurse will take you all to the zoo."

"Run along," Mrs. Chalmers ordered, when they hesitated.

"He's chewing gum," Lydia said triumphantly.

"Here," Charlie said, handing Lydia the rest of his pack. "Share it with your sister." He glanced at his watch. "You'll have to excuse me, Mrs. Armitage, but I have an appointment at twelve. I'm afraid I'll have to run along."

"Just like Jolly Roger," Mrs. Armitage answered, with the manner of the woman who was both ugly enough and rich enough to say whatever she wished. "Cold fish, both of you. How do you stand him, Lucy? I suppose you're running the family business, Charlie."

"Yes, I am," he answered, noting Mrs. Chalmers' expression as he spoke. Then he added, "Actually, I'm merely Mr. Chalmers' assistant."

"Businessmen are horrible creatures. Necessary, but horrible. Run along. We women will never miss you."

Nor did she miss her son Jolly Roger, Charlie thought while Forbes was taking him down in the elevator, as long as the four-dollar dividend plus the yearly extra came in on time. He might loathe Mrs. Armitage if she were his mother-in-law and he were running the mills. As it was, he just envied her son Jolly Roger.

Just outside the entrance to Nate Taylor's office, on East Thirty-eighth Street, a newly planted sycamore clung tenuously to life, the grillwork that covered its root system clogged with cigarette stubs and trash. Its leaves were wilting in the intense heat. Inside the brownstone building the lobby was dark. A girl sat at a desk, working a switchboard which apparently served the whole building. When Charlie told her he wished to see Mr. Taylor, she waved him casually up the stairs.

Nate's office was on the second floor at the rear of the building. A shingle hung over the door, with "N. Taylor. Promotion and Advertising" stenciled in black paint.

Charlie knocked on the frosted glass window and then walked in. He saw Nate sitting at his desk against the window. He was talking on the phone. He mouthed a soundless greeting and pointed toward a chair.

Through the window behind Nate's desk, Charlie looked out into a court filled with laundry lines. The office itself was crowded with filing cabinets, bookcases, and equipment—a television set, a radio, a dictograph, a typewriter, and an adding machine. It was all an organized mess, the floor clean and recently waxed, and walls freshly painted.

"Where are the kids?" Nate asked as he hung up the phone.

"Uptown with their grandmother and Lucy. My trip to New York turned into a family outing."

"Donna will be disappointed." Nate came around from behind his desk and shook hands.

"Donna?"

"My slave. She was all primed to take your girls up the Empire State Building. Come on. I'll introduce you." He walked across the office and opened a side door. "Donna, this is Mr. Webb. Mrs. Shaw is my genius in residence. I couldn't get along without her."

"He says this, but he doesn't mean it," she answered, shaking hands. She was in her mid-fifties, a thin, drawn-looking woman, with blue circles under her eyes. Her office was nearly as large as Nate's. At one end was a large table, a sheet of heavy plywood supported by six legs. Shelves from the floor to the ceiling held bound magazines.

"I cheat," Nate said, following Charlie's gaze. "When I run out of ideas of my own, I go back twenty years to see how someone else did it. Advertising is like music. There are only three or four basic tunes. The problem is to dress it up in modern clothing."

"And this is all there is?" Charlie asked, looking around the two offices. Even though Nate had warned him, he had expected something more impressive.

"Disappointed?" Nate asked.

"Just surprised."

Nate nodded. "So was I when you told me The Hadley Company still operated on water power."

Charlie grinned sheepishly and said, "Touché."

"There are lots of bigger places than mine, if that's what you want."

Nate was obviously on edge.

"Let's see what you've thought up for us," Charlie answered.

Nate turned to Donna. "Bring in your Hadley work of art, and then go eat your lunch. Take as long as you want."

A moment later she laid a large rolled-up piece of art paper on Nate's desk.

"I hope you like it," she said to Charlie. "It's difficult to work from a photograph."

"If this is all part of the build-up," Charlie answered, "it's successful. Can I see it?"

"All in good time," Nate answered. "First comes the introduction."

He waited until Donna had left the office. Then he turned about in his chair and gazed out the office window onto the laundry lines.

"I'll be honest with you," he said, "and admit that this is the first account I've really been excited about since I started in this business. Somewhere along the line I've picked up a reputation as a master of the hard sell, and that's how I've made my living up until now—pills, deodorants, and detergents." He turned again and rested his elbows on his desk. He had lost his tan, and he looked tired.

"I'm as nervous as a cat about what we've done for you. I'd like your account in the worst way. Not just because I see a little money in it for me, either. I look on you and The Hadley Company as a way of getting me out of a rut. When you see this," he added, tapping the roll of art paper, "and when you read the copy that goes along with it, your first reaction will be No. At least I hope it will be No. I hope what I've done will scare you." He pushed the roll toward Charlie. "Go ahead and look at it, and keep in mind that this is just a drawing. Eventually it will be a photograph in four colors. Donna just worked this up from a picture I took in your father-in-law's office."

Charlie unrolled the drawing on Nate's desk, and weighted the ends with the telephone and an ash tray. It was Mr. Chalmers sitting on the edge of his desk, looking benignly at a knife he held in his hand. His expression was one of pure love, like a mother gazing at her child. Behind him, through the window of the office, Donna had drawn in the dam, the river, and the distant hills. On the dam a small figure of a boy was fishing with a pole. She had included a few details of the office, the clock, and the old Hadley sign.

"This is marvelous," Charlie said. "Mr. Chalmers will buy it just as it is."

"That's not what I'm trying to sell. Now read the copy that goes with it. But before you read it, let me warn you that I operate on the theory that people really do read advertisements. It's copy that persuades people to buy, not a picture. I've tried to keep this in character. I tried to put the same feeling in it that I felt when you showed me through your father-in-law's house. O.K. Read it." He handed Charlie a typewritten sheet of copy.

"Wait a minute," Charlie shouted. "Are you trying to tell me you plan to have Mr. Chalmers pose for a thing like this? Do you actually plan to use him in your advertisement?"

"Right."

"Then I don't even need to read it. No matter how good it is, it's out. He wouldn't appear in an advertisement in a hundred years."

"I think he will," Nate answered, undisturbed.

"He won't, Nate. I know him, and I know everyone like him up there. Life isn't a stage. It's not a place to take a stand and make a public display of yourself. It's a closet where you keep a strongbox filled with bankbooks and stock certificates. My God, Nate. Modesty is the byword up there. Even obituaries have to be modest."

"I think he'll do it," Nate answered.

"Take my word for it, he won't."

"I'm so confident he'll do it that I've already tentatively reserved the entire back page of the *New Yorker* for the first week in December. That's where he'll be. In four colors."

"You're mad," Charlie shouted. "Stark, raving mad. Mrs. Chalmers would die of embarrassment. People are more afraid of making fools of themselves up there than they are of cancer. It's one of the commandments. Thou shalt not make a fool of thyself."

"What's Mrs. Chalmers got to do with this?"

"Everything. None of us do anything up there without first asking permission of our wives. Why do you think we never get divorced?" Charlie shook his head. "It's out, Nate. I'm sorry, but it's out."

"So far, so good," Nate answered. "I hoped you'd react this way. Now listen to your Uncle Nate. I've done a little research on your father-in-law. I wrote one of your bookstores up there and ordered all his books. I read them. They're good. I mean he's a writer, even though he doesn't dare admit it. He works and sweats over words, even though he's only writing about his wife's family and some old canal. Your father-in-law has the bug, Charlie. He has it bad."

"I know it. That's all he does all day in his office."

"All right. I know something about people who paint pictures or sweat over words, or act. They've never quite grown up. They still are children shouting, 'Look at me, look at me.' That's why they paint, and that's why they write, and that's why they act. They want people to look at them. I don't care if your father-in-law does live in a closet with his stock certificates and his bankbooks. I don't care if he does have a million dollars invested at six per cent. He would like to be famous. He would like to walk along Fifth Avenue and have people recognize him."

"Fame, yes, but not notoriety."

"The dividing line is obscure. Both need an ego, and that your father-in-law has. It's obvious from his books. He thinks he is someone worth looking at, and I know he'll be tempted to do this if he has the slightest excuse."

"But what excuse will he have?"

"You'll just tell him that the success of the entire advertising campaign depends on it."

"But does it? Why not a professional model?"

"If you'd read my copy you'd know why. Because I'm going to stress just one thing in every ad I do for The Hadley Company. The family tradition of quality. Hadley knives are like diamonds. They get passed from one generation to the next. The factory still operates on water power because your grinders like the feel of water. Quality. Quality. Quality. That's *all* I'm going to talk about, and you can't find quality in a professional model. Your father-in-law has just the proper amount of snobbish arrogance to really put this thing across. I want a man who looks like he knows good diamonds, and good antiques, and good steel knives. I don't want some fathead who's working for fifty dollars an hour as a professional model. I want your whole family."

"The whole family?" Charlie asked nervously.

"When the river freezes over I want a shot of either Lucy or one of her sisters skating by the dam. And I'll have one of you stoking that furnace of yours. Sixth generation of the family starts at the bottom rung learning the business." Nate grinned. "I'm going to make you all tourist attractions, and I'm also going to sell your knives. At the same time I'll be running some hard-selling ads in all the trade magazines, and you'll be sending out promotional material to every store in the country. When your salesmen show up they'll be greeted as old friends, instead of just salesmen. I wouldn't be so enthusiastic about this, Charlie, unless I believed what I was saying. You have a wonderful product, and it will sell. Now do you like it, or don't you?"

"We're still not past Mrs. Chalmers."

"To hell with Mrs. Chalmers. Don't tell her what you're going to do. And I'll bet before long she'll want to get into the act herself. I may not know your mother-in-law, but I know women."

"If you hear an explosion like an atomic bomb when this thing appears in the *New Yorker,* that will be Mrs. Chalmers when she sits down for a quiet half-hour of light reading."

"Will you do it, Charlie?"

"I'll tell you after I have a small family conference."

"Not with Lucy, I hope." Nate looked worried.

Charlie shook his head.

"With sister Polly. I think she might know how to handle her father. And anyway, I've always wanted a good excuse to go see her in New York."

thirty-one

AFTER THEY HAD FINISHED LUNCH AND NATE TAYLOR HAD RETURNED TO HIS office, Charlie made two telephone calls. The first was to Polly.

The phone rang for almost a minute before a voice Charlie didn't recognize said, "Miss Chalmers' apartment."

"Is Miss Chalmers there?" Charlie asked, mystified.

"This is an answering service."

He said, "Oh," more surprised than impressed. "Where can I reach Miss Chalmers?"

"If you will leave your name, sir, she will call you."

"When is she expected back at her apartment?" he asked.

"I really couldn't say, sir."

"What time does your answering service quit for the day?"

"At five."

"Does Miss Chalmers usually call in for her messages before five?"

"I really couldn't say, sir."

He hung up, and called Lucy at Mrs. Armitage's.

"You'd better go on home," he said. "I'll be in New York pretty late."

"Doing what?" Lucy asked. "Charlie, honestly our poor children have had a rotten day. They keep asking me where you are."

"Tell them the next time I'll take them to New York without their grandmother, Lucy. That might cheer them up. Anyway, you go home when you're ready. I'll take the late train and take a cab from the station. I have to see someone after five tonight."

It was evidence that their marriage had reached a ten-year equilibrium when Lucy didn't ask him who he would see. Had she asked him, he wouldn't have told her anyway. He never lied to Lucy, but merely made it a point not to tell her the whole truth. It was lies and whole truths that caused trouble in marriages.

Polly lived at the lower end of Manhattan, on Cannon Street. The neighborhood was a slum, with a swarm of children playing in the street, dodging in and out of the trucks parked along the curbing. The air smelled of fruit stands and rotting wine. It could have been a section of Naples moved as a unit across the ocean, men sitting in doorways, their wives above them leaning out open windows, shouting at their children in the streets.

The number he was looking for was a dark entryway next to a garage. The building reeked of garlic and frying fat, and voices and music from television sets blared through the open doors into the hallway. Polly's apartment was five flights up. She had typed "P. Chalmers" on a scrap of paper and stuck it to her door with Scotch tape. The door was locked, and had an extra padlock and chain.

He waited for a half-hour, sitting on an orange crate, leaning back against the apartment door. When finally Polly arrived, because the hall was dark, she didn't see him. She paused on the landing, fumbled in her pocketbook for her keys, and then lit a cigarette lighter, holding it in front of her as she walked toward her door. In the flickering, yellow light she looked hot and exhausted, her hair sticking to her neck and forehead.

"Oh, my God, Charlie," she gasped, dropping the lighter and jumping back when suddenly he appeared. "You scared me."

"I'm sorry, Polly." He retrieved the lighter and handed it to her. "I should have waited in the street, but I was afraid you wouldn't let me come up."

"I wouldn't have, and I won't. Go home," she said. "I told you not to do this, and I mean it. I'm always glad to talk to you at Christmas, but leave me alone in New York."

"I would like to talk with you, Polly."

"You've picked a terrible time."

"It's business. I'd like to offer you a job."

"In The Hadley Company?" she said sarcastically. "Or are you so rich you're backing a play?"

"A job as a model. We're planning some advertising."

She stared at him for a moment. Then she said, "I don't believe you, but come on in. Will you behave? No ugly scenes?"

"It's your gaunt, aristocratic beauty I'm after, not your feminine charm."

"Hold this," she said, handing him her pocketbook. She unlocked the padlock and then the door. He followed her inside.

The apartment was a shock. It consisted of one large room divided into three sections with screens. At one end, behind a screen, was the bed. At the center were a gas stove and a laundry tub, which was used as a sink, washbasin, and bathtub. At the other end, near the only window, were a couch, a chair, and a lamp. The walls and the ceiling were painted blue. Polly's clothing hung from a water pipe that extended the entire length of the apartment. There was also a Siamese cat, which leaped from a box of groceries onto Polly's shoulder, sinking his claws affectionately into her flesh, rubbing his nose against her cheek.

"Meet Barrymore," she said, handing Charlie the cat. "Barrymore, meet my brother-in-law."

"Is that the smell I smell?"

"I can't let him out because he never comes back. Go sit over there," she

220

said, pointing to the couch. "I'll be with you in a while. I may have a job tonight, and I have to take a bath. We can talk while I bathe."

She lit the gas stove and drew two kettles full of cold water. When the water was hot, she poured it in the washtub and turned on the cold-water tap.

"How much do you pay for this dump?" Charlie shouted from the couch. Polly had pulled a screen around the tub, and her stockings had already appeared over the top.

"Twenty dollars a month."

"It's not worth a nickel more. Where's the bathroom?"

"Down the hall."

"No hot water?"

"What do you expect for twenty dollars?"

He could see her bare feet under the screen. Then they disappeared, and he heard her climbing into the washtub.

"Can I help you with your back?"

"I have a brush, thank you. You might get me a towel. I keep it near the bed, hanging on the water pipe."

He walked to the other end of the room. Polly's bed was her living room. It was seven feet long, and as wide. On it she had her telephone, a radio, a pile of magazines, and a bed tray which she used as a desk. The bedding smelled musty and stale. This was a side of Polly Chalmers he would have preferred not to have seen. At Christmas time, when she came home, she was always bright and sparkling, like a college girl.

"What's the job you have tonight?" he asked, tossing the towel over the screen.

"Just a job. Maybe I'll decide not to do it."

"Acting, modeling? What?"

"You sound like my mother."

"Has your mother ever seen this place?"

"Once. I suppose you think it's awful too."

"I've been wondering what it is you're trying to prove by living here."

She was rubbing herself with the towel.

"Am I trying to prove something?"

"You must be. Why else would anyone with the money I know you have live in a place like this?"

"It's statements like that," she said, "that make me hate you. Sometimes I think I like you, and then you come out with something like that."

"You still haven't answered the question. Why do you live here?"

"Because it's all I can afford."

"Oh, stop it," he said. "I see the dividend checks that go out to you four times a year."

"That's not my money. That's Grandfather's money."

"It's money. Why don't you spend it?"

"I do sometimes. I put it into a bank down here. When I go completely broke, I borrow from it."

"You're getting neurotic," he answered.

She had emerged from behind the screen, dressed in a kimono. She stood looking at him, her hands on her hips, Color had returned to her cheeks. She looked refreshed, clean, and quite beautiful.

"It drives you wild to see someone who won't quit, doesn't it?" she said. "I'm happy doing what I'm doing. Isn't that enough of an answer for you?"

"How can you be happy if you're not productive? What have you done? What are you doing?"

She looked at him as though he had driven a knife into her. "I want to be an actress, Charlie. Don't you have an ounce of compassion in your soul?"

"But you're thirty years old, Polly. Shouldn't something have happened by now?"

The telephone rang, and she disappeared behind the screen near her bed with it. It was the answering service checking out for the day. When she hung up Charlie shouted, "Get dressed. I'll take you out for dinner."

"I was going to suggest that we eat here. I'd love to cook you something. I'm really an excellent cook."

"All right. Can I run out and buy something?"

"Yes. Go get us some Italian bread and some red wine."

He started for the door. "Do me a favor," he said, hesitating. "Wear one of your good dresses."

She peered around the screen. "All right. But why?"

"I prefer you looking prosperous."

She looked at him with distaste. "I've learned something about you," she said. "You're a terrible snob."

"I've also learned something about you," he answered, walking out into the hall.

He took his time buying the bread and the wine. The area was an evening terminal for trucks. They now completely blocked the side streets, jackknifed across the pavement, parked for the night. During the day the city had turned on the fire hydrants along Cannon Street, and children were playing in the puddles of oily water in the gutters. Near the corner grocery store, a blind accordionist was playing Italian love songs, singing tonelessly, a cup partly filled with coins. The whole district throbbed with noise, the shouts of the children, the vibration of the subway under the street, the traffic, and the music from the tavern. If Polly had been born here, Charlie thought, she would do anything, beg, borrow, or steal, to escape. As it was, backed with a legacy from her grandfather, for her to live on Cannon Street was to return to the human race.

By the time he was back in the apartment, Polly had changed into a black dinner dress, high-heeled shoes, and a pair of diamond earrings.

"I did this for you," she said, as he stood in the doorway staring. "Don't you have any comment?"

"If you went out in the street dressed like that you'd be mobbed."

"Not mobbed, just robbed," she answered. "Go sit down. I'll announce dinner when I have it ready."

Dinner was a salad, Italian sausage, bread, and the bottle of wine. As it grew dark outside the noises changed in the street below. Gradually the women and the children disappeared, and the men took over, drunken groups of them standing in doorways, arguing and shouting. Three floors below, in another apartment, someone was playing a piano, practicing scales. Now and then in the distance, out on the river and the harbor, a tug would signal with a blast from its whistle. Barrymore, Polly's cat, paced the window sill, growling and scratching the screen. When they had finished eating, Charlie sat on the couch.

"What sort of jobs do you have, Polly?"

She had dumped all the dishes into the washtub and was pouring hot water over them.

"I have different jobs. Never two the same."

"How much do you earn a month?"

"My Lord, you're persistent. How much do you earn a month?"

"A thousand dollars, more or less."

"It isn't fair," she said bitterly. "You make a thousand dollars for doing practically nothing, and I make nothing for killing myself each day."

"What do you do each day?"

"You're determined to find out, aren't you?"

"What did you do today, for instance?"

She walked to the couch, pulled his feet off onto the floor, and sat next to him.

"All right, Father, I'll tell you. This morning I went to the Ludwig Art School on West Twenty-seventh Street, where from nine to twelve, at three dollars an hour, I posed for art students. After lunch I visited two casting offices where I talked only to secretaries. Then at three I went to my ballet class, which is about like visiting a gymnasium. All it does is keep me in shape, and people always ask you if you can dance when you're trying to get a job in television or something like that. Then I visited another casting office, which was closed for the day, and finally I came back here and found you in the hall. That's a pretty typical day, except I don't usually have you to keep me company for supper."

"So you made nine dollars today. Does that mean you make forty-five dollars a week?"

"Unfortunately I only have that job twice a week, but sometimes I go to the Wits' End at night and pick up a few more dollars in the check room or waiting on tables. It's just a place to be seen."

"Seen?"

"You never know when some director might walk in and like the way you look, or maybe he likes the way you check his hat. Other people have had their start that way."

The reflection from the apartment walls and ceiling made Polly's skin look blue.

"When I was in college," he said, "there was always talk about how we were going to be different, how we just weren't going to end up like our parents. That's why I'm curious about your life. Is it a good one?"

Polly pushed herself away from the couch, walked across the room, and sighted into the wine bottle. She returned with a glass full of dregs. "You have an uncanny knack of putting me into a box. My life is lousy, and you know it."

"But hasn't it gotten to the point where you have to make a decision about yourself? I mean, isn't it like selling insurance or brushes or knives? If you can't make sales, you either go into some other line of business, or you starve."

"You can say that so glibly," she answered, "but it's different when you're trying to sell yourself, in person. In this case, I'm the merchandise."

"Well, could it be that you don't have talent, that you're no good? If you were ever going anywhere as an actress, wouldn't something have happened by now? You're thirty years old." When she drew in her breath in a convulsive sob, he said, "Oh, My God, don't cry. I'm sorry, Polly."

"It's all right," she answered, instantly in control of herself. "It's red wine. It always does this to me." She reached for his arm and wiped her eyes on his sleeve. When she saw the lipstick she had smeared on his cuff, she giggled. "Now, you'll have to leave your shirt in an ash can somewhere. Lucy will never believe you stayed in New York on business."

"I really did come here to offer you a job. Do you want to hear about it?"

"All right," she answered, obviously not taking him seriously.

He walked across the room and picked up the drawing he had brought with him from Nate Taylor's office. He handed both the drawing and the typewritten sheet of copy to Polly. Then he waited while she read it.

Her first reaction was an explosive laugh.

"You don't really plan to run this, Charlie? Mother would resign from the Garden Club."

"That was my feeling too. But Nate suggested that we tell your mother nothing about it. After this we plan a whole series. You're to be next. You told me once you wanted to return home in triumph. Here's your chance."

"There's a hitch to this somewhere," Polly answered, looking at him curiously.

"Yes, there is. I'm counting on you to persuade your father."

"Me persuade him?"

"You've always had a way with him. You're the one member of his family he really wishes well."

Polly rose from the couch and spun about on her toes, her dress flying out horizontally.

"Mother will have a heart attack," she giggled, her face beaming.

"This might be a break for you, Polly. Your picture will be all over the country. Polly Chalmers, beautiful young star of stage and television——"

"Ha," she interrupted.

"You read what Nate wrote about your father. 'Distinguished author and historian.' When Nate is finished with you, the casting directors will come storming to your door."

"Is this your way of giving me a handout, Charlie?"

"Hell no," he answered. "I need your help, and it's the Company I'm thinking of, not you. I was hoping you could persuade your father to make a public display of himself."

"I can do it just like that," she answered, snapping her fingers.

"How?"

"Do you know what my father does about three times a year when he comes to New York?"

"I hear he goes to the Grolier Club meetings."

"That's what he tells my mother. But he doesn't. He comes here."

"Here?"

She nodded. "He sleeps right here on the couch. We go night-clubbing together, and I take him around to the Village dives and introduce him to some of the phony artists and writers. He gets pleasantly drunk, and tells me about the book he hasn't got the guts to write."

"Why, the old snake," Charlie shouted, laughing with delight.

"I love him," Polly said soberly. "I love him because he's so unhappy. I can get him to do this," she added, glancing at the drawing. "I'll just ask him to do it for me. He'd commit suicide if he thought it would help me. He wants me to succeed as an actress more than I want to succeed myself." She walked across the room and stood in front of him. "Do you have to go home tonight, Charlie?"

"Yes, I do," he answered. "Why?"

Polly took both his hands and put them on top of her shoulders.

"I thought we might go out and celebrate."

"Celebrate what?"

"Does it have to be something specific? Don't you ever just feel like *celebrating?*"

He moved away from her and looked at her from across the room.

"The only thing I celebrate these days," he said, "is children's birthdays. All right," he added harshly. "So I've become one of the dull ones. That's what you're thinking, isn't it?"

She sat wearily on the couch.

"I really don't know what I'm thinking any more," she answered. "Perhaps my trouble is that I *don't* ever think."

"I feel responsible for all of you, Polly."

"Responsible," she echoed.

"Your family is breaking up, and you're all too blind to see it. The only real talent any of you have is being part of a family. And you're squandering it. The only place you amount to a damn is at home. Here in New York you're nothing, and you never will be anything."

"You can be terribly cruel," she gasped. "Really, terribly cruel."

"It's a good life up there, Polly. You ought to try it."

She didn't answer for a moment. Then she looked at him soberly.

"But can't you see I'd like to try it? I'd like to go home."

"Then why don't you go?"

"I've burned too many bridges. I'd have to go home on my knees."

"Getting married is hardly the same as crawling on your knees."

"Yes," she answered, "but where can I find some cold-blooded opportunist like you who will marry me for my family? Someone like you is just what I need."

It was dark outside in the street. In the apartment below a baby was crying, and down the hall a door slammed, the sound echoing in the brick building.

"If I'm going to catch my train I've got to go," he said. "But do me a favor. Sometime this week drop up to Nate Taylor's office. He has some plans for our next advertisement that he wants to work out with you." He smiled at her. "He saw your picture on your father's desk. He'll recognize you." He paused a moment. "You don't happen to have a man's shirt around here anywhere, do you? I don't usually return to my wife covered with lipstick."

"You're in luck," she answered, patting his arm. "Father keeps two or three of them here. How about socks?"

He shook his head. "Just a shirt. My socks have holes, but they're fine."

thirty-two

ONCE EVERY YEAR, ON THE FIRST FRIDAY IN DECEMBER, LYDIA CHALMERS would be reminded that since 1914 she had been perpetrating a fraud. It was a harmless enough deception. If discovered, her only punishment would be embarrassment. But falsehood, whether large or small, was evil, and Lydia didn't like it. The fact of the matter was that every report she had ever read in front of the Garden Club had been ghost-written for her by her husband Lowell.

It had all started back in 1914 when she made the mistake of showing him her report on new members.

"In this I've tried to be more or less witty," she warned him. "We hope to keep our annual meetings light."

He read it and returned it to her without comment.

"Haven't you anything to say?" she asked, disappointed.

"Mahogany, my dear. Pure, pure mahogany." She had glowed with pride until he had added, "You write like a wooden Indian."

She should never have let him rewrite it for her. His paper had immediately established her as the club humorist, and that was a reputation she found impossible to maintain without him. Over the years she had become completely dependent on him.

"We all can't wait," the other members would tell her when the day of the annual meeting drew nigh. "We can't wait to hear what wicked things you'll have to say about us this year."

It was a little frightening, Lydia thought, as she sat at her desk examining the beautifully typewritten script that Lowell had handed her the evening before. All because of her husband's glib pen and his facile mind, she had become a national authority in the field of amateur gardening. Over the years, and over her signature, he had written five articles for the *National Bulletin*—"The Small Greenhouse," "The Care and Culture of Lawns," "How to Have Color in Your Garden Twelve Months of the Year," "Wild Gardens," and "The Principles of Grafting." The ridiculous part of it all was that Lowell hated gardening. After an evening spent picking her brains and sifting through her masses of unrelated notes on a subject, he could turn out in a single day a witty and informative paper which would bring gasps of admiration from women whose husbands had more to do. Women, after all, expected to be bored to tears by papers. When they weren't, their gratitude knew no bounds.

Sometime, Lydia thought, before she died, or perhaps just as she died, she'd admit that it had been Lowell who had written her papers for her. It would be ticklish, however. If the club members found out that she didn't do her own writing, they might also think she didn't do her own gardening either, and that wasn't true. She loved to garden more than anything else in the world. She could garden but she couldn't write, whereas Lowell could write but he couldn't garden.

This was another one of his clever jobs, she thought, as she glanced through the report. He had called it, "The Louis and Clark Expedition to Bartholomew's Cobble." Miss Mary Clark, aged ninety-two, one of the cofounders of the club, had organized an all-day outing in search of ferns. Like an ancient beagle on her last chase, she had spent the day scrambling over rocks and through brush, her colored chauffeur Louis always at her elbow, ready with cane and encouragement. When the club heard the title of the report Lowell had written for her, Lydia knew the laughter would be deafening and Miss Mary Clark would laugh hardest of all.

There was a pathetic side to these Garden Club papers of Lowell's, she thought. What a shame he had never exercised his talents in a more challenging way. She had asked him once why he didn't write something and send it out to an editor. His answer had been his last word on the subject. He had, he said, no desire to make a fool of himself.

He was really quite good, she thought, as she read on about Miss Mary Clark. "With the determination of Alexander, with the zeal of Saint Joan, on and on she went, leaving us young things far behind her." It would bring down the house, Lydia knew, and her reputation as a humorist would be secure for another year.

She glanced at her watch. She had a half-hour to familiarize herself with the report. She liked to be able to read it smoothly, and Lowell often used complicated words.

The telephone rang just as she was settling to the task. It might be Lucy, she thought, suggesting that they drive to the meeting together.

However, it was Eleanor Goddard.

"You sly minx," Eleanor cooed. "Why didn't you tell us?"

"Tell you about what, Eleanor?"

"Oh, come now, Lydia. Let's not play games."

"I haven't the faintest notion of what you're talking about, Eleanor."

"Listen to her," Eleanor said, as though she were talking to a large audience. "Am I not addressing the wife of the distinguished Lowell Chalmers, author, historian, and fifth generation of his family to carry on the priceless tradition of quality?" Eleanor burst into a shout of laughter. "My dear, it's simply killing. You must have written it yourself."

"Written what?" Lydia said angrily. "Will you please tell me what you're raving about, Eleanor."

"Then you haven't seen it?"

"Seen what, pray?"

"Oh, my dear, my darling, my dear. Do you take the *New Yorker?*"

"I'm sure we do."

"Have you glanced at the copy which came today?"

"I've been making some last-minute changes on my report, thank you very much."

"Well," Eleanor gushed, "drop your report this instant, and look at the back page of the *New Yorker*. It's simply divine."

In her haste to get downstairs, Lydia forgot her glasses. The morning's mail was still in a pile on the hall table. She unrolled the *New Yorker* and flattened out the back cover. Then she giggled with delight. She hardly blamed Eleanor for being excited. Whoever had posed for the advertisement she saw bore a remarkable resemblance to Lowell. They might almost be one and the same man. She climbed back up the stairs, carrying the magazine in her hand. Lowell would take a good deal of kidding about this, she thought.

Fortunately she seated herself at her desk before she put on her glasses. Otherwise, as she looked again at the picture and read the message that went with it, with her vision no longer blurred, she might have slumped to the floor. As it was the blood drained out of her face, and a hand seemed to grip her throat.

"It's a joke," she giggled out loud. Lowell must have arranged some sort of a practical joke, and had asked Eleanor to spring the trap for him. She'd heard of people who printed up dummy newspapers with preposterous headlines. Obviously Lowell had done the same thing with the *New Yorker*.

She opened the magazine and glanced at the inside pages. The *New Yorker* looked as it always did in December, cartoons, stories, and pages and pages of advertising. It was at that moment that she went numb with horror.

For a full minute she sat reading over and over again, "Lowell Chalmers, author, historian. Lowell Chalmers. Lowell Chalmers. Lowell Chalmers."

"Lowell Chalmers," she gasped. Was he out of his mind? Was he mad? No wonder he had been acting so odd lately, like a boy who was hiding a nasty secret. And she had thought all the time that he had merely been tired, and she had tried to be particularly nice to him.

Then she reached for the telephone and dialed Lucy's number.

"Darling," she said, her voice tight, "can you come over here immediately? Something rather terrible has happened."

"Good Lord, what?" Lucy asked, frightened.

"I'd rather not talk about it over the phone, darling. Can you come right away?"

Lucy didn't finish zipping up the side of her dress until she was halfway to Lawn Street in her car. She ran in through the kitchen entrance, nodded at Elsa who was calmly polishing silver, ran through the hall and on up the stairs. She found her mother sitting at her desk, staring bleakly out onto the terrace.

"Mother, what is it?" she gasped.

Mrs. Chalmers handed her the *New Yorker*.

"It's Father," Lucy shouted.

She was intensely relieved. She had been sure it was a heart attack. The time for heart attacks had arrived, she knew. Her father was nearly seventy, and some year it would happen. All the way over from Highcliffe Road she had steeled herself for the worst. Merely to find a full-page picture of her father on the back cover of the *New Yorker* was a pleasant surprise.

"What a marvelous picture," she added, when her mother didn't answer.

Lydia Chalmers turned on her daughter fiercely.

"Do I gather you approve of this cheap commercialism? Our family has never been one to make a display of itself. You should know that."

"It really could be worse, Mother. It all seems in rather good taste. And he is an author, isn't he?" Lucy giggled.

"I've never been so ashamed in my entire life, Lucy. This is frightful."

It was a side of her mother Lucy hadn't known existed. Her mother, to her, had always been as calm and as confident as the Rock of Gibraltar.

"But it's just advertising, Mother. People do these things all the time."

"*We* don't do these things, Lucy. Our family doesn't have to do these things."

Lucy glanced down at the bottom of the page. "It says here that this is the first in a series of full-page advertisements which will dramatize one of the fine families that has kept New England the stronghold of quality that it is today." She looked at her mother thoughtfully. "Does this mean they're planning to have us all pose for these advertisements? I wonder who's next?"

"There will be no next," Mrs. Chalmers answered frostily. Then suddenly she wilted. "Eleanor Goddard called a few minutes ago. She was licking her chops. How can I possibly read my report today with this disgraceful thing staring me in the face?"

"But you've *got* to read it, Mother. The Garden Club just wouldn't be the Garden Club without you and your yearly report. It's the high point of the year. Everyone says so."

"Do they really, darling?" Mrs. Chalmers hesitated, gazing out the window. "Then I suppose I'll have to go through with it." She rose from her desk, her face pale, her jaw set, her expression that of the soldier who has just been ordered to the front.

The younger members of the Garden Club often asked each other what would happen when all the big houses were gone. Lucy, for instance, would have loved to have a meeting at her house on Highcliffe Road, but with an active membership of ninety, many of them quite large, her living room was simply out of the question for a regular meeting. A cocktail party was one thing, but Garden Club meetings were sober affairs, and when generations were mixed, space was a prime requisite. The day might come, of course, when they would have to hire the Hill and Dale Club for the afternoon and hold meetings there. Flower and Bower used the Hill and Dale, as did the Junior League and most other sizable organizations. But there was more to the Garden Club than was written in the by-laws. It was, for instance, the occasional visits to homes like the Goddards that made membership in the club such a joy.

The Goddard house, its style known locally as "Post-Civil War Monstrosity," occupied a six-acre tract at the juncture of Bond Street and Outlook Avenue. The house was a period piece, complete and preserved in every detail, from the freshly painted black iron fence along the sidewalk, the recumbent lions that guarded the entrance, the white gravel driveway, to the large portico that had once protected the carriages and their occupants from the rain. The house itself was yellow stucco, four stories high, trimmed with brown wooden gingerbread. Its windows were large, vacant panes of glass.

Over the years the house had remained inviolate, a fortress against the sweeping tide of the city. Across Bond Street was a new insurance building, brick with a small gold dome. To the north, across Outlook Avenue, was a solid block of stores. To the south, just beyond the Goddards' woven cedar fence, was a parochial school.

For a generation, and particularly since the war, "Senior," as the elder Newell Goddard was called, had rebuffed a parade of real estate agents who had knocked on his door, urging him, as they put it, to bow to the inevitable, offering him a steadily mounting sum of money to deed away his house and his acres of mountain laurel and dogwood trees. He was always polite, and he always refused.

His reason baffled the real estate men. He liked, he told them, to wander about his property, assailed on all sides by power and gas lines, by streets and sidewalks, by buildings and noise; he liked the feeling that he was still an individual in a society that was taxing the individual to death. They dismissed him as a character and eagerly awaited his death. However, when they examined his tax records, they always found them marked "Paid."

"Perhaps I might just pretend I haven't seen it," Mrs. Chalmers whispered to Lucy as Joseph let them off at the Goddards' front door. "If only Eleanor doesn't make a big thing of it."

"She will," Lucy whispered, as she rang the bell. "You know Mrs. Goddard as well as I do."

Eleanor Goddard was waiting in the hall. She had torn off the back cover of her *New Yorker*, and she waved it triumphantly as Lucy and her mother entered.

"Ta-ta-ta tum, ta tum," she sang out in a loud vocal fanfare. "Rise for the Queen," she shouted into the huge living room where most of the club had already gathered. Then she enveloped Lydia with her large, plump arms, and hugged her. "Isn't it marvelous?" she giggled at Lucy with malicious delight. "Aren't you proud of your father, author and distinguished historian?"

"My, isn't this lovely," Lydia Chalmers said, breaking away from Eleanor Goddard's grasp and admiring a sickly ivy plant on the hall table. "You do have such a touch with potted things, Eleanor."

She then walked resolutely into the living room and tried to lose herself in the throng.

Before the formal part of the meetings got under way, there was a period of general garden gossip. This consisted of news of family and friends, weather and sickness, deaths and pregnancies. Lucy headed for Mary Robinson, who was standing with a group of the young.

"Don't say a word," Lucy warned when Mary grinned at her. "Mother's fit to be tied."

"She is?" Mary asked, obviously surprised. "Ed called me from the office about it. He said that's all everyone was talking about this noon at lunch. He thinks it's the most brilliant bit of advertising he's ever seen."

"Are you serious, Mary?"

"I couldn't be more so. He said he had ten calls this morning about Hadley stock, which is ten more than he had all last year."

"I mean you're really joking, aren't you, Mary? Mother's sick about it."

"Sick about it? Sick about what?"

"She thinks it's rather cheap."

"Then she's the only one who thinks so. We're all as envious as sin."

Lucy might have thought Mary was joking until Bushy Sedgewick joined them and said enthusiastically, "You're famous. May I touch you?"

Bushy was from Boston, and had an annoying attitude of being able to take things local or leave them. Until that moment Lucy had disliked her intensely. But when Bushy added, "I called Shreve's this morning and ordered an entire set of Hadley carving knives for my father for Christmas," Lucy almost fell on her neck with love.

Perhaps it was just the young who weren't shocked, she thought, glancing about the Goddard living room, searching for her mother. Her mother might be dying of embarrassment with her own friends. She saw her standing by the Goddard piano in the midst of a giggling, laughing press of her friends. She seemed flushed with pleasure. Lucy wandered over and listened for a moment.

"I'll confess," she heard her mother say, her face as radiant as that of a sixteen-year-old girl who has found herself the belle of a ball, "I'll confess that when Lowell first broached the idea to me I was dead against it. In fact I was horrified. But Lowell insisted, and what Lowell wants to do, of course he does. Once he gets his mind set on something there's no changing it." She paused, listening to old Mrs. Wooley. "Yes, you're quite right, Eudora, al-though a month ago I might not have agreed with you. I suppose I'm a little too conservative for this modern world. You see Lowell has made a complete study of advertising during the last year or so, preparing this thing, and he learned that . . ."

At that moment Miss Jennie Loomis approached Lucy and said, "We're all terribly proud of your father. I called Doubleday's and ordered every one of his books."

Miss Loomis was a kindly old soul, noted in the club for her seventy-eight varieties of miniature cactus.

"Did they have them?" Lucy asked.

Miss Loomis' answer was drowned out by Eleanor Goddard calling the meeting to order.

"Can I say something nasty, Mother?" Lucy asked when they were riding home after the meeting.

"Please do," Mrs. Chalmers answered gaily, the cheerful lilt back in her voice.

"I think Mrs. Goddard was wild with envy."

Her mother was silent for a moment. Then she said, "I hardly know how to put this without making it sound as though I didn't like Cousin Eleanor, which of course I do. She's one of my oldest and dearest friends, and I don't know what I'd do if anything ever happened to her. I mean that, Lucy. I love Eleanor Goddard dearly."

"Of course I know that, Mother," Lucy answered, anxious to have the niceties out of the way.

"But you see," her mother continued, "poor Eleanor has always been a little jealous of me." Mrs. Chalmers hesitated a moment. "No. That's not exactly fair. She's been jealous of our whole family. We do things, darling. There's a spark in all of us that has long since died out of the Goddard family." Mrs. Chalmers lowered her voice to a whisper. "This is cruel of me to say, Lucy, and it has nothing to do with the fact that poor Newell Junior has no children—that's a shame, isn't it?" she said, interrupting herself.

"What were you going to say that you thought might be cruel?" Lucy asked impatiently. "Yes, it is a shame."

"Eleanor," Mrs. Chalmers continued, still whispering, "is utterly bound by convention. She would no more have allowed Newell Senior to pose for an advertisement like that than she would allow him to swim the English Channel. She's dead up here," Mrs. Chalmers said, tapping her forehead. "As a family, the Goddards have run out."

They rode for a moment in silence.

Finally Lucy said, "Mary Robinson told me that Ed thought the advertisement was brilliant."

"Well, darling, of course it was brilliant. Your father happens to be a brilliant man."

"Don't you think we might give Charlie just a little credit for it?"

"By all means," Mrs. Chalmers answered generously, squeezing Lucy's wrist. "Your Charlie deserves a great deal of credit. Your Charlie is full of admirable qualities, darling. But when it comes to your father's flair, his spark, his willingness to take chances, I'm afraid Charlie still has a number of things to learn. And of course, when it comes down to your father's ability to write, to express himself in words, whether it be an advertisement or . . ." she paused, looking at Lucy thoughtfully. They were nearing Lawn Street and Lucy's car. "If I tell you a secret, darling, will you swear never to tell another living soul?"

Lucy nodded. All conversations with her mother were preceded by an oath of secrecy.

"Would it be too immodest of me to say that over the years I've gained quite a reputation in our Garden Club for my reports and my papers?"

"You were wonderful today, Mother."

Mrs. Chalmers took a deep breath.

"Your father wrote my report, Lucy. He's written every single word I've ever written since 1914, including all my articles for the *Bulletin*."

Joseph had stopped the Chrysler in the driveway and was moving around to open the rear door.

"Now I'll tell you a secret, Mother," Lucy whispered. "I've known all about that for years, and so has every other member of the Garden Club." She patted her mother's hand. "Tell Poppy I'm proud of him, and I've got to run. I'm going to get Charlie a decent meal for a change."

"Is Mrs. Chalmers at home, Elsa?" Lowell Chalmers asked at five that afternoon as he came through the kitchen doorway.

"Yes, sir," Elsa nodded. She tilted a bowl of hard sauce at him, knowing well he liked it.

"Does she have visitors?" he asked hopefully, not commenting on the hard sauce.

"I believe madam is waiting for you in your study, Mr. Chalmers. She's been at her Garden Club meeting all afternoon."

"Oh, my God," he muttered. It was going to be worse than he expected. He should have disappeared for a week, slunk off down to the Island or gone to New York to stay with Polly.

How could he best handle this? he wondered, as he walked on through the hall toward his study. There was, of course, an outside chance that Lydia hadn't yet seen the advertisement. However, that seemed unlikely. Even if she had missed it, one of her Garden Club friends would surely have spotted it.

Judging from the number of calls he had received that day at the office, the entire city had seen it. He could have become no more notorious had he committed an ax murder. Fred Baird had been the first on the line shortly after ten that morning.

"I gather you don't believe in letting your directors know what's in the works out there," Fred said as his opening remark. "Whose brain storm was this?"

"My son-in-law Charlie's," Lowell had answered. "He got himself involved with some damn fool advertising agent down in New York, and they sold me on this before I knew what I was doing."

"Then it wasn't your idea, Lowell?"

"Not a bit of it, and I can assure you, Fred, it's the last time I'll let Charlie handle any advertising for us."

"Then you tell Charlie something for me," Fred Baird answered. "Hadley opened at three hundred and ten this morning, up thirty points from the last sale yesterday, and I've already had over a dozen calls from New York asking about you people out there."

"Just because of one silly advertisement, Fred?"

"My personal opinion is that it was a rather brilliant advertisement. It even made me want to buy some of your damn knives, and I've got a house full of them. You tell Mrs. Fleck to send me in about two hundred annual statements. This is going to stir up a lot of interest, and I want to be ready for it."

When Joe Pritchard called, asking whose idea it was, remembering his conversation with Fred Baird, Lowell said, "You might say we all had a hand in it, Joe. We work pretty much as a team out here."

Then when Newell Goddard called from the bank and asked the same question, Lowell admitted modestly, "Naturally, I didn't do all the detail work, Senior, but the conception was mine. Not that I wanted the personal publicity," he added hastily. "But the logical approach seemed to be to start with me. We plan a whole series of these things right on down the line. We have a good product to sell, and advertising is the modern way to stay abreast of an expanding market. The country is too large these days to cover by old-fashioned means."

Lydia, however, would be quite another matter. She would no more approve of him posing for an advertisement than she would approve of his wearing a hand-painted necktie to church.

He found her sitting near his study fireplace. A small fire was burning brightly, and on the table, next to a decanter of sherry, two wine glasses were waiting. In her lap she was holding a copy of the *New Yorker*. He stood in the study doorway, looking at her miserably.

"Well, Lydia, say it. Get it over with. I'm every bit as ashamed of myself as you must be."

She closed the magazine and placed it on the table. Then she crooked a finger at him, motioning him toward her chair. When he stood next to her, she reached for his necktie and pulled his head down close to hers. Then she kissed him on the cheek, her lips cool and dry.

"You, Lowell, are a naughty boy."

He straightened up, astonished.

"Is that *all* you have to say?"

"What else would you have me say, you vain creature? That you look good enough to eat in four colors, which you do? Why, oh why, Lowell, didn't you wear your dark brown suit? Your new one. It's far more becoming to you."

"You amaze me, Lydia," he answered, still unable to believe his good fortune. "I thought you'd be furious with me."

"But, dear one, why should I be furious with you?"

"I just thought you would be." He reached for the sherry decanter and poured both glasses full.

"Naturally, I was a little hurt that you didn't tell me about it, Lowell," Lydia said, sipping her wine. "It came as a surprise, even if a pleasant one."

"You really mean you're happy about this, Lydia?"

"Of course. I'm delighted. Tell me. What results has it brought?"

He looked at the ceiling, a smile coming into his eyes. "One rather fantastic result, Lydia. Did I ever mention a girl named Dodie Germond to you? I took her to the Yale freshman dance. No, of course. That was long before I met you, wasn't it. Anyway, she saw my picture, and called me all the way from St. Louis."

"How fascinating," Lydia answered, without enthusiasm. "What I really meant was, how effective was the advertisement for the Company's business?"

Lowell waved his hand impatiently. "You'll have to ask Charlie about that. He handles all the incoming orders these days. I did notice, however, that he seemed quite pleased. Incredible, isn't it, about Dodie Germond. I haven't thought of her in over forty years. She's a seven-time grandmother, she tells me." He turned and grasped Lydia gently by the shoulders. "I can't get over the fact that you're not angry with me. I've known you for a long, long time, and I thought I could pretty well fathom your mind. I was sure you'd be horrified when you saw that advertisement. But apparently I was wrong. After more than forty years of marriage I can still be fooled by my own wife. I really don't know you at all, do I, Lydia?"

She smiled happily. "Life would be rather dull, wouldn't it, if you ever knew anyone completely? Drink your sherry. I'd like to tell you about your paper that I read at my meeting today."

"Oh, yes. How did it go?" he asked, sinking into his reading chair. "I hope no one was too upset when I compared Miss Clark to Joan of Arc."

"They loved it. As usual, you provided just the right touch to liven up the meeting. And now I'm going to confess something to you, Lowell. I am a wooden Indian. You were quite right when you told me that years ago."

"Why Lydia, that's ridiculous. If I said it, and I don't think I did, I must have been out of my mind."

"You said it, and it's true. I'm a wooden Indian, and I married a brilliant man." She rose from her chair. "I'm going to leave you to your papers. I hoped you would notice we're having your favorite dessert for dinner."

"I did see the hard sauce," he admitted. "Elsa showed it to me. What's to go with it? Nothing, I hope."

It was a joke they had together of forty years standing, that one day he would be allowed to eat nothing but hard sauce for dessert.

"You're a naughty boy," she said, smoothing his hair as she passed him on her way to the hall.

thirty-three

Nate taylor stepped off the new york train on christmas eve dressed in a chesterfield and a dark Homburg. In one hand he carried a new leather suitcase, and in the other a bundle of what appeared to be Christmas presents.

"No Polly?" he asked, allowing Charlie to take his suitcase. "She did come up from New York, I hope."

Charlie nodded.

"She's back at the Chalmers, coiled on a couch waiting for you. For reasons best known to the female mind, she asked me to fetch you."

They walked together down to the street, using the outside ramp. The station was jammed with Christmas Eve arrivals, large family groups hugging sons and daughters, everyone cheerful and happy.

"It's nice to see where everyone goes," Nate said as they were getting into Charlie's car. "I've always just seen the other end of it, people leaving New York. By the way," he added casually, "I hope you know that Polly asked me up here."

"She told me two weeks ago."

"I don't want you to think I was crashing a family party."

Charlie eased the car out into the avenue and headed west.

"I would have asked you myself if I'd thought you would have come."

"If you had asked me I probably wouldn't have come. I find Polly rather difficult to refuse."

Charlie nodded. "She's quite a girl," he said, keeping the subject open. "Even when your interest in her is only professional."

Nate didn't answer for a moment. Then he said, "I might as well admit that I'm crazy about her. I have been since the night you introduced us last summer."

This, Charlie thought, was a development he hadn't counted on, even though it ought not to surprise him. Why shouldn't Nate Taylor be crazy about Polly? Everyone else was, or had been at one time. He wasn't worried about his sister-in-law. She could take care of herself. But could Nate? Polly might end up hurting him more than he'd ever been hurt in his life.

"Remind me to tell you about Polly sometime," he said.

"Why not tell me about her right now?"

Charlie turned off the avenue onto Lawn Street. In another four minutes he'd be at the Chalmers' driveway.

"There's another problem I'd like to discuss with you first," he said. "You're acquainted with female jealousy, aren't you?"

"I know it exists."

"My wife Lucy feels rather left out of our advertising plans. I told her I'd

236

suggest something to you where we might be able to use her as a model. Wait a moment, Nate. I just promised to talk to you about it. I'm not going to insist that you do it. You're in complete charge, and I'm not going to interfere."

"Lucy would like to have her picture taken by a professional photographer. Is that it?"

"She's envious of Polly. I know it all sounds silly, but I have to live with it."

"We'll arrange something," Nate answered.

"And that isn't all. Even Mrs. Chalmers has been hinting around about a picture of someone using our Hadley garden scissors. She doesn't come right out and say it, but I know she's suggesting herself as a model."

"We can arrange something about that, too. I'll take care of the whole thing."

"But how can you satisfy them without spending fifty thousand dollars of Hadley money?"

"We will. Leave it to me."

"How?"

"I'm having Sid Tenner come up here the day after tomorrow to work out some shots of Polly on skates. I'll tip him off on Lucy and your mother-in-law, and he'll take a few shots of them doing whatever they want to do. Later we'll explain to them that the pictures didn't fit in exactly with our plans. We'll soften the blow by sending along some enlargements. Sid knows the score. He has to do this sort of thing every day. All it will cost us is Sid's time and a roll of film."

"You're a genius, Nate."

"Hardly. Let's return to Polly. Tell me about her."

They had nearly reached the Chalmers' driveway. Charlie drove to the side of the street and turned off the motor.

"All right, Nate, you asked for it. Did you ever have a cat?"

"My mother had one."

Nate had removed his hat and placed it in his lap. He extracted his cigarette holder from an inner pocket and gripped it in his teeth, making no move to put a cigarette in it.

"Cats," Charlie continued, "are like Polly. They are amusing as long as they are amused. They're sleek, smooth, and decorative. But they also like to hunt for the sheer sport of it, and they seldom eat what they catch. They just play with dead bodies."

"So I'm just a dead mouse?"

"Polly can be both fickle and cruel."

"I've already figured that out myself."

"You havn't seen her enough to figure anything."

"You could be wrong. I've seen no one but Polly for three months. I've taken her to dinner every night she'll go out with me. We've seen every museum in New York, Central Park at midnight, the Empire State Building, and Grant's Tomb, like two tourists, the Staten Island ferry, and half the dives in the Village. She's also met my mother and my father. I think I know Polly Chalmers quite well."

Charlie hesitated. It was ridiculous, he thought. Nate knew what he was thinking, and he knew what Nate was thinking, but neither of them dared put it into words.

"Just let me urge you not to fall in love with her, Nate."

"I've already fallen in love with her."

"She'll hurt you. Perhaps not in New York. People from here make it a point of being liberal when they live in New York. But up here where her roots are, she'll hurt you. We'll all hurt you."

"How about you?" Nate asked.

"What about me?"

"Polly thinks a hell of a lot of you. She says you were the only good thing that has happened to the Chalmers family in a generation."

"Polly knows I wish her well."

"She feels a particular attachment to you. She's told me all the things you've said to her. You register with her, Charlie."

"What are you getting at?"

"I'm going to ask Polly to marry me one of these days, and when I do, and before she says yes or no, I think she'll come to you for advice. I'm just curious as to what you're going to tell her."

"I don't think it will ever go that far. She may have an affair with you, but I don't think she'll consider marrying you."

"She won't have an affair with me, because I won't have an affair with her. And I am going to ask her to marry me, and I'm pretty sure she'll go to you for advice."

"All right," Charlie answered angrily. "Then you tell her this for me. That if she comes to me for advice I'll tell her to go to hell. It's her problem, and yours. Not mine. You tell Polly to make up her own mind."

Nate considered the answer for a moment. Then he said, "Then I'll ask you myself. How would you feel about having me a member of the family?"

Charlie knew the question was coming since they'd begun the conversation. He said, "I'll just say this much—the Chalmers as a family have a great deal. They have money. They have what is called social standing. They're respected. They're educated, and they're all healthy. The only thing they lack is brains."

"Meaning?"

"You might bring some brains into the family."

Charlie started the car and headed into the driveway. The headlights reflected from a figure standing by the garage.

"Speak of the devil," he said, "complete with blue jeans and mink. Consider yourself warned, friend, and I hope all this won't ruin a profitable arrangement for The Hadley Company. That's what really worries me."

"Hi," Polly said, pulling open the car door on Nate Taylor's side. "My, don't you look formal? Are you going to a funeral?"

238

"When in Rome be natural," Nate answered. "And furthermore, I don't have any informal clothes."

"Charlie," Polly said brightly, "Lucy called. Ordered me to order you not to linger. Seems you have a Christmas tree to decorate."

"I'd like to introduce Nate to your mother, Polly."

"Won't be necessary. I'm in charge of Mr. Taylor. Run along to your happy hearth." She put her hand on Nate's arm. "Ready, Mr. Taylor?"

"Ready, Miss Chalmers." He leaned in through the car door. "Thanks, Charlie."

"Yes, thanks, Charlie," Polly echoed, guiding Nate toward the kitchen door.

The dregs of Christmas, Charlie decided, always tasted the same. Inevitably, late in the afternoon, he and Clyde would end up alone, out in the kitchen, him sitting at the kitchen table, Clyde staring out the window, both of them wondering what to say to each other.

"Are you depressed by the thought of your long drive back to Philadelphia?" Charlie asked after one lengthy period of silence.

"It's not driving to Philadelphia that depresses me," Clyde answered. "It's just Christmas with the Chalmers."

Here we go again, Charlie thought. The chip was still on the shoulder. Every year when he saw him, he hoped Clyde would have matured. The annual chamber music from the living room had ceased. Anne and Lucy, he knew, would be sitting on the couch talking with their mother. His three children would be talking in separate corners, examining their presents. Mr. Chalmers would be in his study with a book. Polly and Nate had left the house a moment before, heading for the park with skates. Nate was dressed in a pair of Mr. Chalmers' tweeds and a sweater. It was a cold, gray Christmas afternoon, the temperature well below twenty.

For a moment he stared at Clyde's back. Every profession placed its stamp on a man, he thought. If businessmen were inclined toward fat, and doctors turned sallow and gray, ministers too had a trade-mark over and above their clerical collar. Clyde's hair was now completely white. He made a virtue of it, wearing it long, like an eighteenth-century statesman. He was a striking man, Charlie admitted, lean and straight, with bright, intelligent eyes. Somewhere inside Clyde was a person worth knowing, a person worth trying to reach.

"If you feel this way toward the Chalmers family," Charlie asked, "why do you keep coming up here every year?"

"Anne seems to feel the need of family ties."

"And you don't?"

Clyde didn't answer. He left the window and sat opposite Charlie at the table.

"You look more successful every time I see you," he said, smiling faintly.

"I realize you consider that an insult."

"But don't you have any particular goal? Is your day-to-day business enough to keep you contented?"

"I set goals for myself all the time," Charlie answered. "Right now I'm trying to double The Hadley Company's business, and I'm trying to organize a larger sales staff. That's my present goal."

Clyde frowned, as though he found the answer repulsive. "And what new world will you conquer after that?"

"This reminds me of my sophomore year at college."

Clyde continued to smile. "I'm sure when you were a sophomore you were concerned only with memorizing answers for your next test."

"May I make a personal remark about you, Clyde?"

"Please do. I'd welcome it." Clyde sounded like a moderator in a discussion of international affairs.

"You're an ass."

Clyde's smile didn't waver.

"I'd rather be an ass doing worthwhile work than a success walking a treadmill."

"You've probably repeated that to yourself so often you actually believe it. It's damn lucky for you that I do walk my treadmill. Otherwise, what would you and Anne live on down there in Philadelphia in your retreat from the world?"

"That's a little unfair," Clyde answered, flushing. "If you refer to the dividends from The Hadley Company, I think you'll admit we put them to good use."

"That's just what I don't admit. You're just pouring good money down a rat hole. I visited you and Anne down there, didn't I? You once told me that I should come and see what you and Anne were doing, and I made a special point of doing just that. As far as I could see, you aren't doing very much. Your so-called private mission is a failure. The reason you resent my success in my business is because you're a failure in your own. And let me finish. You can criticize the way I live, but you can't take criticism yourself. You and Anne ought to stop hiding from the world, and go out and compete in it."

Clyde stood up, his face pale. "Is that all you can say of the work Anne and I are doing?"

"From my observation in Philadelphia, you're running a bankrupt business. If you decided not to go back there, not a soul would miss you."

Clyde started toward the pantry door.

"That's right," Charlie called after him. "Rush off to Anne and tell her it's time to run back to your cave."

Clyde stopped. "This is completely incredible," he said. "I thought that you might be one member of this family who liked me."

"I do like you," Charlie answered. "In fact, I was even going to suggest that you leave Philadelphia and come to work in the town of Hadley."

"As one of your salesmen?" Clyde asked scornfully.

"No. As a minister. That's what you're supposed to be, isn't it? The Hadley Church is looking for a younger man. Mr. Worth is retiring in six months."

"I really couldn't consider anything like that," Clyde answered, startled.

"Why not? Why don't you and Anne spend the night with Lucy and me at our house? Perhaps we might get together on something if we were away from this Lawn Street atmosphere. I don't like it either."

"Thank you, but we can't," Clyde answered, obviously touched. "I'd like to, but I know Anne feels we ought to get back tonight."

"If I can persuade Anne to stay over, will you?"

"I'd like to very much," Clyde answered. "Actually, we have nothing too important to do back in Philadelphia."

As Charlie passed the study door he saw Mr. Chalmers dozing in his chair, a book open, resting against his Christmas stomach. In the living room Mrs. Chalmers was sitting on the couch between Lucy and Anne, with Ruthie asleep on her lap. Lydia and Roswell had made a cave under the piano with Christmas boxes.

"I do hope you're not planning to go home quite yet," Mrs. Chalmers said as Charlie entered. "It's not often I get the chance to see my two older daughters together."

"I'd like to talk to Lucy, if I might," Charlie answered.

"Why all the mystery?" Lucy asked, not stirring.

"Can I see you a moment in the hall?"

When Lucy joined him, he said, "Ask Anne to spend the night with us. Clyde has agreed if Anne will do it."

"I wouldn't think of it. Mother has been asking her to stay here, and she's refused. Anne says Clyde feels he has to get back."

"Clyde told me he doesn't have to get back. Ask Anne."

"I won't," Lucy answered. "If I did, Mother would be furious."

"Ask her. Please, Lucy."

"I will not. It's been a pleasant Christmas, and I won't ruin it."

She started back toward the living room. Charlie grasped her firmly by the elbow.

"Ask Anne to spend the night at our house," he ordered.

"Charlie."

"Ask her. I mean it."

"Yes, lord and master," Lucy answered with angry sarcasm. "And if she refuses?"

"Don't let her refuse. I want to have a talk with Clyde."

Lucy had put the children to bed the moment they all had returned from Lawn Street. By the time the girls left the Chalmers' house they were already snapping and snarling at each other, Roswell in tears, accusing both Lydia and Ruthie of stealing her presents. There had also been a bloody scene in the upstairs hall when Lydia yanked a piece of rat-tail licorice out of Roswell's mouth, taking with it a front tooth. Finally, however, the evening's blood stopped flowing, tears gave way to sleep, and all bedrooms were quiet.

"Why mothers get gray," Lucy had sighed as she went wearily down the stairs.

"Ah yes, but everyone gets gray," Clyde answered thoughtfully, glancing at Anne, who was waiting for them in the hall. It was a hint of what would come, of what was on Clyde Harbert's mind.

That they all should have something to drink had been Charlie's idea.

"Why not," he asked, "put off eating for a while? I'm not hungry anyway. Would a drink and an open fire interest you and Anne?"

"Anne and I sometimes have a sherry together. But nothing stronger, thank you," Clyde answered.

"Good. Sherry it will be for all of us." He walked toward the kitchen.

"Make mine an extremely small sherry," Anne called after him. "It makes me sleepy."

Small it would be, Charlie mused to himself in the kitchen. Small and lethal. He removed two bottles from under the kitchen sink, where he kept his liquor supply—one of whisky, the other two-thirds full of sherry. Then he inserted a funnel into the neck of the sherry bottle and added six inches of whisky to it. It was at that moment that Lucy joined him.

"What in God's name are you doing?" she asked in an angry whisper.

"Mixing a drink," he answered blandly.

"Whisky and sherry?"

"Good for people with problems." He tapped her on the shoulder. "No comment, please. This is my party."

"I will not sit by and watch my sister be plied with alcohol."

"Then just don't watch, because that's exactly what I plan to do."

"Anne is high strung, Charlie," Lucy pleaded. "Something like this might do terrible things to her."

"It might even make a human being out of her. Excuse me," he said, stepping past her with the fortified bottle of sherry and a tray of wine glasses. "Will you join us?"

Lucy followed him into the living room, her mouth a firm line of disapproval.

"A lump of ice in each wine glass. What a unique idea," Clyde exclaimed.

"Doesn't ice ruin sherry?" Anne asked, sniffing her drink suspiciously.

"Not *good* sherry," Charlie answered. "Nothing can hurt good sherry. Ah, peace and quiet," he sighed, changing the subject. "The end of another year."

A fire in the fireplace complicated the heating system. In order not to be blasted out of the living room with heat, it was necessary to turn the thermostat down to fifty-five, which cooled off the rest of the house and left but one room warm, the living room. A draft of cold air crept in along the floor from the hallway until Charlie stood up and closed the living room door.

"Well, what shall we talk about?" Anne asked after a while, holding her glass for a refill. "Do you mind, Clyde? It's terribly good."

"Not at all. I'm ready for more myself."

"Let's not all get drunk," Lucy said nervously.

"A little sherry never hurt anyone, not even a minister," Charlie answered, filling both Clyde's and Anne's glasses to the top.

"Anyway, let's talk about something cheerful," Lucy added.

242

"Let's see. What do we know that's cheerful?" Clyde asked, after a moment of silence.

The room was again quiet.

"This is ridiculous," Lucy laughed. "Can't any of us think of something cheerful?"

"Yes, I can," Clyde said. "I'm going to loosen my collar."

"What an excellent idea," Anne answered, removing her shoes and stockings. "I haven't felt as pleasantly sloppy since my college days."

"Ah, college days," Clyde echoed. "Now there's something cheerful. Dreams, fresh, new, and untarnished." He gazed into his wine glass. "I looked at your little girls tonight, Lucy, and I thought, there they were, so young and innocent, no scars and no disappointments. Then I projected them thirty years from now, and thought of the messes all of them would make out of their lives."

"Clyde," Lucy gasped, horrified, "why should they make messes out of their lives?"

"Of course they will. We all make messes out of our lives."

"Is your life a mess?" Charlie asked quietly. Anne was watching her husband from the couch, sipping steadily from her glass.

"Why don't we all go eat something?" Lucy asked hopefully, rising to her feet.

Charlie answered by refilling both Anne's and Clyde's glasses. Lucy resumed her wary vigil on the chair.

"Is my life a mess?" Clyde asked himself, his face already bright red from the fire and the alcohol. "What do you think, Anne? Is our life a mess?"

"Why rope Anne into this thing?" Lucy interrupted. "I've just thought of something cheerful. Don't Mother and Father look well?"

"Everyone looks well," Clyde answered, "but is anyone really well inside?"

"You're positively morbid," Lucy said, laughing gaily, almost wildly. "Christmas is no time to be morbid."

"What better time?" Charlie asked. "What better day in the year to ask ourselves where we're all going?"

"Yes, and when you ask yourself that, how can you help but be morbid?" Clyde added, "I refer to myself, Charlie. Not to you. I envy you your life."

Anne spoke then. She was looking at the ceiling through her glass. "What do you envy about Charlie's life, Clyde?"

"Perhaps I envy him his wife," Clyde answered. Then he giggled, already a little drunk. "It rhymes. Wife. Life."

Anne lay motionless, a stricken look on her face.

"Let's eat, everyone," Lucy said firmly. "I'll go make some sandwiches."

"Food for the body but not for the soul," Clyde mused.

"Clyde Harbert, you're drunk," Lucy said nervously.

"Is that what I am, Lucy? It all started when Anne mentioned college days. I wish I had the last twenty years to live over again."

"What would you do with them?" Charlie asked.

"Why don't you come on out to the kitchen, Anne?" Lucy insisted, tugging at one of her sister's bare feet. "We'll let the men cry in their beer."

"I want to listen," Anne answered. She held out her glass toward Charlie. "Is this really sherry?" she asked.

"Look at the bottle," he answered. "Duff Gordon. The best."

The fire had burned down. He put on two more logs.

"What would you do with the twenty years, Clyde?" It was Anne who asked the question.

"I'd marry some dumb girl who thought God meant women to bear children. That's the first thing I'd do."

"Clyde," Lucy shouted, "what a nasty thing to say!"

"Is it so nasty? Ask your sister Anne if it's a nasty thing to say."

"I'm sure Anne wants children just as much as you do."

"Now, perhaps, but not fifteen years ago, when she should have wanted them."

"Now wait a minute," Lucy answered angrily. "I happen to know what you're referring to, because Anne told me all about her not wanting to have children when she was married. But didn't you agree with her? Didn't you both discuss it before you were married?"

"Yes, we discussed it," Clyde answered sadly, "and I agreed. But what's a man know about things like that? I may have been a fool, but Anne was a monster. For a man not to want children is bad enough, but for a woman not to want them is . . ." he hesitated, staring at his wife. "You should have known better, Anne. We're forty-one. Forty-one," he repeated bitterly. "Look at us. We're gray and old. Does that look like a fertile woman there?" he said, raising his voice, pointing to Anne. "Does your sister look fertile to you, Lucy? She doesn't to me. She looks old and sterile."

"Merry Christmas, everyone," Lucy muttered, glaring at Charlie.

Anne had rolled onto her side and had buried her face against the back of the couch.

"I hate children now," Clyde continued. "I hate all children, and I hate everyone who has children. I hate your children, Lucy, and I hate you because you have them."

"I'm really not interested," Lucy answered coldly. "I just wish everyone would come eat."

"Why don't you adopt?" Charlie asked.

The room was quiet for a moment. Then Clyde said, "Why don't you tell him, Anne?"

"I will not stand for this for another instant," Lucy shouted. "This is my home, and I won't have a discussion like this on Christmas night. It's disgraceful."

Charlie looked at her. "Do us a favor," he said. "Shut up."

Clyde giggled with delight. "That's what I should have told Anne when I first met her. Shut up." He repeated the phrase as though he liked the sound of it. "You just shut up, Anne Chalmers."

Anne spoke from the couch, her voice muffled. "Why haven't you left me, Clyde?"

He waited until she looked at him. "Because I loved you when I married you, and I still love you today. Silly, isn't it?" A drunken grin spread over his face. "I've just thought of something cheerful for you, Lucy. My wife has the prettiest feet in the world."

"Lucy's are prettier," Charlie protested. "Her arches are better."

"Why doesn't everyone go to bed?" Lucy asked miserably. She was near tears.

"Lucy's not as drunk as we are," Charlie explained patiently to Clyde.

"A pity," Clyde answered. He stumbled across the room and wrenched off one of Lucy's shoes. "Now both you Chalmers girls stand side by side," he commanded. "Up, Anne Chalmers. Up, Lucy Chalmers. Place your feet side by side, and we'll just see whose wife has the prettiest foot. Admit defeat, Charlie," he shouted a moment later, when the two women were standing shoulder to shoulder and foot to foot. "Anne's feet are white and pure. Lucy's most definitely have the inferior pedal extremity."

"By God, you're right," Charlie muttered.

"Friends. Friends. Please watch your language," Clyde giggled. "A man of the cloth is present in this humble domicile. Two people of the cloth," he corrected himself. "One man of the cloth, and one woman of the cloth." Then he added, "Woman of the cloth, and very good in bedclothes as well."

"Clyde, stop it," Lucy ordered. "Please go to bed. You're drunk."

"Look at her," Clyde shouted, paying no attention to Lucy's outburst. He carried a lamp from the corner of the room and set it next to Anne. "Don't move, Anne. I'm putting a spotlight on you. Did you ever," he asked, turning toward Charlie, "see a better forty-one-year-old figure than the one you're gazing at now?"

Charlie had never really looked at it before. Anne's stocky figure was excellent. Flushed and drunken, she looked almost wanton.

"I loved her for her body fifteen years ago," Clyde giggled, "and I still love her body today. Feel this body," he insisted to Charlie. "Feel how hard it is. Nothing sagging about Anne. Hard, firm, and strong. One hundred and twenty pounds of vibrant flesh. Feel her, Charlie."

"Where?" Charlie asked. Anne looked ready to be felt.

Lucy shot across the room and grabbed his arm. "*We* are going upstairs," she shouted. "You two can do as you wish." She propelled Charlie out of the room and pulled him up the stairs. When they reached the hall landing the lights went off in the living room, and the back of the couch hit the wall. A moment later Anne giggled.

"I hope you're satisfied," Lucy hissed, as outraged as Charlie had ever seen her.

"I am," he answered. "Completely."

Two and a half months later, around the middle of March, in the course of two days, Lucy and Charlie received two long-distance telephone calls. The first was from Philadelphia, for Lucy.

"You don't mean it, Anne," Charlie heard her shout. "That's simply marvelous news!"

"What's marvelous news?" Charlie asked, walking out into the hall.

"Hush," Lucy hissed at him, waving her hand for silence. "Go easy, Anne. Make Clyde wait on you hand and foot."

"What's the news?" Charlie asked again, moving closer.

"Will you please be quiet," Lucy ordered. "No, I was just talking to Charlie, Anne. Don't forget to sign up a good doctor, and use him. They charge enough. And you've got to stop working so hard. Being pregnant takes a lot out of you."

"Oh, no," Charlie roared, reaching toward the heavens. "Good old alcohol."

"Shut up," Lucy snapped in exasperation. "Not you, Anne. Charlie was just being male." She held the receiver toward Charlie. "Clyde wants a word with you. And don't be crude. Please, Charlie."

"Bingo, Reverend," Charlie shouted. "We knew you had it in you."

"Is that all you can think of to say?" Lucy hissed. "Tell him how thrilled we are."

Charlie waved her to silence, listening. "Certainly I meant it, Clyde. I'll call the head of the committee tonight."

"What committee?" Lucy asked, lingering.

"Absolutely," Charlie said to Clyde. "I think they'll consider themselves lucky to get you, and you and Anne will like Hadley. It's a nice little town."

"What are you talking about?" Lucy asked, reaching for the phone.

He twisted away from her. "Not at all," he said to Clyde. "And I think you're making the right decision. A good man will do a lot with the Hadley Church. And don't worry. They'll want you. I can just about promise it."

Lucy snatched the phone from him, and Charlie walked back into the living room, grinning with delight. When Lucy joined him a moment later, she put her arms around his waist and hugged him.

"I prayed, Charlie. I prayed they would have a baby."

"I just kept my fingers crossed," he answered.

"Is Clyde coming to the Hadley Church?"

"I think they'll appoint him if I suggest it. Most of the trustees work for The Hadley Company."

Lucy released him and sat on the arm of the couch, her face radiant with happiness.

"You can say what you want, Charlie, but things do come out all right. Things do have a happy ending. I mean you always think things with happy endings are just trash, as though they couldn't happen. Well, it did happen," she said, looking at him defiantly. "It did."

The second call, the following night, came from Polly in New York. It was for Charlie.

"Hi, Pol," he said, seating himself at the hall table.

"Prepare yourself for a shock," she said.

246

He had been prepared for a shock since Christmas, since his discussion with Nate Taylor.

"I'm ready," he answered.

"I'm going to be on 'Robert Montgomery Presents.'"

"Well, well," he answered, relieved. "Is that all?"

"Well, how many times have you been on television?" she asked angrily.

"Never, and I think it's great. I just expected some more personal news."

She hesitated a moment. "No. That's the only news I have at the present time. I hoped you'd be pleased."

"You know I am, Polly. I'll organize a family party. When is it?"

"A week from tonight on NBC."

"What was that all about?" Lucy asked, when Charlie had returned to the living room.

"Polly's going to be on 'Robert Montgomery Presents,' a week from to-night."

Lucy sniffed. "It's about time."

"Such sisterly loyalty is touching. Anyway, let's ask your mother and father over to watch her."

"Oh, by all means," she answered airily. "A star is born. Let's ask the whole world."

At quarter to nine on the evening of Polly's debut, Mr. Chalmers arrived at Highcliffe Road in a state of high anticipation. Not only was it to be the first time he had ever seen a daughter of his in anything besides a school play, it also was the first time he'd ever been able to watch television without feeling guilty about it, as though he were committing a mortal sin. Mrs. Chalmers, however, came into the house with an expression of lofty disdain, as though she were being forced to attend a midnight showing of the *Folies Bergères*. For her, television was the culmination of all that was bad in the modern world.

"Mother," Lucy had blurted out a year before, at least three years after every other housetop on Highcliffe Road had sprouted an aerial, "we bought a television set."

"I see," Mrs. Chalmers had answered, her expression one of determined tolerance, as though Lucy were again sixteen and had just confessed she were no longer a virgin. "Doubtless you felt you just had to succumb."

"It was a matter of keeping our children or losing them to the Robinsons," Charlie answered, annoyed that he had to apologize.

"Nonsense, Charles. If you'd merely place a few good books in front of your children, they'd feel no need for television." She turned to her husband. "Don't you agree, Lowell?"

"Don't rope me in on this, Lydia," he protested. For years he had always eaten a box lunch during his noon hour at the Hadley Library. Lately, however, he had been eating a leisurely afternoon meal at the Hadley Diner, where he could watch Mary Margaret McBride.

"All right. I won't say another word about it. I have no desire to interfere in the lives of others. But it distresses me to know that my grandchildren will grow up as illiterates with bloodshot eyes."

Had radio passed through a similar stage in its infancy? Charlie wondered. Had those who spent the early '20s with batteries dripping acid in their cellars and earphones pressed to their ears felt the need to apologize? No one dared admit that they bought a television set because they wanted to. It was the children who wanted it, or there was one program on Sunday afternoon called "Omnibus" that was worth watching, or perhaps Maurice Evans in Shakespeare.

It was all a lie, and it fooled no one, everyone having spoken the same lies when they first bought their set. The moment television arrived at the house, Charlie had indulged himself in an orgy of watching. From Roy Rogers to Jane Wyman and back to Gene Autry again. The fights, the wrestlers, the one-armed detectives with English accents, Crunch and Des, and even, loathing himself as he watched it, "The Lux Video Theatre." They had rationed the children to an hour a day, but had gorged themselves until suddenly they had sickened of it all, and television had taken its place along with the rest of the electronic gadgets in the house—the dishwasher, the mangle, and the washing machine—a servant and not a master. As awful as it was, however, as fashionable as it was not to give in, like alcoholism and the *Reader's Digest*, television seemed destined to last.

"I would like to make it perfectly clear," Mrs. Chalmers announced as she came into the living room, "that if it weren't that my own daughter were appearing——"

"Relax, Lydia," Mr. Chalmers interrupted, waving her to silence. "What's on now, Charlie? I mean, can we see something good before Robert Montgomery?"

"We might warm up the set at that," Charlie answered, winking.

"You'll do nothing of the kind, Lowell. We'll all sit right here and have a little intelligent conversation. You've said often enough yourself that conversation is a lost art."

"Bah," he said scornfully. "It always was a lost art." He turned to Charlie. "How about 'Gunsmoke'? We couldn't get that now, could we? Joe Pritchard's been raving about it."

"Not tonight, Mr. Chalmers. But let's go see what's on." He winked again at his father-in-law. "Perhaps we can tune in the United Nations."

"Did you hear that, Lydia? Charlie says the United Nations might be on."

"I prefer to visit the United Nations in person, thank you," she answered coldly, seating herself next to Lucy and plunging immediately into the topic of Anne and her forthcoming baby.

They had placed the television set in the room originally known as the library because there was a small bookcase in it. Gradually the room had become known as "the room where the television set is," and finally just "the television room." Eventually, to make room for more chairs, the bookcase had been moved to the upstairs hall.

"Mrs. Chalmers is hopeless about this," Mr. Chalmers muttered, watching avidly as Charlie adjusted the set.

"Lucy and I were toying with the thought of giving you a set for your birthday."

"Oh, my Lord, don't do that. Mrs. Chalmers would smash it with an ax."

"Why don't you give Elsa and Joseph a set? Mrs. Chalmers would then be faced with keeping the set or losing her help. Furthermore, she'd probably be sneaking out to Elsa's room on Sunday afternoon herself, to watch Alistair Cooke."

"But you see, Charlie, it's the aerial Mrs. Chalmers objects to."

"We just have these rabbit ears. She couldn't object to that."

"Lydia," Mr. Chalmers shouted back into the living room, "you don't have to have those hideous aerials on your roof. You can have these little rabbit ears. Come look. They're quite presentable."

"I've seen rabbit ears, and if anything I think they're worse," she replied.

"She's hopeless," he repeated.

"They're going to televise the National Open this summer, Mr. Chalmers."

Mr. Chalmers sighed mournfully. Then he leaned forward and whispered, "Did you ever see this Dagmar?" He grinned foolishly, and brought his hand up along his chest. "Was she as something as they say?"

Charlie shook his head. "Her star had set before we had our set." Then he yelled into the living room, "We'd better all gather. The program is changing."

Mrs. Chalmers walked stiffly into the room and sat on a straight wooden chair.

"I trust someone will tell me when it's time to watch."

Lucy giggled, and Mr. Chalmers said, "Relax, Lydia, when it's time——"

"Dear me," Mrs. Chalmers interrupted, "what is Mr. Montgomery doing on television?"

"Earning a living," Charlie answered.

"As what, pray?"

"They call him a host. He sets the scene and generally runs things."

"Mr. Montgomery runs *television?*" she asked incredulously.

"Just this program, Mother Chalmers."

Mrs. Chalmers looked coy. "I met Mr. Montgomery once."

"You did, Lydia? And where was I?"

"At home, dear one. I sat next to him on a train to New York," she smiled fondly. "He offered me his copy of the New York *Times*. He was most charming." She pointed distastefully toward the screen. "That's why I find it rather surprising to find him there."

"I suggest we all stay quiet," Mr. Chalmers insisted. "The play is beginning, and we don't want to miss Polly."

"We certainly don't," Lucy agreed. "Not after all this."

The play was a light, witty comedy, handled with all the usual Montgomery polish and skill. The action, what there was of it, took place for the most part in a telephone booth.

249

"Well," Mrs. Chalmers exploded at the end of the first act, "Polly must have had a rather insignificant part, or did I miss her?"

"Two more acts to go," Charlie answered. "Can I get everyone something to drink?"

"Beer?" Mrs. Chalmers asked sweetly. "Isn't that what people usually drink when they watch television?"

"A beer would taste quite good," Mr. Chalmers agreed.

"You can get me one too," Lucy said.

"Mother Chalmers?"

"Nothing, thank you, Charles."

Charlie was nearly to the kitchen when he heard Lucy's shout.

"The commercial! The commercial!" she yelled. "There's Polly in the commercial."

Charlie made it back to the room just in time to see Polly's long, graceful leg being shaved by an electric razor. It was Polly all right. There was no question about it. She was wearing a dressing gown, and she looked as though she had just emerged from a bath, hot, flushed, and steamy.

"Dear Lord," Mrs. Chalmers crooned, as Polly faded into an announcer holding the razor in his hand. "Dear, dear Lord."

"She was quite good," Mr. Chalmers said loyally, obviously shaken.

Lucy propelled herself across the room and turned off the set.

"Big deal," she said triumphantly. "The commercial."

"Wouldn't you think Polly would have had more pride than to do a thing like that?" Mrs. Chalmers said. "I'm thoroughly ashamed of her."

"Now Lydia," Mr. Chalmers said, his voice lacking conviction, "even Sarah Bernhardt had to get her start somewhere."

"I know very little about Sarah Bernhardt, Lowell, but I feel quite certain she never shaved her legs in public."

"Times have changed, Lydia."

"They certainly have. And for the worse."

"Shall I get the beer now?" Charlie asked. "Or is everyone going home?"

No one answered, because at that moment the phone rang.

"I'll get it," Lucy said, starting for the hall. "Hi, Pol," she shouted a moment later. "You were terrific. We're all just sitting here absolutely agog." She paused. "Well, maybe a little, but she'll get over it. Wait a minute. Ask her yourself. Mother, it's Polly," Lucy shouted.

"That was a most interesting performance you gave, darling," Mrs. Chalmers said stiffly. "I hope you were well paid for it. Will you," she paused, searching for the proper verb, "will you be shaving your legs like this every week?" She paused. "I see. Well, I must say I'm not sorry." Mrs. Chalmers was then quiet for nearly thirty seconds. Finally she gasped, "Polly. You're not serious." For a moment she seemed about to faint, her face pale, her hand gripping the receiver, her knuckles white. Then without another word she cut off the connection.

"Lydia," Mr. Chalmers shouted, "you've hung up, and I wanted to talk to her."

"Polly," Mrs. Chalmers whispered, staring at her husband but not seeing him, "is married."

The room was quiet for a moment. Then Lucy shrieked, "Not to that awful Nate Taylor?"

"Yes, Lucy, to that awful Nate Taylor."

"Well, now," Mr. Chalmers said.

Again the room was quiet.

"What a night," Lucy said, her expression gleeful. "Polly makes her debut shaving her legs, and she's married to a——"

Mr. Chalmers whirled on her fiercely. "Stop that," he ordered. "What's done is done, Lucy. I want no more discussion about it. Is that clear?"

"Whatever you say, Poppy," she answered blithely.

"Charlie," Mr. Chalmers continued, "go get us all a drink. The least we can do is to raise a glass to Mr. and Mrs. Nathaniel Taylor."

At his words Mrs. Chalmers wilted, as though the truth had finally been driven home. She took her husband's arm and walked dejectedly into the living room.

"Why did she do it?" she said quietly, although not quietly enough. "Why couldn't just one of our daughters have married someone we liked?"

For whatever reason Polly had done it, Charlie thought as he walked into the kitchen, she had chosen the right way. At best, a formal wedding would have been a mockery, the parents of the bride and groom united only by their mutual downcast hearts. Friends would have come out of curiosity and not to celebrate the event. A formal wedding would have opened wounds with both families that would never have healed.

"What shall I open?" Charlie muttered to Lucy when she joined him in the kitchen. "Champagne?"

"Heavens, no," she answered cheerfully. "Beer. It seems far more appropriate."

thirty-four

LATE THAT SUMMER MRS. FLECK STEPPED INTO LOWELL CHALMERS' OFFICE and announced that there was someone in the outer office who wished to see him.

"Not a salesman, I hope, Mrs. Fleck. If it is, tell him Mr. Webb will be back from Detroit at the end of the week."

She shook her head. "It's your daughter, Mrs. Harbert."

"Come in, Anne," he shouted, striding toward his office door. "I was afraid you were a salesman."

"No, it's just me," Anne answered, stepping past Mrs. Fleck and maneuvering herself toward a chair. "I hope I'm not disturbing you."

"Not at all. Not at all. I was just putting a little polish on my desk. There's a great deal of dampness out here in Hadley. I suppose it's the river."

His daughter Anne had reached that final stage of pregnancy which Lowell preferred, if possible, to avoid. Advanced pregnancy made him jumpy. He must either stare or avert his eyes completely. God, he decided, had played a rather ugly trick on the female of the human race.

"I gather you don't like salesmen?" Anne said, shifting herself uncomfortably in her chair.

"It isn't a question of my not liking them, Anne. I just feel sorry for them, and that's no way to be with salesmen. I let Charlie take care of them when he's here. Charlie has an interesting theory about salesmen," he continued, beginning to wonder why Anne had come. "He's been building up a sales staff lately, and he likes to get boys who were interested in dramatics."

"Actors make good salesmen?"

"Charlie thinks so. He says that to make a sale is nothing more than getting a favorable reaction from an audience. That's my trouble, you see. I'm an actor's best friend. I laugh when I'm supposed to laugh, and I cry when I'm supposed to cry. Unfortunately, I also buy when I'm supposed to buy. 'No' has never been a word that's come easy to me."

Again Anne shifted her position, and a pocketbook she had been carrying fell off what was left of her lap onto the floor.

"Incidentally, what's Clyde done to himself lately?" Lowell Chalmers asked. "He looks different."

Anne smiled wanly.

"He met with the board of trustees. They suggested he cut his hair shorter because they felt it made him look like a Communist, and they ordered him to get rid of his round collar because people might think he was a Catholic."

"Capital," Mr. Chalmers roared, pounding his desk with his fist. "And now he looks like the good Congregationalist that he is."

"We hope to be good Congregationalists," Anne answered, looking at her father intently.

He had never felt at ease with Anne since the day she had been ordained as a minister. It had placed her in the ranks of the pious, and he felt no more kinship with the pious than he did with the poor.

"Well, now," he said briskly, "what brings you to my office? Things continue to go well here in Hadley, I hope."

"Extremely well, Father. Clyde and I love it here."

"I'm happy to hear it. We have a pleasant little village here. How do you like the old parsonage?"

"After Philadelphia, it's heaven."

"Good. Excellent." He paused, waiting. "Well now, what can I do for you?"

"I've come to apologize to you, Father."

He stared at her in amazement; then he said, "Apologize to me, Anne? What on earth for?"

"For the way I've acted for the past fifteen years."

"Nonsense," he sputtered, "you've never done anything which calls for an apology. What foolishness is this, Anne?"

"When I think of how patient you have been with me all these years, I am so ashamed of myself."

"Anne, Anne, Anne," Mr. Chalmers answered, shaking his head. "Let's have no more of this. What do you think families are for? We all knew that you had certain personal problems that you felt you must solve in your own way before you were ready to take your place in the world. Perhaps a few times all of us were a little sharp with each other. But that's over and done with now. You're back here in Hadley. Clyde has his own church at last. Before you know it you'll have a child of your own, and then you'll discover how wonderful life can be."

"I just had to clear the air," she said. "All the blame for the mess Clyde and I made of the last fifteen years should be placed on my shoulders. Clyde has wanted his own church for a long, long time, and I held him back. Clyde wanted me to tell you that he thinks you and Mother are two of the finest Christians he has ever known. That's from his heart, Father, and from mine."

Tears welled into Lowell Chalmers' eyes, and he turned his head away quickly.

"Let's leave it at that, shall we, Anne? Your mother and I wish you and Clyde well. We want to do everything in our power to keep you near us and to make your life a good one. You're our child, and very soon now you'll realize what it is to love a child."

That, he hoped, would end the matter. To feel love for your family was right and proper, but to be forced to profess it was intensely embarrassing. Yet Anne continued to sit in her chair, her eyes never leaving his for an instant. He was beginning to feel trapped.

"I'd like to ask a favor of you right now, Father."

"Well, ask away," he answered. "Anything at all. That's what a father is for."

"How long have you and Mother been members of the Lawn Street Church?"

He thought a moment. "Well, of course, your mother has been a member there all her life, and I've been a member since we were married. Why?"

"Do you consider your membership there a tradition that shouldn't be changed?"

"Well, I'd hardly say that. The Lawn Street Church is convenient, and that's important these days when so many other things occupy your time. Then I admire old Doctor Eaton, although I must say he should have retired years ago. That reminds me of something," he said, interrupting himself. "And you discuss this with Clyde. A reluctance to retire is a common failing among all men, but it seems particularly prevalent among ministers. When our Doctor Eaton was sixty-five or so, he called a meeting of the trustees and announced his retirement. We wouldn't hear of it. We insisted he stay. We saw no reason why a man in the prime of life should put himself out to pasture." Mr. Chalmers smiled wistfully. "That was over fifteen years ago. Doctor Eaton is now eighty-two years old. A year ago the board of trustees called a meeting. We made it quite clear to Doctor Eaton that if he offered his resignation again, this time we'd accept it. However, now it was his turn to refuse." He paused, waiting for the moral of his story to register. "You tell that some time to Clyde," he finished.

"I shall," she answered vaguely. "Then I gather you and Mother feel no strong attachment to the Lawn Street Church?"

"Well," he answered, "no one can be a member of a church for over forty years without developing a feeling of loyalty."

"But don't you also feel loyal to the town of Hadley?"

"Ah," Mr. Chalmers said, "at last I begin to see what all this is leading up to."

She nodded. "Clyde and I would feel honored if you and Mother would join the Hadley Church."

"What can I say?" he asked, suddenly panic-stricken.

"We hope you'll say yes."

"Of course it's a rather long trip out here. Thirty-six miles if one includes the drive back, and one must."

Anne was ready for him.

"I want you and Mother to join me at the parsonage each Sunday for dinner. The time has come when I should take over a few of the family responsibilities."

"Have dinner at the parsonage each week," Mr. Chalmers gasped, unable to mask his horror.

"I think it's what I really need, Father. The feeling of being an essential part of a family."

"Well then, by all means, you and Clyde must eat Sunday dinner with us."

She was also ready for that.

"We can't, of course, because Sunday is Clyde's day of labor. We have to be out here on Sunday. Won't you and Mother join me both for worship and later for dinner? Mother must relax a bit. She must hand over some of her family chores to me."

"Chores?" Mr. Chalmers echoed. "By Jove, you don't know your mother very well, Anne. She would no more relinquish her role at the Sunday dinner table than she would relinquish life itself."

"But isn't this just like your Doctor Eaton," Anne interrupted. "Couldn't you hint to Mother that——"

"If I even suggested such a thing," Mr. Chalmers interrupted, "if I so much as hinted at it, your mother would be deeply hurt." He raised his eyebrows as a sudden thought struck him. "And by George, for the first time I know how poor old Doctor Eaton must feel. Just because a person is getting on in years doesn't mean they like to be pushed aside." When Anne's expression registered disappointment, he added quickly, "But that doesn't mean we won't consider joining your church."

"Would you, Father?" she asked eagerly. "Clyde and I will be so pleased."

He hadn't felt as trapped since the day he'd sat next to a Christian Scientist on a train. He stared for a moment at the ceiling. "Of course," he said, "your mother will have to make the final decision about this." He paused, thinking, stalling for time. He had talked himself into a hole. He knew that if he joined Clyde's church, he'd have to attend services. For the rest of his life he could then look forward only to a bleak succession of ruined Sundays. He had nothing specific against church, but he demanded the right to feel relaxed about it. That was the basis, the keystone, of his Protestant faith—that only Truth, or God if you must, was worthy of his awe, whereas a church was merely an organized opinion. For years he had neglected Doctor Eaton's services with complete peace of mind, but with Clyde as his pastor, embarrassing complications would inevitably arise.

"Anne," he said, a fresh note of determination in his voice, "because you've been open with me, I'll return the favor. Sunday has always been a sacred day for me."

"That's as it should be, Father."

"You misunderstand me," he went on hastily. "You see, I write things. Foolish things, I admit, but it's a hobby which over the years has meant a lot to me. For instance, right now I'm working on a project—well, never mind about my project. It wouldn't interest you anyway. But I do my best work on Sunday. It's the one day of the week which belongs to me, and to me alone. If I had to drive out to Hadley to attend church in the morning, and then back again at noon, then Sunday dinner, good Lord, by the time I was able to sit at my desk, the day would be shot. I'd have no time left to myself at all. Surely you can understand this."

Anne looked sunk.

"But I have another suggestion," he continued. "Do you know what it is to be on a board of directors?"

"Not really," she answered.

"Well, often organizations need advice and counsel from men in other fields of endeavor. For instance, here at The Hadley Company we have a broker, a banker, and two lawyers on our board, along with certain members of the family who hold large blocks of stock, such as your mother. The point I'm making is," he continued, "why don't you have Clyde put me on the board of directors of your church? Make me an unofficial trustee."

"Clyde and I are ambitious for our church, Father." Her voice was fraught with determination.

"And you should be."

"We need certain improvements in the church building itself. Obvious things like paint, and a new roof, and a new organ. I've been planning to organize a Sunday school. That's something which has been sadly neglected out here. I'm hoping Clyde will be able to double his budget next year, and keep doubling it until we have a church the town can be proud of. I see this as a challenge, a——"

"Fine. Wonderful," Mr. Chalmers interrupted. "I'm behind you on this one hundred per cent. And I know this will take money. Lots of it. And I also know this money must come from somewhere. God has a clever way of leaving the practical end of religion up to the parishioners. Am I not right?" He smiled ruefully.

"It will take money," she agreed. "And Clyde and I plan to work day and night to raise it."

"You can count on me, Anne. As of this moment, consider me one of the directors of your church. When you have a few objectives clearly in mind, call on me again. You'll find out how generous I can be."

When his daughter had gone, Lowell Chalmers rested his forehead wearily on his desk blotter. How much would this cost him, he wondered? A thousand? Five? Ten? He shuddered. How much poorer in pocket would he be by the time Anne and Clyde had rebuilt the Hadley Church? It had cost him nearly twenty thousand to put the Hadley Library back into shape. But then he loved books and believed in them. He pressed the buzzer for Mrs. Fleck.

"Please don't send me any more salesmen," he said, when her head appeared in the doorway.

"But Mr. Chalmers," she protested, "surely your own——"

"I was merely making a joke, Mrs. Fleck. How is my son-in-law Mr. Harbert doing? Does the congregation like him?"

"I've heard nothing but praise," she answered.

"Good. I'm glad to hear it." He looked at her mournfully for a moment. "Did it ever occur to you," he said, "that banks and churches are very much alike?"

"Banks and churches," she echoed blankly.

"Banks and churches," he repeated. "Call the people worshippers, or call them depositors, the need for their money is equal, and the competition for it just as keen."

"Yes, sir," she answered. "That's very interesting, Mr. Chalmers."

"I didn't mean it to be interesting. I was merely commenting on the human scene. No matter," he added, when it was obvious the poor woman was confused. "Just remember when you see a new coat of paint on the Hadley Church to give praise to the Lord, and give thanks to me."

"Yes, sir," she answered, backing out of the office. She had been Mr. Chalmers' secretary for twenty years, and there were still times he could baffle her.

At Thanksgiving that year, between the main course and dessert, when she rose to recite what over the years had become known as "Mother's Thanksgiving poem," Mrs. Chalmers found herself facing nine members of her family, including, besides herself, her husband Lowell, Lucy, Charlie, Lydia, Roswell, Ruth, Clyde and Anne, and Aunt Roswell. Not at the table, but very much part of the family gathering, was Anne's new baby boy, born on the seventeenth of September.

Mrs. Chalmers' poem was a Chalmers tradition, a painful and embarrassing interlude in an otherwise pleasant meal. Each year she would choose what she considered to be the outstanding family event of the year and render it into doggerel. In 1943, for instance, the year Mr. Chalmers had published his long essay on George Borrow, Mrs. Chalmers had recited,

> "Soon after we were married
> To me my husband said
> That t'was much to his sorrow
> That George Borrow was dead."

It continued for three more stanzas, to be followed by polite family applause, and then vanilla ice cream.

She declaimed in a singsong voice, punctuated by giggles and mischievous glances at whoever was responsible for the event of the year. All in the family except Mrs. Chalmers hated it.

"Hail to thee, little Ros," she sang when Lucy's second baby was born. "Bundle of pink and blue, bright star of the future, God's promise of something new."

Against all his critical judgment, and only to remain on good terms with his wife, over the years Lowell Chalmers had added Lydia's poems to his family diary. Had he dared, he would have incinerated them with the rest of the household trash. Cute poetry appealed to him no more than did white wagon wheels at the end of a driveway. However, if Christmas belonged to Jesus and the children, Thanksgiving belonged to Lydia, and her poem was as inescapable as the turkey and the cranberry sauce.

"Are we all ready?" Mrs. Chalmers asked now as she rose and fixed her eyes on the cradle by the dining room window.

"As ready as we'll ever be, my dear," Mr. Chalmers sighed.

"Ready for what?" Aunt Roswell asked, holding her hearing aid toward Charlie, who sat next to her. She asked this same question each year, either to be stubborn, or perhaps to delay the inevitable for a moment longer.

"Mother Chalmers' poem," Charlie answered.

Aunt Roswell nodded, her ancient eyes glazing. Then, with no attempt to be subtle, she turned off her hearing aid.

Midway through her turkey, Ruthie had slipped from her chair, and was crawling about under the table pretending she was a tiger, growling and untying shoelaces. This also was a part of Thanksgiving at the Chalmers', a tiger under the table—first Lydia, then Roswell, and finally Ruthie, her older sisters finally having mastered the adult art of being bored and yet well behaved. Lucy could be strict with her children when she felt it necessary, but in years past the family had always thought it fun to have a small tiger under the table, as entertainment in a long session of overeating. Not so Anne, however.

"Can't you please control her?" she asked Lucy, as Mrs. Chalmers adjusted her glasses.

"Control who?" Lucy asked blankly. She had reached the stage of motherhood where a child of hers could be setting off dynamite and she wouldn't be aware of it.

"Ruthie," Anne announced. "She's being terribly rude to Mother."

"Oh, poof, Anne. She's not hurting anyone." Lucy didn't like criticism of her children from anyone, and particularly not from a sister who until two months before had been childless.

"This year," Mrs. Chalmers began, "two terribly important milestones have taken place."

"A milestone doesn't take place, my dear. Milestones are passed."

"No more interruptions, if you please," Mrs. Chalmers answered cheerfully, waving her husband to silence. "First, there was our Polly's wedding last spring." She hesitated, building the suspense. "But, as exciting as Polly's marriage was, something far more exciting happened in September." She gazed fondly at the cradle.

It was at this moment that Clyde leaped to his feet with a cry of anguish.

"The child bit me," he exclaimed. "Right on my leg."

"That does it," Anne answered, diving under the table and dragging forth Ruthie by one arm. She sat her niece roughly in her chair. "Now sit there and behave yourself," she ordered. "Perhaps your mother is incapable of disciplining you, but I'm not."

"If you please," Lucy shouted, putting her arm around Ruthie's shoulders. "Ruthie isn't a biter, and she never has been. Did you bite your Uncle Clyde, Ruthie?"

Ruthie shook her head and burst into tears.

"I didn't think so. As usual, Clyde and Anne are just being neurotic."

This was more than Anne would take. "Your daughter may not be a biter," she said angrily, "but neither is my husband a liar. Did this child bite you, Clyde, or did she not?"

"Stop it!" Mr. Chalmers shouted. Family dinners were always a disappointment to him. When he and Mrs. Chalmers ate alone, he was apt to be sad that the whole family wasn't present, but when everyone did gather at the table, he then longed to be eating alone. "You, Anne, be quiet, and you, Lucy, you be quiet also. And you, Clyde, please sit down." He waited, his jaw set. "Now, Lydia. Your poem. The ice cream is melting in the pantry."

"Uncle Clyde has hair on his legs," Ruthie interrupted, triumphantly holding aloft a pinchful of dark hair.

Lucy snickered and emptied Ruthie's fingers out onto the dining room floor.

"Your children are just animals," Anne said, staring at her sister in cold disapproval. "Just undisciplined little beasts."

"Silence," Mr. Chalmers roared, pounding the table with his palm. "Lydia, if you please, your poem."

Again Mrs. Chalmers adjusted her glasses and looked toward the cradle. "O Muse," she giggled, "here is my poem. May it find favor in your heart.

"In his cradle, fast asleep
Lies our infant boy
With open arms, we welcome gladly
To our family, Little Hadley."

"Dear, dear Lord," Mr. Chalmers sighed, tilting his head toward the ceiling, his eyes closed.

Lucy winced openly and wrinkled her face. There woud be three more stanzas to go.

"You're all being terribly rude," Anne interrupted. "Let poor Mother go on."

As she listened to the remainder of the poem, Lucy's expression settled into one of bitter resentment. Her bitterness had been building inside her since the day Anne had arrived home from Philadelphia, and particularly since the seventeenth of September, when her sister's son had been born. Clyde had phoned the good news from the hospital at forty-five minutes after midnight.

"Hadley Chalmers Harbert the First," he shouted, naïvely believing that Lucy would share in his exultation. "Eight pounds, eleven ounces, and all solid man."

"How wonderful," Lucy answered dully. She had stumbled out of bed after having been asleep for two hours, and she was sitting at the hall telephone, shivering and drugged with fatigue.

"Well?" Charlie asked, when she returned to bed.

"Boy."

"Happy day. What are they going to call it?"

"Hadley Chalmers. And you should have heard Clyde," she sneered. "Anne was so brave, he said. So brave," she repeated. "Honestly, what's so brave about having a baby? I've had three of them, and I didn't consider myself brave. I hope you didn't go about telling people how brave I was."

"Hadley Chalmers?" Charlie mused. "That's rather clever of them at that."

"Yes, isn't it. And I'll bet Mother gives them the Hadley cradle."

"Let them have the cradle," he answered. "We'll take the stock."

"But it isn't fair," she protested. "The family antiques mean a lot to me, Charlie, and Mother's never given me a single one of them. Not one. Just because we had girls."

"I repeat," Charlie had answered, anxious to go back to sleep, "if it comes to a choice, we'll take the Hadley stock."

But Lucy would not be comforted. From the instant she had arrived home, her sister had been treated like a returning prodigal. Two truckloads of furniture had left the Lawn Street house and were now in the Hadley parsonage. Clyde's salary was so small, her mother explained, and the parsonage was so huge, and poor Anne did so desperately need things.

It wasn't a question of need, Lucy insisted, although only to herself and to Charlie. She didn't dare face her mother with the accusation. These were family pieces which were being given away so casually, furniture which by all right and by all law should change hands only by inheritance. By these gifts her mother seemed to announce that one day she expected Anne to be the head of the family, Anne who would still be rotting in the slums of Philadelphia, childless and an utter failure, had it not been for Charlie.

Then there was the Hadley Church. Her mother and father were supporting it, body, checkbook, and soul. There were a new coat of paint and a new bell, plans were being made to restore the steeple, there was talk about an electric organ, and there was joking about renaming it the Chalmers Memorial Chapel.

When young Hadley had arrived, the gifts had increased to a flood. First, as Lucy had predicted, had gone the cradle, the Hadley cradle, the prize family antique, the only remaining possession of John Hadley, who had arrived from the Bay Colony in 1634. It was just an oaken box fitted with crude rockers, and an antique dealer would have ignored it. But to the family it had always been the Holy Grail. As one by one Lydia, Roswell, and finally Ruth had arrived, the Hadley cradle remained where it was, in the Lawn Street attic. But when Hadley was born, the cradle was waiting for him at the parsonage when he and Anne returned from the hospital. Had her mother placed a hand on young Hadley's brow and announced, "I name you my sole heir," Lucy could have felt no worse.

The rest of the gifts had merely twisted the knife. The Hadley silver cup went out to the parsonage, as did the Hadley spoons; Great-Grandfather's gold watch; Great-Grandmother's sampler of Ruth gathering the wheat, which Lucy had been sure her Ruthie would get; the Hadley chest, a carved oak blanket chest which had been rescued from New York, where it had been sold by Ledyard Pittman when he needed funds; the Hadley mirror; the Hadley mantel clock; and the Hadley footstool. In young Hadley's name Anne was collecting everything, just because her child had been a boy.

It was not only material things that were at stake here, Lucy thought. It was a matter of principle. Who had been her mother's faithful servant and companion, who had put up with her domineering ways during the last ten years? Not Anne. Who had been on hand to help open up the houses at the Island? Who had attended the rites of Sunday dinner year after year? Who had catered to her mother's every whim? Who had stayed at home and had always been available? Not Anne. Anne had been just a problem, a source of worry and despair. By what right did she now step on the stage at the final curtain and receive all the praise?

If her sister thought she could take over this way, Lucy said to herself as she listened to the end of her mother's poem, if her sister thought the family mantle would pass to her by default, perhaps the time had come to warn her otherwise. If Anne expected to take over as head of the family, she would have to fight.

By this time Mrs. Chalmers had finished her poem.

"Is that all, my dear?" Lowell Chalmers asked hopefully, his hands poised, ready to clap.

"Hurrah," Roswell shouted. She had noticed Elsa loitering in the pantry doorway with the ice cream.

"Hush, child," Anne snapped. "That was lovely, Mother. May I have it for my scrapbook?"

"Well darling," Mrs. Chalmers answered, turning toward her husband, "in the past your father has always wanted my poems."

"That's perfectly all right," Lowell Chalmers said hastily. "If Anne wants it, she's more than welcome to it."

Lucy now rose to her feet. "I have a poem too," she announced.

"Oh, good Lord," Anne said in weary surprise. "This is Mother's house, Lucy. Not yours."

Lucy began, smiling at her sister sweetly:

> "Hadley is a clever name,
>   As are Fred, Joe, and Perry,
>   But Anne, to be really fair
>   Shouldn't you call him Sherry?"

"What's that?" Aunt Roswell interrupted. She had tuned in again. "Sherry? We've never had a Sherry in this family."

"Anne and Clyde are both very fond of sherry," Lucy answered looking more cheerful than she had in months.

"Elsa, if you please, the ice cream," Lowell Chalmers said, beckoning toward the pantry door.

thirty-five

THE TOWN, LUCY THOUGHT AS SHE WANDERED DOWN THE STREET TOWARD THE Yacht Club pier, was like a desert after a summer rainfall, bursting with life and color. A sun-tanned horde of people were surging through the streets, going nowhere, having come from nowhere, on bicycles, in cars—blond hair, dogs, children, all healthy, and all glad to be alive on an August day. There were the people off the boats, seared dark brown, in their shorts and tee shirts. There were the three-day excursion tourists from the mainland, clutching their wallets, regretting their budgets, gazing longingly in the window of the Country Store at the cashmere they couldn't afford. There were the summer residents like herself, with eyes that had seen it all before, sedate, superior, awed only by the natives, those runout salt-water Yankees, ruthless and greedy, with a year's income to be gathered in two frantic summer months.

It was blistering hot, heat shimmering off the street, the sun reflecting from the white clapboard walls. The air smelled sweet with honeysuckle, fresh paint, and sun-tan lotion. Lucy walked slowly, hoping to spot someone she recognized. Everyone looked young, years younger than she suddenly was. It was the Appian Way, she thought. The crowd in the street was always young. Only she grew older.

As she passed the liquor store Johnnie Marshall burst through the swinging door, his arms laden with bottles.

"Hi, old girl," he said in greeting. Johnnie called everyone "old girl" or "old boy," particularly when he was vague about a name.

Johnnie should have been killed in the war, Lucy thought cruelly as she looked at him. Eighteen summers before he had been fiercely handsome, tall, muscular, and dark, with a magnificent barrel chest, always bare from June to September, except for a mat of black hair. But now, eighteen summers later, he showed every one of his thirty-eight years. Under his August tan he was reddish blue, and his eyeballs were mottled with blood, watering in the bright light. To be stylishly out of style, he wore only a pair of army suntans cut off above his knees with pinking shears. His body was ruined. His muscles were flabby and soft, laden with fat, and his hand was unsteady. Now, without a shirt, he merely looked naked, and had he been a woman he would have been arrested for indecent exposure.

"Hi, Johnnie," Lucy answered, lingering for lack of anything else to do.

"Listen, old girl," he said, herding her against the store window, poking her in the shoulder with a bottle of gin. "We're having a little gathering at our place tonight. Bring your husband and join us."

"Can't," she answered, making a face, "he's working."

"During Race Week? You must have married a positive drudge." He leaned toward her, nuzzling an ear. He smelled strongly of deodorant and breath. "Then come alone," he murmured in a Charles Boyer accent.

Lucy slid away from him. Eighteen years before, she had been mad about Johnnie Marshall. One entire month she had spent lurking about the harbor, hoping and praying that he would ask her to help him scrape barnacles from his catboat. Why did he have to live past that summer? she wondered. He might then have remained a beautiful memory, a dark god astride his phaeton Ford. But he had lived, just as she had lived, and what had made him so exciting at twenty, at thirty-eight was the vice that made him a bore. It was proper and expected of Williams students to get drunk every night, but Johnnie Marshall had been out of Williams for seventeen years.

"Does your silence mean you'll come?" he asked, leering at her confidently, like a bull.

"I really can't, Johnnie."

What did he do with himself all the time, she wondered, besides live on the Island and drink? He had gone through all the Marshall money, which had once been considerable, and if he worked at all he wasn't willing to admit it.

He shrugged as though he really didn't care if she came or not. "So be it, old girl. Gotta go. Ta ta, and hip hip. People there are at my house who need a drink." He started to walk away.

"How's Delia?" Lucy called after him.

"Delia?" he asked, turning about and affecting an exaggerated expression of surprise. "Oh. Delia. You must mean my wife. You know, I haven't seen the dear old girl in days." He leered at her again and edged away into the crowd.

How could she ever have been so crazy about him? Lucy wondered. He had taken her to a Yacht Club party just once. She had bought a new dress and had washed and combed herself for days. Then at midnight, just before he had slid unconscious to the floor, he had deposited nine cups of undigested rum punch in her lap, and this had been the night she had planned to kiss him.

A group of tourists was bulldozing its way up the narrow sidewalk, driving everyone else out into the street or against the wall. Lucy flattened herself against the Driftwood Shop and let them pass. The Island had gone to hell since the war, she thought. The ferry had made it much too easy to reach. In the old days zoning laws had contained the spots of disease, but now the whole Island was becoming cancerous. Soon it was to be almost as bad as Cape Cod.

As she stepped off the curbing to cross the street, the strident warning of a Bermuda carriage bell sent her leaping backward. A light yellow Thunderbird convertible with the top down and no muffler roared up the street, leaving a blue haze of exhaust. Driving it was a boy of college age, dressed in bathing trunks and a blue beret. With him were three girls, blonde, sunburned, and pretty, wearing shorts and halters, their smooth skin the color of maple sugar. Along with two more boys perched on the top of the back seat they were all singing, "Hey, Mr. Banjo." On the rear bumper of their car was a cube of ice, embedding itself as it melted, dripping water onto the pavement.

Even now she could envy a group like that, Lucy thought. If she could be born again she would choose to be blonde, with blue eyes and a cherub mouth. What difference if the cherubs ended up at thirty-seven washed out and faded, like puddings, soft, stale, and unattractive. It was better to have an interesting and strong face, her mother had told her when she'd sit home on the night of a party, than to look like an orchid and act like a butterfly. Orchids fade, and butterflies live only for a season. True, Lucy thought. True. But it would have been nice to have been pretty for a season, with a few wild rides on open cars to remember when you were thirty-seven and a few warm, sandy kisses to look back on.

She passed the bicycle shop, the hardware store, and finally the fish market. Then the pavement merged into the wooden pier, and splinters like daggers curled up off the planks. When she had been sixteen, and had been going to her first Yacht Club dance, she had worn a pair of open-toed slippers. In the darkness a splinter from the pier had stabbed her just under a toenail and had run six inches through the top of her foot, leaving a dark scar of tar and creosote. These were her memories, she thought. Not warm afternoons of singing, "Hey, Mr. Banjo," with a cube of ice melting on the bumper, while someone in shorts and a beret was plotting to get her alone behind a sand dune, but Johnnie Marshall vomiting into her lap and a splinter under her toenail.

At that moment her three children ran across the pier toward her. She had left them with crab nets and pails. Roswell was carrying a small dead mackerel.

"Where did you get that?" she asked in motherly horror.

"It was floating on the water," Roswell answered. "We're going to eat it for supper."

Lucy took the fish by the tail and threw it into the harbor.

"It's been dead for days, silly. Now go jump in the rowboat, all of you. We're on our way home."

Roswell perched herself on the prow of the boat. Then came Lydia, struggling with the oars, and at the stern Lucy sat next to Ruthie.

"If you row us across the harbor without catching a crab," Lucy told Lydia, "I'll let you go out in the boat alone."

"Can you catch a crab with an oar?" Roswell asked, her literal mind coming to the fore.

"It's a figure of speech," Lucy answered.

"I want to see the boats," Ruthie piped.

Ruthie would be the prettiest of her three daughters, Lucy thought, looking at them critically, one by one. Roswell and Lydia would succeed through grim determination, while Ruthie would just be pretty. Lucy glanced at her watch. It was nearly four.

"Lydia will row slowly," Lucy answered, "and we'll take a long way home."

The sun was glittering off the water through the forests of masts. There were at least a hundred yachts in the harbor, everything from a long black monster as large as a destroyer to a high, fat, commercial cruise boat, all decked out with meaningless flags and pennants.

"The *Louella*," Roswell read out loud as they passed a sea-green fishing yacht. She had recently learned to read, and she was proud of it.

"Hi," Ruthie called to the elderly man who sat on the rear deck.

"Ahoy," he answered, waving an ice-filled glass at her.

"We're going faster than you are," Ruthie yelled. Being cute, she had always been sure people wanted to talk to her.

"You have a better motor," he answered, returning to his drink.

"We don't have a motor at all," Roswell whispered from the bow.

"He was just being funny," Lucy answered wearily. "Try not to be so literal about everything."

"What's literal mean?" Roswell asked.

Lucy was saved a long and elaborate explanation by a sudden question from Lydia.

"Why are sailboats better than motorboats?" she asked.

"Who said they were?"

"You did."

"That wasn't exactly what I said, Lydia. I just expressed the opinion that people who owned sailboats were usually better than people who owned motorboats."

"What's it mean when some people are better than other people?" Roswell asked.

"Some people are, that's all."

"What makes them better?" Roswell persisted.

"Well," Lucy answered, hoping to end the subject, "some people are flashy."

264

"What's flashy?" Lydia asked.

"It's something we aren't and don't wish to be."

"Let's drift," Ruthie said. It was a new word she had recently learned. She had trouble with her "R's" and pronounced it "dwift."

"All right, we'll dwift," Lucy answered, smiling fondly at all her children.

She leaned back against the stern of the rowboat, listening to the waves lap against the bow. Music was filtering across the water from one of the yachts, and in one of the houses along the shore people were laughing. The image of Johnnie Marshall, with his bloated face and his arms filled with bottles, returned to her mind. She had once wanted desperately to marry Johnnie Marshall, and had felt cheated when he chose Delia Deland. But now she wouldn't trade her life for Delia's for all the gaiety in the world. She had often felt resigned to Charlie and what seemed to her his senseless desire to work himself to death, but it had taken just a brief encounter with Johnnie Marshall to make her know how lucky she really was.

And how about Charlie? she wondered. Did he consider himself lucky too? For all she had helped him during the past ten years, he might have done much better with someone else. Suddenly she felt guilty. She ought to be home, she thought, with her husband, helping him do whatever it was he wanted to do. She really didn't know what Charlie did want to do. She had never taken the time nor felt the interest to ask him.

"Hi," Ruthie called out to another man on another boat.

"We're going faster than you are," Roswell said. She sometimes worried a phrase for weeks, like a dog with a rubber bone.

"Hush, children," Lucy whispered.

"I thought people in boats always waved at each other," Lydia said.

"Out in the ocean, yes, but in a harbor, no. And anyway, we're not much of a boat."

"Someone is looking at us with a telescope," Roswell said, pointing over the stern.

Lucy turned around and looked toward the motorboat. A man in demin shorts and a white shirt stood by the tiller, gazing at them through a pair of binoculars. His boat was less than a hundred feet away.

"Why is he looking at us, Mother?" Lydia asked.

"I wouldn't know, darling. He apparently has nothing else to do."

Lucy hoped her words would carry not only to Lydia but to the young man with the binoculars.

"But why is he looking at us?" Roswell repeated.

"I said I didn't know. Start rowing please, Lydia."

"Hi," Ruthie shrilled, her voice as penetrating as a gull's. "Why are you looking at us?"

"Because you're worth looking at," he answered, lowering the binoculars.

"We're dwifting," Ruthie shouted.

"Well, dwift over here. I'd like to speak with your mother."

"He wants to speak to you," Lydia whispered, holding the oars out of the water.

"I have ears, darling. Keep rowing, please."

"But he wants to speak with you, Mother."

"And I don't wish to speak with him. We don't know him. Keep rowing, please."

"My mother doesn't want to speak with you," Roswell shouted. "We don't know you."

"I don't know you either, but I still want to speak to you."

"He still wants to speak to us," Roswell repeated.

"Lydia," Lucy whispered angrily, "if you don't start to row, I'll take the oars myself." The tide was carrying the rowboat closer to the motorboat.

"What's your name?" Ruthie shouted.

"Rod. What's yours?"

"Ruthie, and my sisters' names are Roswell and Lydia."

The rowboat was now less than thirty feet away.

"My children seem to think they can talk to absolutely everyone," Lucy said, finally addressing the man directly. "You'll have to excuse us."

"Do you children want to know why I was looking at you?" he asked, paying no attention to Lucy.

"Yes," they shouted in unison.

"All right. Come on over here and I'll tell you."

"I'm sorry," Lucy answered firmly, "we have to go home."

His manner annoyed her. He stood at the stern of his boat, his hands on his hips, his white teeth gleaming in the afternoon sunlight, an arrogant smile on his face, as though he expected no argument where women were concerned. He was tall and thin, with a narrow face and a jutting jaw. He was younger than she was, Lucy decided, with none of the softness about his middle and under his chin that she expected in men her own age.

"Please don't go home," he coaxed. "I need you and your children."

"What *are* you talking about?" she asked, allowing the rowboat to drift closer. He immediately hooked his leg over it.

"I'm a professional photographer. I'm working on a film for a television program. I need some models. Seriously," he added, when by her expression it was obvious she didn't believe him. "I'm quite harmless. I just want to take some pictures of you and your three pretty girls."

"What sort of pictures?" Lucy asked, by now curious.

"Just pictures. You and your children could sit on the bow of my boat, and we'd ride around the harbor once or twice. I need some background shots of the boats and so forth. It always works better to have something pretty in the foreground."

"Please," Lydia whispered fiercely. "Please say yes, Mother."

"Of course I'd be willing to pay you. How about it, kids? Do you want to take a ride and get paid for it?"

"I'm sorry, but we simply can't," Lucy answered. "We have to hurry home."

Ruthie burst into tears, and Lydia wailed, "Oh, Mother."

"I feel rather foolish saying this," Lucy said over the noise, "but I'm really

266

not in the habit of taking rides with people I've never seen before. Are you really a photographer," she added, "or is this just some sort of a joke?"

"Don't move," he answered, disappearing into his cabin. He returned with a movie camera. "Satisfied?" he asked. "I assure you that this is only business with me, and I'm offering to pay you for your time."

"He'll pay us, Mother," Roswell said, as though this should settle the matter. For two years she had been filling a clay elephant with coins.

"Do you really want to take a ride, children?" Lucy asked.

"Yes," they shouted in unison, sensing victory for themselves and defeat for their mother. They leaped out of the rowboat shouting with joy.

"I'm Rod McNeil," he said, helping Lucy into his boat. "You don't realize how much I appreciate this."

There was a wedding ring on his left hand.

"You'll be sorry," Lucy giggled. "I look like an old witch on film."

"That I doubt," he answered. "Not with a face and figure like yours. I've been in this business long enough to recognize the real thing when I see it. Incidentally, what's your name, or shall I just call you, Hey you?"

"I'm Lucy Webb," she answered, flushing and feeling terribly young for a change.

"All right, Lucy, how about ten dollars? Will that be enough, and perhaps a dollar apiece for your children?"

"Don't be ridiculous," she answered. "We should be paying you."

"Well, at least let me take you all fishing some day."

"We'll see about that," she answered. "What would you like us all to do?"

"Just follow me," he said. He took her hand casually, and led the way toward the bow of the boat. "Now here's the idea, Lucy. First I'll circle the harbor, shooting the general background. Then we'll maneuver in through the boats, trying to get a picture or two of the town. You and your children just sit up here and forget all about the camera."

"But what do you want us to be doing?" Lucy wailed.

"Nothing in particular. Just pretend you're going for a ride. If you see something unusual, like a seagull or a buoy, point it out to Lydia here. You won't be in the picture all the time."

"I feel utterly ridiculous."

"You needn't. I'll tell you a trick to remember when you're having your picture taken. Pretend there isn't any film in the camera."

He turned, and moved to the stern of the boat.

"Are we arranged all right?" Lucy shouted, wetting her lips with her tongue.

He sighted at them through the camera.

"Move Ruthie about a foot to the left. There. Perfect. Now hold it just about like that."

He started the motor and headed for the opposite shore, occasionally slowing when he noticed something he wished to record on the film.

"Which is your house?" he shouted a while later, when they had completely circled the harbor.

Lucy pointed.

"Good. Hold your arm out like that and say something to your children. Fine. Now we'll go in close to some of the big boats, and perhaps you can wave as we go by."

"Can I smoke, Mr. McNeil?"

"Call me Rod. Yes. Of course you can smoke. I want you to feel completely natural."

After a while he throttled down the motor and headed toward the Chalmers dock.

"Now we'll get a last sequence of you and the children climbing over the side. Good Lord," he exclaimed, as though he were seeing the Chalmers summer house for the first time, "does your husband own a bank?"

"It's not his. It's my family's."

"What's your family's name?"

"Chalmers," she answered, joining him at the tiller. "But actually this is still called the old Hadley place. That was my grandfather. He discovered the Island before the public did."

"Hadley? Isn't there a street back in the town by that name?"

"Hadley Street," Roswell interrupted.

"Wait a minute," Rod McNeil said. He reversed the engine and held the boat steady in the water a few feet off the dock. "Something is beginning to add up around here. Are you this company I've been seeing on the back cover of the *New Yorker?*"

"The Hadley Company," Lucy answered. "Why?"

Rod McNeil hit his forehead with his fist.

"Here I've been ordering you around like . . . seriously, Lucy, I've been making a fool of myself. Why didn't you tell me who you were?"

"You're the first person who ever thought I was anything, and anyway I've enjoyed being ordered around, if that's what you've done to me. We had a nice time, didn't we, children?"

"Do we have to go in, Mother?" Lydia asked.

"Yes, we do. Now don't beg, girls," she said, putting her fingers across Roswell's lips. "We've had an exciting afternoon, but it's over. We do have to go," she added, smiling at Rod McNeil.

He eased the boat against the dock and ran toward the bow, looping a line around a post. Lucy took the line from the rowboat and leaped onto the dock.

"Now thank Mr. McNeil," Lucy said to her children, "and then run along into the house. Your supper is waiting for you."

She lingered a moment, feeling she ought to say more than just thank you and good-by. Rod McNeil was extremely attractive. In the late afternoon sunlight his face and arms were golden brown.

"I'm sorry this has to end," he said. "I can't remember when I've enjoyed myself more."

"I might ask you in for a drink," Lucy answered, "but I don't think my mother would approve. I'm a married woman, and all that."

268

"Your mother?"

"This is her house, and she's in there waiting for me right now."

"I eat mothers," he said, baring his teeth.

Lucy laughed. "I'm afraid you'd find my mother rather indigestible. She has that reputation."

"I'll risk it, if you will." He was watching her, his eyelids drooping slightly.

"All right," she said, "but don't say I didn't warn you. All you'll get is one small glass of sherry, and then my mother will send you on your way."

"It's been quite a number of years, Mr. McNeil," Lydia Chalmers said stiffly, "since my daughter Lucy brought home a man for parental approval."

Rod McNeil nodded respectfully and did his best to look uneasy, as he knew Mrs. Chalmers expected him to be. He'd have to play it by ear for a while until he could size her up. It would have been simpler if Lucy were present. However, she had introduced him to her mother, and then disappeared into the kitchen to feed the children.

"I gather you are married," Mrs. Chalmers said, glancing at his wedding ring.

"I am married, Mrs. Chalmers, and quite happily, I might add."

"You have children?"

"Yes. Two of them. A boy and a girl." He lowered his eyes. "I think it was your three granddaughters, Lucy's little girls, who made me feel so anxious to be a part of a family group tonight."

Mrs. Chalmers raised her eyebrows slightly. "You could always go home, Mr. McNeil. I'm sure your own wife would be delighted to include you in her family group."

She'd be tougher than he expected. He usually handled mothers according to what animal they reminded him of, snakes, weasels, cows, or geese. But this one was a hawk, with talons extended and sharp, ready to swoop down on him if he made a single false move. It didn't look too encouraging.

"Do sit, Mr. McNeil. I'd gladly offer you something stronger than sherry, but in this family we do not make it a practice to drink cocktails when our husbands are away."

"Husbands would approve of that, Mrs. Chalmers, and actually I never touch cocktails myself. Sherry will be fine."

There must be a flaw in her somewhere, he thought. He'd continue to probe until he found it. He sat waiting for her to speak. When she said nothing, he glanced approvingly about the room.

"This certainly is a lovely house you have, Mrs. Chalmers. I suppose it's always been in the family."

"Oh, yes. We're not a family that buys and sells things. My father built it. He had a small boat that he needed a place for in the winter. You see, originally this was just a boathouse."

"Fascinating. I always love to hear about the history of individual houses."

"It's been altered and added to over the years," Mrs. Chalmers continued. "The room we're sitting in was added in 1910." She pointed to the expanse

269

of small-pane windows that overlooked the harbor. "A window like that was quite unusual in its day, although today everyone has these so-called picture windows."

"Don't they," he agreed scornfully. "And what pictures some of them frame, such as a neighbor's back yard."

"I couldn't agree with you more. Do you have a picture window in your house in Albany? You did say you live in Albany?"

He nodded. "We do live in Albany, but we don't have a picture window. I'm afraid my wife and I are much too conservative, Mrs. Chalmers, or call us traditional. We built for comfort, not for style."

For the first time she glanced at him with a spark of approval.

"Tell me more about yourself, Mr. McNeil." She smiled wanly. "I confess I've never known anyone with your name. What does your family do?"

"There isn't too much of my family left, Mrs. Chalmers."

"But surely there must have been someone in your family, back a few generations perhaps, who was successful enough at something to enable you to float about in a boat taking pictures for television. Or do you actually make a living at it?"

He was beginning to understand her now. Until that moment he had merely been defending himself. But the time had come for the attack.

"Take a deep breath," he said, "and prepare yourself for a shock." He paused, letting his words linger for effect. "My grandfather was a bricklayer."

Mrs. Chalmers laughed with delight.

"How charming. I must say from the way you sounded I expected something far worse than that. What could be, shall we say, more useful than laying bricks?"

He shrugged. "Nothing, I suppose, but in some places it's considered rather plebeian."

"Not in my circles, young man. Scratch any American and you'll find a peasant underneath. My great-grandfather was a blacksmith, and we're all rather proud of it."

"And you certainly ought to be," he said respectfully. "Didn't your great-grandfather invent the Hadley horseshoe nail?"

He had scored. Mrs. Chalmers' eyes opened wide with surprise.

"Now how on earth did you know that? Don't tell me you read these terrible advertisements my husband writes?" She patted the latest copy of the *New Yorker* affectionately.

"I've seen your ads, yes," he answered, "but I knew about the Hadley horseshoe nail a long time ago. My father had race horses for years."

"How absolutely fascinating," she said. "And he used our nails."

"He certainly did. And it's really quite interesting, because I always wanted to meet the people who could turn out as small an object as a horseshoe nail with such exquisite skill. Of course, since these advertisements you mention, I really feel as though I have met all your family."

Mrs. Chalmers waved her hand disparagingly. "I'm afraid some of our advertising rather overdoes it."

He had her on the defensive now.

"Not at all," he answered easily. "There aren't many families like yours left in this country. Take my own, for instance. The brick business is gone. Such things as race horses are a thing of the past. My mother and father are both dead, and our old house," he shuddered, "has become a nunnery. And me, I've become more or less of a sea hobo, you might say, for lack of a better term. What once was a rather thriving family empire has gone up in smoke."

"I find that rather sad, Mr. McNeil. Doesn't it disturb you too?"

"It most certainly does. But not every family has that magic quality which keeps it going on and on, generation after generation, the way yours has done."

"My dear young man," Mrs. Chalmers answered, "our family has survived because of no magic quality. In fact it's the absence of these so-called magic qualities that has kept us all together. We have always been able to recognize our limitations. As a family we are not noted for our talents, but our willingness to plod. I mean exactly that, Mr. McNeil. Every family must have its plodders, or it withers and dies."

"That's brilliantly phrased," he answered, "and you've put your finger on something that's so seldom admitted."

Lucy came through the kitchen door. She was wearing her best purple dress. Her shoulders and arms were bare.

"Darling, come join us," Mrs. Chalmers called cheerfully. "You've brought us a most charming sea hobo." She giggled. "You don't mind me calling you that, I hope, Mr. McNeil?"

"Unfortunately," he said sadly, "that's what I am."

He poured Lucy a glass of sherry.

"What do you think of this sherry I bought this afternoon?" Mrs. Chalmers asked, changing the subject abruptly. "I'd like a man's opinion on it."

He was being tested now in another department.

"Do you want the polite answer of an uninvited guest?" he asked. "Or shall I tell you the truth?"

"Oh dear, isn't it any good?"

"Not very." He sipped the sherry experimentally. "I would say that this is the sort of wine a woman buys when she has very little money left in her purse. It belongs in a melon or in plum pudding, but not in a glass."

"Your friend is positively insulting," Mrs. Chalmers said to Lucy, obviously delighted. She turned again to Rod McNeil. "And what would a man have bought?"

"I always remember a cardinal rule when I buy wine, Mrs. Chalmers. If it doesn't taste good, it isn't good."

"But what would you have me do? Insist that a bottle of it be uncorked so I could sample it?"

"Of course you do run into that problem when you buy only by the bottle," he answered. "I know my father once found a sherry he liked, and just like that, he bought a thousand bottles of it so he'd always have it on hand. My wife and I try to follow much the same policy."

"A thousand bottles?" Lucy exclaimed.

"Oh, Lord no. By the case."

"Darling, I'm beginning to think our Mr. McNeil must find us rather dull. Are there many people like you out floating around in the ocean?" she asked.

"I told you he was fascinating," Lucy said proudly.

"And he is, darling. I haven't enjoyed myself so much in months. Now tell me something, young man. Why on earth did you choose the rather strange profession of taking pictures for television?"

"I'm afraid if I answer that, I'll appear rather naïve and idealistic."

"What's wrong with being idealistic?" Lucy asked, by her expression encouraging him to go on.

"Nothing's wrong with it, but some people don't understand it. Actually, I didn't select my profession. It selected me. From the time I was a small boy I was interested only in two things. Boats and cameras. All right," he said, pointing at Mrs. Chalmers as she was about to interrupt him. "I know what you're about to say. That I should have gone into the family brick business, and made cameras and boats my hobby."

"Don't most people do that, Mr. McNeil?"

"I wish you'd tell your mother to call me Rod, Lucy."

"Do call him Rod, Mother. He isn't that old."

"How old are you?" she asked.

"I'm thirty-nine, Mrs. Chalmers."

"You don't look it," Lucy said admiringly.

"Thank you, but I am. Thirty-nine, and almost forty."

"Go on about your profession," Mrs. Chalmers said. "It's such fun to meet someone different like you."

"I knew you'd like him, Mother. My mother was simply horrified when I told her I'd picked up a strange man," she added, turning to Rod McNeil.

"I hardly blame her, and I am a rather strange man. I'm a failure," he said nodding thoughtfully. "Yes, I am, and don't argue with me, Mrs. Chalmers. I could have sold bricks, and probably I should have, but ten years ago, at the end of the war, I decided I would spend my life doing things I enjoy, and I didn't enjoy bricks. It was as simple as that. So when my father died, the brick business was sold, and here I am with my movie camera."

"This reminds me of a discussion I had early in my married life," Mrs. Chalmers said, accepting more sherry. "My husband told me soon after we were married that he'd never make a businessman. You see, he wanted to spend his life at a college somewhere, writing his books. Oh, yes he did, love," she added at Lucy's look of surprise. "He told me he hated business, and he hated knives. He wanted nothing to do with The Hadley Company when we were first married."

She pointed her finger at Rod McNeil. "But here's where you and my husband differ. He was willing to buckle down and accept his family responsibili-

272

ties. He was willing to make a hobby of his talent, instead of allowing it to make a failure out of him. And don't think I haven't been lenient with him and his writing. I didn't forbid him to write. I just persuaded him that to make a profession of it would be a serious mistake. And he does still manage to write," she said, moving to a bookcase. "These are all his, and excellent they are. They're not of much general interest, but the talent is still there, as sharp as it ever was, and someday, when he decides to retire and has more time, I know he'll sit down and do something really fine."

She returned to her chair. "It gets back to my theory about families and what breaks them apart. Families are made up of people who buckle down, who put first things first, and those who believe otherwise are riding for a fall."

"Does Mr. Chalmers write stories, Mrs. Chalmers?"

"Oh, dear me, no. My Lowell has no knack for that sort of thing, and I must say I'm glad."

"Why?" he asked.

"He might put me in one of them," she giggled. "And no wife likes to know what her husband really thinks of her."

"Mother's joking," Lucy interrupted. "She and Father get along so well it's almost criminal."

"Of course, we're talking just about talent here," Rod McNeil said. "But genius is quite another thing. I thought I might be a genius once. I actually thought that I might be able to make a permanent contribution to the world." He looked at Lucy, shaking his head. "Your mother has a knack of making me bare my soul."

"I thought you were a genius when I met you this afternoon," Lucy said.

"Did you really, or are you just being kind?"

"At least you baffled me, and aren't geniuses supposed to baffle ordinary people?"

"Poof," Mrs. Chalmers exclaimed. "He doesn't baffle me one bit." She turned to her daughter. "But he does amuse me, love, and I have an announcement to make. You sir, are going to have dinner here with us."

Rod McNeil waved a finger from side to side.

"I'll have to refuse, Mrs. Chalmers. No, don't urge me because I just can't do it. I'm heading back for the mainland tomorrow, and I have a little work to do on my boat while it's still daylight."

"But this is ridiculous," Mrs. Chalmers answered with the air of a woman who does not expect to have her invitations refused. "You can tie your silly old boat right up to our dock, and you'll have plenty of time to do your work after we eat."

"I'm sorry," he said, rising to his feet, "but I'm going to be stubborn. There's supposed to be a hurricane coming, and I may decide to head for the mainland tonight." He extended his hand, half bowing as he did so. "I've enjoyed our conversation, Mrs. Chalmers. I hope you invite me into your home again some time."

Mrs. Chalmers took his hand warmly.

"I do wish you wouldn't run off like this," she said, "but if you must, you must." She giggled. "The next time you visit us I promise you we'll have better sherry."

Lucy walked with him out onto the pier.

"Mother was simply charmed with you," she said admiringly. "How do you do it?"

"For some strange reason mothers find me attractive," he answered. "Old ones, that is," he added quickly.

"I suspect young ones find you quite attractive too," Lucy said, blushing a little as she spoke. "Are you really going back to the mainland tonight?"

"Can you think of a reason why I shouldn't?"

He was flirting with her, Lucy thought, and she was alarmed to discover that she liked it.

"What reason could I think of?" she asked, avoiding his eye.

"Well, if you could give me a reason I might linger a while." He kicked the toe of her shoe gently. "You could always row out to see me after your supper. I could use a little help with my boat."

"What are you talking about?" she asked, more annoyed with herself than with him. "You are a brassy individual, aren't you?"

"Your husband is obviously neglecting you, Lucy. Doesn't he know how nice you are?"

She turned her back to him so he wouldn't see her face. Then she said, "You'd better go. It so happens I'm not a lonely summer widow looking for a fling."

"And if you were I wouldn't like you as much as I do. Row out to see me tonight." He ran his thumbnail down her bare back, leaving a white line against her tan.

"Just go," she said, moving away from him. "I mean it."

"Is that your final word on the subject?" He was mocking her gently.

"Yes," she said quietly. "Go get in your boat. I'll help you cast off."

He shrugged, and leapt easily onto the deck. When she threw the stern line to him she said, "When will the pictures be on television?"

"Pictures?" he asked innocently as he started the motor.

"Isn't that what we were doing out there this afternoon? Taking pictures?"

"Oh, that," he answered. "You aren't very observant, are you. There wasn't any film in the camera." He grinned at her, and then throttled the motor hard, heading the boat out into the harbor.

"Why so thoughtful?" Mrs. Chalmers said to Lucy that evening after dinner. "You've been staring out that window as though you'd never seen the harbor before."

The harbor was dark, lights from the boats reflecting in toward shore over the calm water.

Lucy sighed, and said, "Maybe I've been seeing too much of my children."

"You poor darling," Mrs. Chalmers said sympathetically. She put aside

274

her sewing. "Why don't you go off by yourself tomorrow, and do something that's fun for a change?"

"Such as what?"

"Surely you can think of something. Call Jane and Grayson Lord. Have them take you on a birdwalk."

Lucy considered the suggestion for a moment.

"Would you mind terribly if I did leave the girls with Elsa for the day?"

"Not at all, Child. By all means do it." Mrs. Chalmers resumed her sewing, tipping the shade of her lamp for more light. "It's hardly my place to say this, Lucy, but I don't think you'd be feeling this way if your Charlie didn't neglect you so shamelessly."

Lucy turned and stared at her mother for a moment.

"Does he really neglect me?" she asked.

"I would say that was only too obvious," her mother answered frostily.

Lucy started walking toward the stairs.

"I was just beginning to think," she said quietly, "that perhaps it was I who had been neglecting him."

Lucy reached the Lords' house just before twelve. She slowed her car and glanced in over the privet hedge. What possible release could a day with the Lords bring her, she wondered. Jane was probably making fudge, or baking bread, or polishing her pewter, or weaving. Grayson was doubtless in his workshop, carving today's wooden bird, or mounting yesterday's on a piece of driftwood. The Lords and their hobbies seemed a thousand miles removed from her mood. She was depressed, and playing the recorder with Jane or admiring Grayson's collection of stones and minerals wouldn't help. She went on past the Lords' driveway and turned in at The Retreat.

"L. C. Chalmers," she read out loud from the gatepost. "Private. Keep out."

That was her mood, she decided. She was feeling exclusive. She wanted to be alone for a day, so she could think.

She found the key under the white stone near the porch, where it had been hidden winter and summer for thirty-five years. When she was inside the house she went about pulling the curtains and opening the windows. The air was completely still, and a film of mist had moved in over the land, covering the island like a strip of cotton gauze. It was dark, the atmosphere light gray, as though the sun had moved another hundred million miles away. After a while she lay on the couch, staring at a cobweb on the ceiling, listening to the sound of the surf.

The episode with Rod McNeil the evening before had alarmed her. How could she have found him attractive, she wondered. He was nothing more than a rotting piece of carrion that had washed up with the tide. Everything about him stank, and yet when he had run his thumbnail down her back her knees had gone weak and her flesh had tingled.

What was happening to her, she wondered. How could she have been tempted by this? She had a good life. How could she have toyed with the idea of ruining it?

But was her life so good, she wondered. Had she ever been anything more than a parasite? Would anyone but her three children miss her if she were to die?

Her life had always been made easy by someone else's labor. She had never created anything, she thought, except three children, and perhaps just having children wasn't enough.

She went into the kitchen, and opened the icebox. There was some limp lettuce in a plastic bag, and a few eggs. She made a salad and ate two scrambled eggs out of the frying pan.

While she was eating the rain started, a sudden tropical downpour that thundered against the shingle roof, clogging the gutters, sluicing down the outside of the windowpanes. When she was washing the frying pan she noticed that the windows of her car were open. She ran across the driveway, and was instantly soaked to the skin. Then she stood for a moment by the car, her face tilted back into the rain. Finally she left her car and started walking toward the cliff and the ocean. The narrow path through the brambles was already a stream of muddy water.

She sat on a boulder at the edge of the cliff and looked down at the ocean. The tide was running higher than she had ever seen it. Huge rollers were smashing against the cliff, eating into the sand and clay, the foam stained a muddy yellow. A hundred feet away a section of the land had slid down into the surf, leaving behind a tangle of bayberry bushes. The wind had started to blow, driving the rain in off the sea, mixing with the spray. She could taste salt.

Things did change, she thought, even something as solid as an island. When she had been a girl The Retreat was over two hundred yards from the cliff. In twenty-five years the ocean had devoured a hundred yards; millions of tons of sand, clay, and boulders had gone out to sea.

Behind her she could barely make out the house, and the island had become a solid gray blur of moving mist and water. Suddenly she noticed Grayson Lord's sheep moving in a flock down the hill toward the main road, their fleeces sodden and heavy, their heads close to the ground.

All these things she loved, Lucy thought. The island, her family, the knowledge that her father and her grandfather had loved the same things she loved, and that her children would love them too. All these things were hers, but in her thirty-six years she had never done one thing to earn them, nor had she raised one finger to help preserve them. It could all disappear, she thought. It could be chipped and eaten away just as the ocean was devouring the island.

Suddenly a wave struck a few feet below her on the cliff, and the boulder she was sitting on shuddered from the impact, the ground at her feet vibrating. She moved back from the cliff, and then ran toward the house, the thorns tearing at her bare legs. When she reached her car, a figure appeared in front of her on the driveway. It was Grayson Lord.

"Good God, Lucy, are you all right?"

He was wearing a felt hat and a yellow slicker that nearly touched the ground.

"I'm fine, Gray. I was just looking at the ocean."

He followed her onto the porch. "Your mother called. She thought you were with us. Jane told her some white lie about your being over in Lobstertown. We knew you had come up here."

"I'm all right," she repeated. "I just felt like being alone."

"But you can't stay up here alone. Listen. We're having a hurricane."

The wind was blowing now in gusts, moaning around the corners of the house, driving the rain against the shingles.

"Maybe I just feel like getting wet, Gray."

"Well, you got wet." He took her by the shoulders and aimed her toward her car. "You're going down to our place, and don't argue with me. This kind of foolishness doesn't become you. Go on," he ordered. "I'll drive you down."

"I saw your sheep," Lucy said when they were part way down the hill. "They looked lost."

"Don't worry about my sheep," he answered. "They're probably back in the barn by now. Are you crying, Lucy?" he asked, glancing at her in surprise.

She didn't answer, blinking back her tears.

He patted her shoulder clumsily.

"Hang on," he said. "Jane will fix you up with some dry clothes, and we'll all have a good drink of whisky. O.K.?"

"I'll be all right," she answered, instantly in control of herself. "I guess the ocean just scared me a little."

thirty-six

AT ELEVEN THAT NIGHT, WHEN LUCY RETURNED TO THE HARBOR HOUSE, SHE found her mother sitting alone in the hallway near the telephone table. She was dressed in a kimono and slippers, and her hair hung down her back in long, gray strands.

"I hope you didn't wait up for me," Lucy said uneasily. "The driving was awful."

"I'm afraid I have something far more important on my mind right now than you," Mrs. Chalmers answered. "Will you join me in a cup of soup?"

In times of emergency, where others fortified themselves with prayer, whisky, or a cigarette, Mrs. Chalmers drank soup.

"Is something wrong?" Lucy asked. She was exhausted, and had hoped to crawl into bed.

"Will you have some soup with me?" her mother repeated.

The question was an order. "Of course," Lucy said meekly. She followed her mother toward the kitchen. "Have you ever seen such a rain?" she asked. "The whole Island is awash."

"And it's apparently raining much harder at home," her mother answered, busying herself at the gas range. "Your father called."

"Father called?" Lucy said, alarmed by her mother's calm. "About what?"

"I'll tell you when I have my soup. Not before. How on earth do you operate this thing?" she asked. She had wasted four matches, and the gas was still not lit.

"Let me do it," Lucy said. "You go sit down. What kind of soup do you want?"

"Just soup, please, as long as it's hot. How were the Lords?"

"Fine."

"You couldn't have seen many birds."

"I didn't. Is Father sick, Mother?"

"No, he isn't sick. He called about a flood they're having at home."

"I hope you told him we're having one here too. I've never seen the tide so high. A great chunk of our land fell off into the ocean."

"Will you please try to concentrate on what I'm trying to tell you," her mother said sharply. "They're having a flood at home. A flood," she repeated. "The Hadley Company has been completely destroyed."

"I don't believe it," Lucy gasped, staring at her mother in horror.

"Yes, Lucy. Destroyed. Washed right down the river."

"But that's awful."

"Is that all you can think of to say?"

"But what did Father tell you? Was he out at the plant when he called?"

"Apparently Charlie phoned a message to him at the Lawn Street house. The town of Hadley is completely cut off."

"Is Charlie out in Hadley?"

"How else would he have called from there if he wasn't?"

"I wish you'd stop being so obtuse with me," Lucy answered angrily. "Here's your soup. Now will you please tell me what's going on at home?"

"The factory has been destroyed," her mother repeated. "That's all your father knew, and that's all I know."

"But is Charlie all right?"

"Why shouldn't he be all right?"

"What is the matter with you?" Lucy shouted. "Perhaps you're not concerned about Charlie, but I am." She walked toward the kitchen door. "I'm going home. I'm going to pack up the children right now, and I'm starting for home."

"Don't be ridiculous," her mother answered. "The first ferry doesn't go until six o'clock tomorrow morning."

"Well, I plan to be on it, and I have a lot of packing to do."

"Come back here and sit down," her mother said firmly. "Even if you do go home, you could do nothing to help. Charlie is in Hadley, and you couldn't reach him if you tried. Now sit, please. I want to talk to you."

"But how can you be so calm?" Lucy shouted. "Or is it because Father's all safe and dry back at Lawn Street, while Charlie, as usual, is out doing all the dirty work?"

"That's quite enough of that," Mrs. Chalmers said coldly. "This is no time for hysteria. Would you like to know what I have been thinking about, or shall we wait and discuss it tomorrow morning?"

"You'd better tell me now, because I won't be here tomorrow morning."

"We'll see about that." Lucy had left the gas burning, and Mrs. Chalmers crossed the kitchen and turned it off. "This flood might be a blessing in disguise, darling. That's what I've been thinking since your father called."

"You mean we may end up with a new factory?" Lucy asked eagerly. "Charlie's been talking about that for years."

"I'm afraid I mean quite the opposite," her mother answered. "If the factory is destroyed, I think it's time we did something we should have done years ago. We nearly sold The Hadley Company during the war, and the sale would have gone through if Aunt Roswell hadn't been stubborn about it. That time it was from choice. Now I'm afraid it will be from necessity."

"Sell it?" Lucy echoed. "But it's the one valuable thing our family has."

"You're being naïve, darling. Our family no longer depends on the Company for our income. That used to be so back in my father's and my grandfather's day. But now most of our money is invested in other things, and we've kept the Company going more for sentimental reasons than for anything else."

"But you can't just dispose of it just like that." Lucy snapped her fingers. "Charlie has spent ten years out there working his head off, trying to build the Company back up to where it used to be."

"I'd expect you to be loyal," Mrs. Chalmers answered, "but I'm thinking of our responsibility to the entire family, not just one individual such as your Charlie. A new plant will mean spending all our reserves, and it's those reserves which have been paying us our dividends since my father died."

"But the Company's on the way up, Mother. Charlie has been rebuilding it."

"I won't sit here arguing with you, Lucy."

"I'm not arguing. I'm trying to find out what's at the bottom of your sudden desire to get rid of The Hadley Company. You don't know whether the factory has been destroyed or not, but already you've decided to sell it."

"Let me ask you something, young lady. You've had a pretty good life all these years, haven't you?"

"What's my life got to do with this?"

Her mother pointed a finger at her. "I ask you why your life has been so pleasant. It's been because I have seen to it that we've always been well provided for. Yes, it's been me who has made most of the decisions in our family, Lucy, and it will be up to me to make this decision now. The money left us all by my father and my grandfather is not something we can gamble with. It's a trust fund that we really don't have the right to spend at all. I'm thinking of your children and your children's children."

"I think I know what's bothering you," Lucy answered. "You've been handling all our family problems all these years, and now you're not willing to trust them to anyone else. You know my father isn't man enough to keep the business going, but you won't even let Charlie try. This is a personal thing with you, isn't it? It's going to give you a great deal of pleasure to show Charlie who's boss. You've never been able to push him around the way you push my father around, and you've resented it. You've been waiting for an opportunity like this for ten long years."

"That's so utterly ridiculous," Mrs. Chalmers said haughtily, "I won't even comment on it."

"But you'll admit that my father won't be any good in a crisis like this. He won't know what to do, will he?"

"Your father is sixty-eight years old, and that's hardly the prime of life."

"But Charlie is just thirty-eight, and that is the prime of life."

"I will not see our family trust handed over to your husband, if that's what you're suggesting."

"Then it *is* a personal matter with you," Lucy said triumphantly. "You're going to show Charlie who makes the decisions in the family."

"I think it's time we both went to bed," her mother answered. "I've said all I plan to say on the matter."

"Charlie will fight this, Mother. He won't take this without a struggle."

"What a delightful prospect," Mrs. Chalmers answered. She laughed without mirth. "You really are terribly naïve about business. What can he possibly fight with? His bare hands?" She smiled at Lucy compassionately. "You're upset, and you'll see it all more sensibly in the morning."

"I'm sick about this," Lucy said. "Sick and ashamed. Charlie is the best thing that's happened to our family in years, and all any of us have ever done is to try to knock him down. We've been afraid of him because he does have guts. We don't deserve him. None of us do, and especially me. I've been the worst of all."

Mrs. Chalmers was obviously amused by her daughter's passionate outburst. "Whether we all deserve Charlie or not," she said, "I think it's still me who must make the decisions in this family, which reminds me I plan to start for home myself the day after tomorrow, and I'll need your help in closing up the house. If I have to go home to straighten out a mess there, I have no intention of leaving an even worse mess down here. You can expect to go home when I do on Saturday morning."

"I'm planning to catch the six o'clock ferry tomorrow," Lucy answered. "You can close the house alone."

As she glared at her daughter, Mrs. Chalmers' eyes narrowed, and deep creases appeared between her eyebrows. Her mouth set itself in a thin, angry line.

"You are not going home tomorrow," she said, her nostrils flaring slightly. "You will leave when I say you can, and not a moment before. Do I make myself quite clear?"

"I'm sorry," Lucy answered. "For a change you'll have to manage without me."

She turned and ran swiftly up the stairs.

280

Ralph Henry's call had come through shortly after eight o'clock, and in the nearly ten years that Charlie had known him, it was the first time he had ever known the foreman to sound scared.

"You better get out here right away," he shouted, his voice crackling over the phone. "We got trouble."

"What kind of trouble?" Charlie asked, hoping to calm the old man down. When he had left the plant at five that afternoon, everything had been a little damp from a week of wet weather, but there had been nothing to cause such hysteria.

"Can you hear that?" Ralph Henry shouted at him.

"Sounds like you're down near the grinding machines."

"I ain't. I'm in the front office. That's water coming over the dam. We already lost the warehouse, and water's knee deep in the main shop."

"I'll be right out," Charlie answered, hesitating no longer. He grabbed his raincoat and a flashlight as he ran out toward his car.

Outside, Highcliffe Road had reverted to its original status of a swamp. Water was standing inches deep on the pavement, and the culverts were geysers, muddy rain water boiling up and over the sidewalks. As usual, the Robinsons were having a party. He saw Ed escorting a couple in from their car, the wife shrieking with delight, the husband less pleased, wading ankle deep across the Robinsons' lawn, carrying his shoes.

Three miles west of the city Charlie began to see cars and trucks stranded along the highway, stalled in the gutters, wet and dead. It must be fairly serious, he thought, as yet unaware of what was happening. The rain was pouring down, beating against the roof of his car, dripping in through the air vent, soaking the car floor. Now and then the motor sputtered, drops of water being driven against the spark plugs by the fan. After a while he turned off the windshield wiper. The rain was coming so fast he could see better without it.

Still this was nothing to become hysterical about, he decided when he reached the mile-long level stretch of farm land just east of Hadley. There had been heavy rains before. The rivers and brooks overflowed their banks every spring, and twice since he had been working at The Hadley Company, there had been water in the powerhouse. Ralph Henry must be getting old. The warehouse couldn't be gone. It was ten feet above the highest level the river had ever reached, and it was made of brick, with walls two feet thick.

Suddenly, without any warning, the steering wheel spun in his hands, and the car wrenched violently to one side, shuddering as though it would break apart. A spume of muddy water poured against the windshield, blinding him for an instant. He jammed on the brakes just as a front wheel sank into something soft. The motor was coughing and sputtering, and he raced it to keep it alive. Then he inched the car backward, stopping when all four wheels once again were on the pavement.

All the windows of his car were smeared with muddy water. He took his flashlight and stepped outside. As far as he could see ahead, and off to both sides, there was nothing but water, a vast moving lake. He had often admired this little valley on his trips to and from the factory. A geological age before, it had been a river bottom, just one of the thousands of channels the melting glacier had carved with its runoff to the sea. As the glacier had retreated to the north, the valley had filled with silt, and finally, thousands of years later, with soil, black and fertile. Every year corn, grass, and alfalfa grew thick and dark green, and a large herd of cows grazed along a lazy, meandering brook, all that remained of the glacial river. It was a small brook, with never too much water to be contained in a four-foot concrete pipe running under the highway. Now it had become a river again, nearly a half-mile wide.

He edged across the road, feeling for the shoulder, the water above his knees. The shoulder had turned into mud. When he stepped onto it he lost a shoe, and had to retrieve it with his hand. The lights of his car were still shining, and ahead he could see debris floating over the road—staves from a wooden silo, the roof of a building, and a film of leaves and hay. He waded back to his car, not certain what he should do. There was another way into Hadley, but the other road crossed the same valley five miles farther north. If the valley was a river here, he knew it would be a river everywhere. He'd either have to gamble that he could make it through the water, guessing the location of the road by the fence posts along the side, or return to the city before he lost his car.

The water was rising fast. Already it was gurgling over the bumpers, nearly up to the car floor. How straight was the road? he wondered. He'd driven it thousands of times in the past years, but still he couldn't remember if there was a bend in it or not. At least he knew the valley was level. If he hurried, the water should nowhere be over the tops of the tires.

He climbed back into the car and started forward, a few feet at a time. Suddenly, a hundred feet out in the water, the headlights picked up something alive and moving. It was a cow, bellowing and terrified, moving toward the light. This was a break, he thought, pressing down on the car horn and racing the motor, forcing the cow to turn about, bumping it along in front of him down the road, watching the depth of the water as it crept up on her flanks. Two hundred yards ahead he saw a flashing light. Someone was trying to guide him safely through the river.

It was a policeman, his car across the highway as a road block. He leaned in the window and shone his light in Charlie's face.

"Can I get to Hadley?" Charlie asked him.

"You better stay out of Hadley," the policeman shouted at him. "The river's going wild."

Everything was going wild, Charlie decided as he drove on up the hill to the east of the town. The brooks and the streams had become rivers, and the river had become an ocean, all of it moving toward the sea, carrying everything along with it.

"This is bad," he muttered out loud to himself, feeling the need of a human voice even if it were only his own. "This is bad," he repeated as he started down the hill toward the town. All the water that was falling must pass through the Hadley gorge. The factory would be like a cork at the mouth of a vast funnel. "This is bad," he muttered over and over again, scared for the first time.

He heard the sirens as he came into the town, a sodden, mournful wail. George Wyatt, the head of the Civil Defense Committee, would be pleased, Charlie thought. George had been hoping for a real disaster since the day he had been appointed. The whole town was dark, only the firehouse on the green, with its emergency power unit, with lights.

The main street had become a brook bottom, heaps of gravel and ripped pieces of pavement piled up along the store fronts. The town looked stunned, as though no one in it yet realized what was happening—the streets deserted, the houses dark, rain pouring out of the sky and down the hillsides, sweeping everything into the maelstrom that had once been a quiet, peaceful river.

He parked his car by the firehouse and ran toward the factory, the roar of the water plunging over the dam soon drowning out the moan of the sirens. It was a sound that he had never heard before, an ugly, sucking roar. The whole dam had become a spillway, and the factory had become the dam. The bottom of the span, which in dry weather was more than thirty feet above the river, was now invisible in a foaming, muddy whirlpool.

When he reached the front office, he felt the ground vibrating under his feet. The bridge was gone, he noticed casually, as though it were the most natural thing in the world. He could see the twisted steel wreckage draped against the side of the span. He flashed his light out over the river. A small house had become lodged along with the bridge, against the span, building up the pressure, backing up the water even higher. He didn't need to be an engineer to see that the span would soon be torn off its foundations and would be pulverized by the current and rocks below.

The floor of the front office was still above water. There was a light in Mr. Chalmers' office, a candle, with Ralph Henry sitting in Mr. Chalmers' chair, smoking his pipe.

"This is bad, Ralph," Charlie shouted when he burst into the office.

"It ain't good. That's for damn sure."

"How is the main shop?"

"Every machine we got is under water."

"How about the forge?"

"Gone half an hour ago."

"How about all our steel?"

"I expect that's gone too. I couldn't get close enough to see." If Ralph Henry had been hysterical when he called an hour and a half before, he was now much too calm.

"It looks to me as though the whole dam will give way," Charlie said.

"I kinda think you're right."

"You seem pretty calm about all this," Charlie shouted at him, suddenly boiling with rage. "If the dam goes, good-by factory."

The foreman nodded. "Good-by factory is right. Maybe it's good-by factory anyway."

"Where the hell is everyone? Where's Harvey? Where's Leo? Are you all alone here?"

"Taking care of their own, that's where they are," Ralph Henry shot back at him. "There ain't a house left anywhere along the riverbank. That's Leo's house out there against the span, and one of Leo's kids was in it."

"Jesus Christ," Charlie muttered.

"And it won't do no damn good to pray neither."

"I'm not praying. I'm swearing. What'll we do?"

"I was hoping you'd know what to do. Me, I'm just sitting here waiting for someone to tell me what to do."

"Does everyone know this is happening?" Charlie said, shouting to make himself heard over the roar of the river. "How about the fire department? The place looked empty."

"Goddam it, it is empty. I tell you everyone is taking care of his own. If the river don't stop rising the whole town will be under in another six hours. I been sitting here watching it. It's coming up about two feet an hour."

"How are you feeling?" Charlie asked.

"Me? I'm feeling fine. Don't I look it?"

"How would you like to carry our records up to the firehouse? You'll have to wade through about five feet of water."

The foreman pounded his fist on Mr. Chalmers' desk. "Goddam it, I knew there was something I should of been doing while I was waiting for you. The records." He strode toward the outer office and the filing cases. "Old Mr. Hadley used to tell me that, and I forgot all about it. Get the records, Ralph, he used to say. If the place burns down you can buy new machines and hire new men, but you can't replace the records." He wrapped his arms around a cabinet and hoisted onto his shoulder a hundred and fifty pounds or more of dead weight.

"Carry it to the firehouse," Charlie called after him, "and then come back for more. I'll be right behind you."

"My place is gone too," the foreman told him as they were wading through the factory yard toward the gate. "Just like the *Queen Mary*. If I'd had a bottle of champagne I'd of smashed it on the side when she went down the river."

"What are you going to do, Ralph?"

"How the hell do I know what I'm going to do? What's everyone going to do? How are things back in the city?"

"A little water in the streets. Not much else."

"So old Lowell is back there writing a book and don't know what's going on."

"When I get a chance I'll call him."

"No, you won't, because there ain't no phones. They went out right after I called you. Sure glad I wore my rubbers," he said, stumbling out of the water and climbing through the town toward the firehouse. "It's like I was telling you," he continued. "I was eating my supper when I commenced to hear water. I didn't think nothing about it until I hear it get loud and the

284

house started to twist off its foundations. When I looked out the door I see the whole river bearing down straight at me, and I had to leave in a hurry. I didn't even have no chance to wash my dishes."

They worked an hour carrying the records from the office to the firehouse, each trip taking them ten minutes. On the last trip across the factory yard the water was up to their shoulders.

"Too goddam bad someone can't see what heroes we're making of ourselves," Ralph Henry said bitterly. "I only wish we could carry out the machines."

"We'll buy new ones," Charlie told him.

"Something tells me we won't. Something tells me The Hadley Company is finished."

They were nearing the firehouse. Charlie put down his load and gripped the foreman's arm.

"I don't want any talk being started around town about the Company being finished," he said. "Get that straight. Because I'm telling you we'll build a new plant out here, and we'll buy all new equipment."

"And I'm telling you that Chalmers, and what's left of the Hadley family, won't see it that way at all. When they find out what's happened out here, they'll cash in their chips."

"Then we'll stop them. This may be the best thing that's happened to the Company in fifty years. We've needed a new plant, and maybe now we'll get it."

A crowd was gathering at the firehouse, women in summer dresses soaked to the skin, children clinging to them quiet and subdued. The men were clustered by the door, watching it rain. One of the men grabbed Ralph Henry and pulled him off to one side.

"Why ask me?" Charlie heard the foreman shout. "Ask him, he's the boss. Not me."

"Ask me what?" Charlie said, interrupting.

"Some of the boys are wondering what this means for the Company, Charlie." It was Bill Haney, one of the new hands on the machines. Immediately the rest of the men in the firehouse joined them, listening. "Is this the end for the Company?"

"If this was the end, would we have carried out all our records?" Charlie said angrily. He patted one of the filing cases. "This is our business right here. All this flood means to the Company is that our plant is getting a good washing out, and we've been needing that for years. And don't go around spreading rumors, Bill. When the water goes down things won't look so bad."

Someone ran into the firehouse shouting that the span had gone, and Ralph Henry cursed softly. Charlie stepped outside and listened. Without the span to act as a dam, the sound of the river had changed. It was quieter.

"I'm glad it's gone," Charlie said, returning to the firehouse. "The span was clogging up the whole river like a beaver dam."

Ralph Henry just stared at him bleakly. He seemed to be suffering from a delayed shock. He was sitting now on a filing case, his shoulders slumped with exhaustion, his teeth chattering against his pipestem.

After a while Jim Hartry, the town's first selectman, appeared in a yellow slicker and his rain hat. He looked sick, as though the sight of his town disintegrating before his eyes had affected him physically. Charlie cornered him and asked him about a phone.

"Go see George Wyatt," he answered. "He's got some kind of a Civil Defense rig upstairs." He guided Charlie away from the crowd. "Everyone I meet is asking me about the factory. What's the word? Will this be the end of The Hadley Company?"

"I'm getting a little sick of answering that," Charlie said harshly. "We're going to rebuild. Does that answer your question?"

Jim's expression brightened, as though this were the first piece of good news he had heard in a long, long time. "How about the family?" he asked. "How do you know what they'll do?"

"I'm the family now, Jim, and you've got my promise that we'll rebuild."

He ran up the firehouse stairs and into the equipment room. George Wyatt was sitting alone at his radio, his expression one of demonic ecstasy. A mail sorter by trade, George had been praying for this day for five years. He was a dry, tired little man, with not much to look forward to but old age and Social Security. Civil Defense had become his religion. Every year for five years at the annual town meeting, he had risen to his feet and castigated the townspeople for their indifference. Twice he had tried to organize a practice catastrophe, with negligible results. His sirens had wailed, and the dogs had howled, but only George took the whole thing seriously. A candle flickered at his elbow, exaggerating the lines of exhaustion under his eyes.

"This is G for George Wyatt," he was intoning into his mouthpiece. "Chief of Civil Defense, Town of Hadley. Come in please. Over."

Charlie tapped him on the shoulder.

"Who can you get on this, George?"

"I can get messages to anyone you want," he said proudly, "including the President of the United States."

"I guess we can leave Mr. Eisenhower alone," Charlie answered. "But how about Lowell Chalmers? Can you get a message through to him?"

thirty-seven

AT TWO O'CLOCK THE NEXT AFTERNOON, LESS THAN A HALF-HOUR AFTER SHE had arrived home from the Island, Lucy was staggering down the cellar stairs with an armload of laundry when the telephone rang.

"Get it, will you," she shouted to Lydia, who with her two sisters was in the library watching television.

Lucy was exhausted. She had taken the six o'clock ferry that morning, and all the way from the Cape the girls had fought, whined, and teased like three cats in a barrel. With the washouts, the detours, and the ruined bridges in the eastern part of the state, the trip home had taken six hours. It wouldn't be Charlie calling. She was sure of that. The lines to Hadley were all down. She had tried to reach him the moment she had arrived.

"It's Mr. MacDonald," Lydia yelled down the cellar stairs.

"Who is he, and what's he want?"

"He has some kind of a message for Daddy."

"Write it down carefully and leave it on the telephone table. Get him to spell things, Lydia. It might be important."

Lydia prided herself on her ability to write, but her letters were illegible to all, including herself. Lucy set the dials on the washing machine and stood watching the water soaking the clothes. Then suddenly she flew up the stairs toward the phone. The name MacDonald had registered.

"This is Mrs. Webb," she said, snatching the receiver away from Lydia, who had laboriously been copying down a message. "Can I help you, Mr. MacDonald?"

He had a hearty Midwestern voice. "I've been trying to reach your husband all day," he said. "You probably don't know who I am, but——"

"But I do know who you are," she interrupted smoothly. "I know you're from Detroit, and that you and my husband do business together."

"That's right. Your husband and I are old friends." He paused a moment. "Looks like from what I read in your local paper The Hadley Company has been pretty badly hit."

"I'm sure it isn't as bad as it sounds," she answered calmly. "I mean if you're worried about your money or——"

"The Hadley Company doesn't owe us any money." His laugh hurt her ear. "I'm trying to give your husband some money, not take it away from him."

"In that case I'm sure he'll be glad to see you, Mr. MacDonald."

She closed her eyes, shaking her head, trying to remember who and what Mr. MacDonald was. She remembered only that Charlie had mentioned his name, and that he was from Detroit.

"You tell him I called, will you, Mrs. Webb, and that I tried to see him. I'll be in touch with him by phone from Detroit when he clears the wreckage away out there."

"Where are you now?" she asked, stalling for time. Her three children were lurking at her side.

"Can we watch 'Queen For A Day?'" Lydia whispered.

"Go watch whatever you want," she hissed at her daughters. "Run along. I'm terribly busy."

The children sped toward the television set with whoops of delight. "Queen For A Day" had always been on the family proscribed list, along with soap operas, Fulton J. Sheen, and "The Rosary Hour."

"I'm in sort of a mess here," Lucy said, returning to the phone. "I've just brought my children back from our summer place."

"You sound like my daughter," Mr. MacDonald answered. "How many children do you and Charlie have?"

"Three girls," she answered. "Where are you now, Mr. MacDonald? Or did you tell me?"

"I'm down in the city, waiting to go out to the airport. I had hoped to see Charlie today, but perhaps it better wait."

"If this is important," she answered, "perhaps I could get through to Hadley. The roads may be opened by now."

"I think what I plan to tell him may be pretty important for his future," he answered.

"I'll be right down," she told him. "And you'll have to pardon my appearance. I've had a hard two days."

His laugh sounded nice, like a friendly old grandfather.

"Don't you worry about that. I'm not much to look at myself."

Ten seconds after Mr. MacDonald hung up, Lucy called Mary Robinson.

"Mary," she said breathlessly, "I'm home." She paused. "I know, and I don't have time to talk about anything. Do me a terrific favor. One of Charlie's business friends is stranded downtown, and I have to drive him out to Hadley. Could you possibly keep your eye on my three for a while? I'll leave them here with the television if you could check on them from time to time. And maybe feed them if I don't get home. Lord knows what the roads are like out there. What did Ed say about The Hadley Company? Anything?" she paused. "Oh, Lord. Poor Charlie must be sick. I've got to go. The girls are fine, but if you hear screams or see smoke, check. Thanks, and you're a darling."

Mr. MacDonald smelled faintly of expensive cigars. He was short and bald, with a round, pink face. His suit was wrinkled, and perspiration had soaked through the band of his straw hat. He moved slowly and deliberately, easing himself into the car, as though he might have recently had a heart attack and wished to avoid another.

"So you have three little girls," he said as they were driving out of the city. "How I envy you. My wife and I had just the one." He extracted his wallet from his pocket and removed a picture. "There we all are last Christmas." He held the picture up for Lucy to see. "That's my wife, who passed away two months ago, and there's my daughter Lue, with her husband, and my two grandchildren."

"What a marvelous family," Lucy said, holding the picture against the steering wheel as she dodged through the traffic.

He replaced the picture in his wallet.

"What are your little girls' names?"

"Lydia, Roswell, and Ruth."

"Nice names." He grinned at her. "What I'd call Eastern names, Mrs. Webb."

288

"Why don't you call me Lucy?" she said.

He looked like a man Charlie would want her to be friendly to. It was awful, she thought, how little she knew about Charlie's business friends. His life was really a complete haze as far as she was concerned. He sometimes tried to tell about what he did and who he met on his business trips and his trips to conventions, but she had retained none of it. Mr. MacDonald was talking steadily, as friendly and as unassuming as a puppy.

"They don't come any better than that Charlie of yours," he said when they reached the outskirts of the city. "He's a doer."

"We like him too," Lucy answered, still trying to remember who Mr. MacDonald was.

"Yes, sir, he's a young man of the old school. Did he ever mention to you how we met?"

"Charlie seems to know so many important people," she answered glibly, "I sometimes forget how he meets them all."

"Of course you're acquainted with my concern," he said confidently.

"Isn't everyone?" she asked.

"Well, that's a little steep, but I suppose old DFI's reputation has moved around in the last forty years."

She could see he liked her. Now if she could just figure out the translation of the initials DFI . . .

"How did you run into Charlie?" she asked.

"Charlie ran into me," he answered, laughing. "He snaked a Sears Roebuck account right out from under my nose. So I wrote him a letter. I told him if ever he was in Detroit to look me up. That I had a proposition to make to him. You know that old saying, don't you, about if you can't beat 'em, join 'em?"

"So you couldn't beat Charlie, and you wanted to join him?"

Her answer appealed to him. He tipped back his head and laughed. "I didn't want to join *him*. I wanted him to join *me*. That's my system. If you can't beat a man, buy him. I tried to buy that husband of yours."

"Didn't Charlie go out to Detroit a year or so ago?"

"Sure he did, and I offered him a job."

"Charlie never told me that," she blurted, feeling completely stupid. She really knew nothing of what Charlie did any more. She knew nothing about his life because it had never interested her.

"I told him he was much too good for this little run-down company back here. I told him he'd reach a dead end and never go any further. I offered him the sort of opportunity most young men dream of."

"What did he say?" Lucy asked nervously.

"He said no," Mr. MacDonald answered. He was watching her. "He told me his wife couldn't be happy away from where she was born."

"Why that's ridiculous," she protested. "I'd go wherever Charlie wanted me to."

He nodded. "I'm glad to hear you say that. I'm going to remind you of that when we get to see Charlie. This time he won't be able to use you as an excuse. I want him," he said, pointing a finger at her. "I want him so much I'm even prepared to buy The Hadley Company to get him."

"Is that why you're here?" she asked uneasily. "To buy The Hadley Company?"

"I will buy it if that's the only way I can get your husband in with me."

"Perhaps it isn't for sale."

He waved his hand disparagingly. "That's one thing I've learned in my seventy-two years. There's a price tag on everything and everybody."

"We'll see," Lucy answered coldly.

They had reached the valley just east of Hadley. The water had fallen as fast as it had risen, and the fields on both sides of the highway were shimmering with mud. Nearly a dozen dead cows had been washed into a pile against a barbed-wire fence, and their bellies had already started to bloat in the searing August heat. Crows were feasting, and there was a cloud of flies.

"Poor devils," Mr. MacDonald muttered, gazing in awe.

The corn, which two days before had been growing tall and dark green, now lay crushed, caked with mud and slime, the whole field a tangled heap of tree trunks, branches, tar paper, and ruined bales of hay. At the edge of the field the barn had been twisted loose from its foundation, and an open shed had fallen in, its roof draped over two new tractors. The farmyard was a sea of mud.

"If I was that farmer I'd sell out right now," Mr. MacDonald said.

"And do what?" Lucy asked sarcastically. "Move West?"

"I can think of worse places to go."

"The West was populated by Easterners with no guts," Lucy shot back at him. "There's such a thing as refusing to leave a place because you love it."

"God says to love people," he answered gently, obviously surprised by her sudden anger, "not places."

"I love places," she answered. "I love this place."

"It looks like I'm beginning to see what your husband Charlie meant. He said you were pretty sentimental about your home."

"If Charlie wants to go to Detroit, we'll go to Detroit. But I like it here." She was close to tears.

"That's all I want to hear. You won't stand in his way if he wants to make a change then, Lucy?"

"Of course I won't, but I don't think he'll go. I think he likes it here."

"We'll see," he answered.

They were driving slowly. Sections of the pavement had been washed out, and road crews were filling in the holes with gravel.

"It's a funny thing," Mr. MacDonald said thoughtfully. "It was water that built this section of the country back in colonial days, and now it's water that's destroyed it."

"Destroyed it," Lucy shouted. "Good Lord, you see a few dead cows and one or two ruined buildings, and you talk as though everyone is dead around here. I don't see anyone crying about it. Do you? People around here are tough."

"Tough and practical," he answered. "You'll lose most of your industry after this. The money and the good men will move away."

"You don't know us," she said with a burst of insular pride. "They've been writing us off since the days Detroit was an Indian burial ground or whatever it was. You just watch and see if we don't rebuild."

"Let's get specific," he answered, watching her again. "How about this family your husband works for? They're a pretty typical Eastern family. Do you think they'll risk all their capital on an old worn-out clinker of a factory?" He laughed and answered his own question. "Not on your life. I know these people back here. They've lost that old pioneer spirit."

"I won't talk about it any more," she said, turning away to hide her tears.

"I hope I haven't made you mad, Lucy. This flood you've had bothers me just as much as it does you, but I'm trying to be practical about it, and I hope you'll be practical too. I'll tell you a secret," he added. "My father was born in Maine. He was one of those gutless Easterners you were talking about. He left Maine because he didn't like the cold winters and the stony soil."

They were climbing the hill. When she looked down on the town, Lucy's heart sank. She had last seen the valley in late May. It had then been lush with spring, the orchards in bloom, the woods a pale green, the river a ribbon of placid water flowing down from the hills to the north. Now everything was flattened and brown, the valley a long, twisting scar, as though a giant bulldozer had run wild.

All the houses along the riverbank were gone. Not even a foundation remained. The river had carved itself new banks, undermining the road that ran to the north, a mile of pavement draped over a silt bar. The reservoir had filled up with gravel and mud, and the railroad trestle had fallen on its side, protruding from the sand.

"It's awful," Mr. MacDonald muttered, breaking the silence. "The whole place is ruined."

The factory looked smashed, like an insect that had been crushed under a giant foot. The span had disappeared, leaving only a scattering of bricks along the riverbanks. The powerhouse and the chimneys were gone, along with the warehouse, the railroad siding, and the old forge. At the lower end of the factory, none of the buildings had roofs, and water still stood inside the walls, dark muddy pools. There was a deep gorge through the entire factory yard, and the wire fence had been forced against the office building, driven there by a section of a house that had washed down from above. Three hundred yards downstream the bridge lay twisted and collapsed, like a broken, useless toy. Tons and tons of water still poured over the dam, and a cloud of mist was blowing out over the factory and the town, soaking the streets and the buildings. If a thousand bombs had fallen on the town, the destruction could have been no more complete.

"Actually," Lucy said cheerfully, avoiding the remains of a landslide as she eased the car down the hill, "actually, it's nowhere near as bad as I expected."

Charlie was wheeling a load of liquid silt across the factory yard when he saw Lucy making her way toward him, along with Mr. MacDonald.

"Well for heaven's sake," he greeted her, putting down his wheelbarrow. "I thought you were at least two hundred miles away." He kissed her gingerly, first wiping some mud and perspiration from his face.

"I came right home, Charlie. I wish I'd been here with you."

"There was nothing you could have done except wring your hands. What brings you here?" he asked Mr. MacDonald, shaking his hand. "Not to gloat, I hope."

"Good God, son, I wouldn't gloat over something like this. I only wish I could lend a hand with the wheelbarrows."

"Mr. MacDonald called me from his hotel, Charlie. He'd been trying to reach you."

"I was in New York anyway, Charlie."

"And you just decided to travel up to view the remains?"

"I came up to talk with you," he answered, pointing a finger at Charlie's bare chest. "I told you last year I wouldn't take no for an answer."

"He's the persistent type," Charlie said, winking at Lucy. "Do you want to see what's left of our factory?" he asked, walking back toward the main shop. "We're taking inventory right now."

The afternoon sun was streaming in through a hole in the roof. There was no glass left in any window. The entire work force of the company was busy with hoes, shovels, and wheelbarrows, scraping the silt into piles, wheeling it out into the yard, and dumping it into a washout. Some of the wives had brought coffee, and the Hadley Tavern had donated a keg of cold beer. The shop was alive with activity and noisy with cheerful insults being shouted back and forth between the sweating men. Ralph Henry was moving from machine to machine, taking notes on a greasy pad.

"Everyone seems pretty happy," Mr. MacDonald said.

"What would you expect us to be? What's done is done."

"People are usually quiet at funerals."

Charlie laughed, and again winked at Lucy.

"I'll bet you think you're going to buy us out cheap, Mr. MacDonald. Was he full of gloom on the way out, Lucy?"

"He certainly was," she answered. "He talked about how we were all finished around here."

"Don't let this old bandit fool you. He trades companies like some men trade horses."

"Forgive me if I was crude on the way out, Lucy," Mr. MacDonald said, putting his hand on her arm. "I have a bad habit of telling the truth about things." He turned to Charlie. "Do you have an office where we can talk?"

"I'll run along," Lucy said hastily.

"No you won't," Charlie answered. "I may need you." He led the way toward the main office building. "Things are still pretty wet. We had two feet of water over the floor."

"How about your records?" Mr. MacDonald asked casually.

292

"They're all up at the firehouse, bone dry. My foreman and I got them out just in time."

"You look exhausted, Charlie," Lucy whispered.

"Well, I am. Everyone out here is exhausted. Even your father has been using a shovel in his office. All his antiques are ruined, including your great-grandfather's clock."

"The phones are in," Mrs. Fleck said proudly when Charlie stepped into the office.

"Good," he answered. "Get me Mr. Bemis. I'd like to speak with him when I've finished with Mr. MacDonald."

"That's your little shop out in Cleveland, isn't it?" Mr. MacDonald asked. "Doesn't Bemis run that little place for you?"

"Not so little any more," Charlie answered. "We've had to expand it since we took that Ford account away from you." He grinned. "We're spending quite a bit of money out in Cleveland, and starting to make a little more."

"And speaking of money," Mr. MacDonald answered, sitting on the arm of a wet office chair, "I would say that someone would have to spend quite a bit of money right here, assuming you plan to go back into business."

"Subtle, isn't he?" Charlie said grinning at Lucy.

"Shouldn't I leave you two alone?" Lucy asked.

"I want you here," Charlie answered, his voice harsher than he meant it to be. He had been without sleep for over forty hours.

"So, let's talk turkey," Mr. MacDonald began after a pause. "First of all, I didn't come up here because of this flood. I was planning to visit you anyway. I would have been here today no matter what had happened. I hope you'll believe that." His sincerity sounded genuine.

"Mr. MacDonald offered me a job last year," Charlie said to Lucy. "We would have to move to Detroit."

"I know," she answered.

"I told your wife all about it on the way out here. She says she'll go wherever you'll go, so you can't use that excuse again."

"That means I'll have to think up a new one?"

"You're not going to think up a new one. You're coming in with me. I'm an old man. The job I offered you last year, and the job I'm offering you right now, is the same job I would have offered my son if I'd had one, and provided he was as good a man as you are. You'll go in as my special assistant, and if you want to talk about salary right now, I'm ready."

"Do you know what company Mr. MacDonald owns?" Charlie asked Lucy.

She was standing against the office wall behind Mr. MacDonald. She shook her head.

"It's the Detroit Forge and Iron," Charlie said, "and they operate about a dozen divisions in eight different sections of the country. They make everything we make and a lot more besides, but they don't make it as well." He smiled. "They have the size, but we have the reputation."

"And a smart advertising agent," Mr. MacDonald put in. "That's half your business. More than half now," he added, pointing out the office window at the ruined factory.

"Our advertising has done well for us," Charlie agreed. "If it hadn't, you wouldn't be here now."

"What are we sparring about?" Mr. MacDonald asked. "I'm not here to bargain with you. Will you let me talk?"

"It won't cost me anything to listen."

"All right. Tell me how much they pay you here."

"I earn enough."

"How much?"

"Ten thousand a year, more or less."

"I'll bet Chalmers doesn't pay you more than eight."

"Ten, more or less," Charlie repeated.

"We won't argue about it. Whatever you're getting now, we'll double that figure as a starter. How does that strike you?"

"Very generous. What would I have to do for twenty thousand a year?"

"Exactly what you're doing now, only on a much bigger scale. And if you want to bring in any of your people here with you, that's all right with me. How about that old foreman out there? We could find a place for him in our organization."

Charlie moved away from his desk and walked to a window.

"You sound as though you're sure The Hadley Company won't reopen after this."

"I don't think you will, and you don't either. Be honest with me."

"I thought you might make us an offer for The Hadley Company. You could talk to Lucy's father, Mr. Chalmers, about it. He's in his office."

"Mr. Chalmers is your father, Lucy?" Mr. MacDonald looked at her in embarrassment. "Looks like I ought to do my homework more carefully. Lucy nearly scratched my eyes out on the way out here, Charlie, and now I can see why."

Mrs. Fleck knocked on the office door and then poked her head inside.

"Mr. Taylor is on the line from New York," she said. "He says it's important."

"Excuse me a moment," Charlie said, lifting his phone. "Hi, Nate. What's on your mind?" He listened for a moment, smiling and watching the ceiling. "Free, you say. You wouldn't call it free if you could see us up here. Things are a mess." He paused again. "Of course we'll do it, and thanks." He pushed the phone across his desk. "That was our advertising agent. He persuaded NBC to send a mobile television unit into Hadley. Apparently our little flood has become big news." He pointed a finger at Lucy. "Why don't you go on out and wait for them and lead them down to the factory? Nate thinks we'll get a lot of advertising out of it."

"Do you think it will do any good?" Mr. MacDonald asked.

"Of course it will do some good," Lucy snapped, starting for the office door. "Who ever heard of Chicago until it burned?"

294

"Your wife's quite a scrapper," Mr. MacDonald said admiringly when they were alone.

Charlie nodded vaguely.

"So you want to buy us out?" he asked.

"I'm willing to, if that's the only way I can get you."

"Would you abandon the factory here?"

"Yes. Of course I would. I won't lie to you about that. I'd keep the Hadley name. That's the one thing you've really got that I want. And we'd keep your Cleveland branch. That will fit in nicely. There will be no one out of work here or anywhere else, including your advertising agency. The whole thing can be arranged by an exchange of cash or stock. All that I'll arrange with Chalmers in there. What I really am after is you, and the Hadley name."

"I can only speak for myself, Mr. MacDonald. About the Company, you'd have to talk with the stockholders."

"You'd have to be part of the deal."

"You sound out Mr. Chalmers and the other stockholders first. After you've done that, I'll tell you how I feel about it. And one thing more. Don't imply to Mr. Chalmers that I have anything to do with this. If you tell him that I'm part of the deal, then the whole thing will be off as far as I am concerned."

"Can I take it that your answer is yes?" Mr. MacDonald asked, reaching for Charlie's hand.

"If you can persuade the stockholders of The Hadley Company to sell out their interests to you, then you'll have me as one of your employees," Charlie answered. "Is that enough of an answer for you?"

"You just leave the stockholders to me," he answered. "I have a way with them. And after what's happened out here, they're just lucky they've still got something I want."

thirty-eight

That night, when the children were finally in bed, Charlie joined Lucy in the living room.

"Now," he said, "once again. Tell me everything your mother said about selling out The Hadley Company."

"I don't think she really wants to sell it any more than we do."

"Then why?"

Lucy ran her hand along a moulding, idly examining her finger for dust. Then she said, "It seems to be a personal thing with her, Charlie. She's determined not to let you have it."

He nodded. "I suppose that's partly my fault. I once warned your mother I'd take the Company away from your family. I was mad at her, and spoke without thinking."

"She uses as an excuse that it wouldn't be fair to the stockholders to risk all their money on a new plant," Lucy said. "She knows my father isn't man enough to keep the Company going, and she refuses to think of you as part of her family because she's never been able to squash you, like she has everyone else. You frighten her, and she's determined to show you who's boss."

"I think I'm capable of protecting the family trust fund," Charlie answered. "I resented your family when I first came back from the war, but I don't any more. I consider myself lucky to be part of it now."

"Do you want to go to Detroit?" she whispered. "If you want to go, I want to go too."

"Do you?" he asked.

She sat down on the couch and looked at him fearfully.

"That's a little unfair."

"You'd rather stay here, wouldn't you?"

"Yes. I'd rather stay here."

"So would I. We are something here. In Detroit we'd be nothing."

"But what will you be if Mother sells the Company?"

"Mother," he echoed. "Who's Mother? How much stock does she own?"

"But she controls the rest of the family, Charlie. She makes the decisions. You know that as well as I do. No one dares stand up to her."

"I do," he answered. "I've been waiting for this moment for years, since the day I went to work for The Hadley Company. I told your mother I'd take over the Company, and I'm going to."

"You mean you'll fight her?"

"Of course I'll fight her, and for her own good too."

"But how?"

"With stock, silly. I'll start with you. You own quite a few shares. Are you going to back your mother, or me?"

"You don't have to ask that."

"All right. Next we'll visit all the family stockholders one by one. If anyone wants to sell out, we'll buy his shares."

"With what?" Lucy asked.

"Money. I've already asked Danny Girard about this. The Pearl Street Bank will back me. Banks don't like to see industry leave either. That's how they make their money, by lending it. Danny and his father-in-law seem to have confidence in my judgment. They're willing to bet on me."

"How can I help you?" Lucy asked. "If you're going to fight my mother, I want to fight her too."

"Praise the Lord," he said gleefully, kissing her on the forehead. "I've waited a long time to hear you say that."

"How can I help?" she asked again.

"By calling your sister Anne. Tell her we'll be out tomorrow morning to pay her a little social call."

The Hadley parsonage had been built in the 1840s, during the town's first era of expansion. Of no definite style of architecture, it was charitably called Greek Revival, a white, rectangular, two-story, frame wooden building with a low-pitched roof and protruding eaves and cornices. Its large single-pane windows, always dirty, stared vacantly across the green at the church five hundred feet away.

The parsonage yard, front and back, was a tangle of weeds. Here and there, as a sign that some past minister's wife had also loved the god Pan, there were struggling clumps of phlox and day lilies competing successfully with the ragweed, the chickweed, and the lamb's-quarters. Nothing grew along the crumbling brick foundation except a single wild honeysuckle bush, planted, doubtless, by a careless bird.

"Why are ministers' houses always so unkempt?" Lucy muttered as she and Charlie were walking up the front path at ten the next morning.

"Because they never own them," he whispered back at her.

Clyde and Anne Harbert had made one change in the front yard. They had installed a pile of sand, where young Hadley was listlessly at work with a set of plastic spoons. Around him, driven into the ground, was a short section of snow fence, his play pen.

"Do you think he could be retarded?" Lucy whispered as she was passing her nephew.

Young Hadley had developed a weak eye, which tended to roll in toward his nose. He sat now on his sand, his diapers stained and heavy, his mouth hanging slackly, his bad eye rolling, his good eye regarding his uncle and aunt with neither recognition nor affection.

"Anglo-Saxons are late bloomers," Charlie answered, hoping this was his nephew's only problem. "Hi there, fella," he shouted cheerily, reaching through a hole in the snow fence, patting young Hadley on the head. He was determined to cultivate this boy. As things stood now, he might one day emerge as the sole male heir to carry on The Hadley Company.

"He isn't advanced," Charlie whispered to Lucy, following her onto the porch. "That's for sure."

"Come in, come in," Clyde shouted, shaking hands, beaming with good will. "What brings you two here?" There was a babble of children's voices from the rear of the house.

"Didn't Anne tell you I'd called?" Lucy asked, dismayed.

"Oh, so she did," Clyde answered. "So she did. I have so many things on my mind, with this flood and all, I tend to forget."

"What's with the children?" Charlie asked, looking down the hall toward the kitchen. "Are you and Anne starting a nursery?"

"It's this flood. We've taken in about a dozen of them while their parents look around for new homes." He led the way down the hall, kicking aside toys, diapers, blankets, and a bicycle wheel, clearing a path to the kitchen. "Anne," he shouted. "Friends and relations are here. I'd take you into our living room," he explained, "but Anne has at least a dozen cots set up in there."

"How does she stand it?" Lucy asked.

"She's in seventh heaven. Anne would care for the whole town if she could."

"Anne likes it out here, doesn't she?" Charlie said.

"She loves it, and so do I. I hope you approve of the changes we're making in the church." He beamed. "You can thank Mr. Chalmers for our new steeple. He's been wonderful."

"Hi," Anne shouted, breezing down the hall, "you'll have to pardon our house. As you can see, we're up to our ears in children."

She was wearing a pair of worn-out oxfords, a soiled cotton dress, and a red handkerchief over her hair. She glowed with health and happiness.

"Could we go into your study?" Charlie asked Clyde, when it appeared that was the only place left in the house to sit down.

As they were moving into the study Lucy whispered to her sister.

"Anne, from the looks of him, I think Hadley needs changing. He seemed sort of miserable out there on the sand pile."

"Ha," Anne answered, dismissing the suggestion with a wave of her arm, "he's always miserable, and he always needs changing. I do it on schedule."

"Change him on schedule?" Lucy echoed, amazed.

"It's the only way I can have a moment to myself."

"But the poor child."

"Poor child nothing. That's one of the main faults with most mothers. They do nothing but attend to their children, and never think of themselves. And if that sounds selfish, I'm sorry. But I'm a busy, busy woman these days."

"Sit down, sit down," Clyde said, arranging chairs. "I'm afraid I'll have to apologize for my study. Anne and I just don't seem to have time to arrange anything out here."

Books had overflowed the bookcases and lay in piles on the corners. Clyde had a new mimeograph machine on his desk. He had been printing the church programs, and ink-blotted paper lay scattered over the entire study floor. He had also been writing a sermon. On top of the mimeograph machine were an open Bible and some longhand notes.

"Well," Charlie said, after everyone was settled on a chair, "you're both busy, and so are we. I'll come straight to the point. Have you and Anne heard that The Hadley Company may be sold?"

"No," Clyde exclaimed, obviously surprised, "I hadn't heard a word about it. Have you, Anne?"

"Nothing definite," she answered. "But I'm hardly surprised, and I certainly wouldn't blame the family if they did. There isn't much left of the Company, is there?"

"That's a matter of opinion," Charlie answered. He could see that Anne was hostile.

"It will be a terrible blow for the town," Clyde said thoughtfully.

"I really don't think it will," Anne answered promptly. "Fifty years ago, yes, but today, no. Most of the people who live here work in the city these days, and jobs are plentiful."

"Anne," Lucy said angrily, "how can you be so cold-blooded about this? The Hadley Company has been in our family for over a hundred years."

"Mother called me today, and we discussed the whole thing," Anne answered. "What she told me made good sense."

"What did your mother say?" Charlie asked.

"She just asked me if I didn't think it would be a sensible move, and I said I did. It's hardly as though anyone will lose much money. The way Mother explained it, the factory is really just an incidental part of it all."

"That also is a matter of opinion," Charlie answered.

"Naturally you'd feel that way, because temporarily you'll be out of a job. But I think Mother is looking at it from the whole family's point of view. She said that to rebuild the factory would take just about all the reserves."

"That's true," Charlie admitted. He was feeling his way along. It was obvious that a sentimental appeal would be useless with Anne.

"Does this mean the factory will be closed down?" Clyde asked. "Just like that?"

"That's exactly what it means," Charlie answered.

"But don't we have a certain moral obligation at a time like this to keep it open? Doesn't the whole town depend on it?"

"Poof," Anne answered.

"What do you mean, poof?" Lucy snapped. She was pale with anger.

"Poof. That's what I mean." Anne turned toward Charlie. "You want something, don't you? Mother told me to expect a call from you."

"Charlie wants to take over the Company and keep it in the family," Lucy blurted. "He hopes all of us will back him."

"Let me say something," Charlie interrupted. "Your mother says she is thinking of the family, Anne, and so am I. The only really valuable thing your family has is The Hadley Company. Whether you admit it or not, it's the one reason why all of us are still a family. It's always been there, paying dividends, providing jobs for people like me and your father, and also allowing you to live in the Philadelphia slums. I think to let it go out of the family will be a mistake. We won't be much poorer as far as money is concerned, but we won't be a family any more. We'll all just be a bunch of people named Harbert and Webb and Taylor. Who knows," he added, turning toward Clyde. "Your son Hadley may want a job someday in the Company. A family business is like a home. It's always there."

"I doubt that young Hadley will survive his dirty diapers," Lucy murmured. Charlie put his hand on her arm.

"I can run The Hadley Company, Anne, and I can run it well. I've really been running it for three or four years. I really don't want it sold, and I was hoping you'd back me up."

"What you're really asking is for all of us to turn our money over to you, isn't it?"

"In a sense, yes. I'll be risking it, if that's what you mean."

"Our money, Clyde's and mine. Polly's money. My mother's money. Everyone's money but your own."

"Anne!" Lucy shouted. "Charlie isn't trying to steal anything."

"Doesn't it really amount to the same thing? Isn't he trying to take over the family? Be honest, Charlie. Isn't that what you're really trying to do?"

"I think I'm capable of taking pretty good care of this family, Anne. At least financially."

"Well, thank you very much, but I'll take my chances with my mother in charge. And furthermore, this is hardly the time for Clyde and me to slap my mother in the face, after all she's been doing for us lately. Don't you agree, Clyde?"

"Your family has been generous," he agreed, looking at Charlie uneasily. "But some of what Charlie says makes sense, Anne."

"It makes sense for him, yes, but not for anyone else. I don't blame you for trying, Charlie. We all have to look out for ourselves. If my mother thinks the time has come to get practical about The Hadley Company, I for one intend to go along with her."

The room was silent for a moment. Then suddenly Lucy exploded.

"Is this my sister who once felt so guilty about her independent income?" she asked, her voice dripping sarcasm. "Is this the girl with the big, big heart who wanted to give all her money away to the poor? You sound like a money-lender, Anne."

"I've grown up a little," Anne replied, unabashed. "Having a son," she said, giving the word a special emphasis for Lucy's benefit, "made me see things a little more clearly."

"Just how do you see things?" Charlie asked.

"This money Grandfather left us all," Anne answered, "is not really ours. It belongs to our children and our children's children. We have no right to squander it or to risk squandering it. That's what Mother told me, and I agree with her completely."

"After all Charlie has done for you and Clyde," Lucy interrupted bitterly, "you ought to be ashamed of yourself."

"My mother is the only person in my family who has always been loyal to me," Anne answered, "and I think it's now my turn to be loyal to her."

Lucy reached down to the floor and picked up one of Clyde's freshly printed church programs.

"I hope you approve of my hymn selections," Clyde said cheerfully, obviously trying to relieve the tension in the room. "I like to sing myself, and I assume that everyone else does too."

Lucy wasn't listening.

"Who's James Hartry?" she asked Charlie, pointing to the program.

"He's the first selectman out here."

"He's the one who wants you to run for state representative, isn't he?"

"He's talked about it one or two times."

"And isn't Ralph Henry your foreman?"

Charlie glanced over Lucy's shoulder at the program. She pointed to the names of the board of trustees.

"Well, what do you know," he said, reading down the list rapidly. "Ralph

Henry, Jim Hartry, Doctor Leslie. You've even got old Leo Glenn, our jani-tor. Do all your trustees like the job you're doing here, Clyde?"

"They think he's doing a wonderful job," Anne interrupted. "They think he's the best minister they've ever had in Hadley, and they've told him so."

"I told them he was a good man when I asked them to appoint him," Charlie answered, nudging Lucy as he spoke.

"Wouldn't all these men be pretty angry if they knew Clyde had voted to sell the Company?" Lucy asked innocently, responding to Charlie's nudge.

"Clyde has nothing to do with this," Anne said angrily. "The stock is mine, and not his. And furthermore, the board of trustees like us. They want us to stay."

"I doubt if they'll be quite so enthusiastic about Clyde when they hear how his wife feels about the town's main industry," Charlie answered. "They're likely to take a second look at Clyde, particularly with all the other troubles everyone has around here now. They might think he's being a little disloyal to the town."

"Don't think you can scare us," Anne answered, "because you can't."

"I guess I'd better stop being so subtle about this," Charlie said coldly. "All your trustees either work for me or respect my judgment. That's why they hired you. I recommended you. They'll get rid of you for the same reason."

"You're bluffing," Anne answered, glancing uneasily at Clyde. "I don't think you're nearly as important in this town as you think you are."

"Suit yourself," Charlie answered. "We'll see who's right. You or me. And no matter what happens to The Hadley Company, I can guarantee that Clyde has preached his last sermon in the Hadley Church." He stood up and started for the study door.

Clyde reached out and grasped his elbow.

"I'd appreciate it if you and Lucy would excuse us for a moment," he said. He then tapped Anne on the shoulder and motioned her to follow him out-side.

"What now?" Lucy whispered.

"I hated to do that to Clyde," Charlie answered, "but it's time he stopped Anne from running his life. She's just like your mother."

Clyde reappeared in the study doorway. His face was flushed with the remains of an argument. He moved across the room and sat at his desk. For a moment he toyed with the handle of his mimeograph machine.

"I don't know whether you can understand this or not," he said finally, "but I am a clergyman, not a businessman. Since the day we were married this stock of Anne's has been a curse." He placed his hand on the Bible. "I once took an oath," he continued. "I meant it quite sincerely. An oath of poverty. It's the only way a minister can have the peace of mind we keep trying to instill in others. A minister must stop thinking about owning prop-erty, or having money, or owning stock. I believe in my work, Charlie. I be-lieve people need ministers just as much as they need businessmen."

301

Lucy started to interrupt, but Charlie silenced her with a meaningful glance.

"I like it here," Clyde continued. "I like the people in this town, and they seem to like me. I feel needed here. I like my church over there." He pointed out his study window. "I would like to stay here as long as my congregation wants me to stay."

"I want you to stay too," Charlie said.

Clyde nodded. "Anne and I have had a discussion about her stock. She has agreed to offer it up for sale. If you want it, you may have it."

"I'll buy it, of course," Charlie answered. "Anne will receive the market price for it."

"I don't want to see the check," Clyde said. "Please make it out to my son. Deposit it in his account, if you will. I wish I could give the money away, but I suppose my son may not be a minister the way I am, and money will one day be useful to him. For me, this income of Anne's has just been a curse, and I'm thankful at last to be rid of it. Now perhaps I can make my own way in the world."

"Be sure Anne signs the certificates," Lucy interrupted. "There's a blank space on the back of them."

"They'll be signed," Clyde said grimly.

"Well, I guess that does it," Charlie said cheerfully. "Incidentally, you'll be having two new members of your church before long. Lucy and I are moving out to Hadley."

"Are we?" Lucy asked, when she and Charlie were driving back to the city.

"Are we what?"

"Moving to Hadley?"

He nodded. "Will you mind?"

"Not at all," she answered. "I think the head of The Hadley Company ought to live out here."

"I'm not the head of the Company yet."

"I suspect you will be, after seeing you handle my sister Anne. Where do we go from here?"

"New York," he answered, "and your sister Polly. She shouldn't be so tough."

Since Polly's marriage a year and a half before, Mrs. Chalmers had often felt an urge to explain why she had given her youngest daughter no furniture.

"It isn't that I don't want to give her things," she insisted over and over again, "but then she hasn't asked me for anything, and I assume this must mean she doesn't need anything." Mrs. Chalmers would then pause, and with a sigh reserved for all those unfortunates who must live in New York, she would add, "But then, how can anyone furnish one of those impossible two-by-four apartments? Nothing looks well in them. Not even people."

Therefore Polly's apartment was filled with things she and Nate had

302

bought since they were married—a mechanical chair designed to delay heart disease on which one could neither sit nor lie comfortably, a hideaway bed which was never hidden, metal chairs that sent a chill through a summer suit, and a television set that doubled as a magazine table. As he sat looking about the apartment, Charlie felt, as he always did when he visited in New York, that life here was at best a temporary thing, that apartments were merely places to stay warm and dry until a home could be found elsewhere, preferably at least a hundred miles away. The top of an air conditioner that had been fitted into a window to filter the smog was coated with soot—one day's fall-out, Polly insisted, swearing that she had dusted the entire place to be ready for Lucy's arrival.

"I probably ought to warn you people that we've come more or less on business," Charlie told Nate when he was being given a second cocktail.

"I knew it," Polly groaned with exaggerated annoyance. "And I was hoping you had come to observe my happy domesticity."

Polly appeared to be exactly as she described herself, happily domestic. She seemed completely relaxed. She sat on the couch, her feet curled under her, now and then cocking her ear toward the stove, as contented as a Siamese cat.

"As usual, it's about The Hadley Company," Charlie said.

"Talk your damn business," Polly answered, starting for the kitchen. "Lucy and I will go trade recipes."

"We need you more than we need Nate, Pol."

"Why don't I make a temporary exit?" Nate said promptly. "I'll run down to the corner for a glass of water."

"You're family now, darling." Polly linked her arm through his and returned to the couch. "Anyway, I don't trust my swamp Yankee brother-in-law. He has that greedy look in his eye."

"What's with The Hadley Company?" Nate asked.

"Have you heard from your mother or father lately?" Charlie said, looking toward Polly.

"About a week ago Father sent me one of those Kiplinger letters of his. Full of the usual junk. *Wall Street Journal* editorials and so forth."

"Then you haven't heard that they plan to sell the Company?"

Polly glanced at Nate before she answered. "Nate's been buying stock in it," she said.

"I was investing in you," Nate interrupted. "I know a good businessman when I see one."

"Who wants to buy the Company?" Polly asked.

"They have an offer. I could tell you who made it, but it doesn't make any difference." Charlie stood up and walked to the window, perching on the air conditioner. "The point is, we're faced with a tremendous expenditure up there if we want to stay in business. We can patch up our factory temporarily, but to really get back into production, we'll have to build a complete new plant. I'm telling you this so there won't be any misunderstanding about what I'm going to propose to you."

303

"You were right," Polly said, winking at her husband. "We thought you'd pull something like this, Charlie."

"Frankly," he continued, "I'd like to take over up there. I'm asking for the support of the stockholders. But I have to be honest about it. We may have to spend a lot of cash before we're through, and there may not be any dividends for a year or so."

"Spend a million dollars," Polly said airily. "Who cares?"

"It's your money, Pol."

"What's a little money, more or less? Nate is going to make lots of it."

"Get your patrician wife to focus," Charlie said to Nate. "Explain what I'm trying to do."

"Stop being cute, Pol." There was an edge to Nate Taylor's voice.

"But I know exactly what he's trying to do. He warned me he would do this years ago, and now he's doing it. He's going to take over from the family."

"How can we help?" Nate asked bluntly.

"By telling Polly's mother to go to hell," Charlie answered, equally blunt.

"Then what?" Polly asked.

"Then your father will resign, and another president will be chosen."

"You?"

"I might be the logical choice."

"And you need my stock?"

"I need all the stock I can get."

Polly smiled at him. "I've always wanted to get you in this position someday. What kind of inducements can you offer?"

"Shut up, Pol," Nate sounded angry. "Stop playing the fool."

"I am not playing the fool. Charlie wants something from me. I expect something in return. Isn't that good business?"

"It's also called bribery," Nate answered, "and Charlie doesn't offer bribes."

"What do you want from me?" Charlie asked, disregarding the warnings Lucy was sending his way.

"I want you to make me a promise."

"What promise?"

Polly leaned toward Nate and whispered something into his ear.

"Oh, for Lord's sake," he exploded.

"Make him promise," Polly insisted.

Nate blushed. "She wants to be sure you'll give our son a job if we let you take over the family company."

"Your son!" Lucy shouted. "Are you pregnant, Pol?"

Charlie burst out laughing. "Well, well, well," he said. "So at last the college sophomore is going to bury herself with children."

"You go to hell," she replied, sticking out her tongue at him.

He had never seen her look happier.

"Oh, no," he mocked. "Children weren't for you. They were the curse of all womanhood, the admission that——"

"Go to hell," Polly repeated cheerfully. "Make him stop, Nate. Protect me."

304

"This eludes me," Nate put in, glancing at Lucy, shrugging his shoulders.

"Also me," Lucy said. "But then your wife and my husband always had a secret rapport. Of course Polly's son can have a job in The Hadley Company. Can't he, Charlie?"

"I will hire anyone Polly wants me to hire," he answered.

"Anyone?" she asked, glancing at Nate. He shook his head imperceptibly.

"Anyone," Charlie repeated.

"Then how about hiring Nate?"

"Enough is enough," Nate said, flushing with embarrassment.

"Wait a minute," Charlie shouted. "Let me get this straight. Do you want to leave New York, Nate?"

"This wasn't exactly how I planned to bring it up."

"Of course he wants to leave New York," Polly interrupted, "and I want my children born where I was born. That damn place up there gets in your blood."

"Oh, Pol," Lucy sighed, tears coming into her eyes.

"When do you want to start?" Charlie asked, anxious to nail it down. The visit to New York was working out far better than he had expected.

"I'd have to close out my business here. It would take a few months. But I can start whenever you say the word. You're the boss."

"He's the boss now," Polly said quietly, "but he won't be long. Nate's going to take the Company away from you, Charlie. You wait."

"I'm game," Charlie answered, winking at Lucy. "Only he'll have to start from the bottom where I started from."

"Where is the bottom?" Polly asked warily.

"The furnace room," Lucy answered on cue. "Nate will have to shovel coal. It's a family tradition."

"The hell with that," she answered. "Nate's a businessman, not a day laborer."

Nate reached out and placed his hand over Polly's mouth.

"If it's a family tradition to shovel coal, then I'll shovel coal. And you," he added, looking at his wife with affectionate admiration, "will have to learn to curb your tongue." He released her and pointed toward the stove. "Go check your roast, woman. It smells done to me."

"I hope we won't be sorry," Lucy said later that night, as they were driving home up the parkway.

"About Nate coming into The Hadley Company?" he asked, divining her thoughts. He had been wondering about it himself.

She nodded. "Someday you and he may meet head on."

"Possibly. But by that time, if things go as well as I think they will, The Hadley Company will be large enough for ten people like Nate and me."

"Polly warned you he'd try to take the Company away from you," Lucy said uneasily.

"Nate won't take anything away from me," he answered. "He won't be able to if Aunt Roswell does what I hope she'll do."

"Ugh," Lucy muttered, "I keep forgetting that vile aunt of mine. I just wish I'd been nicer to her all these years."

He patted her hand. "You seem to forget that you had a husband who was taking care of those things. You leave your Great-aunt Roswell to me."

For over a year and a half, in the privacy of the family, it had been generally agreed that Aunt Roswell was finally dying. There had been no sudden, dramatic change in her physical condition. She still managed her own housework, and she still engaged in her monthly altercation with her landlord. She attended the Flower Show in March, she had missed no Sunday in church, no Tuesday night symphony concert. It was her mental state, however, that gave the family cause for alarm—or relief, as the case might be. Just as old men lose their powers of concentration in their final months on earth and sit about dozing and dreaming in the sun, so Aunt Roswell too was showing the telltale signs of decay. She was giving away her things.

In June, at her apartment in New York, Polly had received a collect shipment of fifty-four African violets, along with two dozen extra pots and a small bale of peat moss. Polly had long had her eye on Aunt Roswell's collection of family jewelry, and she needed African violets and peat moss just as much as she needed a full-grown circus giraffe.

Anne, who always needed furniture, received Aunt Roswell's books, which she didn't want and didn't ever bother to open, carting them intact to the Hadley Library, which didn't want them either, particularly the two hundred pounds of back issues of the *Literary Digest*.

Mrs. Chalmers, who had always had far too much furniture and who never wore jewelry, received both the furniture and the jewelry, including a long necklace of more than one thousand tiny glass beads strung on a rotted string, which parted on arrival, showering particles of glass down the stairs, across the hall, and under Lowell Chalmers' feet for the next ten days, until he ordered the entire house cleaned and the gleanings removed with the trash.

However, Lucy, who would have accepted just about anything, received nothing except a bad jolt one morning at breakfast as she was reading the morning paper.

"Why the old bitch!" she had shouted in a rare outburst of profanity. She crumpled the paper and threw it onto the floor.

"Who's a bitch?" Charlie asked.

"Aunt Roswell. She's given one hundred and fifty thousand dollars to the Society for the Restoration and Preservation of Historical Landmarks."

"There's always her hearing aid," Charlie answered philosophically.

Aunt Roswell had always amused him. He was sure that when she finally chose to die, she would manage to leave the family at each others' throats with rage and frustration. If Aunt Roswell craved immortality, he knew she would have it, bitterness being a far more lasting memorial than a stone.

"Let me do most of the talking," Charlie whispered to Lucy now, as they knocked on Aunt Roswell's door. "She'll know why I'm here, and she won't expect me to be subtle about it. I've never played games with her. It doesn't pay."

The apartment was nearly bare. In the past it had resembled a summer antique shop, tables, benches, highboys, lowboys, bookcases, and her two pianos all jammed together into her living room. Now everything was gone except for one piano, a desk, a wing chair by the Franklin stove, and a single upholstered stool.

For a while they sat side by side on the stool, listening to the latest list of sins committed by Aunt Roswell's archenemy, her landlord. The most recent fight had centered about birds, the landlord objecting to the pound of peanut butter that Aunt Roswell had smeared on the outside of her window sills.

"I hope you never end up like I am, a helpless old woman," she whined to Lucy, her blue hands anchored in her lap, her long head occasionally resting against the back of her chair, as though her neck had at last lost the strength to support it.

"The poor old soul is fading fast," Lucy whispered.

"Turn your head away when you whisper," Charlie muttered. "She can read your lips."

"I don't need to read lips," Aunt Roswell shot back at him. "There's nothing wrong with my ears, and there never has been."

"I always thought you were faking," Charlie answered, still shouting out of long habit.

She grinned at him with malicious delight, her gold fillings visible for an instant. Unless someone in the family dared pick her teeth, a sizeable part of Aunt Roswell's fortune would go with her into her grave.

"Fooled you for years about my hearing, didn't I, Lucy? You and your fool mother thought I was deaf."

"We really did," Lucy answered, glancing toward Charlie for guidance.

"How else can a useless old woman know what her blood relations think of her? There's just one way. Pretend you're deaf. Remember that when you're as old as I am."

"I shall, Aunt Roswell."

"Well, what are you two after?" she snapped impatiently. "I've given away all my things except that piano there. Take it if you want it. It's no good anyway."

"I didn't think you'd offer us anything if it was any good," Charlie said.

"You're after something, aren't you? You don't fool me."

"Have you heard about the flood, Aunt Roswell?"

"Of course I've heard about the flood. What about it?"

"Do you know it nearly destroyed our factory?"

She nodded vaguely, and again her head rested against the side of her wing chair.

"She seems to be tiring," Lucy whispered. "Shouldn't we have come earlier in the day?"

"They're talking about selling The Hadley Company," Charlie shouted. "They don't think we should rebuild."

"They? Who's they?" she snapped, opening her eyes.

"Mrs. Chalmers."

"Maybe she's right. That fool husband of hers isn't man enough to keep the business going."

"But I am, Aunt Roswell, and that's why I'm here. I want to take over the Company."

"You don't think you fooled me, do you?" she asked.

"I'm not trying to fool you. Either you vote your stock with me, or The Hadley Company will be sold."

"I saw through you years ago," she snapped at him. "You and your visits over here to admire my plants. You never fooled me."

Lucy put her hand on Charlie's arm. "We were all terribly pleased with your gift to the Society for the Preservation and Restoration of Historical Landmarks, Aunt Roswell. That's a worthy cause."

She opened her eyes wide for an instant. Then she sniffed. "I'll bet you were pleased. I suppose you thought I'd give that money to you, just because you named one of your girls after me."

"She's utterly impossible," Lucy muttered. "We might as well go home."

"How about it?" Charlie asked. "Are you going to vote to sell the Company or not?"

"Wouldn't you like to know."

A television set was blaring in the apartment above. As usual, Jackie Gleason was shouting at his wife.

"That's what I have to listen to all day," Aunt Roswell whined. "I complain to Mr. Adkins, and I get nothing but insults. It's no joy to be a helpless old woman these days. You get no respect from anyone. Not even your own family."

"How about your stock?" Charlie persisted. "What do you plan to do with it?"

"I don't plan to do anything with it. I've already signed it away."

"To whom?" Charlie shouted, suddenly pale with anger. "How could you have done a thing like that?"

"It was mine, wasn't it? Or do you think I'm incompetent?"

Charlie didn't answer.

"Answer me," she ordered harshly. "Do you think I'm incompetent?"

"I know damn well you aren't incompetent," he said grimly. "And that's what hurts. You were the one person I felt sure I could count on. I left you to the last," he added bitterly. "I thought you would know how much The Hadley Company meant to the family."

"It's just lucky for you you don't think I'm incompetent," she sniffed at him, "because I signed all my stock over to you."

"To us?" Lucy gasped, her fingers pressing into Charlie's arm.

"Not to you," Aunt Roswell snapped. "To him. He's the only one in the family with any backbone. It's all down at the bank waiting for you," she added, turning again to Charlie. "You could have had it a year ago if you'd asked me."

308

"I suppose you expect me to thank you for this," Charlie said, grinning. "But I'm not going to. I've earned it fighting with your landlord, fixing your doors, and riding you around the countryside."

"Now that you're in charge," she asked, "what are you going to do with The Hadley Company?"

"Just what you and your brother would have done," he answered. "Rebuild it."

She nodded. Aunt Roswell no longer looked as feeble as she had when they first entered the apartment. She was now sitting up straight in her chair, her eyes wide open and alert.

"You run along outside," she said curtly to Lucy. "I want to talk to Charlie alone."

Lucy hesitated a moment, wondering if perhaps she should shake Aunt Roswell's hand, or even kiss her. Then she thought better of it and headed for the door.

The moment Lucy was gone Aunt Roswell rose briskly from her chair and strode to her desk, her back straight, her head erect.

"I'm planning a trip," she announced, glancing defiantly at Charlie over her shoulder. "And don't you try to stop me."

"Heaven forbid," he answered. "A trip? Where to?"

"I want you to decide that for me," she answered. "You've been to Europe, haven't you?"

"During the war."

"I sent for all these travel folders." She pointed in annoyance to a sheaf of paper on her desk. "I can't make up my mind where I want to go."

"How about a bicycle trip across France?" Charlie asked.

"None of your impudence," she retorted. "I'm too old for that sort of thing."

"No wonder you've been giving away all your things. You've been afraid you'd meet someone on this trip who wanted to marry you for your money."

She snorted. "I'm not that much of a fool. Plan me a trip," she said, dropping the travel folders into his lap. "I want to leave the day after to-morrow."

"The day after tomorrow?" he echoed in amazement.

"My lease runs out. My landlord thinks I plan to renew it because I always have. He'll get a little surprise when he finds me gone."

"How long do you want to be in Europe?"

"Six months. A year. You plan the whole thing for me. Now that I know The Hadley Company is in good hands, I'd like to enjoy myself before I die."

Charlie stood up and tapped her on the head with a travel folder. "You'll never die," he said. "You're much too mean to die."

His remark delighted her, and she was still smiling when he went out the door.

thirty-nine

On wednesday, a week later, when charlie returned from the factory at six, Lucy greeted him with the statement that her mother wanted them over that evening after supper for a conference.

"Only she called it a chat."

Charlie nodded.

"Nothing can go wrong, can it?" Lucy asked nervously. "I mean, you do have enough of the stockholders on your side."

"Just about everyone is on our side except your mother. Ed Robinson has been calling a lot of our small stockholders, getting their views on the subject. If they sound uneasy about anything, he makes them an offer for their stock. We're ready to play games with your mother, and we have the loaded dice."

On the way over to the Lawn Street house, Charlie glanced at Lucy. "You look rather miserable."

"This won't be an ugly scene, will it?" she asked desperately.

"I can promise you it will be all sweetness and honey. A nice mixture of sugar and arsenic."

"You won't tease her, will you?"

He hesitated before he answered. "So help me, I'd like to, Lucy. I've waited a long time to box your mother in. But now that I have, I find I don't relish it. I really admire her underneath it all. If she'd been a man, The Hadley Company and General Motors would be competitors."

Mrs. Chalmers met them at the front door. She was gushing over with good will, a sure sign she was feeling organizational.

"Darlings," she cried, "why so formal? I usually expect you through the kitchen door."

"We thought you had probably planned a formal evening, Mother Chalmers." As he spoke, Charlie decided that never again would he call his mother-in-law Mother Chalmers. She would be Mrs. Chalmers from here on out.

"I hear you've been doing a truly magnificent job at the factory, Charles." She linked her arm through his and led him toward the study. "Both Mr. Chalmers and I agree that you must take Lucy away on a long, long vacation when all this is over."

"Charles thrives on hard work," Lucy answered.

"And when all this is over I hope I'll be working harder than ever," he added.

She cocked her head at him, and said nothing until they stepped into the study. "Here they are, Lowell. Right on time, as always. There's something I've never complimented you on, Charlie. Your promptness. My father used to say that to be prompt is the only sincere compliment."

310

"Well now," Mr. Chalmers said, advancing toward them and shaking hands as though he hadn't seen either his daughter or his son-in-law for a month. "Mrs. Chalmers and I are having a spot of brandy. Will you join us?"

"Nothing for me, Mr. Chalmers."

"Nor me," Lucy said, following Charlie's lead.

"Of course you will, children," Mrs. Chalmers insisted. "We have it all ready for you." She gave each of them a glass.

"How do you handle situations like this?" Charlie asked, smiling at Mr. Chalmers. "How do you make it clear to Mrs. Chalmers that you mean what you say? I really don't want any brandy," he repeated, turning again to his mother-in-law.

"Nor I," Lucy echoed. She took her glass and Charlie's and handed them to her mother.

Mrs. Chalmers merely raised her eyebrows and returned the brandy to the tray.

"Actually, Lydia," Mr. Chalmers said thoughtfully, "I don't think I want this brandy either." He poured all three of the glasses back into the decanter, obviously glad to have something to do.

They arranged themselves about the study, Mr. Chalmers at his desk, Mrs. Chalmers on a straight wooden chair, Lucy on the radiator, and Charlie standing at the fireplace, his shoulders against the mantelpiece.

"Well, Lydia, why don't you begin?" Mr. Chalmers said, avoiding Charlie's eye.

"I think you could just read your letter, Lowell. It covers the entire situation far better than I can do."

"I think you should give Charlie some of the background thinking on this. Tell him some of the things you've told me in the last week or so."

"Let's see," she began. "Now what are some of the things we've been talking about. You must at least suspect why we've asked you over tonight, you and Lucy."

"We don't have the slightest idea," Charlie answered. He was determined to make it as difficult for Mrs. Chalmers as he could. "Lucy just said you and Mr. Chalmers wanted to chat."

"Well, we do want to chat. We want to chat about The Hadley Company and how much it has always meant to our family. Mr. Chalmers and I have really been talking about nothing else for the past week, have we, Lowell?"

"Why don't we come right out with it, Lydia?"

Mrs. Chalmers reached for Lucy's hand and patted it.

"When Lucy and I were at the Island a week or so ago," she began, "and we received the awful news about this flood, I warned her that no matter how we felt about it personally, we might be forced to become practical about this company which has meant so much to us all for so many generations."

"Perhaps I'd better handle it after all," Mr. Chalmers interrupted. He turned toward Charlie. "Do you remember a conversation we had a number of years ago in my office, when you first came to see me about a job? I warned

311

you then, didn't I, that if The Hadley Company ever became a threat to our family's security, we'd dispose of it whether we wanted to or not. You remember our conversation, I hope?"

"I recall it vaguely," Charlie answered. "I think I told you I hoped that day would never arrive."

"Well, the point is, it has arrived," Mrs. Chalmers said, taking over again. "Because of this flood and the complete job of rebuilding we must do out there, The Hadley Company, instead of an asset, has suddenly become a liability. None of us like to think about it, but it's true. I've been trying to decide what my father would have done in a case like this."

"He would take every cent he owned and rebuild," Charlie interrupted.

"Ah, but there's a difference," Mrs. Chalmers replied easily, as though she were ready for him. "My father owned nearly all the stock himself. When he took risks, when he gambled, he was gambling only his own money. Now, however, we have to think of quite a large number of people. We have to think of our whole family, not just one member of it."

"But isn't this a poor time to sell out?" Charlie asked. "What are we really offering for sale, and who would buy it?"

"We have an offer," Mr. Chalmers said. "And it's from a responsible source. It's really the reason I've gone along with Mrs. Chalmers' thinking on this. If we turn this offer down, we may never receive another one as good."

"Read your letter," Mrs. Chalmers said. "It covers the situation so thoroughly."

"Well, now," Mr. Chalmers answered, fumbling for his glasses and removing a sheet of paper from his desk. "This is a preliminary letter that will go out to all stockholders, warning them of a special meeting we'll hold early in November, and telling them the subject to be discussed at the meeting, which is what we've been discussing here tonight." He looked at Charlie. "The sale of The Hadley Company."

"Then you really do plan to go through with this, Mr. Chalmers?"

"I'm afraid there's no alternative," he answered.

"There is one."

"Charlie feels he could rebuild the factory and keep it running," Lucy said, speaking for the first time.

"Of course we're all proud that you have such confidence in yourself," Mrs. Chalmers answered. "And it's not that we don't have an equal amount of confidence in you too. But what you're really asking us to do is to turn over all our family assets to you. Mr. Chalmers and I would do that gladly. But we must consider the whole family and all our other stockholders."

"You're not being fair, Charlie," Lucy whispered. "You promised me you wouldn't do this."

"I just hoped your mother didn't plan to go through with it," he answered, "but I see she does." He turned toward Mrs. Chalmers. "I suppose I'd better tell you now about what I've been doing lately. I visited all the large stockholders except you during the past week or ten days. They seem to have great confidence in me. Anne was reluctant to go along at first, but Clyde persuaded her to sell her Hadley stock to me. Clyde wants to be a minister, not a businessman. Then we went down to New York and talked with Polly and Nate about it. Nate wants to move up here and work with me in the Company. He's a good man, and I think we'll be lucky to get him."

"Polly's pregnant," Lucy blurted. Then she put her hand over her mouth. "Oh, damn, I promised her I'd let her tell you that, but she is. She said she wanted her children born near home, that she misses it terribly."

"Polly's coming home?" Mr. Chalmers said, his eyes lighting up with pleasure. "By George, Lydia, that means our whole family will be together again."

"Then there was Aunt Roswell," Charlie continued. "I'm not sure what her motives were, but she has signed over all her stock to me. Perhaps she considers The Hadley Company a historical landmark. Anyway, she didn't want it to be sold. Speaking of selling the Company," he added, turning to Mr. Chalmers, "I may know something about that offer you had that you don't know."

"Mr. MacDonald really wanted Charlie," Lucy interrupted proudly. "He offered him twenty thousand dollars a year."

"You didn't tell me that, Lowell," Mrs. Chalmers said.

"I knew nothing about it, my dear. Twenty thousand dollars a year, Charlie! Great Caesar's ghost, how could you refuse it?"

"What, and take our Lucy to Detroit?" Mrs. Chalmers said haughtily. "Her roots are here." She again reached for Lucy's hand.

"My roots are here too," Charlie said. "Everyone seems to forget that."

"I didn't forget it," Mrs. Chalmers said vehemently. "I told Mr. Chalmers you'd fight this thing." She crossed the study and put her hand on Charlie's arm. "I've been against selling the Company from the start. After all it's in my blood. It was my great-grandfather who founded it. But I didn't think it was fair to saddle you with the family problems. By agreeing to sell, I only hoped I was doing you a favor."

Charlie had never admired Mrs. Chalmers more than he did at that moment. She had turned her defeat into victory.

"I appreciate that," he said, stifling a smile, "but I'm quite willing to take on a few family responsibilities. I think it's just about my turn."

"So Polly's going to have a baby," Mr. Chalmers mused. "Our youngest, Lydia. What do you think of that?"

"It makes me feel old," Mrs. Chalmers answered bleakly, her thoughts obviously elsewhere. She returned to her chair and sat down wearily. "Does anyone know where Aunt Roswell is?" she asked, looking hopefully about the room. "I went over there yesterday with some soup, and her landlord said she had gone."

"Gone?" Lucy echoed. "Gone where?"

"She's in Rome," Charlie said. "She plans to spend a month in Italy, a month in France, a month or two in England, and then she's flying on to Japan if she feels up to it. I know, because I planned the trip for her."

313

As he spoke, Mrs. Chalmers seemed to wither, and buried her face in her hands.

"Why doesn't my family tell me what they're doing any more?" she sobbed, her voice catching. "Aunt Roswell goes off all by herself, without a single word to me about it. Polly is coming home to have a baby I know nothing about. Why should I have been left out of all this news?"

"None of us knew about it, Mother," Lucy protested, putting an arm around her shoulder.

"Charlie seems to know everything," Mrs. Chalmers answered. "Why does he have to keep everything a secret from his own family?"

"Why don't we all have a spot of brandy now?" Mr. Chalmers interrupted. He paused, waiting for Mrs. Chalmers to pull herself together. "I suggest, as a toast, that we drink to our family." He held up his glass. "May we all be together for a long, long time."

"I'd also like to toast Aunt Roswell," Charlie added. "May she enjoy herself abroad."

Mrs. Chalmers' composure had returned as quickly as it had left her. "Who cares about Aunt Roswell?" she sputtered. "She's a stubborn old fool." She turned toward Lucy angrily. "Did you see that notice in the paper about her gift of——"

"We saw it," Lucy interrupted. "Isn't that just like her?"

Mr. Chalmers took Charlie's elbow and guided him out into the hall.

"Of course I'm happy about all this," he said. "Extremely happy."

"I'll probably have to call on you for lots of advice, Mr. Chalmers."

He nodded. "Any time at all. Naturally I'll be stepping out."

"Only if you insist on it," Charlie answered.

"I do. It's time I retired. You can figure on taking over officially at our December meeting." He hesitated a moment, as though he knew he ought to say more.

"I probably ought not to ask this," Charlie said, "but what will you do when you retire?"

"My dear young man," Lowell Chalmers interrupted. "I happen to be working on a project that may take me years to complete. If you're worried about my having enough to do you can put your mind to rest on that score."

"Another old canal?" Charlie asked quietly.

Before answering, Lowell Chalmers stared at Charlie for a moment, his pale blue eyes steady and unwavering, the corners of his mouth turned up in an amused smile.

"No," he said. "Not another old canal. This project of mine concerns——" He paused. "Well, no matter what it concerns. In due time I'll show it to you and all the rest of my family." He put his hand on Charlie's arm. "Come along. Let's join our wives, shall we? As usual they're in there gossiping about Aunt Roswell."